Weary after the war, he was looking forward to getting home quickly—in peace and alone...

In the time it took them to ride back to the wagon, Bitter's left eye swelled shut, and the knuckles on his hands puffed up. Bitter thought he might have broken the knuckle of his trigger finger.

His broken nose gave Bitter's voice a nasal sound when he allowed it would have been a lot easier to simply shoot Peale.

"Yep," said Anthony. "But you know damned good and well neither of us would have shot the boy. And he'd of just kept coming after you. You did the smart thing."

"Why do smart things hurt so much?"

Books by Rod Collins

FICTION

Bud Blair Mysteries
Spider Silk
Stone Fly
Bloodstone
Mariah's Song
Not Before Midnight

John Bitter Series, Post Civil War
Bitter's Run
Abiqua

NON-FICTION

What Do I Do When I Get There?: A New Manager's Guidebook
Rogue River Diaries

Bitter's Run

Rod Collins

Bright Works
Press

BITTER'S RUN

Bright Works Press
Redmond, OR
www.brightworkspress.com

Cover & Interior book design by Jeffrey W. Duckworth
www.duckofalltrades.com

Publication Management by Eva Long
www.longonbooks.com

Print ISBN: 978-0-9965394-8-7
eISBN: 979-8-9875768-5-2

Printed in the U.S.A.

To Vi
(Forever, Wife, forever.)

Contents

"Nothing in the world is so exhilarating
as to be shot at without results."

~ Winston Churchill

"Nothing in the world is so exhilarating
as to be shot at without results."

~ Winston Churchill

Book I – Missouri

During the American Civil War, citizens of Missouri were divided, some loyal to the North, some loyal to the South, and some declining to support either side. Formal state government was led by a Missourian who vainly proclaimed Missouri a neutral state.

By war's end, Missouri suffered 1,200 armed conflicts ranging from skirmishes to major battles, ranking only behind Tennessee and Virginia in that dubious honor, and had provided approximately 110,000 men to the North and about 40,000 men to the South.

Underlying the Civil War in Missouri was a prolonged intrastate conflict over slavery that lasted from 1854 until about 1889. That private war ended only when the last of the outlaw gangs and guerillas turned outlaw like the James brothers were extinguished.

1

Harley and the Pig Sticker

ROCKFORD'S EARS SHOT FORWARD AND the big horse stopped dead in the dusty track called the Hound Dog Run, an east-to-west highway and byway in Northern Missouri.

Three years of soldiering for the North had hammered into his rider's subconscious those reactions that were by any practical definition instinctive. In one fluid motion John Bitter drew his pistol and kicked Rockford in the flanks, an urgent order to get behind a huge boulder that some prehistoric geologic event had stranded in the middle of an otherwise brushy, but flat, piece of land. The splatter of a mini-ball against the big rock sent him diving from the saddle and crabbing through a thin screen of scrub oak to find cover behind the rock.

Rockford, the meanest, blackest horse Bitter had ever ridden, ran a few dozen yards and then stopped in the middle of the dirt track when a front hoof stepped on a loose rein. Rockford was mean, but he wasn't stupid.

A pistol barked and a limb over John Bitter's head shook from the impact of the large caliber ball. He peeked around the side of the rock in time to see his old friend Harley Eagen edging through the trees beyond a small clearing.

"Harley? Is that you?" he shouted.

"It's me. I've come to take your scalp, John Bitter! You danced with the devil. Now you have to pay the fiddler. Nobody trifles with the Eagen women."

"Harley," he hollered back, "all I did was go for a walk in the Orchard with Morgan. There wasn't anything else going on. I didn't even get a kiss."

"She says you did."

"I don't believe she said that, Harley. She's just mad because I won't take her with me." He waited, and when Harley didn't answer he said, "Well, what if I was to marry your sister? Would that make it all right?"

"She said she wants nothin' to do with you anymore, Johnny. So that won't work."

Bitter grinned at the picture of saucy redheaded Morgan Eagen, hands on her hips, blue eyes snapping, her tongue lacerating his hide, mocking his manhood when he had the temerity to tell her he was going back to Oregon…alone. She held her tongue until he added he wasn't going to send for her either. Then there was pure hell to pay.

"Harley! You wouldn't shoot an unarmed man would you?"

"You're armed, Johnny."

"No. My guns are on my horse. Only thing I've got is my knife."

"You wouldn't lie to your old friend, now, would you Johnny?"

"No. We're friends, Harley. I wouldn't lie."

Harley's voice came a little to his right. "Yep," Bitter muttered, "trying to flank me."

He stood up from behind the rock, hands outspread. "There you go, Harley. No guns. Just my pig-sticker."

Harley stepped from behind a big cottonwood, pistol held in front of him. "You'd actually knife fight me?"

"Guess so, since that's all I got, Harley," Bitter said quietly.

"You know you can't beat me with a knife, Johnny."

"I guess I'm gonna have to try…unless you shoot me first."

Harley's intelligence, reduced to a little under par by the hard skip of a rebel rifle ball off the top of his head at the battle for

Franklin, worked over-time. His sense of honor pulled and tugged in two directions at once. On the one hand, he owed John Bitter for hauling him from the battlefield to an aid station. That was for sure. He figured he owed his life to John. On the other hand, family honor had to be protected.

Harley stood in the clearing, scratching his scruffy red beard, forehead furrowed from the struggle that thinking always brought. "I don't know what to do, Johnny," he confessed.

Finally he laid his dirty felt hat on the ground, his red hair sticking up in greasy spikes. The hat might have been blue once, but time and abuse had eaten holes in the wide brim, and sweat and grimy hands had turned it nearly black.

Harley holstered his pistol, unbuckled the gun belt and laid it carefully on his hat. His gun belt and pistol were the only things about him in good repair. He pulled an Arkansas toothpick from his right boot top and started a lumbering walk across the forty or so yards that separated him from Bitter. The knife in Harley's big hand looked to be at least a yard long, maybe longer to Bitter.

Bitter pulled his knife, a common wood handled hunting knife he used for common purposes…whittling toothpicks from wood splinters, cutting meat, trimming his fingernails…common uses… held it in his left hand and started a slow, resigned walk to meet his friend. *Former friend*, he reminded himself.

They both stopped when they were about ten feet apart. "Damn, but that's a big knife, Harley. You fixin' to stick me with that thing?"

Harley looked like he would rather do anything else, but he shook his head and answered, "Don't have no choice. Family honor is at stake."

"Harley, it's too hot for this, and I'm thinking you forgot how many times I saved your life these past years. Doesn't that count?"

"It shore makes it harder, Johnny, but I got 'er to do."

Bitter looked up at the clear noon sky, a few fluffy clouds moving slowly to the north, looked back at Harley and finally said, "Hell, Harley, I can't let you do that. I'm partial to my hide, and it wouldn't be reasonable to survive a war and then get killed by an idiot with a knife."

He pulled a revolver from the small of his back and cocked it. "Drop the knife, Harley. Don't force me to shoot you."

"You said you didn't have no weapon!"

"I lied."

Harley growled and lunged, and Bitter danced aside. The gun barrel sounded like a rock smacking a ripe watermelon when it collided with the side of Harley's head. For a few seconds Bitter thought he might have walloped him a bit too hard. But when he saw Harley's back rise and fall in troubled slumber, he set that worry aside.

Bitter walked up the dusty track to Rockford and picked up a rein, and then walloped him across the nose with his hat when Rockford tried to bite him. "You danged fleabag!"

He led the horse back to the small clearing, tied the reins to a scrub oak, and then went looking for the sway-back skin-and-bones gray mare Harley called a horse.

Harley came to, sort of, lying on his face in the dust, arms bound and stretched by rope to a stout stake John had cut from a two-inch oak sapling and driven firmly into the ground with a big flat rock. He struggled enough to know his feet were also tied to a stake. He turned his head to the side and spotted Bitter sitting in the shade, his back against the trunk of a small cottonwood, smoking a roll-your-own, staring at Harley.

"Wondered when you were gonna come around. Feared I might have hit you too hard."

"You just gonna leave me tied up?"

"Yep. And I'm gonna let the sun burn your butt." Bitter stubbed the cigarette in the dust, rose like the agile young man he was, and walked over to Harley. He shook his head and then cut the rope that stood duty for Harley's belt and pulled his pants down around his ankles. He pulled up the back flap of Harley's long johns and let the sunlight warm Harley's hairy butt. A big blue bottle fly immediately buzzed around Harley's backside.

"I figure between the time your horse wanders home and the time Morgan takes to find you, your butt will be so sun burnt you can't ride after me."

"That's meanern hell, John Bitter."

"Not as mean as shooting at me or wanting to stick me with a knife. Enjoy the sunshine, Harley." Bitter paused and then added, "It was one hell of a war. I'm glad we made it through, and I'm glad you were with me. So long, friend."

Bitter wrapped the reins around the horn of the old saddle Harley rode, pointed the gaunt mare in the direction of home and swatted her on the hip with his hat. She trotted a few yards, puffs of dust rising to meet each hoof, and then settled into a shuffling walk that carried her up the track and around a thicket of scrubby trees.

"Probably fall asleep before she gets there," he said to Rockford as he stepped in the stirrup and swung up into the saddle. Rockford humped up, fixing to crow hop like he always did, but Bitter didn't have the patience for it today, so he slapped Rockford between the ears with his hat. "Not now, you idiot!"

He turned Rockford up the track, headed for the ferry at St. Joseph to carry him across the big Missouri and on to the Oregon Trail.

2
Misery

I T WAS WELL BEYOND NOON before Morgan found the old mare standing in the shade of the leaning pole shed that barely passed muster as a barn. The reins hung loosely around the saddle horn, and she noted the empty rifle scabbard. She opened the pole gate and shooed the old gal into the corral.

"This isn't the first time you came home alone, Misery, but it's the first time you tied the reins to the saddle horn. Guess we better go find him 'cause Harley don't have any sense of direction what-so-ever."

Morgan walked to the fruit cellar her daddy had dug into the hillside behind the house. Careful to look for sneaky copperhead snakes hiding in the shelf straw, she found a ripe apple and then whistled up Lucifer, a big rangy mule with a reputation for mean-ness. He shuffled up and warily lipped the apple from her palm.

His dark color seemed to match his temperament. The tavern crowd allowed as to how if it came to a tussle between Lucifer and a bear, they'd bet on Lucifer.

While Lucifer crunched away at the apple, Morgan took her well-oiled saddle from the tack room, a lean-to shed that carried more spaces than boards. She led Lucifer by a hank of mane to a stump that gave her five-feet-four-inch frame enough reach to smooth the saddle blanket and heave the saddle up on his back. He turned his head to watch as she pulled the cinch tight.

"No you don't," she said and rammed a knee in his belly. He sometimes practiced the bad habit of puffing up when he was about to be saddled. That left the strap a bit loose when he let go, a good formula for a slipped saddle and a dumped rider, unless the rider caught a foot in the stirrup. Then it was up to the animal to decide whether the rider would live or just get dragged to death.

As much as she respected the big mule's intelligence, she didn't trust him enough to let him decide such important things as life and death. Lucifer half-stepped sideways and exhaled. Morgan took up another two inches on the strap and tucked it back in against itself. "Good boy, Lucifer."

She stepped off the stump and walked back to the corral with Lucifer padding along behind her. Her big mule had no truck with anything wearing pants and standing more than three feet tall. But for some unknown and probably unknowable reason, he liked or at least tolerated Morgan. Not one other person had ever managed to ride the big brute.

Throughout the war, Morgan had managed to keep Lucifer out of the hands of both armies, the Blues from the North and the Grays from the South, as well as rapacious raiders and acquisitive neighbors. Once a Union cavalry patrol had come close to finding Lucifer's corral in a thicket of spiny blackberry vines, but a Rebel sharpshooter winged the young lieutenant leading the patrol and sort of distracted the Union boys. Morgan thought it a miracle Lucifer had refrained from braying his disgust with life in general and with humankind in particular.

The young lieutenant, a farmer from Ohio when he wasn't working to prevent the South from seceding from the Union, sat on Morgan's front step while she cleaned and bandaged his neck. She dismissed the wound as she pulled the wrap around his neck. "Just barely burned you."

He grinned at her and said, "Not too tight, missy. I still need to breathe."

In spite of herself, she smiled back and said, "North, South… you soldier boys are all the same. The North put Grandpa in jail for a Southern sympathizer, the same jail the Confederates put him in for being a Northern sympathizer. All we want to do is farm."

"I see you got your fields plowed. Do that with a stick? I don't see any draft animals."

She pursed her lips and said, "No. What the South didn't take, you Union boys did. My neighbor's still got an ox we plow with. If you take that we can't farm, none of us. And if we don't farm, you haven't got any food to steal."

He flushed at her outburst, partly because he was offended that she thought so little of the Union army, but mainly because it was true. "We pay for what we take," he retorted.

"In scrip that won't buy anything! I put Confederate dollars and Yankee scrip in the outhouse where it'll be of some use."

His sense of honor ruffled by the fiery redhead, the Lieutenant stood and dug a silver dollar from his watch pocket. He gripped her right hand in his left and slapped the silver dollar in her palm. "For your trouble, Ma'am," he said stiffly.

She was too startled and frankly too hungry for currency to protest. She watched him mount and lead his patrol away, and then she turned and walked the path to the orchard. A fruit jar in a deep, hollow cavity of a decadent apple tree served as bank and security for Morgan. With the addition of the silver dollar, she had a nest egg of over one hundred Yankee dollars.

3
Sore

WITH MISERY ON A LEAD rope, Morgan backtracked the old mare to the trail leading to the Hound Dog Run, north of her family's Missouri homestead. After that it was simply a matter of following the hoof prints in the trail dust.

She heard Harley at least 200 yards before she rode into the little clearing next to the track. His threats roared through the woods and across the hillsides. He was a fine cusser and he could be heard for a mile when he was using his best hollerin' voice.

"I'm gonna kill you, John Bitter!" It seemed to Morgan it took him a full minute to get the word "kill" rolling across the hillsides. At the sight of Harley all staked out, she stopped Lucifer, quit dragging Misery, and just sat, hands crossed on the saddle horn, and gazed in amazement.

A small giggle bubbled up at the sight of Harley's sun-red bottom. She tried to force it down and then finally gave up and let the giggle turn into a full-scale laugh. John Bitter, she decided then and there, had intelligence and a fine sense of humor.

Harley switched from cussing John Bitter and started growling about sisters making light of older brothers.

Morgan shook her head and swung down off Lucifer. While she sawed with a hunting knife at the ropes holding her brother prisoner, she asked, "What happened here, Harley?"

When he related Bitter's denial of wrongdoing, she said, "You idiot. I told you to get him back here. I didn't say he tried to have his way with me. I said he tried to kiss me. That's not worth shootin' or stabbin' someone over."

She watched as he sat up, rubbing the raw marks on his wrists.

"Well, get yourself down to the creek and wash up. You smell awful." She handed him a canteen of spring water. "The creek water will be good for your rear end, but don't drink it. You'll get the worms for sure."

It was a full ten minutes before Harley started complaining about his backsides being cold.

"I swear, Harley. You've turned into a whiner. Well, get out of there and let's head for home."

Harley hid behind a tree, gingerly settled his hat around the big lump under his greasy hair, fumbled with the button on his long johns, just one since the other button had gone missing a couple of months back, and, satisfied his modesty had been restored, pulled up his britches. His wrists were sore from trying to break free from Bitter's stake rope. And his throat was raw from all the impotent roaring he had sent Bitter's way. Gingerly, Harley tied a knot in the cotton rope that served as belt.

When he stepped from behind the tree, Morgan said. "Don't forget your pistol," and pointed to the gun belt and holster hanging from a broken limb on an oak tree. "And I put your rifle in the scabbard. I also reloaded it. What were you thinking, shooting at John Bitter?"

Harley didn't answer, just swung up into the saddle and pointed Misery toward home. He yelped, and no matter how he tilted or turned, his backsides rebelled against the pressure of the saddle. He tried standing up in the stirrups. He tried leaning forward. Nothing seemed to help, and no matter how he grumbled and growled about it, he still had to swing down and settle for leading the old mare by the reins and shuffling down the dirt track that wound through the scrub oak to home. Misery had a look in her eyes that seemed to ask, What have I done to deserve this? Two trips in one day?

Morgan was quiet for the first half mile, and then she asked, "Which way did John Bitter say he was going back to Oregon? The Santa Fe or the Oregon Trail?"

Harley wrinkled his forehead in concentration and after a dozen plodding steps said, "He didn't say. But I'd bet on the Oregon Trail. Why?"

She gave Harley a grim smile, but failed to keep the mischief from her eyes. "Cause I'm going with him."

"He's gone, Sis."

"Even that big black horse of his can't outlast Lucifer. Pick up the pace, Harley. I have things to do."

4

Stinging Worms

TWICE MORE DURING THE HOURS after the run-in with Harley Eagen, Rockford's ears suddenly swiveled forward to give Bitter early warning of riders, and twice he had eased the big horse off the track to hide in the brush. The war might have ended for Bobby Lee and the Northern Army of Virginia, but there were still plenty of armed men who either didn't know the war was over or who were, in Bitter's opinion, too stupid to give it up.

Once he and Rockford watched from their hiding place in a blackberry thicket until a party of five scrofulous, hard eyed men had ridden on around a bend in the twisting track. "You know, Rockford, they remind me of Willard Allison back home. That big Indian who lives on Abiqua Creek whipped Willard every Saturday night. But there Willard was again the next Saturday, telling himself he'd get 'er done this time."

Bitter shook his head. "Too stupid to quit. And some are just plain mean, war or no war."

He considered the comfort of two Remington.44 cap and ball revolvers hanging from saddle holsters, a third revolver in a belt holster, and the sixteen-shot Henry repeating rifle in the saddle scabbard. The first time he saw the Henry in action, he knew he had to have one, and when the chance came, he bought one with his own money. He figured the rifle had saved his hide at least twice during the war.

He stared down the track where the riders had gone and shook his head. Although he was a fair shot, he didn't think he could handle more than two or three bushwhackers at a time if they were close. Out in the open, assuming long-range shooting, he had a better chance, especially with the Henry.

A puff of wind, the smell of rain and the distant rumble of a thunder storm drove horse and rider from the track and into a wide, shallow ravine. A narrow slough eased through big, leafy Bam and willow trees. Bitter spotted a likely camp against two downed cottonwood trees maybe three feet in diameter, the second on top of and perpendicular to the first. When he was new to the Oregon country, he asked a neighbor, one of the early settlers in the Willamette Valley why they called the big cottonwoods that grew along the streams "Bam" trees. The neighbor laughed and said, "Cause when they fall they're so damned big they go bam."

"What do you think, Rockford? If we tie a tarp over the one on top, we'll have ourselves a fine shelter. Might even be room for you." For answer, Rockford started to hump up, ready to crow hop a bit just to express his opinion it was time to call it a day.

The leafy detritus made for quiet going, and Bitter reached for his pistol when he heard a small voice cussing and muttering something totally unintelligible. Rockford jerked his head up, ears pointed front and center.

Bitter swung down, wincing at the creak of saddle leather and patted Rockford on the shoulder. "Shhh," he whispered. Pistol at the ready, he soft footed to a big black walnut tree and peeked around the rough trunk.

He was in time to see a small barefoot boy, maybe ten years old, pants rolled up to his knees, wearing a man-sized gray cotton shirt with the sleeves cut off at the elbows, swing a long cane pole and chunk his bait in the slough. The boy let the line sink slowly in the water and then waited for the ripples on the polished surface to disappear against both shores of the slough. When the line started moving steadily upstream, the boy waited a good four seconds and then set the hook.

"Fish on," the boy said to no one in particular, and with all the finesse of an ox pulling a plow, he simply backed away from the water and pulled a nice largemouth bass up on the grassy bank. Bitter judged it to be maybe three pounds. The boy propped the cane pole against Bitter's walnut tree, and walked to the fish flopping in the grass. He picked up a heavy two-inch willow club polished by hard use and whacked the fish on top of the head. "Six," the boy counted, and pulled a cotton rope-stringer from the water.

"Six what?" Bitter asked and stepped around the tree.

The boy was startled, but he picked up his club and his mouth took a hard, defiant set. "Six none of your business, mister."

Bitter tried to stifle a grin and then simply gave up. He slipped his pistol back in the holster, cocked his head sideways like he was pondering what to do next, and said, "Nice fish. I tell you what, I'll give you a penny for the last one. I'll cook him for my supper."

"You ain't gonna' rob me?"

"No. I aim to pitch camp and cook me one of those fish. If you'll sell me one."

The boy brushed dirty blond hair away from his blue eyes, turned his head slightly sideways and said, "A nickel."

Bitter laughed. "Why you rapscallion. I'll tell you what. I'll give you two pennies for the fish and a spoonful of sugar. But first you gotta put your club down. What do you say?"

"Well, I can't give you none of these. I already got 'em sold to the neighbors. Just me and Ma now, so I sell or trade my fish for hen's eggs or apples or whatever else I can. I got some nice hard cider from Uncle Tol the other day."

"How much do you get from the neighbors for your fish?"

The boy's eyes sparkled with mischief, and he grinned as he said, "A penny."

"I ought to paddle your butt," Bitter said. And then he laughed. "Well, okay, catch another while I pitch camp."

Bitter watched with curiosity as the boy reached into an old wooden bucket, jerked his hand back and uttered words no ten-year-old boy should use. The boy shook his hand and then reached into the bucket again and grabbed a small black worm that wriggled like an eel. He held the wiggler in one hand while he ran a hook through its head.

"What're you using for bait?"

"Stinging worms," he said in a huffy tone that meant anybody with a lick of sense would know that.

Bitter looked in the bucket, pulled back in a start and said, "Uh, son…these are baby cottonmouths."

Bitter shook his head and set the bucket down. "Let me see your hands."

The boy laid his pole on the grass, wiggler still protesting from the end of his line, and held out his hands. Bitter turned the dirt-covered hands over. Several small red spots marked wounds on the boy's fingers and the heel of his right hand, but none seemed to be swelling much beyond what one would expect from a bee sting.

"Let me put some baking soda on those bites. Then you catch one more fish, and that's all. Understood?"

The boy waited while Bitter dug in his saddlebags for baking soda and a tin cup. Bitter blew dust from the cup and set it on top of the cottonwood log. He poured a dab of water from a bullet canteen with U.S. stitched in the faded blue wool cover and added baking soda from a powder horn he used to keep the soda dry. While he mixed the paste with a twig broken from a dead limb he asked, "Your mama know where you are?"

The boy swallowed hard and looked away, but not before a tear pooled in the corners of his blue eyes. *Uh oh*, Bitter thought. He held up the twig and pretended to study a dollop of paste sticking to the end. "You don't suppose," he said, "I could sleep in your barn tonight?"

There was a catch in the boy's voice when he said so softly Bitter could barely hear him, "No barn. Raiders burned it."

"Well, maybe I could roll my bedroll out in front of your fireplace."

"Mama wouldn't like that."

"Well, maybe we could ask her. I got some Arbuckle coffee, some flour, some soda for soda biscuits, some sugar and some Borden's. With that bass you promise to catch, we could eat pretty good."

The boy looked suspicious and asked, "What's Borden's?"

Bitter laughed, and said, "Show me those bites again." While he patted the soda paste over the bites on the boy's hands, he said, "Borden's is canned milk…the sweetest stuff you ever tasted. Got three cans from a sutler just before General Lee gave up the fight. Makes coffee taste pretty nice."

"I never had no Borden's."

"Well…tonight could be your lucky night."

5
The Fox and the Hound

THE CORN SHUCKS IN THE cotton tick on the narrow bed in the corner of the room rustled under Harley as he shifted his weight, groaned, and worked at the doomed business of trying to make his butt feel better.

Wrinkles creased his forehead while he watched Morgan climb the ladder to the loft and toss down big, canvas saddlebags. She set the twin bags on the kitchen table and stuffed one side with her prized iron skillet, a hot cake turner, a big kitchen knife, three spoons and three forks, and a tin cook pot.

She opened the flour bin under the kitchen counter and filled a cotton sack with maybe five pounds of corn meal. She spilled what little salt remained in the pewter salt cellar onto the cutting board and divided it. Half went back in the salt cellar and half went into a small medicine bottle with a cork stopper.

"Sis, what are you doin?"

She turned, hands on her hips, to stare at the pathetic creature she called Brother. She shook her head, pushed a wandering strand of red hair away from her eyes, and sighed as a smidgen of guilt crept into her mind.

"Harley, I'm going to Oregon. There's no life here for me. I'm leaving you half the cornmeal, half the flour, some beans, and some winter apples in the root cellar. You'll have to hunt for the rest.

"Now, the corn is in the ground and starting to sprout. I think Lucifer and I put in about six or seven acres. If you can keep the deer and the raccoons out of it, you'll have enough cornmeal to sell and plenty left for winter.

"You can kill a wild hog for bacon. You're good at the smoking. And render the lard. You make lye soap and you can sell some of that. Put away the red apples for winter and make cider out of the yellow ones. Think you can remember all of that?"

"Don't matter. I'm goin' with you."

"No. You need to keep this place safe for Daddy."

Harley winced at the pain, but he rolled over and then sat on the edge of the cot. "You know he ain't coming back, Sis. Been gone too long. I think he got hisself killed in one of those big battles in Virginia."

"Or captured," she countered. "No. You need to stay here and hold this place. If he doesn't come back, it'll be yours. And you need something you know how to do. Farming is what you do best. So you stay on. When Daddy shows back up, then you can think about Oregon. Understood?"

Harley wiped at a tear that puddled in the corner of one eye, but he nodded. He didn't say anything until he thought he could use his voice without crying, but he had to stop and swallow hard a couple of times before he could croak, "Okay, Sis. But why start so late in the day?"

"I need to find the track of that big black horse and get some sense of where John Bitter's headed.

"Now, one more thing. You clean up, take a bath, comb your hair, put on your best clothes, and trim your beard. Or better yet, shave it off. Then you go see Sarah Macbeth. Her Orin got himself killed. And the raiders burned her house, so she's been living in the root cellar. She's a strong woman. She put a stove in the root cellar, made herself a cot and just stays hidden away most days. Sarah will make you a good wife."

And she's smarter than you, big brother. You need her brains, and she needs your muscle.

Harley didn't say anything, just sat and gave the business of having a wife some troubled thinking. He was used to Morgan telling him what to do, but he wasn't sure he could stand some strange female giving him orders.

Morgan recognized the scrunched look thinking painted on his face. "Harley, go put the pack saddle on Misery and bring her up to the house. I'm giving you $40 for that worn out old gal. That's enough to get you another one. I need her for a pack horse until I can buy a younger animal."

When Harley led Misery up to the front porch, pack saddle cinched to her back, he found Morgan in a faded blue shirt that belonged to their daddy and light canvas pants patched in both knees and in the rear. She had her red hair tucked up in a faded gray railroader's striped cotton cap. An old beat up pair of riding boots about two sizes too large came almost to her knees.

He was startled. He had never seen Morgan in anything but dresses and aprons. "You look like a boy!"

She nodded. "Good. That's the idea, Harley. Safer if nobody knows I'm a girl."

It wasn't until Morgan's bedroll was lashed behind the saddle, a canteen slung over the saddle horn, and her trail gear loaded on Misery that Harley finally shook off the shock of losing his little sister and focused his mind enough to unbuckle his pistol and hand it to Morgan.

"You'll need this." When she started to object, he said gently and more intelligently than Morgan had ever seen him, "I still have my rifle. Wait here."

He hurried into the house and came back out carrying a leather pouch. Lucifer turned his big head and watched him slip the strap over the saddle horn. Harley pointed a grubby index finger at the pouch. "There's a dozen paper cartridges and some caps in there."

Morgan leaned down and handed Harley forty silver dollars. He looked surprised, but she didn't offer any explanation about where they came from. Instead, she patted Harley on the cheek and said, "You mind what I said. Keep this place for Daddy. Tend Mama and Grandpa's graves, and the graves of the little ones. And go see Sarah. She needs you and you need her. I'll write when I get to Oregon."

Misery protested at the load, at the heat, and at the blue flies that buzzed her nose, eyes and ears. Morgan pulled the lead rope tight and said, "Come on Misery. No use protesting." But Misery had her mind on going back to dozing in the shade of a tree, not on making one more dusty trip away from the farm. So she dug her heels in until Morgan wrapped the lead rope around the saddle horn, and started Lucifer moving.

6
Ethan Sharp

THE SEVENTH BASS WAS SORT of a mean critter. Just wouldn't cooperate at all. When it bit the wiggler in half and left the rest, the boy again muttered cuss words Bitter wasn't sure he'd heard at any point during the war.

"Where'd you learn to cuss like that?"

"Like what?"

"Like no boy should cuss. I'll bet your mama would paddle your butt if she heard you. And I'm thinking I'm gonna stand in for her if you cuss again. Understood?"

The boy glared at Bitter, but he didn't say anything, just headed for the stinging worms bucket.

Bitter dropped the canvas tarp he was stretching over the downed cottonwood, and snatched the bucket away. "No you don't. You use what bait you have on the hook. That old bass will be back for the rest of that little snake."

Bitter had Rockford unsaddled and staked out, a tarp tied over the top of the downed cottonwood, saddle and gear tucked away under the back of his shelter, and a small fire going before the boy caught the seventh bass. It wasn't as big as the others, but Bitter thought it would do.

"Want to see a trick?" he asked the boy.

"What trick?"

"I'll show you." And with that, Bitter used the trunk of the downed cottonwood tree as a cutting board. Slick as anything, he filleted the bass and laid the two halves in his skillet.

"I can do that."

"Not without a knife. You got one?"

"Left it home," he said with a finality that told Bitter he probably didn't have one.

The boy watched Bitter straddle the big log with a heavy saddlebag and then place a salt shaker, a powder horn hoarding dry soda, a canvas bag that kept his flour dry, an Arbuckle's coffee bag, a waxed paper bag protecting some brown sugar and a Borden's milk can, all in a nice neat row on top of the log. Bitter fished for a coin purse tucked away in his saddlebags. When he saw the coppers Bitter was holding, the boy held out his hand.

John Bitter, war veteran, a man who had seen the mean side of human nature, and who had seen other men do cruel things to each other he was sure God had never intended, squatted down by his fire and pushed a limb further into the coals.

"Thanks for the fish, son," he said gently, and then asked, "You sure you got a mama waiting on you? If I was to take you to your place, would she be watching out the window and wondering if you were okay?"

The boy looked at the ground and sort of stirred the grass with his toe. A stalk of wild yellow hair fell over his forehead. He brushed it out of his eyes and, without looking at Bitter, said, "Well, she's probably not there right now. Probably gone over to the McAllister's for a visit. They're our close-by neighbors. But she'll be back by the time I get my fish sold and get home."

Bitter didn't push it, but his mind was working like fury on the worry he had stumbled onto.

"Well," he said as he rose to his feet, "my name is John Bitter." He held out his hand to the boy and asked, "What am I to call you?"

The boy shook Bitter's hand with a strong jerk and a quick release, like he was touching a hot stove. He looked at Bitter with suspicion, but his need for friendship overtook his wariness, and with a sudden smile he said, "I'm Ethan Sharp."

"Well, Ethan Sharp. That's a nice strong name for a strong boy. Now, how long will it take you to deliver your fish? If you can be back here in an hour, I'll fix you some soda bread, some nice bass, and a cup of Arbuckle's with sugar and Borden's in it. If your mama is off visiting, then I'm sure she won't mind if you eat with me."

"I can be back in an hour. Will that be okay?"

"You bet, Ethan Sharp. That would be fine."

The boy hesitated and then said, "About that spoon of sugar. I'd like that now, if you don't mind."

Bitter shrugged and said, "Okay." He dug for a spoon in a saddlebag, found one, dusted it off on his pants leg and opened the sugar bag. He packed the spoon with a rounded portion of sweet, moist brown sugar and handed it to Ethan. To Bitter's surprise, Ethan dumped the sugar in his shirt pocket, and then licked off the few grains still sticking to the spoon. "For later," he explained, holding the spoon out to Bitter.

When he reached for the wooden bucket, Bitter said, "I took care of the snakes. You find something else for bait next time."

The boy shrugged, picked up his pole and wrapped the line around the butt end until he could push the hook into a crack in the bamboo. And then, bucket and pole in one hand, fish stringer in the other, Ethan slung the stringer over his shoulder. With fish slapping the back of his bare legs, Ethan Sharp, Bitter's newest friend walked the narrow path along the slough.

Rockford and Bitter both watched until the boy was out of sight, and then Rockford went back to cropping grass. The distant rumble of thunder broke into Bitter's thoughts, and he focused on the practical business of making camp. A drop of rain patted the tarp and he hurried to get a pile of dry limbs under a corner of the shelter. He spooned some flour into a small tin-pot, added a splash of water from his canteen and went about the business of making soda bread.

Rockford raised his head and looked at Bitter as if to ask, What are you going to do about this?

Bitter stared at the big horse for a long twenty seconds before saying, "I don't know, you flea bag. I just know I can't ride away from this. I hope that boy comes back, and at the same time I hope he doesn't need to. I've heard too many stories of raiders gathering up youngsters and selling them to mean-hearted homesteaders for me to be easy about our friend Ethan."

He shook his head while he mixed the bread. "This could sure complicate the business of getting back to Oregon."

7
Trail Broke

MORGAN SMILED AS LUCIFER WITH Misery in tow trotted past John Bitter's let-the-sun-burn-your-butt stakes sprouting from the hard earth. She studied the tracks Rockford left in the dust, and satisfied she knew the right direction, settled back in the saddle.

After Harley and her father took up the art of soldering, the almost daily chore of rounding up their stubborn Guernsey heifer fell to Morgan. That particular critter, Bossy by name and bossy by temperament, was a cantankerous beast that treated all fences as a challenge. She would walk right through a split rail fence, and jump the tougher ones. It didn't seem to matter how sweet the grass in her home pasture or how cool the water from the spring, the old cow had the wanderlust.

And she had given Morgan plenty of practice in the business of tracking. Morgan could never decide if the milk and butter from the cream-rich milk was worth the trouble. On occasion Morgan was heard to declare in frustration, "We should just butcher that old cow."

That was before raiders or maybe some unknown covetous neighbor had determined the Guernsey would be better off in a new pasture…or in a stew pot. Morgan's anger at the theft convinced her she missed the cow after all.

She pulled Lucifer to a stop and studied the tracks near the big rock John Bitter had used for shelter from Harley's rifle ball. Rockford's right rear shoe was just a little crooked. It was subtle and didn't count for much in the loose trail dust, but in firm ground, Morgan was dead certain she would recognize the track.

The mule, rider and pack horse, or what passed as a pack horse made almost seven miles before Misery's stumble-jerked the lead rope. Morgan looked back in time to see the old horse regain her balance, but a hint of lather stained the mare's brown hair, turning it almost black along the straps of the hackamore that crowned her head.

"Oh, Misery, I'm so sorry, but I need one more mile. Just one more." The distant rumble of thunder in a mass of dark, boiling clouds to the west, and the smell of rain in a sudden light breeze settled the issue for Morgan. "We'll camp in Eunice Crawford's old barn and you can get some rest."

Morgan had met Eunice at the occasional camp meeting and the regular church socials that brought neighbors together in rural Missouri. A strong, opinionated woman, Eunice frequently offended others, male and female alike. Morgan nonetheless took a liking to Eunice and her forthright manner of looking at life. Eunice was important to Morgan, especially in the first couple of years after Morgan's mother died from the flux.

And in better, safer times Morgan had frequented the Crawford farm to enjoy a woman-to-woman chat. In a very real sense, Eunice had become Morgan's surrogate mother, or at least an elder aunt and they had become the closest of friends.

Her father was half tempted to forbid Morgan to visit Eunice, but he lacked the moral conviction to be a total bigot. And truth be known, he was just a little afraid of Morgan when she became angry. Morgan's stated opinion and growing conviction that a woman had as much right to property, independence, and free thought as any man was a constant irritation to his sense of propriety and the proper order of things. Besides, her attitude forced him to consider issues he had long considered settled, and in fact hadn't given much thought to in the first place. As Morgan grew in stature and in conviction, what had been settled in his mind was now unsettled, and he didn't like it. Not one bit.

The fact that Eunice refused to accept the attention of any of the local bachelors after her husband left for sunnier climates, and the fact she worked her farm alone…or at least without a husband… since no one counted her hired hand Ephraim as much help…was a subject of consternation to some of her neighbors.

On the few occasions he had taken a dram or two of the devil's brew at Rumford's Tavern in Hamilton, their closest town, Morgan's father was known to state with conviction, "Women should never be allowed to vote. Now take that Eunice Crawford, for example…" Deep in the privacy of his mind and soul, he wasn't quite so certain. But he certainly wanted to be.

The wagon road leading to the Crawford farm was overgrown with weeds and thistles, and with hardwood suckers sprouting from low stumps peppering the road. Eunice's husband considered the road building done when the stumps were low enough to make clearance for a wagon axle.

At one point Morgan had to force Lucifer through a stirrup high patch of brush to get around a downed willow tree.

The border raids and Missouri's own private war with Kansas, a war that lasted from the mid-1850s until the big war cranked up, were enough for Eunice to pack her belongings in two wagons, and with Ephraim driving one team and Eunice driving the other head for the more peaceful world of her sister's farm back in Ohio. She asked Morgan to go with her, saying, "I'll come back when the fuss is over, which it will be eventually. Civilized men always finally get fed up and impose peace on the brigands. Until then I think you will find it safer with me in Ohio." Morgan declined, but regretfully because she had come to take Eunice's presence and support for granted. "I'll write," Eunice had promised.

A half mile off the main track, she pulled Lucifer to a stop at the edge of the timber to study the abandoned fields straddling the road leading up to the house. Morgan was shocked at the speed with which Mother Nature reclaimed untended farm land.

She felt tears pooling in her eyes at the sight of a lone broken chimney standing in an overgrown yard surrounded by fire killed willow trees, spidery sentinels and witness that here once stood the Crawford house. The rail fence built to protect Eunice's rose bushes and kitchen garden was broken in half a dozen places, but winding up and around the lone gate post, in bright testimony to better times, was one of Eunice's prized climbing roses. And somehow the crisp yellow blooms hit Morgan harder than the ruins of the place.

She didn't know if accident or raiders were responsible for burning the house, but gone it was. And it looked to Morgan as if only half the barn was still standing. "Poor Eunice," was all she could think to say.

Enough barn roof remained to provide shelter for Morgan, the tired old mare, and the indefatigable Lucifer. Time and visitors, raiders or not, had spared the cast iron Gould's pitcher pump standing in wait over Eunice's well. And miraculously Eunice's two-holer outhouse remained upright.

The blackened circle of stones on the open barn floor, evidence of recent use caused her some worry, but Morgan drew comfort from the sag of the heavy pistol strapped to her side. She tucked the saddle and the packs in against the only solid wall, and led the animals to the well.

The pitcher pump squealed as she started working the long handle. She was beginning to think the well was dry, but just short of wearing out her strong, young arms, a last pull on the handle primed the pump and a full stream of water splashed into the wooden watering trough. She kept pumping until the animals had drunk their fill, and with one final push on the pump handle, she snatched a drink and splashed the cool water on her cheeks before the flow stopped.

She staked Misery on a piece of green pasture with a 30 foot picket rope, and simply turned Lucifer loose to graze. He had long ago expressed his dislike for hobbles and picket ropes. It didn't make much difference to Lucifer if he mashed a slow foot, or got a little flesh mixed in with a shirt sleeve when he took a bite of his tormentor. He just wasn't going to put up with ropes or hobbles.

It may have been pure obstinacy, or maybe it was simple memory of a time when a former owner tried to beat the big mule into obedience with a length of knotted rope. A timely roll under the fence rails and out of the corral is all that kept Lucifer from stomping the man to death.

Morgan knew he wouldn't wander too far, and she also knew she could count on him to give warning if anyone or anything had a bad case of the stupids and wandered onto his turf. Misery he tolerated, but all other critters need beware.

By sunset a few drops of rain rattled off the cracked and curling shakes keeping the standing half of the barn partially dry. One drop found a way through a narrow gap in the roof to die with a pop and a sizzle in the bacon grease melting in Morgan's skillet. She set the skillet off the fire, and in the manner of people who lived alone much of the time, said, "I guess I better get Misery out of the rain."

8

Michael and Rusty

LIGHTNING LIT THE CHURNING MASS of clouds bunched over Bitter's camp. Thunder followed a few seconds later, and it sounded to Bitter like it was going to last forever as it rolled across the dark Missouri skies. A sudden wind snapped Bitter's tarp just to let him know he better get ready for a tussle.

Rockford looked at the sky and decided to ignore the fuss. Like most horses, at least like most of the survivors, he simply turned his tail to the wind and went on grazing. He shook his flanks as a light rain began to fall.

Bitter squatted under the tarp and poked another small limb into his fire. Soda bread, rolled into a yellow rope and wound around a green willow limb was slowly browning over the fire. The sizzle of bass frying in bacon grease was just barely audible over the sudden symphony of frogs and the patter of rain on Bitter's tarp.

Bitter liked the whole thing; the hint of campfire smoke, the scent of cool, rain scoured air, the reflected warmth of the campfire, the croaking of the frogs, the whole business. He might have been content but for the nagging worry about Ethan. He kept thinking, "Ethan can take care of himself," but no twisting and turning of his mind would let him duck the truth. Morally he knew he was on the hook to do more than ride on in the morning. Besides, he liked the boy.

Rockford suddenly snorted and, head up, ears pointed at the campfire, pulled at his picket pin. And Bitter jerked his hand away from the wet nose of a big, smelly hound that slipped up behind him without alerting either Bitter or Rockford. Ethan stepped into the campfire light, just emerged without preamble out of the near dark created by the spreading limbs of the big walnut tree, storm clouds and twilight. "He won't bite," he said, pointing at the big dog. "He's just hungry."

The big hound circled the fire, nose dripping and twitching at the scent of cooked fish and fresh soda bread, tail banging first against Bitters leg, and then against a tent pole rigged to hold up one corner of the tarp. "What's this critter's name?" Bitter asked.

Clothes damp from the cold rain, Ethan stepped under the edge of tarp and gratefully stretched his hands to the small fire. "We call him Rusty on account of his red hair."

Bitter heard a child's cough coming from behind the big walnut tree. He looked at Ethan and shook his head slowly from side to side. "Mr. Sharp," he said, "I'm thinking you haven't been telling me the whole truth. I reckon there's another hungry belly to fill. Am I right?"

Ethan didn't say anything, just walked over and pulled a little boy by the hand from behind the big walnut tree. "It's okay, Mikey," he whispered, "Mister Bitter won't hurt us. Promise."

My Lord, an urchin, Bitter thought. Aloud he said, "Come in out of the rain, boys."

Bitter couldn't tell if the little blond boy, obviously a twig from the same family tree as Ethan, was shivering from the cold or from fear. John Bitter, hardened veteran and war hero, knelt down and held out his hand to the child, baby really, and said, "What's your name, boy?"

"Mikey don't talk much, Mister Bitter," Ethan said, "Not since the raiders took Mama. He just cries at night." He wiped angrily at silent tears with the back of his hands, and then broke into sobs.

In spite of himself, Bitter's eyes started watering until he had to wipe the left one, always the left one, and mutter about the damned campfire smoke. And then he wrapped both little boys in his big, strong arms and held them while they cried. Bitter swore softly through clenched teeth, "Those sonsabitches. Those sonsabitches."

He wasn't too sure which sonsabitches they were, but he was sorry he couldn't just kill them right on the spot. And he wasn't too sure whose grief he was sharing, the grief of orphan boys, or his own grief for friends lost to war.

The wet nose of the big hound pushed into the tight little circle and nudged Bitter's arm, and he slipped a big hand around the back of the dog's head.

Cried out and dried out a bit by the fire, the little boys sat in front of the fire on Bitter's saddle, scootched in against each other for comfort. Bitter pulled a blanket from his bedroll and tucked it around their thin shoulders.

He tore off pieces of soda bread, one for each of the boys and one for the dog. For some reason, Bitter wasn't hungry. While the bass filets cooled on his one tin plate, he asked, "How have you two been living?"

Slowly between bites, Ethan told a story all too familiar to the farmers in northern Missouri, a story of raiders stealing livestock and food at first, and then later sinking to killing the men and taking the women. It was late in the war before they started selling youngsters to cold hearted settlers or shop owners as cheap labor.

"We hid out," Ethan said, "cause I didn't want me and Mikey sent off to be orphans. I just told the neighbors Mama was sick so they wouldn't wonder why she hadn't been to church for so long."

He took a sip of Borden's from Bitter's tin cup and handed the cup to Mikey.

"So big Rusty here guards Mikey while you fish and trade with the neighbors?"

"Yep."

"How old is he? Four? Five?"

"He'll be six come August. I forget the day."

"Where's your dad, Ethan?"

"Gone. Mama said he got killed in some big battle in Tennessee."

"I'm sorry, Ethan. Don't you have any other relations?"

"Well," Ethan pondered, "there's Mama's sister, Aunt Quilla, but she moved back to Ohio someplace. I don't know where."

"Do you know her married name?"

Ethan shook his head. "Mama never told me."

Mikey drank the last of the Borden's from the tin cup, belched and then yawned.

"Your house still standing, Ethan?"

"Yes, but me and Mikey sleep in the springhouse in case anybody comes around."

"In the morning, we'll go see if we can find any letters or anything that'll let us know where your Aunt Quilla went."

All the soda bread was gobbled up, both filets of bass devoured, followed by a whole can of Borden's, because Bitter figured growing boys needed milk, and he wasted two spoons of brown sugar on the orphans before Mikey fell off the saddle in a dead sleep. Bitter rolled out his ground tarp, spread the blankets, and slipped little blond headed Mikey under the top blanket. Ethan didn't need an invitation to bed. He just slipped under the top blanket and pulled a corner over his head. But when Bitter started to crawl in between the boys, the big hound moved onto the blankets and just stared.

"Judas, Rusty! Where do you expect me to sleep?"

9
Lucifer's Revenge

A T GRAY LIGHT, MORGAN SETTLED in the saddle, thumped Lucifer in the ribs with her heels, and pulled on Misery's lead rope. Morgan was encouraged to find the old mare rested and looking years younger than the beaten, drag foot she had been the night before. Morgan pulled Lucifer to a stop by the broken gate, nipped a blossom from the climbing bush, and tucked the stem under the band of her cap. A wisp of red hair uncoiled and rode companion to the yellow rose.

She had no idea how unlike a boy she looked.

In the first hour, Morgan gained almost four miles on John Bitter. Unlike Bitter, she hadn't felt the need to let two little boys sleep an extra hour. Or brew any coffee because she didn't have any in the first place. And she had never gotten used to chicory coffee in the second.

It was the kind of morning young Miss Eagen drew into her soul for its life giving energy and optimism. The air was cool, the rain had pounded the trail dust into submission, and Misery's head was up, eyes focused on the trail.

For an hour Morgan wool gathered while Lucifer and Misery did the work. She rehearsed the first words she would say to John Bitter when she found him, words like, "John, even if you don't want me for a wife, I'll pay you to take me to Oregon." Or, "You'll need a wife in Oregon. I'm strong, I'm young." Or, "I can ride, I can shoot, and I can cook. Take me with you." She could imagine his joy at seeing her. Maybe he would try to steal a kiss again.

Lucifer's sudden stop in the trail and Misery's collision with the mule's rump brought Morgan out of her reverie. A lean, gapped tooth, stubble-faced tobacco dribbler stepped into the roadway. He walked up and grabbed a handful of Lucifer's bridle.

"Well," he said with a drawl that marked him as an Arkansan, "What have we here, Lige? A boy with flowers in his hair."

"Don't reckon it's a boy, Pa," a voice said from behind her. "I sees a woman."

Morgan was suddenly grateful for the morning chill and the wisdom of wearing the light cotton duster once belonging to Harley, and grateful it was several sizes too big. It hung to her knees and hid the pistol holster. She slid her right hand under the duster and decided she would shoot the man in front first, and then shoot his son.

She started to ease the pistol from the holster when Lucifer settled the issue. The big mule twisted his head and bit Lige's daddy just above the beltline hard enough to come away with some tender hide. The man yelped and jumped aside, but he wasn't fast enough to dodge a heavy front hoof that knocked the chaw clean out of his mouth along with the last three or four of his front teeth. He was dead before he hit the ground. The big mule started stomping on the body just to make sure.

Lucifer's sudden turn freed Morgan from the necessity of shooting from the saddle. She sailed about six feet in the air before descending once more to Mother Earth. Fortunately, she landed butt first on a leafy carpet of old leaves and other detritus that cushioned her fall shy of a bone breaking impact.

Lige shouted, "Pa!" and raised his old musket to shoot Lucifer. Morgan sat up, swept the duster back and finished her draw. She steadied the pistol in both hands, cocked the hammer and pulled the trigger. The pistol ball shot a shower of leaves up between the man's legs. Startled, it was a good three seconds before he swung his rifle in her direction.

The recoil had nearly torn the pistol out of her hands, but she grimly cocked the pistol and fired again. The big .44-calibre ball packed enough wallop to shatter an ankle and knock the man flat on his back. Howling in outrage and sudden pain, he tried to level his musket at Morgan just before she triggered another round. This one caught him just above the beltline and lodged somewhere north of his liver. The rifle sagged to the ground. Good old Lige sighed once and then had the good manners to die quietly.

Morgan cocked the gun once more and got to her knees, trembling and frightened, but hunting another target. At the sight of Lucifer, his flanks twitching, nostrils flared, sniffing the mangled body of Lige's pa, she got to her feet. She took a deep breath to keep the nausea from spoiling her breakfast, and with trembling hands used both thumbs to let the hammer down.

She walked quietly over and patted Lucifer on the shoulder. She took one look at the body and knew the man was dead. "Good boy, Lucifer. You saved my bacon."

When her shakes stopped and the adrenalin burned out, she searched the two men. The old musket belonging to the son was just too used up to be much good, but she hung his powder flask and bullet pouch over her saddle horn.

The older man was carrying a good breech-loading Sharps carbine, probably stolen from a Union cavalry soldier. She made sure it was loaded, added the four extra cartridges to her bullet pouch, and hung the rifle, barrel down, on the saddle horn with a loop made from the man's shoe laces. As soon as she could, she would either buy or make a saddle scabbard. A quick search of the men's pockets failed to turn up any identification…or any money for that matter.

Grateful to Harley for the pistol, she sent a silent prayer of thanks in his direction while she reloaded the cylinder and tucked the gun back in its holster. She took a long pull from her canteen, let out a deep breath to steady her nerves and swung up in the saddle. Lucifer looked at the torn corpse, snorted, and then turned and started down the trail. He looked back once to make sure Misery was still following along behind.

Morgan knew she was supposed to feel bad for killing Lige, but no matter how she searched her conscience there just wasn't any guilt to be found. She knew what those two bushwhackers had in mind, and as sure as the sun comes up, it involved more than robbery. Nope. She didn't feel like she had done anything wrong. In fact she had felt more remorse over the last copperhead she killed down by the fruit cellar. That critter at least was just going about the business of hunting a meal, not bringing evil to the world.

Even if she had been inclined to do so, without a shovel there was no way to bury the men. She reached forward and patted the mule's neck. "Well, Lucifer, since I can't bury them and you can't either, I guess I better tell the sheriff in Hamilton so he can send somebody out and tend to those two."

10
Hooked

MIKEY WOKE FIRST. HE ELBOWED Ethan in the ribs, and when Ethan raised his head to look at him, Mikey, eyes big, just pointed at the fire.

The sun was casting morning shadows as Bitter poked a fork at the strips of bacon sizzling in the skillet and then set about the business of mixing water, flour, soda and brown sugar for fried bread. He wasn't too sure what prompted the impulse to make a special breakfast for the boys, and he wasn't sure he wanted to think about it too much. He finally settled for a shrug of resignation. *In for a penny, in for a pound.*

He was tempted to save the second can of Borden's for another day, but the sight of the gaunt, skinny yawners pricked his conscience and he set one of the two remaining cans on the log.

"Morning, boys. Did you sleep good?"

Mikey didn't say anything, but Ethan rubbed sleep from his eyes and said, "Fine."

Bitter asked, "Where's the red dog?"

Ethan crawled out of the blankets and stretched his hands to the coals. "He hunts his own breakfast. Good thing, 'cause me and Mikey ain't had any extra."

Bitter spooned Arbuckle's into a pot of boiling water, waited until the roil started again and then set the pot on a rock to cool down. He added a dash of cold water to settle the grounds.

"Well, as soon as we eat, let's get to your place and see if we can find out where your Aunt Quilla went. Okay?"

Breakfast over, Bitter put Ethan to scrubbing the tin plate, cup, and eating utensils with water boiled in his skillet. Ethan seem to know what he was about, so Bitter started breaking camp, rolling ground cloth and bedding, lashing the bed roll into a tight bundle, folding the tarp, and coiling rope.

Rockford's rumbling chuff caught Bitter's ears, and he looked up just in time to see Mikey walk in front of the big horse and stare up at him. Heart in his throat, Bitter started to warn Mikey away, but afraid to startle Rockford, he held his breath until the brute of a horse nudged the boy with his big velvety nose and took a sniff of his little boy scent. Mikey reached down and pulled some grass and held it out to Rockford who lipped the grass and started chewing.

"I'll be danged. Rockford's never taken to anybody before."

Ethan looked up from drying the dishes on a piece of rag Bitter had given him for that chore. "Oh, don't worry about Mikey. Animals like him. He always knows what they're thinking."

"Scared me, he did. Rockford is just as likely to take a bite as not."

The big horse nudged Mikey again and set him to giggling and falling backwards in the grass. And then the big red dog was standing over Mikey, hackles raised, crouched to attack. Rockford put his nose close to the dog, and then, somehow satisfied with his inspection, dropped his head and went back to feeding. The dog moved in closer and touched noses with the horse.

Rusty's hackles flattened out, and Bitter let out another held breath. "Ethan, I don't know what I just saw, but it looked like some kind of animal treaty. Dangest thing I ever saw. Mikey scared the peewaddin' out of me."

Ethan nodded wisely and said, "Not to worry, Mister Bitter. Those two will protect Mikey."

The search of Ethan and Mikey's house turned up an old family Bible and a list of names tied to marriages, births, deaths, and locations, almost all in Illinois.

He read the list to Ethan. "Recognize any of the names?"

"Ransom sounds familiar, but I don't know where those folks live."

There were no letters to be found. "Dang," was all Bitter said, but he slipped the Bible in a flour sack he found hiding under a night jar on the back porch. He felt his anger rise up again at those "sonsabitches."

Caught her on the way to the outhouse to empty the thunder mug. I get a chance, I'm gonna kill 'em.

He helped the boys pack their few belongings in the flour sack along with the Bible, and wrapped them all in the one good blanket Ethan retrieved from the spring house. Bitter tied the bundle behind the saddle, took a long look at the load on Rockford and let out a slow sigh. There just wasn't room for all of them on Rockford's back. Not with the saddlebags, Bitter's bedroll and tarp and the boys' things.

He picked Ethan up and set him in the saddle, and then put Mikey in the saddle right in front of Ethan. "You hang on to him."

He wrapped his big hands around the reins and said, "How far to the next town, Mister Sharp?"

Ethan shrugged and said, "Maybe fifteen miles, I guess. I ain't never been there."

"Does it have a name?"

Ethan brightened at that question, one he knew the answer to. "Yep. It's called Hamilton. It's a big town."

"Well, then" Bitter said, "I guess we better get started."

"Wait, Mr. Bitter," Ethan said, and slid down from the saddle, "I want my cane pole."

And so, with a cane pole in one hand and Rockford's bridle reins in the other, Bitter started the long walk west toward Hamilton and his farm in the state of Oregon.

11

A Fair Country Stroll

MISERY STARTED OUT STRONG, BUT in five miles she was back to kicking up spirals of dust with her drag foot pace. The hint of summer heat didn't do anything to help her frame of mind or her energy for that matter. A stumble and a near fall jerked the lead rope against Morgan's leg.

Morgan pulled Lucifer to a stop and dismounted. She coiled the lead rope as she stepped over to the old mare and patted her on the neck. "I don't know if I should cuss you, or give thanks you made it this far.

"Well, there's nothing else for it. You and me, old gal, will just have to walk and let Lucifer carry the load."

Morgan was a fair walker, faster than Misery for sure, but it took nearly an hour to make the next three miles. She led the animals to an inviting pool of shade offered by a big oak as sanctuary for road weary travelers.

Lucifer's long floppy ears swiveled forward, early warning that someone or something was headed their way.

Morgan didn't know it at the time, but she would never again fully trust strangers, especially men, and she had developed an intense dislike of tobacco chewers. She slipped behind the big oak and loosened the pistol in her holster.

A middle aged couple sat on the seat of a heavily loaded freight wagon. A four horse team of black Shires pulled the load, their white fetlocks working in easy rhythm on the level road.

The man nervously pulled the team to a stop at the sight of Lucifer and Misery. He reached for a shotgun and laid it across his lap. "Hello?" he said. "We're just travelers, not outlaws."

Morgan eased around the oak to put her animals between her and the wagon. "Well, then," she said, trying to pitch her voice an octave lower than her normal voice, "just keep traveling and we'll have no quarrel."

The man said, "Your horse looks played out. I seen your foot track in the dust. You must be headed for Hamilton."

When Morgan didn't answer he said, "We're headed to Hamilton, too. Now the war is over, we plan to move back on our farm."

In spite of herself, Morgan said, "Just because the war is over, it doesn't mean the fighting is."

"Is that what happened to the two men back yonder? You do that?"

"I don't know what you're talking about," Morgan said. "I didn't see anybody."

The woman spoke up and said, "No blame in defending yourself."

She looked at her husband and said, "Karl, offer the boy a ride. We can hitch his horse and mule to the wagon."

"Would you like a ride to Hamilton?" the man asked.

Morgan eyed the couple and could feel no threat, but their beady eyes and unblinking stares made her uncomfortable. She couldn't put her finger on it, but something was off kilter here. "I'll walk," she said.

"Suit yourself." He slapped the reins and the team leaned into the harness and the wheels pulled spirals of dust from the road.

She watched the wagon until it rounded a gradual bend in the road. "You must be crazy," she said to herself, "walking instead of riding."

She picked up the reins and led her animals to the road. "All right, you mangy critters, let's get moving."

12

Hamilton

PARCHED WAS THE ONLY WORD that came to Bitter's mind. *May and already turning hot. Disgusting is what it is.* At about the five-mile point, Bitter's boots were turning from comfort to blisters.

He stopped Rockford in a shady spot, looked up at Ethan and said, "Your turn. I'll ride a while."

Bitter swung Ethan down, gathered the reins, slipped a sore left foot in the stirrup and mounted up. Mikey twisted to look at him, leaned back, and in a few plodding yards fell asleep. Bitter had to catch him to keep him from falling off the saddle.

At the ten-mile point Ethan and Bitter swapped again and shared the last of the spring water in Bitter's canteen with Mikey.

It was late afternoon before the small cavalcade limped down the main street of Hamilton. The war and the fuss along the Kansas and Missouri border led Hamilton's residents to exercise a high degree of caution around strangers. But the sight of two blond-headed boys perched high on a big black horse, led by a tall, foot-sore stranger wearing faded Union-blue britches and a battered cavalry hat, didn't long hold the attention of shoppers and shop keepers in the little town.

The big red hound padded to a water trough, lapped his fill, and ignored the warning bark fired his way by a wire-haired mutt standing safely on the boardwalk in front of the Hamilton Emporium. Rockford did likewise and drank his fill without so much as a flicker of his ears in the mutt's direction.

Named after Joseph Hamilton…or maybe Alexander Hamilton of Founding Father fame…or maybe after both men since nobody was quite certain about the matter…the town boasted almost twenty-five houses, a half dozen or so stores selling various goods, a church, a school house, two saloons, a courthouse, a livery, and a barber shop, the proprietor of which also served as the local dentist and undertaker.

The saloons paid service to a company of the 50th Illinois Infantry posted in Hamilton to help the local Home Guard discourage bushwhackers, thieves and confederate sympathizers.

It spoke to the strength of their male character that, although berated by the good Christian women of the Temperance League, who spoke long and loud against the use of tobacco and alcohol—the protection provided by the Home Guard and the Union Army not withstanding—no soldier had been dissuaded from the use of tobacco or alcohol.

A hint of fresh baked bread floated by the water trough and set Bitter's stomach to growling. He pulled Rockford down the street and followed the scent to a single-story, whitewashed restaurant.

A tall, lean woman in her mid fifties, grey hair in a bun, wearing a bright yellow apron to protect her long print dress, eyeballed the cavalcade and then leaned her broom against the doorway.

Sparkling clean windows, backed by gauzy white curtains, carried gold gilt letters proclaiming the establishment "Wanda's Eatery." A neat hand-printed sign advertising homemade pies leaned in a front window.

"Come a ways, I'd guess," she offered in greeting.

Bitter nodded and said, "Some."

"Those ragamuffins yours?"Bitter had worked out an answer to that question, one he figured the local sheriff might ask, so he nodded and said, "My nephews. My sister Ellen's boys."

The woman Bitter took to be the Wanda of fresh baked bread and homemade pies, shot a glance at Ethan and asked, "What's your name, boy?"

"I'm Ethan and this is Mikey, and we're hungry."

"Got a last name?"

"Bitter," Ethan said. "Same as my uncle."

"Your mama didn't marry or change her name?"

Ethan was wary, but he said, "Nope. Kept her birth name. And I'm glad because Daddy was a mean, worthless son-of-a-bitch."

Bitter caught himself in time to stifle a laugh.

It was obvious from the amused look in her hazel eyes, a dubious frown and a "tsk, tsk," the woman didn't believe a single word of Ethan's story, but all she said was, "Well, you get down off that horse and I'll feed you. But if you cuss again, I'll wash your mouth with soap. And for now you'll have to eat out here on the porch until you two get a bath."

Bitter swung Ethan down and then caught Mikey as the little boy reached his arms out and leaned out of the saddle. "Come here, you little rascal," Bitter said and set Mikey on the porch. Rusty jumped up on the porch and was rewarded with a hug from Mikey.

"Ma'am, would you mind keeping an eye on these two while I stable the horse? I'll be right back." Bitter handed her a four-bit piece. "I think this might stand half a chance of covering what these two hungry boys can eat."

"More than enough with some left for you. I'll keep an eye on 'em."

Bitter, Ethan's cane pole in hand, led Rockford toward the livery stable just as two hard-eyed, red bearded riders cantered up the street toward the Boston Saloon and Gambling Parlor. They swung down, tied their horses to the hitching rail, adjusted pistol holsters sagging from gun belts, and stepped up on the boardwalk. They stopped and peered into the bar over the batwing doors and then stepped inside.

Bitter spat and said in disgust, "Bushwhackers. I'd bet on it."

Bitter gave the hostler at the livery stable a dollar for hay and grain and a place to sleep in the loft. He piled the gear in a corner of the tack room and unsaddled Rockford who immediately rolled in the dust of the corral. Bitter failed to mention the boys.

The owner of the café was standing outside the door looking down the dusty street when Bitter came out of the livery stable. The boys were nowhere in sight. Sore feet be damned, he started running up the street.

"Where's the boys?" he hollered.

The woman pointed said, "Down there."

Bitter dropped to his knees and peeked under the porch. He could hear Rusty growling and Mikey crying.

"What's going on, Ethan? What set Mikey off?"

Ethan was shaking, but his eyes were dry. "It's them, Mister Bitter, the ones who took Mama."

"Where?"

"They went in the saloon. The ones with red beards. I seen 'em coming up the street. And I recognized the blaze-faced roan and the Buckskin. Mikey seen 'em too. That's why he's crying."

Bitter stood up and dusted the knees of his britches. Wanda asked, "What did the boys mean about taking their mother?"

"They're the bushwhackers who stole her from the boys," was all the answer Bitter needed to give. "Where's the sheriff's office, Ma'am?"

"Two blocks up and then a left. But Sheriff Tucker isn't there. He and his deputy rode out while you were stabling your horse."

Bitter's shoulders sagged a bit and then he looked up at the tall woman standing on the porch. "Keep an eye on the boys for me, please." He turned and started walking towards the Boston Saloon.

"What are you fixing to do?"

Over his shoulder, Bitter said, "Read 'em from the Good Book."

13
Justice Served

BITTER STOPPED ON THE BOARDWALK, pulled his pistol from the holster and checked to make sure each nipple on the cylinder still held a cap. When he was satisfied the pistol was ready, he holstered the gun, took a deep breath and let it out, steeling his nerves and firming his resolve. He pushed on through the batwing doors and stopped to let his eyes adjust to the darker light. The saloon was empty except for the red beards sitting at a table, sipping whiskey and teasing the dark-haired floozy who worked the saloon for a living.

The bartender looked at the hard set of Bitter's jaw and the way he was staring at the two men. He scooted down the length of the bar and was reaching for a sawed-off shotgun just as Bitter stuck a pistol barrel between his eyes.

"Huh uh," he said quietly, "not a good idea. I'll just borrow that."

The bartender, known to the locals as Little John, a big, dark-eyed, balding man with a graying handlebar mustache, handed the shotgun to Bitter without a word. He hadn't survived all these many years by being stupid.

Bitter walked to the table hosting the bushwhackers, and without so much as a "by-your-leave," busted the closest one over the head with the barrel of the shotgun. The man fell backwards out of the chair, either unconscious or dead. Bitter didn't care which.

When the second red beard, the larger of the two started clawing for his pistol, Bitter stuck the big muzzle of the shotgun in his face and said, "Go ahead. I plan to kill you anyway."

The man flinched and stopped his draw. "What's going on? Do I know you?"

"Not yet, but we're going to get acquainted."

Bitter gave a hard look at the woman who was frozen in place. "Did these bastards ever talk about taking a woman from a farm about twenty miles east of here?"

She shook her head, found her voice and asked with a slight quaver, "Why would they?"

"Well, cowardly dogs like these like to brag about how tough they are, and sometimes they tell their whores things they shouldn't."

The woman straightened her back and glared at Bitter. "I may work the bar, but I ain't no whore."

"Okay. You're no whore, but the question stands. Did they ever talk about stealing a woman from a farm east of here?"

She shook her head.

"You sure?"

"Of course I am," she snapped at him.

"Then get back over against the bar."

The man on the floor stirred and moaned. Somehow that prompted the second man to suggest Bitter had it wrong. All that got him was a shotgun pointed straight at his face.

"Now…what did you do with the woman you stole?"

"I don't know what you're talking about!"

"Yes, you do. There were two witnesses you didn't see when you took Mrs. Sharp."

"You mean those two kids that…oh shit."

"Bartender, you heard that, didn't you?" Bitter asked.

"Yes, I did. Go ahead and shoot the son-of-a-bitch. Anybody who kidnaps women has got it coming. If you don't want to shoot him, I'll go get a rope."

In panic, the red beard shoved the table hard against Bitter and slapped a hand on his pistol. But that's all he managed before Bitter triggered both barrels and tumbled him like a rag in a windstorm. The dead man lay sprawled on his back halfway across the room.

The woman screamed and started for Bitter. "You killed him! You bastard! You killed my Bill." She slapped Bitter about the face and shoulders until the bartender pulled her off.

"You had no right," she shouted. "They just wanted to have a little fun with that woman, but she tried to run away and Little Bill shot her before Big Bill could stop him," she explained to Bitter.

"And that made it all right?" Bitter asked.

"That made it Little Bill's fault," she said.

Bitter pointed at the man he'd clubbed with the shotgun. "That worm is called Little Bill? And he's the one who shot Mrs. Sharp?" It was statement, more than question.

She nodded and said defensively, "Big Bill felt bad about it, but they decided to just bury her and not say anything."

"Just leave two orphans and go on like nothing happened, huh?"

Little Bill or whatever his name was rolled over on his stomach and pushed himself to his knees. In anger, Bitter grabbed the bushwhacker by the shirt collar and pulled him to his feet. Bitter turned him to face the body of Big Bill.

"From man to corpse, in the blink of an eye. Take a good look, Little Bill, because in about sixty seconds that's gonna be you."

Little John and the dark haired woman backed away until the dark mahogany bar stopped them.

"You can't just shoot me. I got rights!"

"Yes, you do. You have the right to defend yourself." Bitter slowly backed up. "Anytime you're ready, draw your weapon."

Little Bill, slightly under par from the whack on the head, and slightly demented when he wasn't under par, grinned and said, "You're a dead man."

Little Bill managed to lift his pistol out of its holster, and he even managed to thumb the hammer back…just a split second before Bitter's first slug punched a hole in his chest somewhere between his heart and his liver. The second slug broke his neck, and the third slug, fired as the man lay kicking on the floor, penetrated his pelvis. Had he lived, he might have developed a high pitched squeaky voice.

The bartender would later say in admiration that John Bitter's draw was the quickest he'd ever seen. "He let Little Bill pull his pistol before he even started his draw, and then nudged Little Bill on out of this life with three big slugs. Little Bill had it coming on account of killing the woman, but the shootout still amounted to cold-blooded killing. Little Bill was as good as dead even before he started his draw. Of course that put the Big Bill's gang on Bitter's trail looking for revenge. It was a sorry day, because most of them never lived to see another sunset."

14
Almost Arrested

MORGAN WAS LIMPING AND TRYING to talk herself into loading enough gear on Misery so she could ride Lucifer, but her conscience just wouldn't let her burden Misery with more than the pack saddle.

"I don't know why I thought you were worth forty dollars, Misery, but I know I'd better get you rested up before I trade you for a younger pack horse."

She figured she was about three or four miles from Hamilton when a horse and rider, followed by a wagon with a young man driving a team of horses, trotted around a bend in the road. Morgan pulled Lucifer to the side of the Hound Dog Run and waited.

As the rider drew closer, Morgan saw the star pinned on the big man's left shirt pocket. Mounted on a large roan gelding, the sheriff was used to intimidating people who had the misfortune of riding smaller animals. In this case, however, Morgan's mammoth mule stood sixteen hands high and put Morgan at eye level with the sheriff. He just wasn't used to not having an edge, and he didn't like it.

He startled Morgan by pulling his pistol and pointing the ugly bore of his revolver at her. "Don't move, son. You're under arrest. I have witnesses who swear they saw you shoot two men back down the road a ways."

She stiffened and said, "Were these witnesses driving a freight wagon pulled by four black Shires?'

The Sheriff nodded, "Yes."

"Then they are liars, aren't they," she answered. "For all we know, that beady-eyed old man could have been the killer."

"They were pretty convincing. Said they saw a young man with a big mule shoot both of the dead men with that carbine you carry."

"Nonsense. This weapon has not been fired," she bluffed. "Check it. And as far as seeing a young man goes," she pulled the cap from her head and treated the men to a profusion of shiny red hair, "I know even an unobservant man like you can see I'm not a boy. So put your gun away and clear the road. I don't know why those people are lying, but clearly they are. I demand their arrest."

The young man in the wagon pulled the team to a stop and grinned as the sheriff's ears turn red. In a huff, the sheriff growled and said, "Walter, you take the wagon and see if you can find any dead men. I plan to take this boy…er…ah…this young woman back to town, and get to the bottom of this."

Walter, nearly nineteen years old and nearly dumb struck by the cascade of red hair and the sudden revelation of feminine beauty, finally found his voice. "One question, Ma'am. Did you shoot anybody today?"

"Yes," she said, "I did. Two bushwhackers who promised me harm. Actually, I only had to shoot one. My mule killed the other one."

"And you expect us to believe a little thing like you bested two bushwhackers?" the sheriff said.

"A minute ago you were ready arrest me. Now that you find I'm not a boy, you don't believe me."

"You sure don't look the type, Ma'am," Walter said apologetically. He looked at Sheriff Tucker and said, "Brother Bob, I think we should both go and see if we can find any bodies. It'll be easier to load 'em if there are two of us. And I'll bet we can finish that chore and still beat her back to town."

The sheriff chewed one end of his black handle bar mustache, ruminated a minute and then said, "Okay. We'll do 'er that way. But you better be in town when we get back, Miss…ah…whatever your name is."

"I'm Morgan Eagan. Now, I have a question for you. Have you seen a tall, clean-shaven young man wearing Union blue and riding a black horse?"

The men looked at each other and shrugged. "Why?" Walter asked.

"Well, I'm supposed to meet him in Hamilton," she lied. "We're going to get married and then move on out to Oregon."

Sheriff Tucker shook his head and said, "Nope. We didn't see anybody on the way out here, but that doesn't mean he couldn't have gotten into town before we rode out."

"Oh," she said in disappointment, "I thought I recognized a hoof print belonging to his horse back down the track a ways."

Walter, a smidgen of jealousy of the unknown stranger working on his mind mainly because he was starting to believe in love at first sight, looked up at her and said, "Ma'am, if you was to offload that gear on the mule into our wagon, you could ride the mule and not have to walk the rest of way."

"If I was a man, would you make the same offer?"

"No, Ma'am," he said and smiled, "because you'd be under arrest."

15
Family Ties

MORGAN DECIDED TO TRUST THE young deputy with her goods. Maybe it was his winning smile and deep blue eyes, or maybe it was because he was a lawman. Whatever it was, she took him up on the offer to offload Lucifer. But kept the carbine and her pistol.

"This way," she said as she looked at the sheriff, "you'll know I'll still be in town when you get there."

After Walter helped her load her pack in the wagon, Morgan offered her hand, which Walter gallantly held a little longer than necessary before bashfully and somewhat stupidly saying, "Thanks."

In embarrassment he leapt into the wagon, and he almost made it, but a left foot hooked the top of the wagon wheel and he sprawled in total loss of dignity on the wagon seat. His hat spilled into the wagon box and his brother, the sheriff, laughed and said, "Walter, you take the cake. A pretty girl smiles at you and you turn into a clubfooted idiot." He also said some unkind things about his manners and his agility.

Walter retrieved his hat, pulled it down about his ears, red faced and totally humiliated, and without a glance in Morgan's direction clucked the team into motion.

Morgan had the decency to hold her laughter until the wagon was out of sight. Her laughter went beyond amusement. An observer might have concluded it was born out of relief the sheriff had not checked the rifle she had taken from the older bushwhacker because she had no idea if it had been fired or not. Or maybe it was letting go the tension of having killed a man.

The ride to Hamilton rested her blisters and let her speculate a bit about her accusers. She was sure the sheriff and young Walter would find the dead men. What she wasn't so sure about was whether they would believe her over the lies of an outwardly respectable older couple. She still hadn't figured out a motivation when Hamilton came into sight, but she had decided to dislike the old couple as intensely as she could.

The smell of cool water in the horse trough drew the big mule to a halt in front of the Hamilton Hotel, a two story structure with a balcony decorating a false front. Both animals drank their fill and let the water drain from damp muzzles.

Lucifer jerked his head up as the muffled sound of gunfire rolled up the street from the direction of the Boston Saloon.

16
A Reason to Run

LITTLE JOHN, EARS RINGING FROM the concussion of the pistol shots, waded through the drifting, sulfurous cloud of gun smoke to look at the bodies. There was no doubt in his mind the red beards were dead, but it was in his nature to be sure of such things. They were disgusting creatures in life, and death hadn't improved them much, a little maybe, but some things just can't be improved.

He nibbled the wax on the left end of his drooping mustache, took a deep breath of the smoky air, coughed, and let a resigned sigh slowly escape pursed lips.

He glanced at Bitter and said, "You're kind of sudden, aren't you?"

Bitter shook his head. "You don't talk to skunks unless you plan on getting sprayed. Where I've been, those who stop to talk generally wind up dead."

Bitter pushed his hat back on his head and pulled a tobacco sack from his shirt pocket. He quickly rolled a cigarette, thumbed a match, and lit the tobacco. Little John saw a slight tremble in Bitter's hands, but all things considered it wasn't much of one.

Little John would later tell the story of a man whose nerves were steel, and whose hands were steady as a rock while he built a smoke and reloaded his warm pistol.

"You intended to kill 'em from the get-go, didn't you?"

Bitter sounded exasperated when he snapped back at Little John. "I intended to see the sheriff do his duty until I found he was out of town. I was afraid these bushwhackers would get away before he got back."

"He'll be back, all right, but you better be gone by then. I don't know the tie between the sheriff and these two, but I hear they be some kind of shirttail relations to Gertrude, the sheriff's wife." Little John paused and then added, "And that's the good news."

Eyebrows raised in question, Bitter asked, "And the bad news?"

"Rumor has it these two rode with Anderson. Rumor also says Big Bill pulled a gang together out of Bloody Bill's crowd."

Bitter nodded, his brown eyes serious for a minute as he studied on the news. "Heard of Anderson. I also heard he got killed last year." He took his Union Cavalry hat off, dusted the brim with an elbow, held it out at arms length to look at the braided band and the crossed sabers, and then he grinned.

"You don't seem worried."

"I noticed an army post across the tracks. Whose outfit is it?

"We have a company of the 50th Illinois stationed here. Why?"

"Then you have to understand. I have a lot bigger gang than Big Bill. I fought with the 40th Missouri. I think I can get help if I need it."

A curious twelve-year-old truant, a frequent school skipper, peeked under the batwing doors, and Little John said, "Boy, I'll give you a dime to fetch the barber. Tell him we got two bodies for him."

The boy disappeared without a word.

"Barber?" Bitter asked.

"Yeah. Gruesome Arnold. He's also the dentist. That's how he got the name Gruesome. He also gives terrible haircuts, and no one in town wants him to give them a shave 'cause he's a little cross eyed. He doubles as the undertaker. Or maybe that's triples as the undertaker."

Bitter was working hard not to smile when Little John finished his recitation of Gruesome's talents. "I see. What does he charge for burying?"

"Six-bits, but he charges five dollars for a coffin."

Bitter shook his head and dug change from his pants pocket. "No. I'll pay for burying, but I'll be damned if I'll buy coffins. Here."

The bartender shook his head in refusal. "On the house."

The floozy walked over to the body of Big Bill, wiped tears with the back of her hands and said, "I hope Big Bill's gang gets you, you blue-bellied coward! And you, Little John, wait till they hear about you wanting to hang Big Bill."

Little John reached for the shotgun. "I'll take that scatter gun now." He looked at the dark-haired woman and said grimly, "You tell them I'll be here. In the meantime, you better pack your bags, Rose, because you can't work here no more."

Bitter looked at the bodies of the men he had just killed, and without another word walked out the door. A four-man squad in Union blue, led by a burly sergeant quick marched up the street, little puffs of dust trailing behind each step.

"You there," the sergeant shouted in a voice that could carry a mile, a trait among sergeants that always amazed Bitter, and which seemed to him to be the number one requirement to be a member of that rank. "Stay right there."

17
Caught

THE GUNSHOTS AND THE FUSS created by the appearance of the town's undertaker and a squad of union soldiers stirred the curiosity of the citizens of Hamilton who started drifting in small groups toward the Boston Saloon.

Morgan tied Lucifer and Misery to the hitching rail and followed along, an ill-defined premonition of trouble sending her mind racing in speculation about the-who-and-the-what of the gunshots. When the lean, blue-clad figure pushed through the doors of the saloon and out on the porch, she involuntarily said, "John!"

A small man, wearing a derby, and an ink stained vest, toting a big camera and tripod, pushed her rudely aside, saying, "Make way. Make way!"

John Bitter stopped in surprise. "Morgan," he managed to yell a second before the sergeant and his squad of Union soldiers stopped in front of the saloon.

"Come down here," the Sergeant ordered.

Bitter said, "Attention!" And somehow the authority in his voice brought the sergeant and the four man squad to a stiff halt. "What's your name, sergeant!"

"Bellamy, sir. And if I may ask, what's your name and rank, sir?"

Bitter ignored the question, and instead said, "We need to talk. For now keep everyone out of the saloon including the undertaker.

And that one," he said pointing to the man with the camera, "keep him here until I get back. I have someone I need to see."

The sergeant hesitated, looked the young man over, eyed the blue uniform, unmarked by rank insignia, and decided John Bitter was, or least had been, an officer in the Union Army.

"What regiment, sir?" he asked.

"I served with the 40th Missouri."

"Good outfit. Were you at Franklin?"

"I was."

"Mustered out?"

Bitter nodded. "Two weeks ago."

"Then you have no authority, sir."

"True, but I'm hoping you'll look past that for a few minutes and humor me."

Even though the assumption of command didn't make a lot of sense, the middle aged sergeant gave Bitter a smile and uttered a reassuring, "Yes, sir!"

Bitter didn't know exactly what he was doing, but he knew he had to somehow legally disentangle himself before the sheriff got back to town. He knew he couldn't spend any time in either a civilian jail or a military stockade. He had Ethan and Mikey to take care of.

While the sergeant, in obeyance of an illegal order, set his men to block the entrance of the saloon, Bitter pushed through a crowd of Hamiltonians who were asking each other what was going on.

Without any factual information whatsoever, a bleary-eyed member of the tavern crowd said, "I think the sheriff's been shot," a rumor that reached the sheriff's wife in less than ten minutes. The sheriff would find the local minister and the minister's wife comforting his presumed widow when he returned home.

Bitter trotted over to Morgan and said, "Am I glad to see you!" He took her by the elbow and pulled her down the street in the direction of Wanda's Eatery. "Come with me. I got somebody I want you to meet."

It wasn't exactly the greeting Morgan had imagined, but the touch of his hand and the "I'm glad to see you" part sounded very encouraging. The other part was a little confusing, however.

"Who do you want me to meet?"

"You'll see."

Wanda had Mikey and Ethan hidden in a back room when Bitter ushered Morgan into Wanda's Eatery. "Ma'am," Bitter said, "where are the boys?"

"I hid them in the store room."

"Boys," Bitter called, "come on out. It's safe now."

Two scruffy blond headed urchins and a big red hound peeked out from behind the storeroom door, glanced at Morgan and then back to Bitter. Bitter knelt down and Mikey pulled loose from Ethan's hand and ran to the safe harbor of Bitter's arms. Bitter, a lump in his throat, whispered, "It's okay, Mikey. The bad men are gone. You're safe now." Rusty padded over and pushed his nose between Mikey and Bitter. John wrapped an arm around the dog's neck and said, "Good boy, Rusty."

Ethan stood by the storeroom door, ready to run if necessary. "I heard some shooting. Did you kill them, Mr. Bitter?"

"I'm afraid so, Ethan. It's a sad thing, but at least they won't bother anyone ever again."

"And our mother?"

Bitter blinked back tears and said quietly, "She's gone Ethan."

Ethan swallowed and fought back tears until Wanda picked him up and put his head on her shoulders. And then he couldn't hold the tears back anymore.

Morgan was simply bewildered by the scene. She had no idea where the boys had come from. And she was amazed by the transformation of John Bitter from the carefree steal-a-kiss charming rascal she knew to this strange, tender-hearted man.

Where did he find the boys? And whose are they? The little one is especially attached to John.

"Mikey," Bitter said, "I've got some things I need to do. Will you be all right with Wanda?"

In answer, Wanda put Ethan down, dried his tears with a corner of her apron and picked Mikey up. Morgan noticed Wanda's eyes were moist like she was holding back tears of her own.

Bitter took Morgan's hand and pulled her out to the raised porch fronting the café. "I don't have time to explain everything, but I have to ask you to watch the boys. I shot the outlaws who killed their mother," he said, nodding in the direction of Mikey and Ethan, "so I have to clear that up. Will you do it?"

She took a deep breath and said, "I have trouble of my own."

He frowned and nodded for her to continue.

"I…uh…how to put this? You see, two bushwhackers jumped me earlier today and I killed them. Well…Lucifer stomped one and I shot the other. But the sheriff told me to wait in town because some people said they saw me shoot the men in cold blood. Of course, they didn't know I was a girl so they said it was a boy, which I'm not, of course, but I don't know why they would lie… and the deputy has my gear…so I have to wait."

Bitter blinked and shook his head at her breathless recitation. "What are you doing here?"

Morgan blushed so hard the freckles on her nose nearly disappeared. Her rehearsed speeches fled at the sudden terror of actually telling John Morgan she intended to marry him and move to Oregon. So she just blurted it out. "I'm following you."

John Bitter stared at her for a few seconds and worked hard to swallow the smile working the corners of his mouth. "You followed me. I'll be danged."

"Yes I did. And now you need me to help take care of those two little boys. Whose are they?"

"I'll tell you that tale another time. Right now I have to get back to the saloon. As soon as I take care of that business, we'll hunt up the liars you told me about and get them squared away. And then when the sheriff gets back, you can get your things and go back home where you belong."

Hands on her hips, a defiant look on her face, Morgan stomped her foot and gave him an emphatic, "No."

"At least stay with the boys. Okay?"

"All right, but you have to introduce me first."

He pulled her none too gently back inside the café. "Boys," he said. "This young lady is Miss Morgan. She'll stay with you while I tend to business."

He pointed to the bigger boy and said, "That one is Ethan. The little guy is Mikey. Mikey doesn't talk, so don't waste time trying to get him going."

"Hello." Morgan said.

Neither boy said a word until Ethan looked up at Wanda and said, "We're still hungry."

18

An Undertaking

THE SQUAD OF UNION SOLDIERS was still blocking the entrance and the sergeant was trying to talk reason to a tall, gaunt, clean-shaven man Bitter took to be the barber-dentist-undertaker. Over the rumble of the crowd he heard the man with the camera saying, "Now listen here, sergeant, I'm a reporter. You have to let me in."

Bitter pushed through the crowd and asked the belligerent man with the camera, "You a newspaper man?"

"Yes I am."

"Good. Sergeant, let him through but don't let him take any pictures with that thing. Got it? And you come inside, too. I want you to hear this so you can vouch for me if it comes down to it."

"Yessir," the sergeant answered.

"And you," he pointed to Gruesome Arnold, "are you the undertaker?"

"That's one of my occupations, yes."

"Come on in, then."

Bitter instructed the newspaperman to take notes while Little John explained the situation. Gruesome Arnold and Sergeant Bellamy were to witness Little John's story.

"It was plain self-defense. This feller in Union Blue," he said, pointing at Bitter, "wanted some information and those two balked. Big Bill, that's the one over there, drew his gun and the soldier boy killed him. Drawing his gun didn't make no sense whatsoever since my shotgun was staring at him. Of course," he added hurriedly, "I wasn't holding it. This soldier boy was.

"And I'm getting tired of calling you Soldier Boy," he said to Bitter. "What's your name?"

"John Bitter, late of the 40th Missouri."

"Rank?" Sergeant Bellamy asked.

"Captain."

"Okay, then, Captain Bitter," the bartender said.

"What's the name of the other dead man?" the reporter asked, looking up from his note taking.

"Little Bill," the bartender said.

"Last name, Dent," the reporter supplied. "Wanted for murder."

Little John shook his head. "I didn't know that."

"And what was Little Bill doing while Captain Bitter was blowing Big Bill away?" Sergeant Bellamy asked.

"Well, he was getting up off the floor because Captain Bitter had busted him over the head with the barrel of my shotgun."

The reporter turned to Bitter and asked, "Why did you hit him?"

"Because," Bitter replied, "there were two of them. And because he and his bushwhacking partner stole a woman by the name of Mrs. Sharp from her farm east of here, and then they killed her when she fought to get away. Made orphans out of her boys."

"Are you certain of that?"

The bartender interrupted. "I heard Big Bill admit to it, although Rose said Little Bill was the one who killed Mrs. Sharp."

"Why didn't you go to the sheriff, Captain Bitter?"

"I was told he was out of town, so I had to take matters into my own hands. You got that written down?"

"Yes. Now then, Little John, describe the shooting of Little Bill."

"Well, Mr. Bitter let him get up and then Little Bill pulled his pistol, so Bitter drew and shot him three times before Little Bill got off a shot. But it was purely self defense. Bitter let him get his pistol all the way out of his holster before he even drew. Fastest thing I ever saw."

Bitter frowned and gave the reporter a hard stare. "If you print that business about the fast draw I'll have to shoot you, too." He paused and then said, "Okay, that's enough. You got your story, mister reporter, and I've got my witnesses on record that it was self-defense. Take your pictures and go write your story."

"Lot of curiosity seekers out there," Little John said, "thirsty curiosity seekers."

Bitter walked to the bar and placed two silver dollars on the counter. He said, "First you serve the sergeant and his men, then you let the others in."

He held his hand out and said, "Thank you sergeant. I've got one more snake to kill and then I'm going back home to Oregon."

Little John filled a shot glass with his best whiskey and handed it to Sergeant Bellamy who downed it with one quick swallow. Bellamy slammed the shot glass on the counter, turned and gave Bitter a salute. "It's been a pleasure, Captain Bitter."

Gruesome Arnold had been listening in and hanging back until the interview was over. Now he said to Little John, "Who's paying for the burial?"

"I will. But we're not paying for coffins."

"You can't bury people without coffins," he whined. "It just isn't right."

The reporter said, "Quit sniveling, Gruesome."

He turned and said to Bitter, "There's a reward out for those two. The poster on them says: "William Dent and William Dent, Jr. Wanted Dead Or Alive.""

The thought of two orphan boys and a long expensive trip ahead made Bitter ask, "How much?"

"I think it runs about two hundred dollars for each," the reporter said. "If you buy the coffins, I'll leave out that part about the fast draw. Deal?"

"Like most of those who ply your trade, you are a hornswaggling, conniving, deceitful s.o.b," Bitter said. "Why insist on coffins?"

With a smile the little man said, "Gruesome is going to help me put the deceased in the coffins. We're going to prop them up against the hitching rail, and then I'm going to take a nice picture for my paper. I'll sell my whole run. And you get the reward."

"Like I said before, you are a conniving and deceitful man. Besides, what makes you think the sheriff will pay the reward? The way I hear it, those two are kin with the sheriff's wife."

"He'll pay it or I'll plaster his name all over my paper as a double-dealing dishonest man…which he is. And I can prove it. It just doesn't matter most of the time so I let it go."

Bitter shook his head, nodded at the sergeant and walked out the door.

19

Lucifer Has the Last Word

MORGAN WAS SITTING IN A chair looking out the front window of the café to watch the boys who were eating on the front porch. And she was drinking the first cup of real coffee she'd had in over a year. It tasted wonderful.

She asked Wanda what was going on, but Wanda insisted all she knew was the tall young man had asked her to watch the boys and then had stalked away in pursuit of two bushwhackers.

"And since we are into questions and answers," Wanda said, "why are you dressed like a boy?"

"I thought I would be safer on the road."

"Well, you don't hide very well. You're just too pretty to be a boy. And boys don't have yellow roses snagged in a pile of red hair."

Wanda noted Morgan's frequent glance in the direction of the saloon. She smiled. "He'll be back. He's the type who survives. As my old mother would say, he can dance between the raindrops."

Wanda set a fresh cup of coffee on the table in front of Morgan, and when Morgan dug into a pants pocket, Wanda said, "On the house."

Morgan sipped the coffee gratefully and slowly to make it last. And she kept an eye up the street for Bitter. When he stepped back out of the saloon and started towards the café, his long legs eating up the distance, she felt her pulse quicken. There was a mystery here, a mystery to pique any lady's interest. Of course, she was already smitten by the tall young man.

Wanda said, needlessly, "Here he comes."

When Bitter reached the café, the boys were sitting on the porch, dirty blond hair falling over their foreheads, bowls on their laps, food disappearing like there was no tomorrow. Bitter stopped with one foot on the bottom step and studied the scene. He drew comfort from watching their commonplace chore of eating.

Survivors, they are. But then what choice do they have?

He put the thought aside, ruffled Ethan's hair, and said, "You boys smell a little ripe, but I can see it hasn't hurt your appetites."

Ethan looked up from his bowl of stew, spoon poised for the next bite, and asked, "You goin' to jail, Mr. Bitter?"

"No. What makes you think I'd go to jail?"

"That's what happens when you shoot people. Less it's a war. Then it's all right."

"Well, this time it was self-defense, so I'm not going to jail."

Satisfied he wasn't losing Bitter anytime soon, Ethan went back to eating without saying another word.

Rusty sat at attention in front of the boys, tail thumping the deck, drooling in hunger. Mikey tossed him a piece of bread, and the big dog snapped it out of the air with an audible click of teeth.

Morgan motioned to Bitter to come in and pointed to a chair on the opposite side of her table. "Sit. So tell me," she said in rapid fire fashion, "what happened in the saloon? Why did you shoot those men? Where did you find the boys? Are they related to you?"

"Do you always talk so fast?"

"Men interrupt a woman if the woman doesn't talk fast. Didn't you know that?"

Wanda set a cup of coffee in front of Bitter and smiled. "She's right, you know. My first and only husband wouldn't listen unless I shouted at him or talked right over the top of him. Then instead of listening, he'd get mad and head for the saloon. Finally drank hisself to death. And that was a blessing."

Bitter smiled in spite of himself and without a word took a sip of coffee.

"Well," Morgan said in exasperation, "aren't you going to tell me anything?"

"I'll say this much. You and Wanda have cleared up a great mystery for me. It's no wonder men can't talk to you women. But I don't think any man could ignore you…either one of you. And I'm not sure a man could get a word in edgewise either."

"So answer the question," Morgan insisted.

"Which one?'

"Start with how you came to have the boys."

When Bitter finished his tale about Ethan using stinging worms to catch bass, the sudden appearance of Mikey, and how it all wrapped together when Ethan spotted the red beards, both women had fire in their eyes.

"Good thing you took care of those bushwhackers," was the only thing Wanda said.

Morgan was speechless for a change, but her eyes were shining in admiration of John Bitter, and her determination to be his wife increased with each breath.

If Bitter noticed her admiration, he didn't let it show.

Wanda pointed out the window to a rider followed by a buck-board. "Here comes Sheriff Tucker."

Morgan walked out on the porch and waved the sheriff over. When Deputy Walter pulled the horse team to a halt, she could see the wagon box was empty…of dead men. Her gear was still keeping Walter company.

"So where are the bodies?" she asked.

Sheriff Tucker looked exasperated. "There wasn't any. We found a place with lots of hoof prints and boot tracks, but no bodies. You can't hold somebody for murder if you can't find a body. Guess you're in the clear, but I'd suggest you leave town. If it was kin folks who took 'em away, they'll liable come looking for the shooter."

"And you won't protect me?"

"If I have to, I will. But if you're gone, I won't have to."

Deputy Walter said from the seat of the empty wagon, "I'll help if it comes down to it."

The middle aged, beady-eyed farmer, who swore he had seen "a boy" shoot two men in cold blood, crossed the street and headed for the wagon. When he got closer, he could see the wagon box was empty.

"Where's the dead men I saw that there boy shoot?"

Frustration showed on the sheriff's florid face, and he decided one more time that he'd a' whole lot rather be drowning a worm in the local slough than chasing dead men who weren't there, or dealing with puckered up dishonest citizens. "There wasn't any dead men," he growled.

"I saw that boy shoot 'em. Has to be some dead men. And he's riding my mule."

"What?" Morgan nearly shouted. "Your mule? You're a lying, sneaky underhanded skunk, a miserable excuse for a human being, and a thief to boot." She looked at the sheriff and said, "Wait right here. I'll go get my mule."

While they waited for Morgan to fetch Lucifer and Misery, the sheriff looked at Bitter and said, "What's she up to?"

"How would I know?"

"Well…you're the one she rode all this way to marry, ain't you?"

"Holy smokes," Bitter said in disgust, "not you, too. Now look here, Sheriff, I never promised to marry that girl."

Deputy Walter experienced a surge of hope, and Sheriff Tucker had another attack of frustration. "You one of those gents who promises the sun, the moon, and stars to a girl just to have your way, and then backs out of the deal? We don't take kindly to that here in Hamilton."

"I never even got a kiss."

"And he won't either until we're married," Morgan said as she led Lucifer and Misery to the hitching rail in front of the café. "Well," she said to the farmer and pointed at the saddle on Lucifer's back, "you beady-eyed, lying coward. If you claim this mule belongs to you, get aboard."

Surprise showed in the pinched face of the farmer, but he was game, even if his larcenous nature was partnered with stupidity.

"Lucifer, hold," Morgan said as the man stepped into the saddle. "Lucifer, go!" Morgan shouted. Lucifer reared up, landed stiff legged and bucked the farmer backwards out of the saddle. The awkward fall brought his butt to a pile of fresh, odiferous road apples and his hard head against the iron rim of Walter's wagon wheel. The fall didn't completely knock the man out, but it did confuse him some. One minute he was the proud owner of a big mule, and in the next minute he was on the ground with a bloody lump on the back of his head and horse manure on the seat of his britches.

When Lucifer started for the addle-pated farmer, Morgan jumped in front of the big mule, grabbed a loose rein, and said, "Stop it Lucifer. You've killed enough people for one day." The frustrated mule settled for a soul-scarring bray that rang clear across town, across the railroad tracks, and into the army post.

Morgan gave the sheriff a hard stare and said, "I'm the only one who can ride Lucifer. So you can see he's my mule. And I insist you arrest this man for attempted robbery."

"I believe I will. Of course," he said and sent a hard stare at the farmer who was pulling himself up with the help of the wagon wheel, "you could pay the town a twenty dollar fine, and give this girl…she ain't no boy, you idiot…twenty dollars for trying to steal her mule. That would square it up, and I wouldn't have to feed you while you were in jail. What do you say?"

"Well," the injured farmer whined, "he sure looks like my mule."

"That'll be another ten dollars for lying and another ten dollars for the girl. You wanna keep talking?" Sheriff Tucker asked.

"I…uh…I don't have any money on me," the farmer protested.

"Walter," the sheriff said, "go with this miserable excuse for a man, get sixty dollars from him, and then usher him the hell out of town. And make sure he doesn't come back. Got it? "

Walter, who was prone to grin when his big brother got going, nodded and got down from the wagon. He drew his pistol and said, "March, mister. Lead me to the money." The farmer was still whining and protesting as Walter prodded him around a corner and down a side street that led to a grove of willow trees along a small stream where travelers often camped.

The sheriff dismounted and walked over to Morgan. "Sorry, Miss. That varmint isn't from around here. We have a better class of citizens in Hamilton."

20
Percentages

OSCAR J. HEARST, NEWSPAPER EDITOR and, in his own words, "Reporter Extraordinaire," came puffing up the street. "Bob," he said to Sheriff Tucker, "we need to talk."

"About what?"

"About your future as the sheriff of our fair town."

"I don't know that I want to be sheriff. Maybe I'd rather go fishing."

"And spend more time at home with Gertrude?" Oscar J. Hearst asked.

"You do know how to hurt a man, Oscar. What do you have in mind?"

Oscar pulled Bob Tucker by the sleeve down the street far enough to hold a discreet if somewhat heated conversation. Wanda, Morgan and Bitter looked at each other and Bitter shrugged, but it was clear that some sort of agreement had been reached when Sheriff Tucker nodded and looked their direction. The big man shook his head, let his shoulders drop in resignation, grimaced and walked back to the café while Oscar scurried down the street to the Boston Saloon and his camera.

"It seems, Captain Bitter, you are in line to collect a reward for Bill Dent, and Bill Dent, Junior. Oscar said I'm to forgive you for shooting them because you didn't know they were related to my wife. Oscar also explained it was self defense. I suspect you did us all a favor. Just don't try explaining that to Gertrude."

"I really wish you had been here to arrest them, Sheriff, but since you were out of town I didn't think I could wait."

"I'm not sure I have the moral fiber to face Gertrude if I had arrested them. She's strong on kin folk." He shook his head, "As my pappy always said, 'you can choose your friends, but you're stuck with kin folks.'

"To make matters worse, Oscar is blackmailing me into having my picture taken with the corpses, which he intends for the front page of his newspaper. Says it'll help me get re-elected. When that's over, assuming Gertrude hasn't shot me by then, come on down to the jail and I'll see about getting your reward paid.

"Now, there's a train through here tomorrow morning along about 7:00 a.m. You'll want to be on it."

"Which way is it going?"

"Out of town," the sheriff said in exasperation, "which is the important thing. But it is headed west to St. Joseph, which is also the right direction for you."

"I intend to ride my horse to St. Joseph, not pay the train to carry him. I've got a long trip ahead, and I need to nurse my money."

The sheriff, who was nearly as tall as John Bitter, and about forty pounds heavier, most of that around his middle, squared his shoulders and said, "You'll be four hundred dollars richer here pretty quick, less my fee of course, so you can damned well afford a train ride. Besides, it's quicker to ride the train, and you'll want some distance before Big Bill's friends come hunting you."

"Less your fee?"

"Yep. I get ten percent on account of advancing you the money because you couldn't wait for a wire transfer."

"I couldn't?"

"No," Sheriff Tucker said, "No, you had to skedaddle out of Hamilton to save me the trouble of shooting at people or being shot at."

John Bitter just shook his head in disgust, but he knew better than to say anything. That did not, however, keep Morgan from blurting, "Why you thieving, no account."

"Now missy," Sheriff Tucker protested, "I just saved your mule and got you thirty dollars to boot."

Bitter put a restraining hand on Morgan's shoulder and said, "Morgan, we'll just thank the sheriff and the Good Lord for our blessings and move on."

She nearly said something stupid like "Yes, dear," but caught herself in time.

Bitter turned and looked at Ethan and Mikey. "Now, let's see about getting a bath and a haircut for the boys and some new duds. Even some shoes maybe. And we'll put up in the hotel tonight… assuming they have any rooms."

"I don't wear shoes in the summer time," Ethan said.

"Well, where we're going, you'll want shoes. Miss Wanda," Bitter said, "where can we find a bath?"

Bitter gave Morgan money for clothes for the boys. Wanda traced their feet on a piece of paper so she could get the shoe sizes right, closed her café for an hour and went shopping with Morgan at Penny's dry goods store. While Rusty guarded the door, the boys and Bitter turned hot bath water a dirty brown in two brass tubs in the backroom of Gruesome Arnold's Tonsorial Parlor.

Ethan's protest about not needing a bath ended in a water choked cough when Bitter just picked him up, clothes and all and dunked him the tub.

Mikey giggled and splashed, blew bubbles, and ducked under the water long enough to panic Bitter who climbed out of his own tub to grab Mikey by the arm and pull him to the surface.

"Don't worry, Mister Bitter," Ethan said. "Mikey swims like a fish. He just likes being under water sometimes."

"Well, he scared the devil out of me."

Helped by a setting sun, the willow and cottonwood trees along the town's little creek treated the citizens of Hamilton to long shadows. Sheriff Tucker had given Bitter three hundred sixty dollars reward money. Two rooms had been reserved for the night in the town's hotel, one for Bitter and the boys and one for Morgan.

She turned Lucifer loose to roam the open prairie beyond the Army post, and Misery was doing her best to chew a quart of rolled oats the hostler dumped in the feed trough. The small, gimpy legged man, whose week old stubble had turned salt and pepper, and who smelled of straw and horse manure watched Misery chew and then looked at Morgan. "You know, ma'am, your mare has good lines, but I'll bet she's got a bad tooth. That's why she looks so gaunt. You see the way she chews, she can't hardly eat."

Startled, Morgan, who prided herself on her powers of observation, said, "Oh no! I had no idea. It never occurred to me she had anything wrong. I just thought she was getting old." She reached through the rails to rub the horse's cheek. "Poor Misery. I'm so sorry."

"Well…she's no spring chicken, but I'd guess she ain't much over nine or ten years old. She's got some good years left. I fix that tooth and I bet she starts gaining. Want me to do it?"

"Can you do it?"

He pulled Misery's head up and pinched her nose. When she opened her jaw to breathe, the canker in her mouth was easy to spot. "Well…it ain't pretty, but I'll tie her down and lance it…let it drain and she should be all right."

Morgan eyed him suspiciously and asked, "How much?"

"One silver dollar."

Morgan thought for a few seconds, considered the pain Misery must have endured, and then nodded. "Do it."

Morgan luxuriated in a bed that didn't rustle with corn shucks every time she turned over. It had been an exhausting day and she was soon asleep.

In the room next door, a freshly scrubbed and clean-shaven John Bitter tucked in the soap scented boys, each with a good haircut in spite of Gruesome's reputation as sincerely and inaccurately invented as could be by Little John.

He watched the rhythmic rise and fall of the blanket warming the boys in the unheated room and decided they were handsome rascals. He put his gun belt under the edge of the bed where it would be handy, and then rolled his smoke scented bedroll out on a cushion offered by a thick comforter. The comforter cost him an extra fifty cents, but he thought it was probably worth it. The day, he decided, had been almost as busy as any he lived through during the war.

He worried briefly about what was ahead of him and the boys. He had no idea what he would or could do for the boys with hate-filled bushwhackers on his trail, but he knew a tired mind wouldn't help. So he let his head settle on the pillow and was almost instantly asleep.

21
Bait

HEAVY FOOTSTEPS IN THE HALLWAY brought Bitter awake just at daylight. There was no attempt by the early riser to soft foot it down the hallway. Bitter didn't sense any threat, but when the footsteps stopped outside his door, he reached for his pistol and crawled out of his bedroll.

His bare feet made no sounds, but an errant floorboard creaked under his weight and he stopped dead still, thumb on the hammer of his pistol.

There was a soft knock and a voice said, "Captain Bitter? You up?"

Bitter eased the door open and was greeted by the sight of Sergeant Bellamy. "Up kinda early, Sergeant."

"Not really, sir. I've been up most of the night. You see I figured when Little John kicked her out, Rose, the floozy from the Boston Saloon would head straight for Big Bill's hideout, so I followed her."

"You did? Why?"

"Why don't you get dressed, sir, and we'll have a cup of coffee on it at Wanda's. She opens early. And her apple pie is awful good. Sheriff Tucker and my Major will meet us there."

"Why?"

"I'd not like to have anyone overhear what they want to talk to you about, sir."

"John, Sergeant. My name is John. I'm not a 'sir' anymore."

"Yes, sir. I'll try to remember that. My name is John also, but I'm called Jack, Jack Bellamy."

Bitter held out his hand and said, "Nice to meet you Sergeant Jack Bellamy."

Morgan's door opened and she treated the men to a mass of tousled red hair. At the sight of the two men she automatically brushed her hair back with her right hand. "Is it train time already?"

"Miss," Bellamy said, "I think you can rest today. Captain Bitter is not going to be on the train this morning."

"What's going on, John?"

"I don't know, but it must be important. Can you watch the boys until I get back?"

"Sure. Let me get dressed."

As John slipped an arm into his shirt, a sleepy eyed Ethan peeked from under the blankets. "You leaving, Mr. Bitter?"

"I'll be back, Ethan," he said as he tucked his shirt in his britches and buckled his gun belt around his waist. "Morgan is going to stay with you until I do."

"You sweet on her, Mr. Bitter?"

Bitter grinned and said, "You go back to sleep and mind your own business, Ethan."

Sheriff Tucker he recognized. Hard not to after yesterday's staring match. He recognized the blue uniform even if the Major was a stranger. But Bellamy had made no mention of a third man. The three men looked up from their conversation when Bellamy and Bitter walked in.

Sheriff Tucker nodded and waved them over. He had his big hand wrapped around a warm mug of coffee. "Sit."

He pointed to the Union officer and said, "This is Major Walters, and this gentleman claims to work for the Pinkerton detective agency. I believe him."

Major Walters reached across the table to shake Bitter's hand.

At first glance, Mark Anthony, a medium-sized, clean-shaven man dressed in a tailored black wool suit and sporting a black bowler, looked like anything but a detective. But there was something in Anthony's cold hazel eyes that made Bitter sense he could be a hard and dangerous man.

"I'm Mark Anthony," the Pinkerton said as he rose to extend a hand. "And you are John Bitter. You did us all a favor yesterday by disposing of Bill Dent and his son."

They shook hands, each giving the other an iron grip and a hard appraising look. Assured somehow that the detective was the genuine article, Bitter pulled out a chair and sat at the table. "That business was unfortunate, but necessary. What has this to do with the Pinkertons?"

Wanda poured coffee, sat a cream pitcher and a sugar bowl in front of Bitter, and asked, "How are the boys?"

Bitter grinned and said, "Smelling a whole lot better and sleeping in. Morgan is looking out for them."

Wanda smiled back and said, "Send them in for breakfast when they get up. I make special pancakes with faces for the children who eat here."

"I'll sure do that, Ma'am. And speaking of breakfast?"

"Ham and eggs coming up."

Detective Anthony waited patiently through the exchange between Bitter and Wanda, and when she went back to her kitchen, said, "All right then. We believe Bill Dent's gang was responsible for robbing the train between here and St. Joseph. Twice. The owners hired the Pinkerton Detective Agency to find the gang and put a stop to their depredations."

Bitter looked at Major Walters and asked, "What has this to do with the army?"

Walters gave Bitter a wry smile and said, "Two things. The Dents stole an army payroll. The Army would like its money back. On a personal level it was an act which caused me all kinds of headaches. You're army, so you know how pestiferous the men can get if there isn't any pay on payday. No money means no tobacco and no alcohol and no gambling…and no whores. Anyway, because it was an army payroll, that makes it army business no matter what."

Bitter nodded. "Okay, I get that. What I don't get is what this has to do with me."

Sheriff Tucker grinned and leaned back in his chair, an amused look in his eyes, and said, "I read this story one time about tiger hunting. You stake out a goat, hide in a tree stand, and wait for a tiger to come sniffing at the goat. You killed the Dents, so that makes you the goat. Although the way Sergeant Bellamy sees it, you'll be the fox and the Dent gang will be the hounds."

"All I need to do is put some distance between me and the Dent gang, which I plan to do soon, and then they won't be my problem."

"That's completely unpatriotic," Major Walters said.

"And I don't care. All I want is to get back home to my farm in Oregon."

"Sir?" Sergeant Bellamy said and glanced at Major Walters who nodded. "This won't take long, Captain Bitter. I listened through the cabin window and heard their plans. They'll be coming along in an hour or so looking to kill you. Now…if you was to be saddled and ready to ride, when they come into town from the east you take a shot at them and then run out the other end of town.

"They follow. About a mile out of town a grove of small pine trees narrows the road down. I'll have Lieutenant Newcomb, and two squads of my best shooters hiding in the trees."

"And I'll be there," Mark Anthony added.

"How many outlaws are there?" Bitter asked.

"I didn't want to risk looking into the cabin, but I counted nine good horses," Sergeant Bellamy said. "Which reminds me to ask, sir, how good is the horse you ride? These people have excellent mounts."

"Rockford can outrun any horse alive." Bitter looked at Sheriff Tucker. "What about you? What are you going to be doing?"

"Walter and I will give chase to the gang, sort of herd them along."

"What if they don't run?"

"Well, Walter and I each have one of those new Henry repeaters. We can keep 'em moving."

"Crap," Bitter said and shook his head. "Who cooked this up?"

Major Walters straightened his shoulders and gave Bitter a sharp look. "I did. Why?"

"Look, Major, I mean no disrespect, but a mixed force of Pinkertons and Union Army is the first problem. They're just as apt to wind up shooting each other as the Dents."

Wanda set plates of steaming ham and eggs in front of each of the men, and Bitter started arranging knives, forks, salt and pepper shakers, biscuits and coffee cups on the table, explaining how he would do this and who he would put in charge of each phase. He didn't bother asking why the plan didn't include trapping the Dent gang in town. *Too many innocents, including Morgan and the boys*, he thought. And he didn't ask why the Major didn't just surround the Dent cabin and end it there.

It's easier to defend than attack, about ten times easier. Yep… get them out in the open. The Major got that part right, Bitter thought.

The Major was miffed at first, but as Bitter detailed the plan, he warmed to the idea. There was, after all, some glory for him in this, and he decided to lead the Union detachment in person.

Bitter looked out the window and saw the details of buildings and trees emerge as the light hinted at another sunrise. "Well," he said as he forked the last bite of ham, "I think we'd best be on it. Can you have your troops in place within the next thirty minutes?" He asked Sergeant Bellamy even though he was eyeballing the Major.

Bellamy answered, "We have enough mounts, and I know a short cut, so they won't see our tracks."

"Good."

He started to pay for his breakfast, but Detective Anthony shook his head. "The Pinkertons will pay for this. I'll put it on my expense account."

Bitter nodded his thanks, took a last sip of cold coffee and pushed back from the table. Sheriff Tucker held out his hand and said, "Good luck, Captain Bitter. I hope you live to get the hell out of my town. Between you and that redheaded lass, you've stirred the hornet's nest. When you're safely on your way west, I can go back to fishing."

Bitter shook Tucker's hand and said, "I think you're probably a pretty good sheriff, but you are hard on travelers."

"And you are nothing but trouble," Tucker said, but there was a hint of a smile in his eyes.

22
The Chase

THE SUN WAS GLINTING OFF a store window when nine determined outlaws trotted their horses into town. A smelly, scrofulous lot, some of whom had yet to have a springtime bath, they were nonetheless well mounted and well armed.

Experienced in the art of ambush, they split into two groups and rode single file down each side of the wide street. They headed straight for the livery stable, looking for the big black horse Rose said the stranger rode.

Nearly invisible inside the unlit barn, Bitter watched through the open doors until the outlaws were about one-hundred-fifty yards away, and then he stepped in the saddle, pulled his hat tight on his head, and kicked Rockford in the ribs. Yankee though he was, he gave a pretty good imitation of a Rebel yell as Rockford burst through the open doors and down the street. Bitter turned and fired his pistol over the heads of the startled outlaws and then settled down to run for his life.

At the half-mile point, the outlaws had stopped spraying the roadside with poorly aimed bullets and settled in for a long chase. Bitter eased back on Rockford's bridle to slow him just a bit, hoping to make the outlaws wonder if Rockford was starting to tire and to give them hope they could run Bitter to ground.

The outlaws trailed Bitter and the big black horse by two hundred yards when the thin grove of timber described by Sergeant

Bellamy came into sight. "Now," he said to Rockford and kicked him in the flanks. Rockford loved to run, and he proved it one more time. Bitter would say as he told the story in a later time, "Rockford could bring the tears to your ears."

He caught a glimpse of blue as he flashed by the trees, and then he pulled Rockford to a sliding halt, jerked his Henry rifle from the saddle scabbard and stepped to the ground. He hit Rockford on the butt with his hat and yelled, "Keep going, you fleabag!"

Mark Anthony, a repeating rifle in his hands rose out of the grass, and he and Bitter were waiting in the middle of the road when the outlaws came streaming through the trees.

"Horses," Bitter said grimly, "Put 'em down."

Systems pumped with adrenalin, Bitter and Detective Anthony each managed to miss with the first shots, but each jacked another round into his rifle, steadied up and dropped a horse on the second try. Bitter saw a big sorrel go tumbling and a rider cartwheel out of the saddle. Detective Anthony fired again, and a bay horse fell in a squealing heap, tripped by the lead animals as they went down. One of the lead riders was crushed by a thousand pounds of falling horse. The other rider was knocked unconscious and splayed face down out in the prairie grass.

And then Sergeant Bellamy's shooters opened up. Their first volley spilled all but one rider from the saddle, and the fight was over. The lone survivor of the army fusillade had a broken arm and a hole in his side. He would survive long enough to meet the hang-man. Blood running down one sleeve, he dropped his pistol and held up his one good arm in surrender.

Three of the outlaws' horses, loose reins trailing in the grass, heads high in their panic, galloped free across an open meadow. Sergeant Bellamy shouted an order to round them up and two blue clad riders rode in chase of the loose animals.

Bitter let out a held breath and looked at Detective Anthony. Neither said a word. It had been a planned slaughter, but that didn't make it feel any better. A pistol barked and the squealing of a wounded horse stopped. To John Bitter's ears, the silence was somehow worse than the noise.

Major Walters, more provident than Bitter would have thought waved an ambulance wagon up to the ambush site, and trotted his horse over to Bitter and Detective Anthony. "Well, done, gentlemen," he said, and smiling, he leaned down to offer his hand. "We had only one casualty. Private Jones managed to shoot his horse in the head. But we have two live prisoners. I think they'll lead us to the payroll."

Sergeant Bellamy trotted his horse up the road to Major Walters, saluted, and said, "My best count says five of the outlaws are dead, two are mortally wounded…Doc is tending to them…one is unconscious, knocked out by a fall, and another is shot up, but he'll live."

Major Walters asked, "Is Private Jones hurt?"

Bellamy grinned and said, "Pride only, sir. I sent him back to the post…on foot…carrying his saddle and the rest of his gear."

Bitter laughed. "Dismounted cavalry, maybe?"

Sergeant Bellamy reached back into his saddlebag and pulled out a flat glass bottle filled with a clear liquid. He said, "Snake bite medicine, sir," pulled the cork and handed the bottle to the Major who sniffed and took a swig. He winced, but he swallowed and nodded his approval. "Thank you, Sergeant. I believe a little snake bite is called for."

The bottle made the rounds and wound back up in Bellamy's big paw. He raised the bottle in salute and said, "To the Union Army and Ulysses S. Grant," and then took a generous pull on the bottle. He looked Bitter in the eye and raised the bottle again in toast. "And to Captain Bitter, a man to ride the river with."

In spite of himself, Bitter saluted and said, "Thank you, Sergeant Bellamy. I feel the same."

Detective Anthony walked into the trees to get his mount, a long-legged Buckskin, and Bitter trailed Rockford down the dusty track. Rockford was in a good mood after a satisfying run, so he only made Bitter chase him for five minutes before settling in on a nice patch of green prairie grass.

Bitter caught up the reins and gave the big black's neck a hug and said, "I could damned near learn to like you, you big, ugly brute."

Bitter and Anthony left the cleanup to the Army and walked their horses back to town. The detective was full of questions, and when Bitter told him he had a farm in Oregon, Anthony wanted to know everything Bitter could tell him about the Willamette Valley.

Bitter had some questions for Anthony as well. "How'd you come by the name Mark Anthony?"

Anthony grinned and asked, "You recognized the Shakespearian connection, did you?"

Bitter nodded. "I did wonder."

"My mother, in addition to being a romantic, is a school teacher who read aloud to her sons and daughters every play written by the Bard. And since I'm the eldest of the male Anthony progeny…"

"You were the anointed one," Bitter finished and laughed. "And I suppose you have a sister named Juliet."

"I do, but Father put his foot down after that, so we have one Jeremiah, one Jonah, and one William. Mother didn't tell Father she picked William's name from the William Tell Overture. The girls…after Juliet…are Ophelia and Winifred."

"And how did you become a Pinkerton?"

Anthony laughed and said, "By chance and happenstance."

Bitter waited and Anthony said, "I was in attendance at Princeton College, in earnest study, about to realize Mother's dream of having a Christian physician in the family. But I found study of human cadavers to be less interesting than chasing the living female form, and I found whiskey to be more satisfying than theology.

"Much to Mother's disappointment, I was asked to leave Princeton at the end of my second year, and I found myself cut off from Mother's purse strings. So…through a friend…I met Mister Pinkerton and offered my services as a trained observer and student of human nature. Much to my surprise, Mister Pinkerton hired me."

"And what did your mother think of that?"

"Oh, Mother is a romantic, so even though she still scolds me for my misadventure and my failure to become a physician, I think she is secretly thrilled to have an adventurer for a son."

Detective Anthony changed the subject by asking Bitter, "How did you come to be in Missouri?"

Bitter chuckled, and then said, "To echo the great Mark Anthony, by chance and happenstance. Actually, when word of Southern secession reached Oregon, I joined the Union Army only to find we would not be sent east to take part in the fighting. When my ninety-day enlistment was up, I refused to re-enlist.

"Instead, I turned my farm over to my brother and kept riding east on the Oregon Trail until I found a Union company that stood a chance of getting into the fight, and one that would also let me join up. That was the 40th Missouri. Three years. That's how long I served."

"And went from private to captain?"

"Fortunes of war, and the luck of the draw, I suppose."

Detective Anthony gave him an appraising stare and then nodded. "What would you say to working for us?"

"The Pinkertons?"

"Yes. You would be our agent for Oregon, and you would draw a stipend of twenty dollars a month unless you were solving a problem for us, in which case you would be on full salary with an expense account."

Bitter looked at Anthony and waited for the baited hook.

"And," Anthony added as they rounded a bend in the road, "because you will be a Pinkerton detective, complete with badge and credentials, you would have a free pass to ride the train to St. Joseph…one step closer to Oregon."

Before Bitter could say he would have to think about it, Sheriff Bob Tucker and Deputy Walter Tucker trotted their horses around a bend in the road.

"Howdy," Sheriff Tucker said and he pulled his big horse to a halt. "How did it go?"

Bitter let Detective Anthony relate the story and when he finished, Tucker nodded. He looked at Bitter and said, "You are sure hard on men and horses."

Bitter felt compelled to defend his decision to shoot the horses, but Tucker beat him to the punch. "Riders on foot are easier to round up than mounted riders. And a hard fall can take the starch out of even a tough man."

Walter, who had hoped to take part in the fuss, looked in admiration at Bitter and Anthony and said, "Sure wish I had been there."

Bitter couldn't help but say, "No you don't. No glory in a slaughter."

Private Jones was within a half mile of town before Bitter and Anthony caught up with him. Without a word Bitter lifted the army saddle from the shoulders of the marching soldier and balanced it on his saddle horn. Anthony held out a hand and swung Jones up behind him on the Buckskin. "Don't tell Sergeant Bellamy," he cautioned.

"No, sir," a grateful Jones answered.

23
Baited and Hooked

PRIVATE JONES ASKED TO BE dropped at the edge of town. "I need to walk to the post, like Sergeant Bellamy ordered," he said.

Anthony and Bitter looked at each other and grinned. Jones swung down and reached for his saddle. "Thank you, sirs," he said, "my feet just ain't used to walking."

"Then I'd suggest you moan and groan a little when you arrive," Bitter said with a smile.

They watched Jones, saddle on his shoulder, round the corner of a building and disappear down a side street. Bitter and Anthony nudged their horses in the direction of Wanda's Eatery. They heard Morgan shout and saw her waving from the porch.

She bounced down the steps and threw her arms around Bitter when he stepped from the saddle. "Oh, Lord," she said. 'I've never been so scared. I saw those men chasing you and that big black horse just flying down the street and you shooting back, and I just knew they were going to kill you because there was so many of them."

Bitter, in spite of his best efforts to remain aloof, and in spite of denying any interest in Morgan Eagan, on impulse pulled her to his chest, wrapped his arms around her and kissed the top of her flaming red hair. That stopped her voice, but she hugged hard enough to squeeze the breath from his lungs before she stepped back and looked in his eyes. And then her temper flared and she snapped, "What were you thinking, taking chances like that? And where are the men who were chasing you?"

Mark Anthony, who was grinning from ear to ear said, "I'd grab that one and hang on, if I were you, John."

John blinked hard in wonder at what was happening to his heart. *Why did I kiss her?*

He looked helplessly at Anthony who went from grinning to outright laughter. "Oh my," he managed to sputter. "Now I know what moonstruck looks like."

Bitter's fierce attachment to bachelorhood reasserted itself, and when Morgan moved in for another hug, he stepped back and held her at arms length.

"How are the boys?' he asked.

"Fine. Just fine," she snapped.

"Where are they?"

"Inside, eating Wanda's best hotcakes. She draws a face in the skillet with batter, lets that cook a bit and then covers the face with more hotcake batter. The boys really like them."

"Good."

By late afternoon, Bitter had agreed to work for the Pinkerton Detective Agency, but only if Mark Anthony used the power of the Pinkertons to search for Aunt Quilla.

Anthony copied the names and locations of relatives listed in the Sharp family bible, and he promised to wire Pinkerton agents in Ohio and Illinois with instructions to locate and find any family with the last name Ransom, and to look for a woman whose given name was Quilla.

"This may take some time," he cautioned Bitter.

The two surviving outlaws were in Hamilton's jailhouse, and Bitter, the only civilian in the ambush of the outlaws, was in line for seven hundred dollars reward…minus Sheriff Tucker's fee of ten percent…of course.

"I still want you on the train in the morning. Understood?"

"If I have my business taken care of, I will be. But not because you order it," Bitter said.

"I don't care why you get on the train, and I don't care which direction it's going. Just be on it," Sheriff Tucker growled.

"And another thing. I know you are not related to those boys. By rights they should be sent to the orphan's home down in Springfield. But I hear that's a mean place, and because of the war it's pretty well packed. So we need another answer."

"The Pinkertons are searching for family right now," Bitter said. "That's part of my arrangement with Detective Anthony."

"What kind of arrangement?"

"I'm to be the Pinkerton agent for Oregon."

"Damnation. How did that happen?"

"Detective Anthony likes the way I get things done, so he offered me a job. I can still farm between investigations."

"Hmm. Well, until the boys' relatives are found, I'll ask the judge to appoint a guardian. You and that mule-riding female get yourselves over to city hall. I'll see you there in half an hour. And bring the boys with you."

Tucker paused and said, "You know, that mule she rides is the scariest animal I ever met up with. I sure wouldn't want him mad at me. I think it'd take a cannon to put him down."

Bitter walked into an empty restaurant, but he heard the clatter of plates being stacked on shelves back in kitchen. "Wanda?"

Hands all pruned up from hot dish water, Wanda said, "Back here."

He walked to the open kitchen door and peeked in. "Good morning."

"Get your business done?" she asked.

"Nearly. There's just one more thing to take care of. Where are Morgan and the boys?"

Wanda smiled and said, "Ethan offered to catch me some fresh fish…for a penny each. So they are down on the slough."

Bitter smiled back and said, "That rascal charged me two pennies."

She nodded. "He's a survivor. And he thinks you walk on water. At breakfast he got to talking about you and how you gave him two pennies and a spoon of sugar for a bass he caught. Said he took the sugar back to Mikey. How did he put that? 'Because Mikey hasn't had any sweet in his life since Mama was taken.' I think that's pretty close to what he told me."

The lump in his throat had to be swallowed before Bitter managed to croak, "Character is what Ethan has. I've known grown men with a lot less."

Wanda used her apron to dry her hands, and then gave him a sidelong glance. "They both just wind themselves around your heart, don't they? What are you going to do about them? Take them to Oregon with you?"

"I'm duty bound to see if I can find any relatives that will take the boys."

Wanda set a tall stack of heavy white plates on a shelf, and asked, "What if you can't find anyone who wants them?"

"Then I'll worry about learning how to raise 'em."

"I'm not sure the law will allow a bachelor to adopt, but if they do, just remember what it was like when you were that age. Love 'em, but don't indulge and don't let 'em sass their elders. It shows disrespect."

"That's it?"

"Pretty much. That's how I raised mine."

"Thanks. I'll keep that in mind. Which direction is the slough?"

Bitter followed a well worn path beaten over time into the sod of a twenty acre piece of prairie grass. He heard Morgan's laugh off to his right and followed the path through a stand of cottonwood and willow trees to a mossy bank where Ethan had set up business.

"Howdy," Bitter said so as to not startle them. Morgan, the boys and the big red hound looked in his direction. He noticed Morgan had Harley's gun belt strapped around her narrow waist.

Morgan said, "Hello, John." Rusty barked a friendly greeting and Mikey walked over and held his arms out to be picked up.

Bitter took his big hat off and swung Mikey up on his shoulders. "Catching any fish?"

Ethan set the hook on a fish and started backing up the bank. "This one makes five," he said proudly.

"He's a terrific fisherman," Morgan said.

Ethan backed up and pulled a bass onto the mossy, grass covered bank. The flopping, protesting fish looked to Bitter to be about two pounds. "Nice one."

"I got a bigger one on the stringer," Ethan said, a note of pride in his voice.

Bitter said, "I've got something to tell you."

Bitter, Morgan, the boys, and Sheriff Tucker met with Judge Henry Harvey Harrison in his office. The judge did not offer them chairs.

A short pudgy man with wisps of gray hair surrounding a bald pate, sitting in a battered captain's chair behind a scarred wooden table, Judge Harrison rocked his head back to get a good look at the tall stranger and the pretty redheaded woman. With his red nose and myopic, watery blue eyes, he inspired no confidence. The gravy stains on his vest and a half empty bottle of whiskey on the sideboard, which had been pushed against a wall bearing a portrait of Abraham Lincoln, just naturally tended to reinforce a no-confidence verdict. *A drunk,* Bitter thought.

But as he was about to find out, the judge brooked no nonsense. In a booming gravelly voice that belied his short stature, he looked at the sheriff and said, "Okay, Bob, what's this about orphan boys?"

Mikey edged closer to Bitter and used his tiny hand to grip two of Bitter's fingers. Bitter stroked the tiny hand with his thumb.

Sheriff Bob Tucker told the judge the whole gruesome story of Big Bill and Little Bill murdering Mrs. Sharp and leaving Ethan and Michael Sharp orphans. When he started to explain how Bitter found the boys, Judge Harrison said, "Let the boys tell that part, Bob."

Ethan said, "Mikey don't talk since those men took Mama."

The judge's jaw took a firm set, and he said, "I'm sure sorry, boy. Can you tell me what happened?"

By the end of Ethan's tale, Bitter had Mikey on his shoulder, patting him gently on the back, and Morgan was holding Ethan's hand.

The judge pursed his lips and sighed and then just stared at the ceiling for nearly a minute. Then he pointed to some chairs against the wall and said, "Drag some over here and sit."

Judge Harrison looked at Bob and said, "What are you doing about finding a family for these boys?"

"Not a thing," Bob Tucker said, and quickly added when the judge frowned, "but…Mister Bitter has the Pinkertons looking for Mrs. Sharp's sister." He turned and looked at Bitter. "What was her name?"

"The sister?"

"That's what I'm asking," Tucker said with a grump.

Bitter looked at Ethan who shook his head. "The only name we have," Bitter said, "is her given name. Quilla. That fits with the name in the family bible."

The judge looked at Ethan, and said, "And you don't know any other relatives?"

"No sir," Ethan answered.

"None at all?"

Ethan shook his head, suddenly struck by the enormity of being alone with Mikey, and by the fear of being sent off to be orphans.

"Well, then," the judge said, but didn't say more. He looked at Morgan and finally asked, "And what is your part in this?"

Sheriff Tucker broke in before she could answer. "She told me she had ridden here to meet with Mister John Bitter for the purpose of matrimony and to travel on to Oregon as his wife."

A smile twitched the laugh lines riding the corners of the judge's eyes. "Is that right, Miss?"

"Well, in a manner of speaking, it is," she said primly. "He never promised in so many words to marry me, but we were sparking while he was visiting the farm, and I concluded he had more than a stroll through the orchard in mind."

"What have you got to say to that?" the judge asked Bitter.

As carefully and thoughtfully as he could, he explained to Judge Harrison, that while he was mightily attracted to Miss Morgan, the Oregon Trail could be a mighty dangerous place and he was thinking more about Miss Morgan's safety than about his own desires.

"So you would marry her if you could get her safely to Oregon?"

Bitter was quick to protest. "I didn't say that!"

The judge glared at Bitter and said, "But the picture changed when you took responsibility for two orphan boys. That one," he pointed at Mikey, "stays glued to you. Are you willing to break his heart?"

"What do you mean?"

"I mean, he has taken to you. You are his security. So…until we find a suitable relative for these boys, you will be appointed by me, Judge Henry Harvey Harrison as their legal guardian. But first, you must be married."

"I can't do that!" Bitter protested.

"Then I'll have to send them to Springfield to the orphanage. Is that what you want?"

Ethan wouldn't look at him, and Morgan was beginning to question the wisdom of a shotgun wedding, which is what the judge was edging up to.

And then John Bitter did a remarkable thing. He laughed out loud and picked Ethan up and held both boys in his arms. "You want me to be your daddy?"

Ethan nodded and Mikey put his head on Bitter's shoulder and pat-patted his back with a soft hand.

Bitter looked at Morgan and said, "Do you really know what it means if you marry me?"

Morgan nodded and said, "I think so." *And I think I've loved you from the moment you rode to the farm with Harley.* "I promise to be a good wife and bear you strong children…in addition to these two."

"It'll be a long, rough trip. You better be certain."

"She is," Ethan said, "isn't she Mikey?"

Sheriff Bob Tucker, who spent a lot of his time avoiding problems, smiled his pleasure and approval when the judge rapped his gavel and said, "So be it."

When Bitter started to get out of his chair, Judge Harrison said, "You stay right there."

Without getting up, the judge rolled his chair to the side board, grabbed the whisky bottle, put three whisky glasses on his lap and wheeled back to the table. The glasses were clean but clouded from the lye soap the Judge's wife used to wash dishes, and as a matter of fact to wash everything else.

"Now," he said, "let's get the names right."

It wasn't until after the judge, in stentorian tones, said, "By the power invested in me by the Holy Church and by the State of Missouri, I now pronounce you man and wife," that Bitter saw the cane standing in an empty brass cuspidor by the door. *Now I know why he didn't get out of the chair*. He thought about his grandfather who said, "When you jump to conclusions, make sure you don't land in a manure pile." *I just landed in a manure pile.*

"You owe me one dollar," the judge said to the slightly bewildered groom. When Bitter handed over a silver dollar, the Judge added, "As soon as you kiss the bride, we can have a congratulatory drink."

John gave the smiling young woman, his new wife a bewildered look, but that changed with the soft press of his wife's lips. *Better than I deserve*, he thought.

Judge Henry Harvey Harrison banged his gavel on the scarred table and said, "Enough of that now," and then poured a dollop of whiskey in three glasses with an extra dollop for himself.

When Tucker and Bitter each had a glass in hand, the judge raised his and said, "A toast to Mister and Missus John Bitter and their children, Ethan and Michael. May you have smooth sailing and fair wind at your back."

Morgan and the boys were happy on their trip back down the board walk to their hotel. Bitter kept thinking, *Shanghaied… and blackmailed is what I've been.* But a bright morning sun set brilliant highlights dancing in Morgan's shining red hair, and he thought, *Well, if this is being shanghaied, I can think of worse ships to sail in.*

24
New Friends

WHILE MORGAN TOOK THE BOYS to the Hotel "to change," Bitter hurried down the street to the Hamilton Emporium and Dry Goods in search of a wedding ring. Morgan hadn't complained, but Bitter's conscience, shotgun wedding or not, was pricked by his sense of propriety. A woman should have a wedding ring, and given his new wealth, thanks to the reward money—less Sheriff Tucker's fees, of course—he believed he could afford a nice one.

The clerk, a tall young man with an open face and a winning smile stumped Bitter by asking, "What size should the ring be?"

"Damn," Bitter muttered, and then, with a resigned sigh, said, "I'll be back."

When he walked into the foyer of the hotel, Morgan was coming down the stairs, holding hands with the boys. Unlike the oversized man's shirt and patched cotton trousers she had been wearing, she had changed to a long sleeved, high necked cotton dress.

Somehow the deep green-and-black tartan pattern in the dress worked as backdrop for the long braid of her flaming red hair. She had swapped the scuffed riding boots she had walked blister in for a pair of fashionable lady's lace up boots. The dress did nothing to hide her firm, trim figure.

"Oh, my," he said involuntarily.

She gave him an impish smile and said, "Oh my, what?"

Wide-eyed, the boys stared at the assortment of gold and silver wedding bands in the velvet lined tray the clerk placed on the counter. Bitter urged Morgan to choose the delicate wonder of a thin gold band with a sparkling diamond inset.

"It is a lovely thing," the clerk said.

"Yes," Morgan agreed, "it is, but it's not the ring for a farm wife."

She picked up a plain gold band, and slipped it on her ring finger. When it fit, she said, "I'll take this one."

Bitter paid the clerk ten dollars and then asked, "Is the diamond ring the same size?"

"It is," the clerk said.

"Good. If you have a velvet box, we'll take that one as well."

Morgan started to protest, but he shushed her and said, "You can wear it for special occasions. Let it be a wedding gift."

He turned beet red when she stood on her tiptoes and brushed his cheek with her soft lips.

The clerk, who squeezed every penny he found, overcame his parsimonious nature and generously gave each boy two red striped peppermint candies.

Wanda Crawford laughed until the tears were flowing after an amused Sheriff Tucker related the circumstances of Bitter's marriage.

Sheriff Tucker tipped his chair back and grinned. "The judge wrapped him up nice and tidy. Blackmailed him, he did. Said if he didn't take the boys, they would have to go to the orphanage in Springfield. It looked to me like that scared Bitter worse than it did the boys.

"And then Judge Harrison said he would not grant guardianship to a bachelor, and because young Mister Bitter had misled the young lass...Morgan...he ordered up and conducted the marriage himself...on the spot. The little boys and I were witnesses."

"What did Morgan say?"

"I do," Tucker said, and laughed. "But I think she would rather have had Bitter propose than be forced."

"I think we should have a wedding party this evening," Wanda said, "right here in the café. What do you think?"

Tucker, who liked parties held in places that served liquor, agreed nonetheless.

Sheriff Tucker and his wife Gertrude brought train tickets, purchased with city funds, for Bitter, his new wife and the boys…a gift he hoped Bitter would use to ride tomorrow's morning train out of town.

Detective Mark Anthony brought a gift wrapped box, a handshake and a demand to kiss the bride, which he did with enthusiasm. He looked at Bitter and failed to keep from laughing. "Congratulations, partner," he said. In an aside, he whispered, "Unwrap the box in private."

Judge Harrison struggled up the steps of the café, helped by his cane and the strong arm of his wife Millicent. He had on a clean white shirt, a red string tie, and a dark blue vest without gravy stains. A new bottle of good Kentucky Bourbon, wrapped in a cushion of newspaper, rode in Millicent's purse. Judge Henry Harvey Harrison hoped Bitter would uncork it on the spot.

Smelling of rose water, Sergeant Bellamy, who was on and off again sparking Wanda, wore his best dress uniform, the numerous chevrons of a Sergeant Major in bright yellow contrast to the deep blue of his uniform.

Major Walters and his wife Helen contributed a freshly baked cake. Helen was a small, spritely woman whose warmth and good will was a constant comfort to the major. When she saw the two boys, she bent down and introduced herself. "I'm Missus Walters. And what are you names?"

Ethan didn't say anything, and Mikey cowered behind Morgan's long dress. Morgan said, "Nice to meet you Missus Walters." She touched Ethan's shoulder and said, "This is Ethan, and the little one is Mikey."

Deputy Walter Tucker tagged along with his big brother, hat in hand…and envy in his heart at the sight of Morgan in her green dress.

Walter wondered if the envy he was feeling was the same thing as the sinful thoughts the preacher talked about.

Gertrude Tucker turned out to be a patient, pleasant woman, much maligned as the voice of Hamilton's Women's Christian Temperance Union, and because her husband was known to imbibe on occasion, an irony duly noted by the gossips of the town.

Wanda watched in amusement as the young couple cut the cake and fed each other a messy bite, ending with frosting on Bitter's chin and on Morgan's nose.

Sergeant Bellamy led the clapping and the laughter. He slipped up beside Wanda and said, "You know, love, they're headed for Oregon. We could go along, just to make sure they get there." He laughed and winked. Wanda shook her head, but failed to suppress a smile.

Wanda took over the chore of cutting chunks of cake and setting them on desert plates which the boys passed out to the guests. When they finished, she set two plates on a table and said to the grateful boys, "These are yours."

And the judge's hopes were realized when Bitter uncorked the bourbon. Wanda set out enough glasses for the men, and Bitter poured an inch of golden liquid in each glass. The Judge raised his in salute and said, "A toast!"

"Here, here," Anthony said and started to drink his whiskey. But the judge growled at him, "Not yet. I haven't finished. Where was I?"

Sheriff Tucker laughed and said, "I think you said 'a toast'."

"Ah yes." The judge raised his glass and with just a touch of an Irish brogue said, "Smooth sailin' and fair wind at your back."

Tucker laughed again and decided it didn't much matter that the judge had made the same toast earlier in the day.

Walter choked and coughed on the fiery liquid and was embarrassed at the thought of what Morgan must think of him.

Conversation began to falter after the first congratulations, and Detective Anthony said, "I changed my mind. Go ahead and open the box."

Bitter looked at Ethan and Mikey. "You want to help?"

Bitter cut the twine with a penknife and set the box on the floor. The boys attacked the package, scattering torn bit and pieces of brown wrapping paper on Wanda's floor. Anthony's package held a new Navy .36-caliber revolver nestled in a black leather cross draw holster, a small skinning knife in a belt sheath, a whistle, a soft blue shawl, and a new leather wallet.

"The Navy is for Missus Bitter. I think you'll find, Morgan," he said, "the .36 a little easier to handle than that big horse pistol you've been carrying. The knife is for you, Ethan. It's sharp, so don't cut yourself."

Eyes wide, Ethan reached for the knife and said quietly, "Thank you."

"This is for Mikey," Anthony said, and held up a copper whistle on a leather thong. "In case he needs to whistle up some help."

He smiled at Morgan and held out the shawl. "To match your eyes. It'll go nicely with that beautiful ring you're wearing."

Morgan blushed and stammered, "Thank you." She wrapped the shawl around her shoulders, and Bitter found himself automatically adjusting the folds in the soft material. He liked the feel of her shoulder under his hand.

"And the wallet is for you, John. You'll find a rail pass that will let you ride free of charge on any railroad in the country. There is also your first year's retainer, a badge and a telegram from our home office stating you are employed by the Pinkerton Detective Agency."

"Well, damn," Tucker was heard to mutter. "I wonder if I can get my money back on those train tickets the town bought."

Bitter pumped Pinkerton Detective Mark Anthony's hand, grateful for remembering the boys, and somewhat chagrined he hadn't thought of that himself.

"Thanks Mark. I'll not forget this."

"Here, here," Judge Harrison said and applauded. "Drinks all around."

That earned him a glare from Gertrude Tucker and a dig in the ribs from Millicent. But it in no way discouraged the Judge in his quest for one more drink.

"My legs are ailing," he whispered to his wife.

Gertrude had the final say after all, for who could deny her request to pray for the newlyweds? "Let us. bow our heads," she said.

25
Married But Single

BITTER WOKE BEFORE DAWN, GRUMPY and out of sorts. He had never given the notion of a wedding night much thought. He had never given the thought of marriage much thought either. In fact, he had decided it was a rough world to bring children into, which, in his mind made marriage and the making of babies a fool's errand. Morgan's kiss in the Judge's office had moved his thinking a bit…away from the cynical into more positive channels.

On the other hand, he hadn't known he'd be sleeping with Mikey and Ethan on his wedding night either. The suggestion that Mikey and Ethan could sleep in one room and he and Morgan in the room right next door met with Mikey's tears and Ethan's refusal to be parted from Bitter.

Morgan had kissed Bitter on the cheek and whispered, "We'll work something out…tomorrow."

What that might be remained to be seen.

Bitter had the boys up and packed before daylight. He rapped on Morgan's door and said, "Rise and shine. We need to pack before the train gets here. Need any help?"

A fully dressed Morgan pulled the door opened and said, "Well, you sleepy heads are finally awake. I'm packed. Let's have some breakfast at Wanda's and then go get Lucifer and the horses."

The boys stuffed themselves with hotcakes coated with butter and sugar, devoured scrambled eggs, and ate three pieces of bacon each. And then Wanda, a master of the art of making something good to eat out of almost nothing, set a glass of what passed for chocolate milk in front of each boy. Mikey, a chocolate moustache dripping off his upper lip, didn't say anything, but his wide-eyed stare was thanks enough. And Ethan, who was Mikey's interpreter said, "He likes it. I do too."

Wanda's cuckoo clock sounded 6:00 a.m., a reminder they should be about their business. Morgan hugged Wanda in thanks, and when Bitter held out his hand Wanda pulled him in and gave him a kiss on the cheek. Her eyes were wet with tears. She pushed Bitter back and said, "You two write when you get to Oregon. I'm thinking Sergeant Bellamy and I will be along next year."

"Are congratulations in order?" Morgan asked.

Wanda blushed and nodded. "I decided to say yes to that rascal. He's pestered me about marriage long enough. And I'm thinking we need a little adventure in our lives now that the war is over."

"I like Sergeant Bellamy," Ethan said.

"I do, too," echoed John Bitter.

After another round of hugs and with new promises made, the John and Morgan Bitter family stepped on the porch just as a buckboard driven by Mark Anthony pulled up.

"I thought you might like some help getting to the train depot," was all the explanation he offered.

Bitter grinned and said, "I could grow to like you, Detective Anthony, if you weren't so ugly."

Anthony laughed and said, "You aren't so pretty yourself."

The two men shook hands and then loaded the boys' new canvas backpacks, each smelling of its fresh paraffin coating, Bitter's battered and hard used shoulder pack, and Morgan's huge double canvas saddlebags in the buckboard. Bitter swept Mikey up and set him on the seat. "You get to ride in style, Mikey."

Mark Anthony held his hand out to Morgan and said, "My lady." She blushed at all the fuss, but she stepped up into the buckboard beside Mikey. The curve of her hips in the green tartan patterned dress, and the sour memory of his "wedding night" brought on a fresh round of the grumps. Bitter allowed himself a full minute of self pity before his naturally optimistic nature reasserted itself.

Ethan carried his cane fishing pole over his shoulder as the procession made the short, four-block trek to the train depot. Bitter was startled by the cold, wet nose that bumped his hand, and without looking down he knew the red hound had shown up in time to catch the train. He gave Rusty a perfunctory pat on the head. Somehow the dog gave Bitter comfort that all was right in the world. He was wrong, but at that moment he didn't know it.

26
Arresting Developments

A FOUR MAN SQUAD OF BLUE clad Union soldiers watched the buckboard pull up to the station. Sergeant Bellamy helped Morgan from the buckboard, and then plucked Mikey from the seat and swung him over to the depot porch. "Can you stay right there?"

Mikey nodded and Rusty sat down beside him. Ethan, clutching his fishing pole climbed up beside him and scratched Rusty's ears. "That's a good lad," Bellamy said.

Anthony hopped down from the buckboard and said, "I want to check for telegrams."

"Thank you, Mister Bellamy," Morgan said. "I need to round up Lucifer."

"It's Jack, Ma'am, not 'mister,' and if you are referring to that big mule, he's eating his way through the little meadow just beyond camp. I tried to catch him for you, but he wasn't having any part of my rope. Can I give you a hand?"

Morgan shook her head. "He has bad memories of ropes, I'm afraid. And he hates men with a fury. But for some reason he likes me…or at least tolerates me. I won't have any trouble catching him, but it's something I have to do by myself."

"I wouldn't want him mad at me," Bellamy said.

Perched alongside twin ribbons of steel sat the clapboard depot with a proud sign proclaiming the Hannibal and St. Joseph Rail-road. The war had brought neglect and faded paint, but the depot still carried the filigree and gingerbread curlicues of the owner's prejudice. A metal rooster rode a brass wind vane clinging to a half story tower perched on the middle of the roof.

The station master, one Mister Riley Witherspoon was also the telegrapher, an honor he wore with pride, even though the copper line linking Hamilton to the rest of the world was frequently down, an occurrence cause by raiders, or some times by poverty- stricken farmers needing wire for patchwork repair.

In truth, Mother Nature also played a hand in the destruction of the wire. Lightning, wind, and falling trees were her tools. But those events didn't make nearly as good a story as raiders, so Riley continued to accuse raiders for each and every interruption to his sacred telegraph.

He was impressed with Detective Anthony's credentials. Mr. Riley had in fact been personally instructed by the president of the railroad, Mister Clemens himself, to cooperate with the Pinkertons in any way possible. Unfortunately, there just wasn't any news back from Detective Anthony's telegrams to other Pinkerton agents searching for Aunt Quilla.

"And I just now checked the wire," Riley said, "to be sure it's still working."

Anthony nodded, said, "Thank you," and thought about the search. On a professional level he was slightly disappointed his agents had failed to find Aunt Quilla. But then they hadn't been at it very long. On a more personal level, he wasn't sorry the boys were safe with John Bitter. *And Morgan,* he reminded himself.

Rockford and Misery were tied to the hitching rail outside the train depot…alongside five other horses wearing Union saddles. Bitter and Morgan's saddles sat on the low, scuff-marked wooden porch of the depot.

Rockford, Bitter noticed, was busy trying to bite and paw his way through a burlap sack.

One of troopers said, "Here you, you blamed flea bag, stop that! That's not your cracked corn." He dodged Rockford's efforts to bite him and snatched the sack away.

Without preamble, Sergeant Bellamy said, "Captain Bitter, sir. I took the liberty of bringing your horses and your gear from the livery stable."

"Thank you."

"My pleasure, Captain. But I have a bit of bad news. Trooper Jones was nursing his sore feet and mourning the death of his horse last night at the Boston Saloon. He said two pistol-packing hillbillies asked Little John, the bartender, if he knew the whereabouts of a redheaded woman. When Little John asked why, one of the fellows said she was kin folk, but she run off from her husband, and they had come to take her back. And of course, Little John said he didn't know any redheaded woman.

"Trooper Jones isn't overly smart, but he's smart enough to smell trouble. So when Little John signaled and pointed at the door, he hightailed it back to the post to tell me what he heard. I had Blind Charlie, our Cherokee scout, trail the hillbillies to their camp."

"And?" Bitter asked.

"Well…me and boys sort of dropped in on 'em last night, sort of by accident you understand, to have a little chat. They claimed to be indignant that our sheriff had not arrested Missus Bitter for murder…there being an eye witness and all."

"The farmer," Bitter said.

"I'm afraid so, Captain. It seems he got to flappin' his jaw over in Kidder, the next town west from here.

"I'll say this much for the hillbillies, they had no backup in them. They just glared at us when I said the farmer was a damned liar.

"To which they said, the tracks where they found their dead kin told the story well enough. It was plain, they said, the man they called Uncle Owen and his son Lige had been murdered and their goods plundered…all their money gone and Uncle Owen's rifle, a good carbine. And they intend to set it right."

"Kill Morgan?"

"Aye. I'm afraid that's what they meant. And I noticed that breech-loading carbine with her goods. You don't suppose she actually killed those men?"

Bitter nodded. "She did, but she doesn't want that known. She was only fighting back because they intended her harm. Lucifer stomped one and Morgan shot the other."

"I'll be damned. That little thing?"

"She was big enough to pull the trigger."

"Well, be that as it may, Blind Charlie laid up close to their camp after we left and listened to their talk. It seems they plan to stop the train just down the tracks a ways and do a search. Just to make sure she isn't on it."

"And if she isn't?" Bitter asked.

"They'll send a telegram to kin folks in Kidder and have them watch the road."

Detective Anthony, who had joined Sergeant Bellamy and Bitter after talking to Station Master Riley, said, "You are just full of good news, Sergeant. Any idea how they plan to stop the train?"

"Well," Bellamy said, "a popular method is to simply fall a tree across the tracks, but…"

"But nothing," Sheriff Tucker said from behind Bellamy. He walked up to the circle of men and said, "When was anybody gonna tell me about these bushwhackers? Seems to me it's my business, not army business."

Unruffled, Sergeant Bellamy said, "Up early, Sheriff?"

"Not as early as you, I see. But to answer your question, Little John got to worrying that you boys in blue would forget your manners and neglect to tell me what was happening. He thought it was important enough to get me out of a nice warm bed in the middle of the night.

"It was especially aggravating because he woke Gertrude up as well. I'll hear about that all through supper, just like I heard about the bourbon we nipped…and that's all it was…just a nip…at your wedding, Mister John Bitter."

"Pitiful," Bellamy said, but there was a smile on his face.

Sheriff Tucker glared at Bellamy for a second and then chuckled. He stared at Bitter for a few seconds and said, "But, the good thing is I'm up in time to make sure you get on the train."

27
Cow Catcher

TO BITTER'S SURPRISE, ROCKFORD WAS harder to load in the cattle car than Lucifer. Morgan, a handful of Lucifer's mane for a lead rope, simply walked Lucifer up the ramp and into the car.

But Rockford, as soon as his front feet hit the hollow-sounding ramp, bucked and fought until he nearly pulled Bitter's arm out of the socket. Two troopers pulled a rope around Rockford's rump from each side and pulled it tight while another trooper hit Rockford's butt with a knotted rope. Spooked, the black horse lunged up the ramp where he banged into Bitter and nearly knocked him down.

To aggravate the situation, when Rockford popped through the door, Lucifer pulled his upper lip back and brayed at Rockford. Insulted and challenged by the big mule, Rockford bared his teeth and turned his rump to get in a good kick…which fortunately just fanned the air. An alert trooper dropped a rope over Rockford's head and took a turn around a handy tie-down bolted to the floor. It took Bitter and three troopers to forcibly winch Rockford into the stall in the right rear corner of the car.

Rusty padded quietly up the ramp, sniffed the odors of mules and horses, and eased into the car. When he saw Rockford, he padded over to the stall and stood in a corner, a wary eye on the door.

Rockford leaned his long neck over the half door holding him prisoner and touched the dog with his nose.

"Lordy, lordy," the trooper said. "This is going to be some fun when we get the other horses loaded."

Morgan watched as Misery, acquiescent as always, let Bitter lead her up the ramp. Morgan thought Misery had brighter eyes since the hostler had lanced the gum. *Maybe she's eating again*, Morgan thought.

Mark Anthony showed the conductor his badge and pulled him aside. A man fiercely proud of his job, the conductor ran what he thought of as a no-nonsense train. After the last train robbery, he had taken to carrying a .44 Derringer in a shoulder holster. And he kept a ten-gauge shotgun hidden on the train, "Just in case," he told his wife.

When Anthony explained what might happen, and why the train should roll on through the Kidder station, the conductor's brown eyes were bright with anger…not at John Bitter or Mark Anthony, but at the notion anyone would dare try and stop his train…again.

The conductor, a medium-sized man, dressed in black, trotted to the engine, his black string tie flapping against his white shirt. He shouted and waved at the engineer who leaned through the open window of the cab. Anthony couldn't hear what they were saying, but he was satisfied when the engineer nodded and ducked back inside.

Sergeant Bellamy assigned three seasoned veterans to protect Missus Bitter and the boys in the passenger car immediately forward of the cattle car. The horses, he told the trooper assigned to the cattle car, were to remain saddled and ready for a chase if it came down to it.

At ten minutes after the hour, the Union horses were keeping company with Rockford, Misery, and Lucifer, and all the gear was stowed.

The Union horses wisely recognized Lucifer's ownership of the front half of the fifty foot car and chose to keep company with Misery, Rusty and Rockford toward the back half. Not one horse challenged the big, dark mule.

Once he settled the business of who was boss, Lucifer calmed down, and when he lowered his head to snuff and lip a few stray flecks of oats scattered in a corner, the young trooper assigned to ride with the horses took his hand away from his pistol. Satisfied he wouldn't have to shoot the big brute after all, he tipped a feed bucket bottom end up and sat down to wait out the trip.

The conductor hollered "all aboard," and the engineer eased forward on the throttle to start the belching, steaming iron monster down the tracks toward St. Joseph…first scheduled stop at the little town of Kidder. Under instructions from the conductor, there would be no morning stop in Kidder on this trip, egg and dairy farmers be damned.

Through the window, Bitter saw Sheriff Tucker standing on the porch of the depot. Tucker grinned, pointed west down the tracks, and then he gave Bitter a thumbs-up. Mark Anthony, Bitter's new boss and newest friend, waved goodbye.

Seating in the two passenger cars was in sets of double seats facing forward and double seats facing back. Bitter sat in an aisle seat in one and Mikey and Ethan shared a seat next to Bitter. An empty aisle seat kept company with Morgan who sat facing Bitter and the boys.

Simply beautiful in a gift from Wanda, a sky-blue, long-sleeved, high-collared dress, her red hair in a long braid, Morgan captivated the three troopers assigned to protect her. Bellamy was amused and Bitter didn't know whether to be jealous or not. When a young trooper with a white-toothed smile started to slip into the empty seat next to Morgan, Ethan hopped down from the seat he was sharing with Mikey, jumped into the empty seat and glared at the trooper.

Bellamy laughed and said to the flustered trooper, "I think young Master Ethan has plumbed the depths of your heathen heart, Rumford. I'd mind my manners, if I was you."

Bellamy looked at Bitter and nodded toward the rear of the car. "Let's see if I can get my pipe lit."

Moving at a velocity of nearly twenty-five miles per hour, the train was flying. At least that's how it felt to Bitter despite the fact it wasn't his first train ride. The first had been on an over-crowded, slow moving troop train. But he wasn't headed home that time, and the troop train had never gone faster than a good horse could trot.

Bellamy managed to get his pipe going and touched the match to the end of Bitter's roll-your-own. After a satisfying puff of nic-otine-laden smoke, Bitter asked, "Why is the army helping us ?"

"Because the Major likes you…and because I pointed out the 50th Illinois is stationed in Hamilton to keep the peace and protect the citizens. And when we know certain undesirable elements are planning to kill one of those citizens, we would be derelict in our duties if we did not intervene.

"I also had to point out how important it was for the Major to remain at the post to command our reserve forces should they be called upon. Otherwise he would be looking for another glorious charge."

Bitter laughed. "You mean he would be here to interfere with Sergeant Major Bellamy."

Bellamy took a puff and grinned at Bitter. "He's a brave lad, but a bit headstrong."

"I never thought he was a coward," Bitter said, "but with the war ended, there will be little room for so many officers. I think the Major would like to remain a major and not go back to being a captain or even a lieutenant."

"There's that, for sure," Bellamy agreed.

"We've been kinda busy so I haven't asked, but how did your scout come to be called Blind Charley?"

Bellamy laughed. "Well, you see we were tracking some fellows who robbed the Boston Saloon…not for money…just for some whiskey. One of them was Charlie's friend. So when we set out to recover the whiskey, Charlie kept missing the tracks. I finally got fed up and allowed that if he couldn't follow so plain a track, he must be blind. And he's been known as Blind Charlie ever since.

"Truth be known, he can track fish up a muddy creek. I swear he can even track birds hours after they fly by. I have no idea how he does it."

Bitter laughed, took a last pull on his cigarette and then field stripped it.

"What did you do during the war, Captain?"

Bitter looked at him, head cocked to the side like he was studying on a reply and finally said, "I was a spy."

When Bellamy's eyebrows rose in question, Bitter quickly added, "In uniform, not a civilian spy. I had a well-mounted company of scouts. Our job was to locate and a report back on any rebel forces we found. We weren't guerillas. Just scouts. That's where I got Rockford. I was told to take my pick of the horse herd, but to leave the black alone because he just couldn't be ridden." Bitter paused and added, "I liked the way he was set up, so I rode him."

Bellamy nodded. "And kept him when you mustered out?"

"I traded my mustering out pay for him. None of the other officers wanted him."

The steam whistle rolled across the countryside, and Bellamy knocked the embers from his pipe. He looked at Bitter and nodded. "Looks like we might have some trouble headed our way."

Alert and a bit nervous, the engineer spotted a medium-sized tree across the roadway about half a mile down the tracks. Instinctively he started to pull back on the throttle, but caught himself in time to just let the train keep rolling. At the three hundred yard mark, the tree was plainer to his eyes, and he could see the tree's bushy limbs keeping about an eighteen inch trunk a couple feet off the ground. He grimaced and pushed the throttle forward and the train began picking up speed.

"If you are going to stop our train," he said through clinched teeth to his fireman, "you'll have bring a lot bigger tree."

The train was doing over thirty miles an hour when the cow catcher scooped the butt end of the tree up and out of the way. The engineer had a flashing glimpse of someone stepping out from behind a tree, and then the engine was beyond the ambush.

Glass from a shattered window peppered the passengers in Sergeant Bellamy's car. Bellamy spotted gun smoke alongside the train track and roared, "That tears it! Shootin' at us, the bastards!"

He shouted at the conductor. "Get this thing stopped!"

The conductor pulled the cord running the length of the car and a half mile later, the train slid to a stop.

When Bitter started to follow the troopers to the cattle car, Sergeant Bellamy shouted back over his shoulder, "Begging your pardon, Captain, but this one is ours! You stay with your family and get them safely to St. Joseph."

As the troopers manhandled the ramp into position, Bellamy shouted at Bitter, "You write us. We'll see you in Oregon before the year is out."

28
Kidder and the Devil

WHEN IT WAS OBVIOUS THE train wasn't going to stop, even though it was only moving at about five miles an hour through the station yard, the farmers waiting at the Kidder Train Depot to ship their eggs and butter cream down line to St. Joseph, shook their fists at the engineer. And as the train growled, grumbled, and clacked past the depot, Bitter spotted three grim looking, bearded men running to ground hitched horses. *They mean to chase us,* he thought.

He looked at Morgan and the boys and was suddenly lonesome for the company of Sergeant Bellamy and his squad of troopers, even the one with the pretty white teeth.

Morgan sensed his agitation and raised her eyebrows in question. He let out a sigh and said, "We've got three bushwhackers chasing the train. Where's your pistol?"

"Oh…in my saddlebags. I didn't think it would be lady-like to wear a pistol on the train."

"Normally, I'd say you were right, but not this time."

The conductor came hurrying into the car. He was carrying a ten-gauge double- barreled shotgun. Without preamble he said, "We have some tough looking men following us."

"I saw 'em," Bitter said.

The conductor looked at Morgan and said, "This may sound a bit strange, but are you armed?"

"No."

He pulled his .44 Derringer from its shoulder holster and held it out. "Can you use this?"

"I've been around guns since I was born."

"All right then," he said and handed her the pistol. "Just cock the hammer and pull the trigger."

The boys were wide-eyed and staring at the adults. Without a word, Ethan got out of his seat and ran down the aisle to his cane pole leaning in a corner of the car. He had no idea what he could do with it, but there was some comfort in the feel of it so he carried it back to his seat and leaned it against the window.

Then he pulled the little skinning knife from the sheath, the knife Mark Anthony had given him at the wedding party. He held it in his right hand and sat back down. He reached for Mikey's hand with his left and looked from Bitter to Morgan seeking reassurance. "Don't worry, Mikey. We'll protect you," he said.

If the situation hadn't been so serious, Bitter might have smiled at Ethan's determination. He stood up, reached for Mikey and plopped him onto Morgan's lap. "You stay right here, Mikey, while I go take care of the bad guys. Okay?"

Bitter was glad he had the foresight to stash the Henry in the overhead rack. He pulled it down and stripped the saddle scabbard from the rifle. He checked his pistol and then asked the conductor, "How do I get to the caboose?"

"That's not a problem. There are connecting doors at each end of the cattle car. I'll come with you."

The train's two brakemen were in the caboose playing checkers when the conductor and Bitter opened the door.

The older brakeman looked up and asked, "What's going on, Arthur?"

"Outlaws coming," the conductor said and hurried to the rear door of the caboose.

Even with the increasing acceleration of the train, the horsemen pounding alongside the rail bed were making good time. The lead rider, a lean bearded man wearing a dirty buckskin shirt reached for a ladder rung just as the conductor and Bitter stepped out on the back platform. Without a word, the conductor cocked the shotgun and pointed it at the hillbilly. "Get off my train," he said with tight lips.

The bearded man let go of the ladder rung and settled back on his horse. Bitter studied on the situation for all of one second, and then pulled the Henry to his shoulder and shot the man's horse in the head.

That wasn't where he was aiming, but the results were gratifying nonetheless. Rider and horse went down in a tumbling heap. Through the dust cloud raised by the falling horse, Bitter could see the man struggling to get free of the saddle just before the horse rolled and smashed his rider into the ground.

The other two riders opened fire with pistols from a few yards away until the conductor's shotgun blew one rider out of the saddle. The man's horse ran a few yards more and then went down in a heap, victim to the buckshot that also killed his owner.

The last rider pulled his horse to a skidding stop and shot at them until his pistol was empty. In impotent rage he swore he would kill the conductor and all of his kin.

Although he couldn't understand the words, the threat was evident to Bitter. That was just too much to take. He gauged distance and speed, and jumped from the train, running down a grassy bank to the borrow pit, trying to match his running speed with the momentum of the train. He stumbled and rolled once near the bottom of slope, his hat flying off his head, but he managed to avoid a derelict railroad tie left over from some earlier track repair.

He picked himself up, grabbed his hat and dusted off the Henry with a shirt sleeve. He watched the man work to reload the pistol. "Go back!" Bitter shouted. "There's been enough killing."

The man continued to reload his pistol and started walking his horse in Bitter's direction. "Don't do it!" Bitter shouted.

"You killed my brothers!" the ambusher shouted back across the two hundred yards that separated them. "You shouldn't a done that. We got us a blood feud now. It won't end until we kill y'all."

"Damn," Bitter said quietly to himself, "I'm sure getting tired of all this killing."

He knelt down, tried to calm his pounding heart, took a bead on the man's chest, and hollered, "This is my last warning. Turn around and go back!"

The man's pistol belched a cloud of black powder gun smoke, and a bullet whined off a steel rail to Bitter's right. He let out a deep breath and gently squeezed the trigger. He didn't hear the gun go off and he didn't feel the recoil. All of his concentration was on the man he was trying to kill.

Later he wondered if the dead man was suicidal or just convinced Bitter couldn't hit him at that distance. *Probably figured I'd miss,* Bitter decided.

The lone survivor of the shootout, a compact sorrel gelding about four or five years old stood trembling and confused by the iron smell of blood and the stillness of its owner. In life he had been a hard man, but one who nonetheless looked after his horses and his hounds.

Bitter walked slowly toward the horse, talking quietly. "What am I going to do about you?" he asked when he was about five feet away. The horse shied and stepped back but didn't run. "Now, now, horse. It's going to be all right."

Bitter caught up the reins and rubbed the horse's neck to settle it down. When he was satisfied the sorrel was calm enough to be ridden, he swung into the saddle and started the horse moving in the direction of St. Joseph. He figured the conductor would get the train stopped and come back for him. In the meantime, he wanted some distance between the living and the dead.

Morgan, the boys and the conductor were standing on the rear platform when the train came chugging backwards down the track. The conductor signaled the engine to a stop and stepped off the platform.

"That was a fool stunt," the conductor said over his shoulder as he helped Morgan to the ground.

"It had to be settled," Bitter said, and stepped down from the saddle. He slid an arm around Morgan's lower back when she put her arms around his neck, and with tears in her eyes, kissed his cheek. She stepped back and said, "I was so scared you would get hurt."

Ethan said, "He did. See there?" and pointed at a big rip in the left knee of Bitter's cavalry britches, a blood soaked path working it's way down the pants leg.

"I'll be danged," Bitter said. "I never even noticed."

A little voice asked, "Does it hurt?"

The surprise at hearing Mikey speak stunned them into silence.

Bitter smiled and said, "Yep, a little bit."

"What are going to do about the horse?" the conductor asked, and pointed at the gelding.

Bitter tied the reins around the saddle horn and swatted the nervous animal on the rump. As the horse trotted up the borrow pit back toward Kidder, Bitter said, "I hope he find his way home."

The conductor nodded. "Might."

The setting sun drew leafy shadows in the open meadows as the train pulled into St. Joseph. A telegram from Mark Anthony waited for Bitter at the station. In terms so brief it could be code,

Anthony's message told him Sergeant Bellamy and his troopers had dispatched one of the hillbillies, but two others had escaped into a swamp. Blind Charlie was on their trail.

Bitter shrugged it off and thought maybe their feud with the hillbillies would be over by morning. Favoring his left leg, which had rediscovered feeling, he stepped down and walked back to the cattle car. When he started to help the conductor and the brakemen lower the ramp to offload the animals, the conductor waved him away. "We have this. You take care of your knee."

Rusty trotted down the ramp and went immediately to the corner of the depot where he raised a hind leg and claimed ownership…or at least his relief at being on solid ground again.

Darkness had fallen before Morgan and John Bitter found a large enough pasture for Lucifer and a livery where the horses were stabled, watered and fed.

Bitter found rooms at the large, red brick, three-story St. Jo Hotel. When the desk clerk, an older gentleman with gray hair offered to help carry the bags, Bitter hesitated before saying, "Thank you."

His normal reaction to offers of help was instant rejection, but his knee was beginning to throb in rhythm to his heart beat. He didn't figure anything was broken, but the dent in the knee cap was painful nonetheless.

The clerk eyed the dark patch of dried blood on Bitter's pants and the rifle scabbard but decided not to say anything. It was obvious Bitter had been involved in some sort of dustup.

Eyes big at the ornate patterns in the rugs, the shining crystal chandeliers, and the dark leather overstuffed chairs in the lobby, the boys clung to Bitter's hands as they followed the desk clerk up the stairs. The clerk opened the door to room seven, set the luggage on the floor next to the bed, and struck a match to light the oil lamp. Bitter tipped him with a two-bit piece, enough to buy a modest supper.

The boys bounced on the bed and Mikey giggled until Bitter looked at them and said, "I don't think that's a good idea, do you?"

"You'll spoil their fun," Morgan said, sticking up for the boys.

"And get us kicked out if they make too much ruckus."

Morgan sniffed and said, "Bring your packs and come next door with me. We'll leave old Mister Fuddy Duddy to himself."

Bitter listened to the sound of bouncing creaking bedsprings coming from next door while he changed into the only other pants he owned, a pair of blue wool cavalry britches. He shaved in the wash basin, ran his fingers through his wavy brown hair and put on a clean white shirt. When Morgan and the boys knocked, he opened the door and said, "Who's hungry?"

Mikey said, "Me."

"Me, too," Ethan echoed.

They ate dinner in the hotel restaurant and endured the envious stares of affection deprived husbands, and the glare of jealous wives who knew they were no competition for the young redhead.

Not all of the stares were in envy, however. John Bitter's blue cavalry pants were not welcomed by every St. Joseph resident. Split down the middle by the war, the citizens of St. Joseph, half supporting the Union and half supporting the confederates, had endured several years of Marshal Law. Those in open defiance of the North and those who refused to swear the oath of allegiance to the Union faced jail and heavy fines.

Bitter chose to ignore any veiled hostility and enjoyed a tender steak. The steak was dark colored, and he was suspicious it might be horse meat, but with a coating of flour gravy and a heavy dose of salt and pepper, it went down just fine, so he chose to ignore his suspicion.

After supper, Morgan took Mikey back upstairs to wash his face and hands in the basin the hotel provided in each room, while Bitter and Ethan, who easily fell into the role of co-conspirators, sneaked Rusty up the back stairs to the room Ethan and Mikey would occupy, protected by the big red hound, of course.

Bitter had rented two rooms because he was determined to sleep with his wife this second night of their marriage. What took place between them was never shared with anyone else, but each knew they would never forget the sweet joy they discovered in St. Joseph, Missouri.

29

Getting Trail Ready

AN EARLY RISER, BITTER SLIPPED from the warm bed and dressed as quietly as he could. He smiled at the tousled red hair and the gentle rise and fall of the comforter. *Lordy, lordy,* he thought. *And to think I wanted to stay a bachelor.*

He pulled on his scuffed, black riding boots, slipped into the hallway, and soft footed to room eight. He knocked once on the door, and was answered by a low growl which told him the big red dog was on the job. "Rusty, you be quiet. It's me."

He waited nearly half a minute, and then the door cracked open and a blond head peeked out, a small fist rubbing one eye. A tail-wagging red hound nosed around Mikey and stared at Bitter. "Morning," Bitter said. "You and Ethan ready for some breakfast?"

"Nope," Mikey said, and started to shut the door. Bitter stopped it with his foot. "I'll bet Rusty needs to take a walk."

"I did that an hour ago, Mister Bitter," Ethan said from under the covers. "We're sleepy."

Bitter chuckled and said, "Well, I'll be back in an hour then."

The smell of frying bacon and the thought of hot coffee stirred his hunger as he walked through the lobby and into the hotel restaurant. He chose a table in the corner that gave him a clear view of the street window and the open archway between the lobby and the dining area. Instinctively, he checked his holster to make sure his pistol was there.

He frowned at the prices on the menu and then shrugged. *There aren't many restaurants on the Oregon Trail.*

The waitress, a small woman an inch or two shorter than Morgan's five-foot-four, her gray hair in a bun, walked briskly across the room, her heels rapping on the hardwood floor. She carried a heavy white mug and a black coffee pot to the table without being asked. "You look like a coffee drinker," she said.

"I am," he smiled, "but I'm not sure what a coffee drinker looks like."

She stepped back and studied him. "Well…some of them run about six feet tall, I'd say. They limp a little when they walk. They sit where they can watch the door. They wear blue army britches, and they look to be fresh from the war…tanned and wary. I saw the way you studied the room before you stepped through the arch." She looked him over once more and said, "And some have brown eyes."

Bitter laughed, "I'm impressed. That's a lot to surmise from a glance or two."

"It's a skill I practice," she said, and then added, "just for fun. How did I do?"

"You got just about all of it right."

"I usually do. Now…before you get all fussed about the prices, I have a special "back-from-the-war" breakfast…fried ham, eggs anyway you like them, coffee and toast with Ma Clemens's apple butter. It'll cost you fifteen cents."

"Deal," he said. "And since you are a fountain of knowledge, do you have any idea where I can find a good wagon and a decent team, Ma'am?"

She held out her hand and said, "I'm Ma Clemens. I'll send you to see Rufus right after breakfast. Now who would you be?"

"I'm John Bitter."

Refreshed by breakfast and coffee, Bitter followed the directions Ma Clemens had spelled out to the blacksmith shop owned by her friend Rufus Paul. Rufus turned out to be a medium sized man with salt-and-pepper whiskers for a beard, and enormous shoulders and forearms.

Bitter heard the ring of a hammer on metal a half block from the open double doors of the blacksmith shop. He stepped inside and watched as Rufus hammered a heated iron wagon tire onto a smoking wooden wheel. When he was satisfied the tire would cool and shrink to an unshakable fit, Rufus moved his tools to an iron-topped table and wiped his sweating brow with a grease-stained bandana.

Only then did he acknowledge Bitter. "What can I do for you, young man?"

"Ma Clemens sent me to see you. I'm John Bitter," he said and held out his hand.

"Rufus Paul," the blacksmith said. "So Ma Clemens sent you. That's a good reference, although she's sometimes as fond of rascals as she is of honest men. What do you need, Mister Bitter?"

"I need a good light wagon with wagon bows for a canvas top, two extra wheels for the wagon, and a good team."

"Why?" Rufus asked.

The question rankled, but Bitter knew better than to offend a friend of Ma Clemens. "I'm not sure that should matter, but I'll tell you anyway. I'm taking my family back to Oregon…over the Oregon Trail."

"I see. Well, I have three big Conestoga wagons out back. One is practically new."

Bitter shook his head. "No. We aren't carrying any household goods or farm equipment…just camping gear and grub for us and our horses. We'll need to cover a fair distance each day to get past the Blue Mountains in Oregon before the snow."

"Hmm…well, I might just have what you need. Let's go out back." Rufus led the way through the dark interior of the shop and pushed through a man door into the light. "There she is," Rufus said and pointed to a new army ambulance with red spoke wheels and a dark brown wagon box. "I made that one from scratch…for the Union army…but with the end of the war, the local quartermaster said he couldn't pay for it. Wouldn't is more like it."

Bitter walked around the ambulance, measured the box with his six-foot wing span and judged it to be a little over six feet wide and maybe ten feet long. "How much does it weigh?

"I'd guess it to weigh a little over four hundred pounds."

Bitter grabbed the wagon bed and lifted until two wheels were off the ground. "Closer to five hundred," he said. "How much for the wagon and two extra wheels…mounted on the sides?"

Rufus studied Bitter for a good 30 seconds. "Hmm…I tell you what. If you was to work for me for the next two days, pay for the iron for two new tires and help me build the wheels, I'd let you have the whole shooting match for…say a hundred dollars. And I'll throw in some harness I have in back.

"Let me think. You'll need at least four draft horses to pull the cart…or four mules. I'd recommend mules. They're nasty beasts, but they can find their own forage and they aren't prone to panic. I think Black Jack Jefferson down toward the slough has some he'd sell you. Don't give him more than eighty dollars for a pair, and don't let him sell you the black. Take the grays and browns or walk away."

By the time Rufus had wound down, Bitter was grinning. "You always this bossy?"

Rufus shook his head. "No. Only when I'm trying to help some young fool who is bent on getting hisself killed by rampaging Cheyenne. You do know the Indians is up in arms and making it rough on travelers using the Oregon Trail?"

"I'd heard as much," Bitter said, "but I'm thinking I can travel with a wagon train or an army patrol and move from fort to fort."

"It's a bit late for hooking up with a wagon train, but I did some work for a survey party, about nine men strong. Shod some horses, and fixed that wagon wheel I was working on when you interrupted me.

"From what they were saying, they'll be doing survey work for a railroad that's supposed to cross the entire continent. You might check in with them. That's a strong party, well armed."

He added with a smile, "And surveyors never get lost."

Bitter said, "I thank you, but I don't think they'll move fast enough for me."

"Speed or safety is the question now, isn't it?" Rufus asked.

Bitter found the boys and Morgan in the hotel restaurant at a table near the street window. Their table was the center of Ma Clemens' attention who was amazed at how much the scrawny blond boys could put away. "You'd think they'd never had a meal and were afraid there wouldn't be another one soon," she said to Fanny Troop, her breakfast cook.

Bitter pulled a chair out and said, "Good morning. Getting enough to eat?"

A happy, glowing Morgan laughed and said, "There might not be enough in the kitchen for these two." She reached under the table and took his hand. "Good morning, husband."

He squeezed her hand and nodded. He couldn't quite make himself say "wife," but he wanted to. And he shied away from saying the word "love."

Mikey mumbled through a mouthful of food something that sounded like "good." Bitter wasn't sure, and it didn't matter. What mattered was Mikey's rediscovered voice.

Ma Clemens walked the coffee pot over and poured Bitter a cup. "How did you do with Rufus?"

"Thanks to you, I found a good wagon, and I'll work for Rufus a couple of days to help pay it off."

"Which gives you," he said to Morgan, "a couple of days to round up the provisions we'll need. I'm thinking we'll pull out at daybreak two mornings from today."

He took out his wallet and handed her two hundred dollars and a list of supplies he thought they would need. "I'm sure I didn't think of everything, like sunbonnets for you, caps for the boys, cold weather coats, slickers, skeeter repellent, that kind of thing. And see if you can find a case of Borden's for the boys."

She leaned over and whispered in his ear, "I'll be happy to do all that, but 'please' works better. I don't take orders, husband."

She exchanged a glance with Ma Clemens, who watched with amusement and said, "I think you two will make a go of this marriage business just fine."

Bitter said aloud, "Please." And then he grinned. There was a lot to like about his new wife.

"Who is Rufus," she asked, "and why are you working for him?"

When he explained the deal he made with the blacksmith, she nodded and said, "That sounds like a good arrangement."

"I've got a lead on some mules for a wagon team, and Rufus is throwing in a good set of harness. I just wonder how Lucifer will get along with other mules."

She laughed and said, "As long they don't get uppity and they understand he's the boss, they'll do just fine."

Black Jack Jefferson, a strong young man who claimed to be a descendent of Thomas Jefferson, was a freedman with a certificate to prove it. He and his wife, a pretty young woman he smuggled out of Arkansas two years earlier, lived in a small but sturdy log cabin on a low bluff overlooking the big Missouri. He made a living by breeding mules from a big burro mare and a sturdy stallion.

He also made good moonshine from the corn he grew on a twenty-acre patch of bottom. In truth he made more money from moonshine than from mules.

No one could say Black Jack was lazy, but when Bitter knocked on the door, Black Jack's wife peeked shyly from behind a half open door and told Bitter that Black Jack was down on the slough "cat fishin'."

She pointed south and closed the door before Bitter could ask for directions. He heard a thunk when she barred the door.

When he remounted, Rockford humped up like he was going to do some of his patented crow hopping until Bitter kicked him in the ribs and pulled Rockford's head up. "No you don't. I don't have time for any nonsense this morning."

Bitter heard the singing before he found the dim trail that led off the bluff and down to the slough that marked the southern boundary of Black Jack Jefferson's land. A strong baritone rang through the trees, carrying the words to an old gospel song that startled Bitter right back into his childhood…and nearly brought tears to his eyes.

He could clearly see his mother at the kitchen sink, the sunlight streaming through the gauzy curtains, washing dishes and singing, "Cheer up my brothers, live in the sunshine. We'll understand it all by and by."

Bitter joined in with his clear tenor voice. The singer stopped for a split second and then started in on the next verse, an unspoken invitation for Bitter to keep on singing. He guided Rockford down the path through a thin screen of trees and to the slough.

Black Jack Jefferson was grinning when Bitter pulled Rockford to a halt. "You sing pretty good gospel…for a white man."

"Not as good as you, I think."

"Well, get down off that horse. Anybody who knows the old gospels can't be all bad. Whatcha doin' down here, anyways?"

"I'm looking for a good team of mules."

" Whooeee. You came to the right place. Who sent you?"

"Rufus Paul."

"That old skin flint. And I suppose he told you not to buy the black?"

Bitter grinned. "I take it you two are well acquainted."

"You could say that," Black Jack said. "I occasionally treat him to a little of Missouri's finest moonshine. Which I make, of course."

He pointed to a clay jug sitting by a fishing pole cradled in a forked stick. "You want a taste?"

Bitter grinned and shook his head. "Thanks, but I'll pass. How do you work that out...I mean gospel songs and moonshine?"

"No problem. Each is a joy given to us by the Good Lord. It's sinful to disrespect the good things our Jesus and his Father provides."

Bitter smiled, shook his head and said, "About those mules."

30
Crossing the Missouri

B Y THE TIME THE MULES, a brown and three grays, were harnessed and hitched to the wagon, and all the gear packed away, Bitter's sore muscles were warming up enough to stop protesting. He set Mikey in the wagon seat and said, "Here we go Mikey. Oregon here we come. Can you say yippee?"

Mikey shook his head. "Nope. Don't want to."

Working for Rufus brought two long days of flash burns from the forge and sore shoulders from turning red hot metal into horseshoes, eye bolts, hinges, and wagon tires. Bitter didn't figure the small burns from hot iron sparks to be of much consequence, but they were a nuisance.

In two days of watching Bitter work, Rufus discovered in him a latent talent for working metal, an ability he hadn't seen in a long time. He knew in advance it was a wasted effort, but he felt compelled to offer an apprenticeship.

Bitter's young heart warmed, and he said, "Rufus, I thank you. I couldn't ask for higher praise coming from a master smith like you. But I have a farm in Oregon I haven't seen in over three years, and I'm anxious to be home."

"I figured that would be your answer. But I had to ask." Rufus held out a burlap sack hiding a hammer, a hoof trimmer, a rasp, horseshoe nails, and horseshoes. "Take these with you. Your animals will need fresh shoes before you're done."

"Thank you. I'll not forget what you taught me these past couple of days."

Rufus held out his big hand and said, "Go with God and keep your powder dry."

At daybreak, Ethan had Misery in tow, and Morgan led a saddled Lucifer to the hitching rail in front of the St Jo Hotel. Ethan tied Misery's lead rope to the tailgate of the wagon, and Morgan startled Bitter when she boosted Ethan into the saddle atop the big mule. Lucifer swiveled his long ears and turned his neck to look at Ethan. "It's all right, Lucifer. You mind your manners," Morgan said and gave him an affectionate pat on the neck. She handed the reins up to Ethan who figured he was cock of the walk now.

"Does Ethan know how to ride?" Bitter asked in a worried tone.

"We've been practicing for two days. First, on Misery because she doesn't buck. She just falls asleep between steps.

"Actually that's not fair. Now that she can chew again, she's gaining, and there's a little ginger in her step. Anyway, Ethan asked to ride Lucifer, and Lucifer didn't object. He finds Ethan and Mikey to be…what's a good word…acceptable? He just doesn't like anybody taller than three feet…especially men. I guess I'm the exception to the three-foot rule."

Bitter held his breath, a hand on one of the holstered pistols hanging from the saddle horn, until Ethan, a big grin on his face turned Lucifer around and pointed him down the street in the direction of the wagon road that led down the hill to the St. Joseph Ferry.

Morgan climbed onto the wagon seat beside Mikey. She adjusted her new sun bonnet, picked up the reins and said, "Git, now mules." She snapped the reins and the mules leaned into the harness, and in easy rhythm joined the stream of wagons, horses and mules headed to the ferry. Misery, tied on behind the wagon had her head up and seemed interested in all the fuss, a decided improvement.

Ma Clemens and Rufus Paul stood on the hotel porch and waved. Ma's voice carried over the low rumble of the wagons. "You write us when you get to Oregon. You hear?"

The lean-jawed ferryman charged four dollars for the wagon, a dollar for the team, and four bits each for Rockford, Lucifer, and Misery. The boys got to ride for ten cents each, and he charged two bits each for John and Morgan. When the ferryman started to charge for the dog, Bitter said, "Don't go getting greedy on me." He picked up the big red hound and put him in the wagon. "There, now. He's part of the wagon load."

The ferryman glared at him, sighed, and finally said, "That'll be seven dollars and twenty cents. The Missus can sit in the wheel-house."

All told, there were six wagons and teams, three dozen saddle horses, five mules and about twenty passengers on the ferry. Morgan was the only woman. A worried Bitter thought the ferry was just a bit overloaded.

The young, energetic, and self important man who introduced himself as First Mate of the *Sarah Bell*, a side-wheel, steam-powered paddle boat, took one look at Lucifer and said, "He can load last right after your wagon and your saddle horses. When the freight wagons are loaded, you can come aboard."

"That means last on last off, and I'll be eating trail dust most of the day."

"I'm sorry, but that's the way we'll load, mister. Either that," the first mate said, eyeballing the roiling brown Missouri and the far bank nearly a half mile away, "or you can swim your animals across." Bitter contemplated the idea of busting the self-important runt in the mouth, but a firm hand on his forearm and a soft voice tempered the impulse.

"Thank you," Morgan said to the first mate. "That'll be just fine." Morgan's "thank you" and the look in Bitter's eye sent the man scurrying down the hill to the ferry.

Bitter said to Morgan, "Damn. A thousand wagons have beaten that trail into fine powder. Unless we get a breeze, we'll eat dust until the noon halt."

"The important thing is to make the crossing here," she said. "Not get into a fight."

Bitter took a deep breath and let his ire settle before nodding. "I mean to travel faster than these freight wagons, so we'll pass this bunch when we can."

After the last freight wagon was aboard, Morgan drove the Bitter's wagon down the slope to the dock and onto the ferry, while Bitter and Ethan led Rockford and Lucifer aboard.

A worried Bitter breathed easier when Lucifer settled for just wrinkling his upper lip, stamping his foot, and keeping company with Misery at the rear of the wagon. He wasn't tied, just ground hitched, but an apple from Morgan and a quiet word settled him down. The mules pulling the Bitter wagon hadn't made any fuss about who was boss, and the wagon blocked any effort by strange animals to trespass.

Thawing in the Rocky Mountains hadn't started in, not in earnest yet, but the big Missouri carried enough early snowmelt to float driftwood logs and whole trees that patiently wintered over on mud flats and island shoals. The rising Missouri nudged a number of them into the current to resume their journey to the Mississippi.

The wagon seat gave Ethan and Mikey a degree of safety from the nervous animals and a good view of the brown river. Rusty barked, and Ethan yelled, "Mister Bitter, look there," and pointed upriver.

A big cottonwood came rolling down the main channel like a live, malevolent spirit, skeletal limbs shiny wet from the muddy water pointing to the sky and then turning, being slowly drowned again. Bitter hurried to the little wheelhouse and asked the captain, "See that big tree heading our way?"

A frown on his face, the man nodded and said, "Uh huh. I see it."

The captain opened the throttle as far as it would go. But it seemed like a futile gesture to Bitter. At first the ferry seemed reluctant to move, but then with the engine pounding and the big side wheel boiling the water, sounding like a giant waterfall, Bitter sensed a gradual increase in speed. He watched the tree close on the ferry and tensed, wondering what he could do to help the boys and Morgan if the ferry tipped over.

Just when it seemed the tree would smash broad side into the overloaded ferry, the ferryman turned her head-on into the current and let the big cottonwood slide on by to the noise of scraping, screeching limbs. And then it was gone. The teamsters cheered and one tossed his hat in the air and then watched forlornly as it sailed downriver to land upside down and float nearly out of sight before turning over and giving in to the brown, sucking current.

If the big tree worried the captain, he hadn't let it show. But Bitter wasn't so sanguine. "Just getting started and that big Bam tree nearly kills us," he said to Morgan who had come out of the wheelhouse to stand at the ferry rail, a six-foot fence keeping spooked animals from going over board. "I hope that's not a bad omen."

Morgan laughed and said, "I would never have guessed you were superstitious."

"I'm not," he said defensively. "But this is a hard road we're taking and if there is such a thing as good spirits, I want them watching out for us.

"Now you take that white-headed bald eagle up there," he said looking at the boys and pointing up river. "Do you see him?" They nodded and he said, "Good. Well, if that old eagle flies west, why that means we are in for easy times, but if he flies south, that means bad luck."

"What if he flies north," Ethan asked from the wagon seat.

Bitter winked at him and said, "Why, that means good weather all the way to Oregon."

Morgan punched his shoulder and said, "You stop funning us. That old eagle is just hunting his breakfast."

With the light wagon and strong mules in the traces, Bitter hoped to average twenty to twenty-five miles a day. But the business of loading wagons, animals, and people on the ferry had taken over an hour. *Add crossing the river and repeating the whole business in reverse, we'll be at least three hours just getting across the river,* Bitter thought, *and it puts us at the end of a line of slow moving freight wagons. We'll eat dust all day.*

As the ferry eased into the landing, Bitter set Ethan in the saddle, mounted Rockford and said, "Here we go. Almost home! Heeyah!"

He drew some solace from the sight of a mounted escort, a squad of cavalry led by a lieutenant that drew up alongside the road to confer with the head teamster, a muleskinner from Kentucky who had betrayed his family by joining the North in the struggle to prevent Southern secession.

When Bitter asked about the escort, one of the mule skinners said, "We're hauling supplies to Fort Kearny. But I suspect there's something in one of the wagons no one wants us to know about. Some kind of rapid fire gun if the dance hall gossip is right." He paused and asked, "So where are you folks headed?"

Book II – The Oregon Trail

Between 1840 and 1860, propelled by the mantra of Manifest Destiny, and the promise of free land, more than 100,000 souls set out to travel the Oregon Trail to the Pacific Northwest in search of a new life…and maybe a bit of adventure. Ninety percent would arrive safely. According to historians, a best guess is that about one percent, 1,000 of the immigrants, were killed by Indians, which consigns the remaining 9,000 fatalities to accident and disease.

It is also estimated an additional 100,000 travelers, mostly men seeking California gold followed the Oregon Trail to a fork in the road called the California Trail. Almost none of the seekers found any gold, but some saw promise in land and agriculture. Those visionaries stayed to build an empire to rival that of many European nations.

1

Trail Broke

THE CAPTAIN EASED THE FERRY boat in against the dock on the Kansas side of the Missouri and held it there with the slowly turning paddle wheel until the deck hand, the man who strutted and claimed to be first mate, jumped ashore and tied a heavy hawser to an anchor stump.

Eager teamsters opened the gate on the ferry and settled on wagon seats. Whips cracked, and muleskinners rained curses on the heads of the animals pulling the heavily loaded freight wagons off the ferry boat and onto the road leading up the bluff beyond the landing. At least one animal in each team broke wind as it took up the load, and a swampy river breeze was sweetened by the odor of fresh horse manure.

Each teamster vied with the rest for creative invective, but if you listened closely, you could hear an undercurrent of affection in the fact that each animal had its own name. And a well-tuned ear could detect harsh threats softened by words of encouragement. "Here we go, old gal. Git 'em up the bluff now." Or maybe a variation like, "Old Dobbin's gonna out-pull the whole bunch of you worthless flea bags. Git now!"

Frustrated by being at the end of line, John Bitter missed the cacophonous melody, but perched high on the wagon seat, two wide-eyed boys and a young red-headed woman were thrilled by the parade of wagons winding up the bluff. While they waited for their turn in line, John fussed with the load, checked the yellow canvas stretched over wagon bows, inspected harness, thumped water barrels, and swatted skeeters.

When he finally noticed the rapt attention his wife and the boys were giving the wagon train, he stopped fussing long enough to watch and finally say, "Quite a sight, isn't it?"

Morgan nodded. "Yes it is, but I can't help wondering what a railroad across the country will mean to these teamsters. I heard talk in St. Joseph that one is being planned."

"I imagine it will put some of them out of business, but the train can't take side roads. Goods will still be freighted to towns not on the rail line."

Morgan watched her husband fidget like a school boy and laughed. "John, you're gonna wear out your boots with all the scootching around. Come sit up here with me and the boys. You get a better view."

The boys moved back under the canvas top to make room for Bitter. "What's eating you?" Morgan asked.

"It's just that I planned on covering about twenty-five miles each day. I figure that even with some rest days, we can be over the Blues and home in about one hundred days. And we've already lost half a day because that worthless, no account put us at the end of the line."

Morgan patted his arm and said, "Relax. We'll get past them at the nooning."

"I guess you're right."

A nervous First Mate hollered, "All right there, you with the mules. Get 'em unloaded."

Bitter jumped down and hollered up to Morgan, "Oregon, here we come."

Mikey and Ethan both gave out a fair imitation of Bitter's "Eeehaw!" and a tail-wagging red dog barked as he sensed their excitement. Bitter swung up on Rockford and followed the wagon, Misery, and Lucifer off the ferry, his frustration eased by this small miracle of progress.

Along about noon, the teamsters pulled off the road, and the tall dust cloud that marked their progress drifted away on a welcome breeze. The Bitter wagon made up for a lack of springs by bouncing over humps and bumps and shaking up the load, but the freedom of the empty road was too much temptation for Morgan. She whistled at the mules and popped the reins until the reluctant team broke into a trot. Head up, Misery stretched her tether rope and trotted off to the side of the wagon to watch the open road and breathe clean air.

The wagon wheels pulled a fine wispy rope of trail dust from prairie soil pounded into a fine powder by the passage of thousands of wagons and twenty-five years of travelers.

Bitter rode Rockford along the south side of the wagon and Ethan rode Lucifer along the north...out in the dust-free prairie grass. Ethan gigged Lucifer in the ribs and put him into a ground-eating trot that was a fair imitation of a Tennessee walker. He turned to wave at Bitter, Morgan, and Mikey.

In an unexpected move, Bitter drew alongside the wagon, scooped Mikey from the wagon seat and swung him in behind the cantle. "Hang on, Mikey," he said and put Rockford into an easy lope. "Eeehaw!" he shouted. It tickled him to hear Mikey laugh at the ride.

After a quarter-mile trot, Morgan took pity on the mule team pulling the thousand pounds of wagon and gear and slowed them to a walk. "Slow and steady wins the race," she said to Rusty who chose to travel in the moving shade of the wagon top.

Two hours later they stopped at a shallow crossing where a seasonal stream carried enough water for the animals. A grateful

Morgan climbed down from the wagon seat and rubbed her rear. "We've got to find something besides my rear end to pad this seat."

Bitter grinned. "Wait until Ethan tries to get off Lucifer tonight. He'll be so sore he can't walk."

He watched the animals drink their fill and suddenly realized his stomach was growling. When Ethan knelt to take a drink of creek water, Bitter said, "Huh uh. Use your canteen. Don't drink the water, Ethan, unless it's coming from a hillside spring or from a cold well. More people have died from bad water on the Oregon Trail than from bad Indians."

"It looks clean," Ethan protested.

"It might be, but I don't want to take any chances. If comes to it, we'll boil our drinking water. I had an old Army surgeon tell me he didn't know why it helped, but he said boiled water didn't seem to bring on the flux like plain water. So that's what we'll do if we have to. Okay?"

Ethan stood up and asked, "What about the horses and mules?"

"They don't seem to be bothered by the water unless it alkaline. But even horses and mules prefer clear, clean running water."

Morgan said, "I'm for fixing lunch right there," and pointed to a grassy green knoll a few yards beyond the stream."

Bitter nodded and said, "I think we've got enough lead on those freight wagons to chance it."

Morgan drove the mules to the knoll and pulled to a halt. A ring of fire-blackened stones told the tale of other meals fixed atop the little knoll.

Bitter used picket pins to stake out Rockford and Misery. "You know," he said to Morgan, "I think Misery is gaining. Your livery stable friend may be right. Her coat is starting to take on a little shine."

"At least her mouth isn't hurting too much to eat," Morgan said.

Ethan helped Bitter unhitch the mules and turn them loose to graze on ankle-high grass. It was new purple stem and was reported to carry a lot of nutrition. At the least the mules took to it and it was filling.

Their bacon, nearly one hundred pounds of it, had been cut in ten pound pieces and stored in kegs filled with bran, oats and cracked corn. Morgan knew if they kept the sun away from the bacon it would last them through to Oregon…at least that was the hope.

Bitter started a fire with some dry cottonwood limbs they had scrounged from the Missouri River banks before setting out that morning, and Morgan set a slab of bacon on her cutting board and sliced bacon for the skillet.

Bitter lifted a small keg out of the back of the wagon, placed it in the shade of the wagon top, and used it for a seat. While he made a roll-your-own, he watched Mikey, Ethan, and Rusty walk back to the creek. Blue bachelor buttons, rose-colored prairie lilies, purple bird's bills, and a half dozen other smaller flowers were in full bloom, giving life and color to a sea of prairie grass.

Ethan took off his shoes and waded in the cool water, looking for bright colored rocks. Rusty just waded. And Mikey picked a wad of flowers for Morgan, some still clinging to bare roots, but beautiful for all of that.

Morgan banged a spoon on the bottom of a tin pot and shouted, "Come and get it," as the first of the bacon curled and sputtered in the skillet. Shoes in hand, a hungry Ethan ran up the hill barefoot through the grass. Rusty loped along behind and then stopped half-way to look back at Mikey who wasn't quite so fast.

Mikey waded through the grass and proud as punch thrust a mangled bouquet of wildflowers at Morgan. Morgan thought she recognized some type of primrose in the bunch, mixed in amongst the bright blue bachelor buttons..

Morgan smiled and said, "Why, thank you Mikey. They are really pretty. Want to put them in the shade while we eat?"

Bitter knew he would be sick of bacon and biscuits before the trip was out, but he was content with this first lunch on the prairie.

2
Armed

THEY SOPPED THE LAST OF the bacon grease from tin plates, a practice that softened the hard biscuits. Bitter thought the unleavened biscuits were just a little softer than hardtack, and just about as tasty. But they made for a quick lunch. And he hoped they wouldn't need to eat the whole fifty pounds they brought from St. Joseph. He scratched Rusty behind an ear and fed him a dry biscuit, "I'll bet you could eat the whole barrel."

"You finished?" Morgan asked.

He handed her his empty plate, and said, "That'll do until supper."

By the end of the day, it was clear to Bitter that firewood was going to be scarce. "Too many travelers," he said around their first evening fire. "They've pretty well burned up the firewood. And it'll get worse once we're on the main Oregon Trail." He looked at the boys, their faces painted by the red glow of the coals in the fire pit. "We'll have to scrounge for our wood. I'm depending on you two to help. Look for anything that'll burn, including dried cow chips."

Ethan nodded, a flop of blond hair falling over his forehead. "Me and Lucifer can do it. You can bet on that."

Bitter reached out and ruffled Ethan's hair. "I know you can. You're a good scrounger."

At bedtime, Bitter moved boxes and barrels to level the load in the wagon box and Morgan rolled out blankets and a straw tick for the boys. Rusty bounced up on the wagon seat, but Morgan knew the boys sneaked him onto their blankets as soon as Morgan and John had their bed made under the wagon.

It became a constant habit for Bitter and Ethan to scour the bottoms, break dead limbs from the trees that sprouted in the wet places, pick up any dry limbs they could find, and rope and drag the bigger pieces to the wagon to meet Bitter's sharp axe. "In a pinch we'll burn the dried cow patties," he said.

Bitter made sure Ethan stayed in sight of the wagon, and he carried the Henry in a saddle scabbard in case he needed to do any long range shooting. Morgan kept her new Navy revolver next to her on the wagon seat. She had yet to fire the carbine, and until she did she wouldn't trust it.

Noon of the second day found them some thirty miles closer to Marysville. A trickle of windblown dust marked their progress and added a thin coating of grit over the rear of the wagon. The sun worked to turn the harness black from mule sweat, and Morgan wondered when Bitter would call a halt. A big horsefly found the heat under the wagon top too hot for comfort and sailed away on a puff of wind.

The patchy shade in a string of scrawny willow trees led Bitter a half-mile off the main road to a well used camping spot. There was no water, but subsurface drainage provided enough moisture to feed a few trees and new grass. Deep ruts told the tale of earlier travelers who found the little grove more inviting than open ground.

As the boiled coffee cooled beside the cook fire, they shared fried soda bread sweetened with brown sugar. Bitter said, "Well, Mikey. Do the new mules have a name yet?"

Mikey nodded and stuffed another piece of bread in his mouth.

A smile tugged at the corners of Bitter's mouth while he waited for Mikey to say something. "Want to share what they are?"

"Well," Mikey said, a hint of mischief in his blue eyes, "the brown mule, the one with the gray patch on his rump told me his name is Windy, but the others haven't said yet."

"Windy?" Ethan asked.

Morgan laughed. "I know which one you're talking about, Mikey. He can sure stink up the place."

Ethan and Bitter laughed, and Ethan said, "That's a good one, Mikey."

Mikey looked pleased with his joke, and Bitter noticed the boy was gaining a little weight…that maybe there was a hint of a tummy bulge where there had been a flat belly just days earlier.

Bitter was angry all over again at the men who had robbed the boys of their mother. It didn't matter that Big Bill and Little Bill were dead. "They're still sonsabitches," he muttered aloud without realizing it.

Morgan and boys were startled by his growl and puzzled when he abruptly walked to the wagon, dropped the tail gate, and started unloading gear. It was obvious to Morgan he was searching for something.

When he turned, he had a new saddle scabbard in his hands. He shucked a small, slim rifle from the scabbard, a beautifully worked rifle with a lacquered walnut stock, a hickory ramrod, and a bright brass patch box near the butt of the rifle.

"I was going to wait to do this, but it seems to be the right time. Ruben, our blacksmith friend, ordered this for a woman, the wife of a Union officer. But the officer was killed, and the woman went back east before Ruben could give it to her. So I bought it from Ruben.

"It's made by a man named Clemens…light weight, shoots a .36-caliber ball, and it's well balanced."

He looked at Ethan. "You are a responsible boy, Ethan. So I'm going to teach you to shoot and I'm going to let you carry this rifle when you and Lucifer are scrounging for wood. See that tree with the white scar on its trunk?"

Ethan, nearly dumbstruck by the thought of shooting a rifle, nodded mutely.

"Okay. Good." Bitter pulled a leather bag free of the wagon load and opened it up. He laid a powder flask, percussion caps, linen patches and a pouch of .36-caliber balls on the tailgate.

"This is how we do it," he said, and quickly loaded the lightweight rifle. "Come over here."

Bitter placed the rifle over the lower limb of a tree, anchored Ethan's left hand under the stock, helped the boy pull the rifle snug against his right shoulder, cocked the hammer back and said, "Close your left eye, line the sights up on the scar on that tree and squeeze the trigger."

Ethan closed both eyes and yanked on the trigger. The noise of exploding gun powder and the punch of the recoil scared him, but he managed to ask, "Did I hit it?"

"No, but I think you scared it. I know you scared me."

"I scared me, too," Ethan admitted.

By the fifth shot, Ethan stopped flinching enough to watch his rifle ball skin bark from the edge of the tree. "I hit it! I hit it!"

"Yes you did," Bitter said. "Now, I'm going to show you how to clean it, and then watch you reload it. You and Lucifer ride with me and Rockford this afternoon, and we'll talk about when and where to use a gun. And when and where not to as well."

They weren't meeting the mark Bitter set of twenty-five miles a day, but by noon of the third day Bitter figured they had covered nearly fifty miles, almost half of the distance to Marysville. He also thought they could make another ten miles before nightfall.

For the most part the wagon grade to Marysville was level, a rolling up-and-down level with dips and humps, but with no great gain in elevation. Bitter knew, however, when they reached the

Platte that would change. It was all uphill to South Pass, a water-grade pull that gradually climbed in elevation, a hard-to-see uphill, but about a four hundred mile uphill pull. And he knew they would be glad for the extra pair of mules pulling the wagon.

There was no shade, so they just pulled the wagon off the road and left the mules in the traces to munch what grass they could find. Lucifer and Rockford were ground hitched on some young grass. The excitement of the trip was wearing off so there wasn't much conversation as they ate cold bacon and biscuits washed down with lukewarm water.

Mikey was sitting on the tailgate of the wagon breaking chunks off a cold biscuit and slipping bites to Rusty. Mikey pointed back down the road and said, "Mister Bitter, there's a rider comin'."

Bitter walked to Rockford and fished a pair of French field glasses from his saddlebag. They rode in a scarred leather case that had kept company with Bitter during the war.

The sun pulled phantom, shimmering heat waves from the crest of the hill marked by the wagon road. But still there was something familiar about the wavering image of the rider…even at a distance of eight or nine hundred yards. Bitter finally lowered the field glasses and said, "I think our friend Mark Anthony is heading our way. I can make out a Derby hat like the one he wears, and the horse looks a lot like his big Buckskin. And he's leading a second horse. I wonder what's going on?"

The Buckskin's ground-eating, dust-kicking lope closed the half mile gap in short order and proved Bitter right. It was Mark Anthony, a sweat-and-dust-coated Mark Anthony who still managed to look dapper in his once white shirt and red sleeve garters.

Flecks of lather darkened the long-legged Buckskin's coat, but he was looking strong nonetheless. The led horse, a big bay with a black mane, was obviously having an easier time, but Bitter could see white salt patches on his hide where a saddle had ridden earlier.

Mark Anthony pulled the horses to a slow walk the last hundred yards to let them cool a bit and to keep from stirring the dust any more than necessary. Rockford's head came up and he whinnied a challenge aimed at the Buckskin, but Lucifer stamped a foot and Rockford settled for a stare, ears pointed forward.

Rusty loaned a friendly bark to the excitement until Ethan told him to be quiet, and the big dog hunkered down in the shade under the wagon.

3
Feuding

A TIRED GRIN ON HIS FACE, Mark Anthony slid from his horse and held out his hand to Bitter. "You folks set a fair pace. I crossed at St. Joseph yesterday morning thinking I'd catch you by nightfall."

"As I see it, we are already a half day behind," Bitter said. "We got held up by a train of freight wagons the first morning."

"I'm forgetting my manners," Mark said. He tipped his derby, gave her a sweeping bow, and said, "How do, Missus Bitter. I hope you find the road smooth traveling."

"I can't say that," Morgan laughed, instinctively trying to push a stray red curl back under her sunbonnet. "My backsides haven't caught up to the bounce of the wagon seat."

Ethan edged forward and held out a grubby hand. "Howdy, Mister Anthony. How come you're riding two horses?"

With a smile, Mark shook Ethan's hand. "Howdy yourself, Ethan. And you too, Mikey."

"Well?" Bitter asked.

"Well, what?" Mark said.

"Why are you riding two horses? I can guess, but I'd like to hear it from you."

"I came across some information I need to share with you, information that couldn't wait until you reached the telegraph in Marysville. I decided I needed to catch up with you, so I bought this big bay. When old Buck gets tired, I swap gear and ride the bay a few miles to give Buck a rest."

Bitter raised an eyebrow and said, "I suppose you had some good news that just couldn't wait. Either that or you missed our company and decided to pay us a visit."

Mark nodded. "Something like that. Right now I need a drink of water. The horses used mine up a few miles back."

"Ethan," Bitter said, "I'd like you to walk Mister Anthony's horses to cool them down. Think you can do that?"

Ethan nodded. "Yep."

Bitter smiled and said, "Thanks, Ethan. Mikey, you want a ride?" Without waiting for an answer, Bitter picked him up from the tailgate of the wagon and swung the boy up on Anthony's saddle.

Mikey gripped the saddle horn with both hands as Ethan led the big Buckskin and the bay down the wagon road in the direction of Marysville.

When the boys were out of earshot, Bitter said, "Okay, the boys can't hear us now. What's going on?"

"Well," Anthony said, "two things. First, two hillbillies were asking the ferryman in St. Joseph if he had seen a young redheaded woman riding a big mule. Said she was kin and they were trying to catch up with her.

"That blabber-mouth ferryboat captain told them all about taking your wagon, your redheaded wife, and a mammoth mule across the river. Right now I figure I'm about three or four hours ahead of them."

"How did you get wind of this?" Morgan asked.

"The kid that works on the ferryboat, the one that calls himself First Mate, didn't like the looks of those fellows, so he hot-footed to the sheriff's office. Sheriff Malden and I are good friends, so Malden sent out a telegram to all ticket agents to look for me.

"A special train took me and Buck from Hamilton to St. Joseph. And here I am."

"How do you know where those men are?"

"Loped right on around them about twenty miles back."

Bitter gave him a hard stare. "Why didn't you arrest them?"

"Can't. They haven't broken any laws yet. I guess we'll have to convince them to give up this feud and go on back home.

"Right after I have something to eat, I figure you and I will saunter back down the road a ways to a nice spot I sort of picked out on my way through.

"I figured that if I didn't catch you at noon, I'd have to wander back and read them from the Good Book. But I also figured it would work better if there were two of us. These hill people are first-class fighting men."

"You said there were two things," Morgan reminded him.

"I nearly forgot. One of our agents in Ohio found Aunt Quilla."

Involuntarily, Morgan put her left hand over her mouth and said, "Oh, no!"

Mark Anthony nodded and said, "I sort of felt the same way when I got the news. Especially since all she wants is the farm."

"What?" Bitter asked.

"Telegrams are expensive at three dollars for every ten words, so our agent was...what's a good word for it? 'Cryptic' works, I think. The telegram is in my saddlebags or I'd read it to you. Basically it said, 'Aunt said no brats who gets farm.'"

"That's a mean old bitch," Bitter said. "Those are two of the finest boys a man could want. I'd be proud to call them my sons."

"So what happens, now?" Morgan asked.

"Well, I should have said there were three reasons to catch up with you. As soon as my saddlebags get back, I'll show you an order of adoption drawn up by Judge Harrison. You both sign it, and the boys become your adopted children. The Judge said he would throw Aunt Quilla in jail if he could. Furious, he was."

With something like awe in his voice, Bitter shook his head and said, "You have been busy, Detective Anthony."

"What will happen to their farm?" Morgan asked.

"As for that, the Judge will offer it for sale, and as soon as a buyer is found, he will send the money to you in Oregon to be held in trust until the boys reach their majority."

Morgan shook her head, a red curl escaping from her white sun bonnet. "I surely underestimated that old man. I just thought he was a drunk."

Anthony laughed. "Well…he does drink a lot. I think that's because it eases the pain in his legs. But he's also an honest and honorable if somewhat cantankerous old man. Speaking of drinking, how about that water?"

Bitter figured the boys had gone far enough so he gave a loud whistle and motioned them back to the wagon.

4

Confrontation

IT WAS DECIDED MORGAN AND the boys would fort up right where the wagon sat while Bitter and Anthony rode back to convince good old Lige's kin folk of the futility of further pursuit. "Idiots, is what they are," Bitter growled while he and Anthony stacked barrels and boxes to form a barricade for Morgan and the boys. "Just plumb stupid."

Bitter shook his head at the memory of the dead man who was kin to the Dunlaps, a demented slow learner who just kept walking his horse down the railroad tracks, loading an empty pistol, and cursing Bitter for shooting his brothers. He kept coming even after Bitter warned him to stop.

Bitter paced off fifty yards back down the wagon trail and drove a cottonwood limb in the sod. He paced back to the wagon and nodded.

"I don't expect them to get by us , but if we can't stop them," he said to Morgan, nearly losing his train of thought in the depth of her blue eyes, "…uh…and they get as close as that stick, shoot first with the carbine, then with Ethan's .36, and then with Harley's pistol. Take your time and make your shots count. Remember, it's easier to hit a horse with a rifle than it is a man, and it's no small thing to put a rider on the ground. A hard fall is almost as good as a bullet. I'll also leave you an extra pistol. Don't try to talk to them. Just shoot 'em."

Anthony nodded his agreement, and added, "We'll be back by dark, so if you would be so kind as to have a nice supper waiting for us , I'd be grateful. I love bacon and biscuits. And I'd really like a cup of Arbuckle's with some sugar when we get back."

Bitter bristled at Anthony's presumption of authority until he realized Anthony was simply infusing a mood of optimism into the planned confrontation with the Dunlaps, turning it into a simple, routine affair. *Like going out to plow a field*, Bitter thought.

His admiration for Detective Mark Anthony grew a notch, and Bitter felt a degree of comfort at knowing Anthony would back his play when the time came.

As the two friends mounted up and turned their horses in the direction of St. Joseph, Morgan said, "You come back safe, John Bitter. Both of you come back safe."

"Yeah," Ethan echoed, and then pulled Rusty in close and put an arm around the big dog's neck. Instinctively Mikey edged up to Morgan and grabbed a handful of her dress.

The two men walked the horses over a rolling hump of grass-covered prairie and out of sight before Anthony said, "If we get out of this alive, I think a shot of good whisky in my Arbuckle's would do as well as sugar."

"I will provide," Bitter said and took the makings out of his shirt pocket to build a roll-your-own. Anthony reached back and pulled a well-chewed cigar stub from a saddlebag and stuck it in the corner of his mouth.

Bitter lit his cigarette and gave Anthony an exaggerated once-over. With his riding boots topped by soft uppers, a black string tie, red sleeve garters for his once-upon-a-time white shirt, an engraved black leather holster rigged for a cross draw, an Irishman's black derby, and the cigar stub, he looked the part of a dandy or a riverboat gambler. Bitter nodded and said, "Uh-huh."

"What?"

"You just look too citified to be dangerous."

Bitter didn't think much of Anthony's ambush site, just a simple grassy fold in the earth. When Anthony explained his thinking, which boiled down to Anthony blocking the road and Bitter hiding in the shallow draw behind the shoulder of a rolling hump of ground until he could flank the bushwhackers, Bitter started to smile, and then broke into a chuckle.

"While I appreciate your noble offer, I think they're going to be suspicious if they see the fellow blocking the road who was in such a hurry he was riding two horses. No…you hide in the draw and I'll wait in the road.

"I want to disarm them," Bitter added. "If they won't give up their guns, we'll have to shoot 'em. But all that will do is send more of that clan after us. No…I want to reason with 'em. Killing 'em won't do any good."

Anthony looked skeptical. "Reason with them?"

Bitter nodded. "Yes. I want this ended. Today. Now. No more looking over my shoulder and wondering if somebody has me or Morgan in his sights."

"How are you going to reason with them?"

"I don't know yet," Bitter admitted, "but I'll think of something."

The wait for the two hillbillies lasted over an hour. Bitter smoked two roll-your-owns and scanned his back trail through his field glasses. Mother Nature entertained him with boiling reach-for-the-sky anvil-shaped clouds. Light gusts of prairie wind swept the grass into wave after wave that mimicked the wash of surf on sandy beaches. A meadowlark sang its song, and Bitter wondered if the song was to attract a mate or to warn other meadowlarks to stay away. It was a peaceful time and place, and Bitter might have enjoyed it if the purpose of his wait had been peaceful as well.

Rockford, ground hitched in the grass alongside the road, ignored it all in his quest to fill his belly. He interrupted the business of cropping grass long enough to shake a pestiferous fly away from his eyes.

High overhead a buzzard drifted north on a fast moving current of air. Bitter admired the flying ability of buzzards even though he figured they were about the ugliest of God's birds.

He was reaching for his tobacco sack to make his third cigarette of the hour when Anthony's low whistle focused his attention on the wagon road. On the crown of a rolling hill, maybe three miles away, two horses carrying riders walked up over the horizon. Bitter focused the lenses of his field glasses and studied the men, but the distance was too great to make out more detail than two riders and two mounts.

Must be them, he thought. *Maybe*, he corrected himself.

"Damn," he muttered and then walked to Rockford and put the field glasses in the saddlebags. The big horse turned his head to see what Bitter was doing and then went back to cropping grass.

It seemed an eternity before the two riders were within a hundred yards of Bitter and Rockford. The taller, bigger man, a dilapidated hat shading his face, his black beard drooping halfway to his belly, rode a nice looking bay horse. The smaller, clean-faced man rode a small mule. Bitter saw Mark Anthony ease the Buckskin out of the draw and pull quietly in behind the riders.

At the fifty-yard mark, Bitter stepped into the road with the Henry in the crook of his elbow. As the older man started to pull a rifle from a saddle scabbard, he was startled when Anthony said from close behind, "Huh uh. You don't want to do that. Keep your hands away from your weapons. My friend and I just want to talk."

Anthony shook his head when the smaller rider, the one on the mule turned to look back. "Judas!" Anthony barked. "It's a boy! They're sending out their children."

The youngster looked to be about fourteen, and he looked scared. "Son," Anthony said in a calm voice, "just ride your mule on up to my friend. Like I said, we mean no harm. We just want to talk."

Bitter was as dumbfounded as Anthony when he saw the teenager riding the mule. The two riders pulled to a stop about thirty feet from Bitter and sat, hands on saddle horns. Bitter just stared, at a loss for what to say.

"What do you want?" the bearded man asked.

"You related to the Dunlaps?" Bitter asked.

"We be the Peales, but the Dunlaps are kin."

"Long way from home, aren't you?" Bitter said.

"You seen a redheaded woman rides a big mule?"

Bitter took a deep breath and said, "What do you want with her?"

"She killed cousin Lige and Uncle Owen. We can't let people get away with killin' our kin."

"And they had it coming," Bitter said. "I don't think the Dunlaps...or the Peales for that matter...have enough brains to get to the outhouse and back without getting lost." The more he thought about it the madder he got.

"No" he said grimly, "this business stops today. The woman you are hunting is my wife. Either you turn back and let us go on about our business, or I kill you both right here."

Anthony said from behind the men, "I thought you were going to reason with them."

"Oh, hell," Bitter muttered. "Get down off those animals and let's talk."

Bitter related the story of Lige and his pappy as told to him by Morgan. The two Peales stood quietly until the boy turned to his father and said, "Pa, Peales don't hurt women. I believe this man. I always figured Cousin Lige was twisted somehow. And if this man's wife is telling it true, Lige and his pa had it coming. It's over."

The older man nodded, but he didn't say anything.

"Daddy, we lost enough men on this fool business."

"I sure wouldn't want to lose my son," Anthony allowed.

The bearded man looked hard at Bitter. "I can forgive the woman, but you shouldn't have killed my brothers."

Bitter started rolling another cigarette, licked the paper and twisted the ends. He looked at the man and said, "The ones who tried to stop the train?"

"Yah. They be the ones."

"I tried to warn 'em off, but they just kept coming."

"They would, being Peales. But I have to make it up to them. You and me…a duel."

"No. I've killed enough men to last me the rest of my life. I think your boy would be mighty unhappy if he took you home hanging over the saddle."

Bitter looked at the bearded man with his broad shoulders bulging under a dirty canvas shirt. Bitter thought the man might weigh maybe two-hundred-ten to two-hundred-twenty pounds, a good forty pounds heavier than Bitter, and he stood an inch taller. Bitter let out a deep sigh, "I tell you what. I'll give you a chance. Bare knuckles. You and me. And then it's done."

The man looked Bitter over, decided he could whip him, and nodded. There was a note of relief in Peale's voice when he said, "And then it's done. Agreed."

Bitter was no stranger to brawls, and he had sparred some with a man in the 40th Missouri who, when he wasn't about the business of preventing the South from leaving the Union, was a professional pugilist.

But when the bigger man took Bitter's hard left to the mouth, a blow that broke a front tooth, and then just shook his head, Bitter knew he might be overmatched.

Anthony later described the fight, which lasted a long ten minutes, as a slug fest. "John broke the man's nose with a hard right. A few seconds later Mister Peale returned the favor and knocked John down in the process. And by the way, you never heard such a racket as when I later straightened the bend in John's nose.

"Anyway, Mister Peale let John get back up, and then they punched away until John tried to knock the big man off his feet with a leg sweep. All that got John was a straight right that knocked him ten feet out into the grass. I thought he was done for sure. But, no, he gets up again and wades in, pounding the other man's gut hard enough to back him up. And then John slips in an uppercut and knocks the man down.

"John's breathing hard and goes down on one knee. 'Had enough?' he asks the man. Peale doesn't say anything, just catches his breath and then pushes himself up on his hands and knees, and then finally staggers to his feet.

"John gets to his feet and glares at Peale. They're both a bloody mess…broken noses, a split eyebrow for John, and a left eye that's almost swollen shut, and a split lip and a missing tooth for Peale. So they stagger over to get at each other, both huffing like a wind broke horse, and they each unleash a tremendous roundhouse swing…wobbly, underpowered swing. And they both miss and wind up face down in the grass.

"Me and Peale's boy get to laughing, and the boy says, 'Good one, Pa. You sure showed him that time.'

"John and Peale roll over on their backs and give each other a bleary eyed stare. And then John starts to chuckle. John says, 'I hope you've had enough. I know I have.'

"So they just flop back in the grass and rest a bit. Peale's son gets a canteen and a rag and starts wiping the blood from his pa's face. And I do the same for John. That's when I straightened his nose.

"Peale finally gets to his feet and staggers over to John. He holds his hand out and helps John to his feet. 'Hell of a fight,' he says. 'What's your name?'

"And, so," Anthony always concluded, "that's how John Bitter and Walter Peale settled the feud…and became friends. Sort of."

Bitter watched Peale's son help his father into the saddle. Young Mister Peale didn't offer his hand, but he grinned at a battered John Bitter and said, "Thanks, Mister Bitter."

When the Peale's disappeared into a fold of the prairie, Bitter eased himself into the saddle. For some unknown and unknowable reason, Rockford behaved himself and didn't hump up and crow hop in his usual style. Bitter said, "Good thing you behaved, Rockford, because I might have shot you."

Anthony pulled Buck up beside Bitter and laughed. "Talking to your horse? Peale must have hit you harder than I thought."

"Hard enough." Bitter tried a smile, but it hurt too much.

5
Finished

IN THE TIME IT TOOK them to ride back to the wagon, Bitter's left eye has swollen shut, and the knuckles on his hands had puffed up. Bitter thought he might have broken the knuckle of his trigger finger.

His broken nose gave Bitter's voice a nasal sound when he allowed as to how it would have been a lot easier to simply shoot Peale.

"Yep," said Anthony. "But you know damned good and well neither of us would have shot the boy. And he'd of just kept coming after you. You did the smart thing."

"Why do smart things hurt so much?"

The thunderstorm promised by the cumulous clouds faded as the storm cell blew apart and drifted north. Bitter was glad. He didn't fear much, but he always got a tad nervous at the thought of getting caught out in the open when a prairie thunderstorm cut loose.

Morgan watched the riders until she was sure they were Bitter and Anthony. "Well, they made it," Ethan said.

Morgan laid the rifle across the tailgate, brushed a stray curl away from her forehead, and breathed a sigh of relief. Ethan saw the slight tremble in her hands.

The boys followed Morgan out from behind the barricade and stood beside her. Mikey took her hand, and Rusty barked at the riders until he recognized Rockford. Then Rusty, with Ethan hot on his tail, dashed down the road to greet the men.

"What happened to your face, Mister Bitter?" John just swung Ethan up behind him and watched Rusty treat Rockford to a tail wagging dance. He was still mystified by the friendship between the black horse and the red hound.

"Lordy, lordy," John," Morgan said when she caught sight of his face. "What in the world happened?"

Mark Anthony grinned and said, "He reasoned with our pursuers, Missus Bitter."

Bitter winced as he stepped slowly down from the saddle. Morgan looked at Anthony and asked, "How does the other man look?"

Anthony grinned. "I'm of the opinion the other man, a certain Walter Peale, kin to the Dunlaps, is equally aggrieved."

"We'll camp here for the night," Bitter declared through swollen lips.

Darkness saw the boys tucked in, and Bitter asleep under the wagon with Rusty curled up at the foot of his bedroll. As the coals in the ashes of the cooking fire winked out one by one, Anthony sipped his whiskey-laced coffee and described the fight to Morgan. It was a story he would hone to a fine edge over the years.

When he finished, she glanced at the sleeping figure of her husband and said, "You're a good friend, Mark. Your hard ride may have saved the lives of the Peales…and maybe John's life as well." She paused and then asked, "Do you suppose Peale meant it when he said the feud was over?"

"From a distance," Anthony said, "I might worry about that. But I heard the relief in Peale's voice when John showed him a way out. It's my opinion you've seen an end of it."

"I truly hope so. I just want to get on to Oregon. You know, John has a knack for coming up with interesting solutions."

"He does?"

She smiled and said, "Yes. I don't suppose you know the story of Brother Harley's sunburn."

When she finished the tale, Anthony chuckled quietly and then said, "The more I know about him, the more I like John Bitter."

Bitter rolled stiffly out of bed at gray light to find a clean shirt hanging on the tailgate. He'd been alone for so long, he didn't expect any kind of consideration. He liked it, but he could almost hear Morgan saying, "This is a special circumstance, so don't take it for granted."

Sore muscles, some he didn't know he had, and a bruised sternum made for slow going as he gingerly eased his arms into the sleeves of the clean, blue cotton shirt. He fumbled with sore fingers at the buttons and watched Rusty crawl out from under the wagon, raise a hind leg and stake a claim to the left front wheel.

He couldn't quite make a fist with his right hand, but he decided the pain just wasn't intense enough to think broken knuckles or broken fingers. He studied the battered face reflected in his shaving mirror and grimaced. Morgan's nursing and warm water had soaked the blood off his face the night before, but there just wasn't any short term cure for black eyes, although the swelling in his left eye was down enough to let daylight peek through.

"No shaving this morning," he said to nobody in particular, unless the red hound counted as somebody.

A half hour after sunrise, Anthony grained his horses from Bitter's supply, filled his canteen from the water barrel, gulped a cup of hot coffee, and stuffed dried apples, biscuits, and cold bacon in his saddlebags.

He mounted the big Buckskin, tied the bay's lead rope to the saddle horn, and reached down to shake Bitter's hand. A smile creased his face when Ethan reached up to shake hands as well. "You ride careful, Uncle Mark."

"I will Ethan." He swallowed the sudden lump in his throat and put the big horse into a ground-eating lope that carried him over a rolling hill and out of sight. "Uncle Mark," he said aloud. "Did you hear that, Buck? Uncle Mark. I like it."

The Bitters watched until horses and rider disappeared over the green crest of a rolling hill, and then it looked like the earth just swallowed their friend. Bitter took a deep breath, let it out and said, "Well, let's harness the mules and get this show on the road."

Noon found them approaching a rough-looking sod house parked close to the dusty road. A crude sign declared the premises Barton's General Store and U.S. Post Office. Sun faded gray lodge poles, visible over the rooftop, supported ancient, moth-eaten, leather hides, patched here and there with faded canvas. As teepees go, it barely passed muster as decent shade. A small woman with long black hair, wearing a worn, blue calico dress appeared from behind the store on her way to the outhouse.

"John," Morgan called. "I need some writing paper. I want to send a letter to Harley."

"Okay," John said. "Let's pull over on that patch of grass across the road from the store. We'll noon while you get your letter writing done." He whistled at Ethan who was a good fifty yards out in the prairie grass, staying off the dusty wagon road.

Morgan pulled the mules to a stop and Bitter stepped off Rockford to help her from the wagon seat. "I'll be right back," she said.

"You need any money?" Bitter asked.

"I have enough."

John left the mules in the traces, but hand-watered each mule and fed each a pint of cracked corn. "Ethan," he said, "stake out that Misery horse. And you, Mister Mikey, feed her a half can of cracked corn. She's coming back pretty good. I have an idea you'll be able to ride her pretty soon."

"No saddle," Mikey said.

"You ever hear of riding bareback?"

Mikey nodded. "I can do it."

Bitter dropped the tailgate, broke out some cold biscuits, sliced each biscuit open and added half strips of bacon, cooked that morning. He added some dried apples to the pile and said, "Soup's on."

The boys finished their chores and came running around the wagon to the tailgate. "Biscuits and bacon again?" Ethan said.

"And good biscuits, they are."

"We find some water, I'm gonna catch us some fish," Ethan grumped.

Morgan came back across the dusty wagon road carrying a package wrapped in brown paper, and a small cotton bag with writing paper, an ink well, a bottle of ink, a quill pen and two lead pencils. She was secretive about the contents of the bigger package. All she would say in answer to their curiosity was, "In time, boys, in time."

Morgan sat on a barrel and used the tailgate for a desk while she wrote Harley a letter to let him know she was now Missus John Bitter, and if that wasn't enough, she was also the mother of two orphan boys she and John had adopted.

Ethan was ten and Mikey would be six in August, she told Harley. Ethan was a fine fisherman, she wrote, and added that Mikey could talk to animals. She smiled as she thought about Harley's reaction to that.

She concluded the letter with, "I hope you have approached Sarah about matrimony. She will make you a good wife. I will write again to keep you posted as to our progress on our journey to Oregon."

She signed it, "As always, your loving sister, Morgan."

In spite of herself she felt small tears forming at the corners of her eyes.

John Bitter noticed and said, "Something wrong?"

"It just occurred to me I might not see Harley or any of my relatives ever again. I think I forgot that in the excitement of going to Oregon."

"Riders coming," Ethan said and pointed west.

6
Rebs

A DUSTY CAVALRY PATROL TEN STRONG, led by a middle-aged sergeant, slowed from a trot to a walk, and then followed the sergeant off the road and out into the grass.

About forty yards from the Bitter wagon, the sergeant pulled his mount to a halt and said, "Dismount. Corporal O'Grady, go tell Barton we'll need water. And keep the men out of his bar. No drinking today. Understood?"

"Yes, Sergeant," the corporal replied with a southern drawl. "No drinkin' today, Sarge. No sir. No beer. No whiskey, Sarge. Just water to rust your pipes. Anything you say, Sarge."

Bitter listened to the familiar banter, the corporal's tone half mocking, but somehow respectful all the same, and looked the riders over. Something about the medium-sized, compact corporal looked familiar, and when the noncom sensed Bitter's stare, he did a double-take and said, "I'll be damned." He ignored his sergeant and walked over to the wagon. "You'll be that damned Yankee that surprised me at Franklin."

Bitter grinned and said, "I wasn't sure I recognized you, Reb, but that drawl was a dead giveaway. How in the world did you come to be in blue?"

"I'll have y'all know, I am a dyed-in-the-wool galvanized Yankee, sworn to defend the Union, protect immigrants, and defend women and children against the wild savages. I joined y'all because it got me out of a Union stockade." He held out his hand. "Let me shake the hand of the man who saved my life."

"Easy on the hand," Bitter said and winced when they shook hands. "How do you figure I saved your life?"

"I'm here, alive. If I'd stayed with my comrades in the army of the Confederate States of America, God bless them all, I'd most likely be dead. All I have to do now is dodge arrows and rheumatism."

Bitter laughed. "I never knew your name."

"O'Grady. Liam O'Grady."

"My Lord. An Irish rebel. I thought you Irish all came from New York."

"I'll have you know, I'm a second generation tobacco farmer." He paused, "And now a first generation Yankee. I know it's not polite to ask, but have you been goin' a round or two with a tough Irishman?"

John touched his tender nose. "If you mean this, I ran into a gentleman who let me hammer his fist with my nose until he finally gave up."

O'Grady laughed and then pointed at John's skinned knuckles and swollen fist. "And I suppose he did the same until you gave up?"

Bitter held out his hand again to shake O'Grady's. "John Bitter," he said by way of introduction, "first generation Oregonian. This is my wife Morgan, and my two sons, Michael and Ethan."

Liam O'Grady bowed to Morgan and said, "Ah…another descendant of the Old Sod. And two good looking boys…so soon. I'll bet there's a tale there worth knowing."

Morgan blushed, and in spite of herself nearly curtsied. "There is indeed."

"O'Grady," his sergeant bellowed, "quit your jawin' and get on with your duties."

O'Grady grinned and hollered, "I was just paying my respects to the Yankee that kept me out of the fight at Franklin, Sergeant."

"And cursed me with you," the sergeant said, and walked over to the wagon. O'Grady laughed and said, "Allow me to introduce my sergeant, Sean Callaghan, O'Callaghan until he turned Yankee."

"A rose by any other name would smell as sweet," Sergeant Callaghan answered.

"I don't think you smell too sweet this day," O'Grady said back over his shoulder as he headed for Barton's General Store and U.S. Post Office to arrange water for the horses, pick up any mail Barton had, and buy a chaw of tobacco.

"He's enough to fuss a man," Sergeant Callaghan grinned, "but he loves a good fight. If we tangle with the savages, he's the one I want by my side."

Bitter looked hard at the sergeant, "And have you been tangling with the Indians?"

"They are getting restless. I can't blame them much. Whites keep moving in and claiming land in and amongst them. The hotheads on both sides provoke hostilities and the fight is on. Somehow, the cavalry is supposed to keep the whites out of the Indian lands. And keep the Indians inside theirs. But it's a big damned country and there aren't enough troopers to patrol it all."

"Are the Indians attacking wagons?" Bitter asked.

"Sometimes," Sergeant Callaghan said. "They are a notional lot. You just never know."

Morgan asked, "Any trouble between here and Marysville?"

"A party two days ahead of you said they lost a horse night before last. They think an Indian stole it. Two men are tracking the lost horse, and I pray to God they don't shoot an ignorant savage to get the horse back. That'll mean big trouble."

"Why didn't you help them?" Morgan asked.

"We can't. I have orders to the contrary. And, besides, there's no way to know the horse didn't just wander off."

"Where are you headed?" Bitter asked.

"We're meeting a freight train bringing supplies to Fort Kearney. The other patrol will hand them over to us. Right here."

John nodded and said, "I think they're a full day behind us. But you got some blabbermouths amongst the teamsters. One man told me the load included a new rapid fire gun."

Sergeant Callaghan stared at Bitter with cold blue eyes and then said, "Tell me what he said exactly."

Bitter sighed and then said, "I don't remember the exact words, but he mentioned a rapid firing gun he heard about from saloon gossip. I don't think the information came directly from the teamsters."

"So…a talkative trooper, maybe?"

"That would be my guess. He had to be talking about a Gatling gun. Mean, vicious gun, it is."

"Well," Callaghan said, "Gatling guns are no secret. We just didn't want any unrepentant Rebs to know we had one in this shipment. We thought they might try to steal it. From what we're seeing, some of the guerilla groups intend to carry on the fight."

Bitter shook tobacco into a tissue-thin paper and quickly rolled a cigarette. "Too bullheaded to quit, I guess. They don't want to admit the fight is lost." He fished a wooden match from his shirt pocket, scratched it with his thumbnail and lit his cigarette.

Callaghan nodded and then said, "Some of them have nothing to go back to anyway."

"So that makes it okay to rob and kill?" Morgan asked.

"Of course not! It's just a way to try and understand their thinking."

Morgan snorted and walked to the back of the wagon. Over her shoulder she said, "Thinking isn't what I'd call it."

A lean, dusty, blue clad trooper trotted over, pointing down the road in the direction of St. Joseph. "Sarge," he said, "rider coming. I can't tell from here, but I think he might be one of ours."

Morgan, Bitter and Callaghan turned to look. About two miles off, a rider chased by a small dust cloud rode over the crown of a rolling piece of prairie and then dipped out of sight again. Even at that distance it was obvious he was in a hurry.

"Get my field glasses, Hackett. They're in my saddlebags," Callaghan shouted.

Bitter walked to where Rockford was cropping grass and pulled his French field glasses from the saddlebags.

Together he and Sergeant Callaghan watched horse and rider top another piece of rolling prairie. "He's gonna kill that horse if he doesn't ease up," Callaghan said without taking the field glasses from his eyes. "Yep, he's one of ours. From this distance, I think that's Corporal Sessions." He dropped the field glasses and let them hang from his neck by a leather strap.

"Hackett, ride out there and tell him to quit killing that horse. Whatever it is, it can't be good. But killing his horse won't make it better."

"On my way," Hackett said and ran the forty yards back to his horse. He grabbed the reins, swung into the saddle, and dug his heels into the sides of a big blaze-faced roan that loved to run. The roan was at nearly full speed by the time Hackett rode past the Bitter wagon, dust boiling up behind the heels of the galloping horse.

"Eeehaw! Eeehaw!" Ethan yelled in his little boy voice, caught up in the excitement of the galloping horse, and a sense that today wasn't going to be the least bit boring.

"Private Henry," Callaghan barked at another trooper, "have the patrol take the horses to Barton's well and get them watered. And fill the canteens. I got me a hunch we'll need 'em before the day is out."

Corporal O'Grady walked out the front door of Barton's carrying a suspicious looking package, something wrapped in a yellow bandana. When he saw the galloping horse, he trotted across the dusty yard of the store to where Callaghan and Bitter were staring through field glasses. "What's happening?"

Callaghan looked at O'Grady's scarf wrapped package, grunted and said, "Medicinal, no doubt."

"For snake bite, Sarge."

Callaghan grumped and said, "See that it stays in your saddlebag."

He pointed back down the road at the fain't dust cloud chasing Hackett's horse. "Corporal Sessions is riding our way hard enough to kill his horse. I sent Hackett out to slow him down. We can surmise, however, he's carryin' bad news. So you stick to water."

By the time Corporal Sessions and Private Hackett stopped their mounts in front of an impatient Sergeant Callaghan, the other horses had been watered, cinches tightened and canteens filled.

"Sarge," Corporal Sessions reported without saluting, "we was attacked by about twenty rebs. We forted up among the wagons and managed to dump one reb. But the teamster driving the wagon with the Gatling panicked and ran from the fight. Whipped his horses up and drove the wagon down a big open draw, the damned fool. Should of stuck with us.

"Anyway, the rebs took off after the wagon like they knew what was on it. Chased it until it was out of sight. We heard some shots and then it was quiet.

"We mounted up and gave chase. Never did find the teamster… or the wagon for that matter. Looks like the rebs made off with both. The tracks led north towards the Platte for a ways and then started swinging west. That's when Lieutenant Beverly sent me to find you. He reckoned you could ride north a ways and we might catch 'em between us. With your patrol and ours, we're pretty evenly matched with the rebs."

"You," Callaghan said to Bitter, "I'd like you to ride along. Anybody who could outfox O'Grady is a damned good scout. And I can see a use for that Henry rifle you carry."

Bitter shook his head. "Nope. I'm not in the army. I intend to stay with my family."

"And how safe do you think they'll be," Callaghan said, "if there's a small army of rebs robbing folks traveling this road?"

Morgan was indignant. "How can you ask him to accompany you? Look at him. In the past eight or nine days, he's been in three gun fights and one brawl. He can barely crawl out of bed in the morning."

Bitter was surprised by her sudden defense and maybe a tad hurt by her insinuations about his staying power.

"He shot the men who stole our Mama," Ethan said. "And then he shot the men who came after him, a whole bunch of men. And then he shot three men who tried to stop our train. That was before the fist fight with the kin folk of the men Missus Bitter shot."

With raised eyebrows, Callaghan looked at Morgan who was just about the prettiest redheaded lass he'd ever seen. "The men Missus Bitter shot?"

Flustered, Morgan blushed and said defensively, "I only had to shoot one. My mule stomped the other one."

"Only one, huh?" And then the blue clad sergeant started chuckling. "Well, maybe you two, meaning you and Mister Bitter could just ride out there and take care of the whole bunch for us."

Bitter gave a resigned sigh and said, "If I do this, Sergeant Callaghan, we do it my way. Agreed?"

"You ever been an officer?"

"A Captain with the 40th Missouri. You might say I was Chief of Scouts. Reconnaissance and ambush."

"Expert, huh?"

Bitter paused and thought about how to answer that when O'Grady said, "Yessir. I'd say he was. Anybody who can surprise me like he did is damned well an expert."

"Okay, then Captain. How do you want to do this?"

"I'll take O'Grady and that one…what's your name?"

"I'm Private Hackett, sir. Paul Hackett."

'Okay, Private Hackett. We'll need two extra canteens for the horses. Double issue of ammunition."

He looked at Ethan and winked. "You'll just have to eat something besides cold biscuits and bacon tonight, Ethan. These two troopers and I need what Morgan cooked up this morning."

Morgan shook her head and thought, *He loves this. How in the world is he going to settle down and farm?*

7

Lessons

WITHOUT PREAMBLE BITTER ASKED, "SERGEANT, you ever study the Franklin battle?"

Callaghan looked puzzled. "Can't say I have."

"Well," Bitter said, "I have. If you take the battle as a whole, you can understand why the Confederates lost. First, they attacked fortified positions. It takes a lot more men to defeat fortifications than it takes to defend them. And the Union army had twice as many men to start with.

"And second, by the time General Hood got his troops into the fight, they were exhausted which compounded the problem of being outnumbered."

Bitter shook his head. "General Hood threw away a good third of his men in an open charge against an entrenched army. He was doomed to lose that fight from the beginning."

"What's that got to do with us ?" Callaghan grumped.

Bitter grinned. "Well, small unit action works the same way. For now, let's just say we don't want to wear out the horses or the men before we tackle the rebs. So set an easy pace for your patrol while O'Grady, Hackett and I scout for that bunch. When we find them, I'll send Hackett back for you. Who knows, we might just take them by surprise and avoid a fight."

Three hours later, the hot sun working hard to make animals and men dry up and blow away, Bitter and O'Grady were bellied down in the tall grass at the crest of a big, rolling hill. In the hollow behind them, Hackett held the reins of the horses.

"Look at that," Bitter said in a quiet voice. He handed his field glasses to O'Grady.

"Well, damn," O'Grady said. "They got theirselves a Confederate flag, rifles stacked in military fashion, pickets out…see that fellow bellied down on that hill to the east of them? They act like they're waiting for someone. And it looks like they're putting the carriage for the Gatling together."

"Regular army, not guerillas, wouldn't you say?"

"Appears that way."

"I like it," Bitter said.

O'Grady let the field glasses settle in the grass and glanced at Bitter. "I don't understand."

"Give it time," Bitter said and gave O'Grady a grim smile. "We best send Hackett back for Callaghan, Corporal O'Grady."

Bitter and O'Grady slid down the hill to the horses. Hackett grinned when O'Grady told him they had found the rebs. He shook his head in disbelief and stared at Bitter. "You mean you found those old boys? In this whole big damn country, you ride right to 'em?"

"Got lucky, I guess," Bitter said.

"Hackett," O'Grady said, "y'all ride back and fetch Sergeant Callaghan and the boys. I'm gonna' try and sneak around that old coon hunter they got watching their back trail. I'll lead Lieutenant Beverly's patrol back in on this bunch."

They watched Hackett disappear around the shoulder of a low hill, and then O'Grady asked, "How do you want to play this?"

When Bitter explained what he had in mind, O'Grady nodded. "Might work. Sure hope it does. I'll tell Lieutenant Beverly what you got in mind. We'll do our part."

An hour later while Bitter hid in the grass, and wished for some shade, he heard the soft clink of a bridle bit and the muffled thump of a horse hoof. He rolled over and looked back down the slope to where Rockford stood ground hitched, filling his belly with grass. Rockford, head up, ears forward was watching the little draw that led around the hill to the south.

Bitter breathed easier when Hackett led Callaghan and seven troopers up around the shoulder of the hill, careful to stay off the skyline.

Bitter slithered back down below the brow of the hill and walked to where Callaghan had silently signaled a halt.

"Whatcha got, Mister Bitter? Hackett told me you found them. Plumb amazing is what it is," Callaghan said softly.

"The rebs are camped in the bottom, over that hump," he said pointing north, "about seventeen strong. And you can rest your mind about that teamster. He's very much alive. I think he was in on this from the get-go."

"I'll hang him for a traitor," Callaghan growled.

Bitter grinned and looked around at the treeless sea of prairie grass. "With what?"

Hackett kneed his horse up to Bitter and Callaghan. "Here comes O'Grady."

Callaghan looked at the grin on O'Grady's face when he pulled to a stop in front of the patrol. "What in the world have you got to be smiling about?" Callaghan asked.

"I think I have good news."

"And what might that be?"

"Sarge, Lieutenant Beverly told me Johnny Reb hasn't got any ammo for the Gatling. It was loaded on a different wagon. Ain't that a hoot?"

Bitter just grinned. "Better and better, I think. Now, what we're going to do is win this battle without firing a shot. As soon as Lieutenant Beverly rides into the open," he said to Callaghan, "I think it would be a good idea for your men to show themselves on top of the hill, spaced about ten yards apart, across the skyline. I want the rebs to see you. I don't want any heroic charges, and I don't want any shooting until I say so."

"What's your plan?" Callaghan asked. "Those rebs still have their rifles."

"Why, Sergeant Callaghan, I'm going down and reason with them."

"What makes you think they won't just shoot you?"

"Because that's a regular army unit down there, led and disciplined by an officer. I hope."

When Lieutenant Beverly's troop rode to the top of the low hill to the north of the rebel camp, Sergeant Callaghan led his squad up on the skyline.

The picket watching the back trail must have fallen asleep, Corporal O'Grady thought.

A bandana tied to the end of his rifle barrel as a sign he wanted a truce, Bitter rode to the top of the hill, stopped beside Callaghan and touched off a round. The shot echoed and rolled across the hills surrounding the rebel camp.

A startled Callaghan looked at Bitter who said, "Just to get their attention."

There was a shout from the camp, and men ran to get their rifles. The officer barked a command that sent three men to the rear of the freight wagon. They pulled the Gatling from under a canvas cover and muscled it to the gun's carriage, obviously bent on getting the gun mounted and ready for action.

Bitter looked at Callaghan who sat on his big bay horse and just watched the rebs fuss with the Gatling gun.

"Plumb amusing, is what it is," he said to Bitter, as other rebels tossed wooden boxes from the freight wagon, and busted them open, frantically looking for ammunition to feed the Gatling.

Bitter took a deep breath, let it out, and said, "Well…here we go. I hope I'm right."

A rebel soldier shouted at his officer and pointed at Bitter as Rockford walked off the hill toward the camp.

An officer with captains bars barked, "Hold your fire," and walked out from the wagon. "What do want, Yankee?" he shouted when Bitter was about thirty yards away.

Bitter pulled Rockford to a halt, his rifle butt parked on his thigh, the yellow bandana fluttering in a puff of wind. "I wanted to make sure you rebs understand the war is over. There's no need for all this fuss and bother."

"We heard General Lee surrendered. Is that true?"

"At Appomattox, over a month ago."

"Damn. I'm sure sorry to hear that. We heard rumors, but none of our officers ever sent word."

Bitter looked the rebels over and shook his head. "It looks like you boys haven't been eating too well."

The captain flushed at the suggestion he couldn't take care of his men, and then shrugged. "No," he said in a tired voice.

"I have this dilemma," Bitter said. "You boys can't surrender since that's already been done. And you can't keep fighting 'cause the war is over. That would just make you outlaws, and you don't look like outlaws. At least not to me.

"Now if you look north, you'll see a cavalry troop led by Lieutenant Beverly, and if you look south, you'll see another troop of Union Cavalry.

"I should add, a full company of cavalry is about two miles away and they are pulling a mountain howitzer. I wish to save us all the trouble of needless bloodshed."

The captain tried to blink away his tears. Whether they were tears of sorrow for a lost cause or tears of immense relief, even he didn't know. He straightened his back and shoulders, came to attention as befitted an officer and a gentleman of the South, and said, "What are your terms?"

"They're not my terms, but General Grant let General Lee keep his sword, and he let the confederate soldiers keep their weapons and what mounts they had. Said they'd need their weapons to hunt and to protect their families when they got home."

"That's all?"

Bitter's emotions were swept by sudden relief and a belief he would live to see another day. "That's all, Johnny Reb," he said softly, sad with pity for all the damned fools who fought in this war, North and South. "She's over. You can go home."

8
Galvanized Yankees

THE CAPTAIN WALKED BACK TO the wagon and gathered his men around him. Bitter couldn't hear what the rebel captain said, but he saw nods and spotted a tear or two rolling down grizzled cheeks. He wasn't sure if those tears, too, were simple relief or grief for a lost cause.

The rebel Captain called, "Attention!" and when his ragged band snapped to, he saluted and was saluted in return by his men. He then ordered his men to stack their weapons on the wagon. "I believe this damned Yankee," Bitter heard him say. "We lost. Lee surrendered after all."

A lanky bearded man who looked too skinny to stand asked, "How come they never sent nobody to tell us , Captain Finch?"

"I don't know, Josiah. I just don't know."

Bitter waved at Callaghan and at Lieutenant Beverly and the two groups rode slowly down off the hills toward the camp, carbines at the ready.

"Damndest thing I ever saw," O'Grady said to Sergeant Callaghan as they neared the Confederate camp.

"I'm some relieved," Callaghan admitted. "I wonder what he would have done if those rebs had ammunition for the Gatling."

"I'm beginning to think he'd a thought of something."

Bitter watched the Union horses work down the slopes until the two groups of blue clad riders converged and loosely surrounded the rebs. He edged Rockford over to a compact, sun worn, erect rider in Union Blue. Bitter held out his hand. "John Bitter, Lieutenant."

The officer smiled and shook Bitter's hand. "I'm Lieutenant Beverly."

With a rueful smile, Beverly said, "I would have bet against your chances of living out the day."

"Day's not over."

Beverly laughed and then asked. "What did you tell those rebs?"

"Well, I told them the war was over. And I suggested if they continued to fight, they would become outlaws. And I did sort of hint that a full company of Union Cavalry was just about to come boiling over the hill and start shooting at 'em with a mountain howitzer."

"I'd say that was most persuasive. Whose outfit would that be?"

"Sir?"

"Who is riding to the rescue?"

"Why," Bitter said with a grin, "I made that up. Just seemed like the thing to do."

Beverly smiled. "Well, it worked." He turned his horse and walked it over to where the rebel captain stood waiting for someone to tell him what came next. Lieutenant Beverly saluted and stepped down off his horse.

"Captain Finch at your service, sir. I offer my sword. We are your prisoners."

"I'm Lieutenant Beverly, Captain Finch. I accept your surrender, but you may keep your sword."

"Thank you, sir."

Beverly looked at the group of gaunt, sullen Confederate soldiers standing near the end of the wagon, some with tears streaming down their cheeks, and asked, "When was the last time your men were fed?"

"Three days ago. We were to be resupplied a week back, but the wagons never came."

Beverly nodded, sympathy in his blue eyes. "Sergeant Callaghan," he shouted, "feed these men."

One of the rebs started edging toward the tailgate of the wagon and the pile of guns. O'Grady saw him and pushed his horse between the man and the wagon. The man, a boy really, barely into his teens, glared up at O'Grady and tried to step around O'Grady's horse.

When the boy spat and said, "You damned Yankee," O'Grady pointed his pistol at him. "You don't want to be doing that, son. It would be an awful thing for your mama to hear you were the last soldier killed in this terrible war. Let President Lincoln have that honor."

"Amen to that. I'd shoot the son of a bitch myself if I could."

O'Grady, eyes hard, said, "A man named Booth has taken care of that chore. But you speak respectful of President Lincoln, boy. He was on the wrong side, but he was a great man. So you let it be, now. You hear?"

Sergeant Callaghan assigned two troopers to arrest the teamster that had driven away with the Gatling gun. The teamster glared up at Callaghan, sullen and defiant until Callaghan wondered aloud if he could get enough lumber from the wagon to build a scaffold and "hang this son-of-a-bitch."

"You can't do that! I'm a soldier of the Confederate States of America," he protested, the color draining from his face.

"All I see," Callaghan said, "is a thief working for the rebs."

O'Grady watched in amusement while Callaghan tormented the frightened teamster. "Of course, we'll be needin' the wagon. So I guess it wouldn't make sense to tear it up just to build a scaffold. I guess we'll just have to shoot this poor beggar as a spy."

"I don't know, Sergeant," O'Grady said. "To put a fine point on it, since the war is over he can't technically be a spy."

"But he didn't know that when he stole our wagon and the big gun. So he thought he was a spy."

"I see your point, Sergeant. Is there nothing he can do?"

"In a minute, we'll get to that, O'Grady. In a minute."

Two Union troopers were posted to guard the weapons stacked on the tailgate of the wagon, and then Corporal O'Grady divvied up what rations the boys in blue brought with them.

At first the rebs were sullen, but as the rations were shared and tobacco offered to nicotine-starved men, the Confederate soldiers decided they weren't going to be lined up and shot after all. And the biscuits and cold bacon were the best things they had seen in quite a while. If a man listened he could hear mumbled "thanks" offered around stuffed jaws. One hard nose held out to the last, until Captain Finch barked and said, "Foster, you eat, or by God I'll have these blue bellies shoot your dumb ass." The starving rebel caved, snatched a biscuit and wolfed it down.

Another of them, a gapped toothed scarecrow of a man whose boot soles were tied on with leather thongs, and whose britches wore more patches than original cotton, asked O'Grady, "Didn't you ride with General Hood?"

"I did. You sure look familiar, but I can't place you." O'Grady said.

"I'm David Armstrong."

"My Lord. I didn't recognize you David. Meaning no disrespect, but you look more cadaver than live human being. What the hell happened?"

And so the chatter started. It seemed like each man had a relative fighting for the other side, and it seemed like each man was more interested in news that might tell him his kin folk survived the war than in the fact the war was over.

At Callaghan's orders, two troopers used the broken wooden boxes to start a fire for coffee. One of rebels asked, "Is that for real coffee?"

"Arbuckle's finest," one of the Union troopers said. "We all got a big pot," the rebel said. "Can you make enough for all of us ?"

Lieutenant Beverly told Sergeant Callaghan to post lookouts on hilltops just in case the missing rebel supply wagons actually came, or in case hostile Indians decided to attack the whites congregated in the little valley. A search by two troopers failed to turn up the Confederate sentinel.

"Looks like he took off, Lieutenant," one of the troopers said.

Beverly watched the rebs drink the first coffee they'd seen in over two years. He didn't feel the same compassion Bitter felt. *Each man chooses his own path,* Beverly thought. But he couldn't help but wonder how he would have chosen if he was born and raised in the South.

"All right, Captain Finch," Lieutenant Beverly said, "have your men form ranks. It's time you were educated to your current situation."

A single line of fifteen gaunt, ragged Confederate soldiers, two of whom were barefoot, stood two paces behind Captain Finch. Sergeant Callaghan looked at Lieutenant Beverly.

When Beverly nodded, Callaghan said in a loud voice, "Those of you who wish to go home will be given a pass by Lieutenant Beverly in case you get stopped by Union regulars. You can keep your weapons. If you own a horse, you can keep that, too.

"However, we need good fighting men to help us keep the peace between the Indians and the whites, and to protect immigrants on the Oregon Trail from marauders, outlaws, run amuck Indians and dumb ass rebs who haven't gotten the word that the war is over.

"That said, I'm here to say if you swear allegiance to the United States of America, you may enlist in the finest cavalry unit to ride the plains. You will be given the rank of private, a clean uniform, meals and $13 a month, and a military chaplain to say nice things over your grave."

A skinny runt about five foot four inches tall, brown eyes smoldering, spat and said, "Piss on you, Yank. You can keep your pass, and I ain't gonna fight for the North."

"Me neither," another man said. "I'm for home."

"Well," Sergeant Callaghan fumed, "to think we just fed you… and you ate. Get your asses in motion then. You stick around here I'm liable to go to shooting."

Under the watchful eye of the troopers guarding the Confederate weapons, the men claimed two rifles, two powder flasks, and two possible sacks filled with bullets, patches, and assorted tools used to maintain their rifles.

They glanced at each, caught the reins of two saddled horses and mounted. They galloped their horses up the hill to the east, stopped at the crest, touched off a round at the sky, and gave a defiant rebel yell as they rode on over the top and out of sight.

Bitter shook his head. *For some it'll never be over,* he thought.

Finally, a stocky, blue eyed man took a pace forward, looked at Callaghan, and saluted. "I never thought I'd wear blue, but I don't have nothin' to go back to. I'm your man, Sergeant."

"What about me?" the teamster asked. "I'll join."

"And miss the rope, I guess," Callaghan said. He looked at Lieutenant Beverly and asked, "What do you think, Lieutenant? Can we let this would be spy slip the noose?"

Lieutenant Beverly suppressed a smile, and said, "I suppose if he doesn't mind his manners, we can always hang him later."

While Lieutenant Beverly led his squad back to escort the other freight wagons to Barton's General Store and Post Office, seven ex-confederate soldiers who were now newly minted U.S. Cavalry troopers, mounted on ex-confederate horses, carrying empty ex-confederate rifles, rode in column with Sergeant Callaghan's mounted troop. The wagon carrying the Gatling gun, driven by one of the Union army's newest recruits, and protected by a rear guard, followed the column south.

Captain Finch asked to ride east with Beverly's squad as far as the freight wagons. "I wish to go home," he told Lieutenant Beverly, "to see what remains of my home, and to find my family if I can."

The remaining Confederate soldiers paired off and were last seen traveling east and slightly south. None of them waved good-bye.

When Callaghan's column started for Barton's store, Bitter said to Sergeant Callaghan, "I think I'll go on ahead." He dug his heels in Rockford's ribs and urged him to a ground-eating lope.

O'Grady looked at Sergeant Callaghan and grinned. "Lieutenant Beverly will get all the credit, you know."

"I'll make my report to Major Henry when we get back. I'll see that he knows Bitter's part in all of this.

"You know, Corporal O'Grady, they should have made Captain Bitter a general. The war would have ended a lot sooner, I'm thinking, and a lot of good men might still be alive."

"Amen," O'Grady said quietly, his thoughts taking him back to battles won and battles lost, always at the cost of brave men on both sides. *Even the victories were losses*, he decided.

9
Fellow Travelers

THE LAST CRESCENT OF THE sun was resting on the horizon when Rockford topped the low rolling hill north of Barton's store. Bitter's heart warmed at the sight of his yellow topped wagon, its shadow a good forty yards long. He saw the mules turned out to graze, Misery keeping them company. Off to the west, making his own shadow, Lucifer grazed in regal solitude.

A trickle of wood smoke rose through the smoke hole of the old teepee behind the store, and he could smell meat cooking someplace, a reminder that his stomach was trying to gnaw a hole in his back bone.

Don't know why I gave those rebs my lunch. Pitiful idea.

"Beef, Rockford, I'm smelling beef or something like it. I wonder where the meat came from?"

And then he heard Morgan's clear sweet voice, singing, "Oh my Sally was such a maiden fair, singing polly wolly doodle all the day, with her curly eyes and her laughing hair, singing Polly wolly doodle all the day."

The boys joined in with their little boy voices on the Polly wolly doodle chorus and Rusty tried a howl that brought Lucifer's head up, ears pointed at the dog. The boys laughed, and, Bitter decided if the mule could talk, he'd tell the hound to be quiet.

Bitter walked Rockford across the road to the wagon. As he stepped to the ground he added his voice. In a decent tenor, he sang,

"Fare thee well, fare thee well my fairy fey, I'm gone to Louisiana for to see my Suzy Anna, singing Polly wolly doodle all the day."

Rusty trotted over to sniff Rockford's nose and to nudge Bitter's hand. Mikey and Ethan each grabbed a long leg. Bitter ruffed their yellow hair and smiled at Morgan.

"You're back, I see," Morgan said in a huffy tone. "I hope you are through playing hero."

"And hello to you, too, Missus Morgan Bitter. You know I had to do this."

"No, I don't know that. And I don't know why you quit being a soldier boy if you like it so much."

The boy's eyes were wide as they stared in apprehension at the sudden quarrel.

Morgan stabbed at the skillet with a fork and then said, "Oh, damnation." She dropped the fork on a tin plate and ran to Bitter. He grinned and wrapped his arms around her. While he kissed the top of her head, she said against his chest, "Don't you ever do that again. We need you here with us."

"I know," he said quietly.

She stepped back. "Well, take good care of that black horse. The boys and I found some lambs quarters, so we'll have greens with supper."

Seated on a wooden keg by the dying fire, Bitter watched the dish water heat over the coals, wiped the last of the beef gravy from his plate with a fresh biscuit and asked, "Where'd the beef steak come from?"

Morgan pointed in the direction of Barton's store. "A wagon came through early this morning and traded a year old steer for supplies. Drove off with enough bad whiskey to start a saloon. Barton butchered the steer and his wife has most of it already drying on smoking racks she put up in her teepee. I bought us some steaks before they turned it all into jerky."

Bitter was impressed and said so. "Darned good meat, Morgan. The lamb's quarters hit the spot too. I think they're as good as mustard greens."

"And she made us a dried apple pie," Ethan said.

"Wow. I'd like some of that."

"Rump," Mikey said.

"What did you say?" Ethan asked.

"Rump. The gray mule that teams with Windy. He told me that's his name."

"How did you come up with that?" Morgan asked.

With a twinkle in his eyes, Mikey said, "Well, he told me his real name is Butt. That's not a nice word, so I changed it to Rump. He's okay with that."

They all laughed, and Bitter said, "Well, Mikey, do the lead mules have names, too?"

He nodded. "Yep. But they haven't told me yet."

Morgan sliced the pie in half, quartered the half, used a hotcake turner to slip a piece on each of their plates, and put the rest in the grub box for breakfast. When Ethan asked for a second slice, she just shook her head and said with a smile, "It'll taste better in the morning."

Bitter tossed a slice of cooked beef fat to Rusty who caught it in the air, snapped and swallowed.

It was dark by the time Callaghan's troops pulled into Barton's yard. Barton, a lean old man whose hair and beard had turned silver, lived in buckskins made by his old Arapaho wife. He had given up trapping and traipsing the wild country years earlier, or maybe it was more correct, he was known to say, "The trappin' and traipsing give up on me."

He had developed a taste for trading while among the wild Indians, and he had discovered a knack for it. So he settled for running a trading post. When he found he could contract with the U.S. Government to be a post master, he figured he was set for life…or at least as long as the U.S. Army ran wagons and patrols past his store.

A lantern hanging from a post in the yard marked the water trough, pumped full by Barton's wife in expectation of Sergeant Callaghan's return.

From his warm bed under the wagon, Bitter heard Callaghan quietly give orders to stack arms and see the mounts watered and grained, and then tell O'Grady he was ready for some medicinal elixir.

O'Grady chuckled and pulled a bottle from his saddlebags.

Daylight found Morgan dressed in gray canvas pants, men's size small, her feet in a small pair of army boots, and wearing a cotton calico shirt sewn by Barton's Arapaho wife. The boots were a bit too large, but the addition of an extra pair of socks made up most of the difference. She stirred the ashes with a small stick, looking for coals to start her morning fire. Bitter watched from under half closed eyelids, blankets pulled to his chin, and marveled at the young woman he had married so few days ago. He would never say it aloud, but he approved her choice of practical garments.

She caught his stare and said, "Why ruin my dresses? And I can pass for a man this way."

He grinned, but didn't tell her how unlike a man she looked, pants or no pants. *Maybe it's the long red braid or her shape the shirt fails to hide that gives her away,* he thought.

A trickle of smoke followed a thin yellow flame that seemed reluctant to consume the dew dampened twist of dead grass she fed the coals. But finally the grass dried, caught and carried heat and light to Morgan's cottonwood twigs which snapped and popped as the flame licked the dry wood. The distinct odor of riverbank firewood sweetened the air and greeted the day.

Bitter let the calm ease into his soul, liking Morgan's quiet, efficient domestic activity, knowing that was about to change as they chased the summer season across the plains and over the Rocky Mountains.

10
Marysville

THE BITTER FAMILY ROLLED INTO Marysville at mid-afternoon of their second day from Barton's store, a fact that pleased John Bitter because it meant they were covering about twenty-five miles a day.

He rode Rockford alongside the wagon and said to Morgan, "We made good time the past two days. If we keep this up, we'll be in Oregon by late August or early September. No snowy mountains for the Bitters."

Morgan pushed her railroad cap back off her head and let her red hair and a long shiny braid glow with highlights from a west hanging sun. Bitter thought that was just about the prettiest braid he'd ever seen…or was ever likely to see.

Morgan frowned at her husband. "Easy for you to say. You drive the wagon tomorrow, and I'll ride horseback. The saddle has got to be easier on a person's posterior than a hard wagon seat."

"Rump," Mikey said.

"What?" Morgan asked.

"Rump must be the same thing as prosterrier," Mikey said.

"Posterior."

"That's what I said. Prosterrier."

Morgan gave up and grinned at Bitter.

Ethan, who had edged Lucifer up to the wagon laughed and said, "That's a made up word, Mikey."

"Is not," Mikey said and crossed his arms in defiance of his brother in particular and in defiance of the world at large.

As the wagon rolled by the red brick building that once housed the Pony Express, Bitter said, "This is a lot more town than I thought it would be. Sergeant Callaghan told me where to find good grass and a decent place to camp on the Big Blue just beyond town. We'll stop there, and then I'm thinking we might just find us a café for supper. How would that be?"

"We'll have to spruce up first," Morgan said with a smile. "You think we can afford it?"

"It's several hundred miles to the next café. What do you think?"

She nodded understanding and said, "Let's splurge then."

A thin screen of cottonwood and willow trees offered shade and wood for an evening fire. The animals were unhitched and the harness spread over a big cottonwood log to dry and recover from salty animal sweat. Bitter ran a long picket rope between two trees and tied the wagon mules to the line. He gave them enough slack to graze a bit, and when Ethan and Mikey had grained and watered each of them, he thought it would do.

Morgan gave him a puzzled look, and he said, "Too close to town. Our mules might be a temptation some couldn't resist if they wandered off."

Lucifer walked down to the Big Blue for a drink. Rockford tugged at his picket pin and finally gave up in favor of cropping grass to fill his belly.

While Morgan supervised, the boys scrubbed their faces and hands in a wash basin. Bitter shaved, and was encouraged by his reflection in the little mirror. The black eyes Walter Peale had given him were fading and coming a shade closer to normal. And his trigger finger was working again.

Hair brushed, faces scrubbed, the boys watched in fascination as Morgan who had changed into her green dress recreated her long red braid. Bitter wiped his face dry, ran a hand through his hair, slapped the dust from his trousers, set his hat on his head, and declared himself ready.

When Rusty started to follow, Ethan said, "Stay, Rusty. You guard camp."

The café they chose offered indifferent service and, in Bitter's mind, *piss poor food*. The stew was greasy, and was more potatoes than anything else.

Morgan stabbed at the stew twice with a fork before being rewarded with a little piece of meat she could barely chew. "I can do better than this," Morgan said to Bitter.

Ethan nodded. "I'm gonna go back and catch us some fish."

Bitter tried a biscuit that was rank with rancid bacon grease. "Shit," he said and pushed his chair back. "Don't eat this stuff. Let's go back to camp."

The proprietor, a small man with thinning hair and squinty brown eyes, a paunch pushing at his grease spotted apron, walked to the table. "Everything all right?"

"No," Morgan said. "We're leaving. The food is inedible. I'll not pay you for it."

The man flushed and said, "You ordered it, you pay for it. If you don't, I'll sick the sheriff on you."

Bitter stared at him until the man broke eye contact and started fidgeting. "How much?"

The man said, "Well…how about a dollar?"

"How about fifty cents?" Bitter countered.

The man nodded, and Bitter slapped a four bit piece on the table.

They were a good two hundred yards from camp when they heard Rusty barking and growling. Bitter pulled his pistol and said, "You all stay back. I'm gonna see what's got Rusty excited."

He kept the scattered cottonwoods between himself and the wagon until he was within a few yards of camp. Revolver at the ready he stepped from behind a tree in time to see a tall, well-built black man backing away from camp. "Easy now. Easy boy," the man said to Rusty. "I mean no harm."

"Then you won't mind telling me what you are doing sneaking around my camp," Bitter said.

If the man was startled, he gave no sign of it. He looked at Bitter and said, "Sneaking is not what I was doing."

"Then what?"

"Me and my wife are camped on the other side of the river… up river from the bridge. We're headed for Oregon, but I don't want to risk the trail by myself. So we been watching for a party to join with. The last train through wouldn't take us."

Bitter patted his knee and said, "Come here Rusty. Come here."

The dog backed away and walked slowly over to Bitter, never taking his eyes from the intruder.

"And you thought we would?" Bitter asked.

"Hoping, I guess."

"I don't know you," Bitter said. "Why are you going to Oregon?"

"I have an uncle there."

"Where?"

"Some town in the Willamette Valley called Corvallis. Uncle Reuben wrote us. Told us to come live with him. Said he had a farm we could work for shares."

"Lordy, Lordy," Bitter said, and holstered the revolver. "Well, go get your wife and we'll talk some."

He watched the man walk the riverbank back to the bridge over the Big Blue. "Come on in," he hollered to his family.

"What was that about?" Morgan asked.

"A family headed to Oregon, and wanting company for the trip."

"Us?"

"Maybe. The man said he tried to hook up with another wagon train and they wouldn't take him."

"Why on earth not?

"Well," Bitter said, "it could be because he's colored."

"And that would be reason enough?"

"For some," Bitter said, "it's all the reason you need."

"Boys," he said, "get some firewood gathered up. We're going to have company."

"I'm going fishing when I'm done," Ethan allowed. "I'm sick of bacon."

Mikey said, "Me, too."

"Amen," Bitter added. "All right. You go catch some fish and I'll get the wood."

Laughter in her voice, Morgan said, "A batch of nice, fresh bass would taste good, for sure. Keep your eyes out for snakes. You hear?"

"I need me a bacon rind," Ethan said.

While Morgan sliced a thin strip of rind from a bacon slab, Ethan untied his long cane pole from the top of the wagon bows where he and Bitter had placed it to keep it safe from the shifting load.

Mikey looked up at Morgan and asked, "Can I go with him?"

That he didn't ask Bitter was duly noted by both adults. *A sign that he's starting to heal up? That Morgan might stand a chance of filling in for his missing mother?* Bitter wondered.

"Ask Ethan," she said. "If he's okay with it, then go. But stay out of the water."

Morgan watched Ethan and Mikey trot down a well worn path to the river, the long cane pole over Ethan's shoulder and his cotton stringer dangling from a rear pocket. Rusty bounced down the path ahead of them, tail wagging, excited to be doing something besides trotting down a wagon road. "John," she said, "I don't know if they can swim. Do you?"

"Ethan says Mikey swims like a fish. And the way his belly is filling out, I'll bet he can float too."

They both smiled. "It's a good thing we're here, John. Right where the Good Lord meant us to be."

"Is it okay if I tell God I don't feel up to the task?

The water in the coffee pot was beginning to boil by the time the tall stranger and his tiny wife walked into camp. A boy about Mikey's age and size edged up behind them.

"I'm Ezra Shipley," he said by way of introduction, "and this is my wife Ruth and our boy David."

Bitter put his roll-your-own on the tailgate of the wagon and rose from the wooden keg he had been sitting on. He held out his hand. "John Bitter. And this is my wife Morgan. The boys are down on the river trying to catch a fish."

Ezra looked at his boy. "You want to go see if they be catching any fish, David?"

The boy nodded, his big brown eyes never leaving the ground.

"Okay, then," Ezra said gently. "You run along. I need to talk to these folks."

Bitter waited a full fifteen seconds for Ezra Shipley to have his say and then felt the need to fill the silence. He pulled the wooden keg a little closer to the fire and said, "Why don't you sit here, Missus Shipley?"

Morgan nodded and said, "We'll have coffee going pretty quick."

"Thank you," Ruth Shipley said.

"Well," Bitter said, "tell me what the trouble is."

"No trouble. The last train through just didn't want any colored folks. So they wouldn't take us. Otherwise, I don't think there's any trouble. We have a good wagon that's almost brand new, a strong four mule team, and provisions enough to get us through to Oregon. I just don't want to risk it alone."

Bitter noted the man's erect posture and asked, "Were you a soldier?

"Yessir. I was a sergeant with the 54th Massachusetts. Wounded at James Island. And I could see no future being a soldier. It's a stretch to feed and house a family on thirteen dollars a month."

He laughed and said, "For a while it was seven dollars a month 'cause they took three dollars for uniforms, and they only paid us coloreds ten dollars a month to start with.

"Ruth's teacher pay and her sewing helped. But it was still slim pickings. So when Uncle Rueben's letter finally found us, I wrote back and told him we was on our way.

"When President Lincoln, God rest his poor soul, talked the Congress into paying us the same as white soldiers, we made out a bit better. And my back pay caught up in time to help us buy a wagon and supplies."

Bitter nodded and then asked, "You got a rifle?"

"I do. A Sharps."

"Can you hit anything with it?"

Ruth said proudly, "If Ezra can see it, he can hit it. He doesn't waste his shots."

Ruth was surprised when Morgan said quietly, "Good for you. Wives should stick up for their husbands."

Ruth smiled shyly and nodded without saying anything.

Morgan spooned Arbuckle's into the boiling coffee pot, watched it for a minute or so, added some cold water to settle the grounds, and then set the pot on a rock by the fire to stay warm.

"Would you folks like to stay to supper?" Morgan asked.

"We don't want to be a bother," Ruth said.

"Nonsense. If we are going to Oregon together," she said, and settled the issue with that direct statement, "we'd best get acquainted over supper."

Ezra was puffing on a well chewed cigar, sipping whiskey-laced coffee, and John Bitter was smoking a roll-your-own and drinking a cup of the same brew when the boys walked into camp.

Mikey and David were giggling and Ethan was struggling to carry a stringer of bass that included one that went at least eight pounds.

"Whooeee," Ezra said. "That's some nice fish."

Morgan frowned at Mikey's wet head and his dripping clothes. "You fall in?" she asked worriedly.

"Nope."

"And?" she said.

Ethan laughed and David started giggling. "Mikey got pulled off the log by a big bass, but he wouldn't let go of the pole. So next thing you know Mikey and the fish are headed down the river, and Mikey is trying to swim with one arm and fight the fish with the other. I didn't know Mikey knew so many cuss words.

"Anyway, Rusty jumped in and me and Davey ran down the bank to pull him in. When Mikey came floating by, Rusty got him by the sleeve, and I waded out and got Rusty by his tail and we all pulled Mikey into the shallows. He still had my fishing pole and the bass. He just waded ashore and pulled that old bass right up on the bank."

Ethan pointed to the top fish on the stringer. "That's Mikey's first bass. A good one, I think."

"Nice," Bitter said. "Take them to that log over there and I'll filet em out. There's enough for a couple of meals for all of us and the dog, too."

"Ethan…and Mikey…that was a fine fish dinner," Bitter said later. "You catch and Morgan cooks the finest fish on the Oregon Trail."

"Amen," Ezra added. "Well, Ruth, we best be getting Davey back to the wagon. The dog will be wondering what happened to us."

"I wonder if Rusty and your dog will get along," Bitter said.

Ruth smiled and said, "Should. One's male and one's female."

"That doesn't mean a thing," Ezra grinned. "Why, look at the fuss we have trying to get along."

"I'll get a lantern and walk you folks back to your wagon," Bitter said. "Ethan you keep Rusty here. Okay?"

Morgan handed a pie tin loaded with cooked bass filets to Ruth. "For breakfast. We always eat cold leftovers and only take time to heat the coffee. John likes an early start. Says we aren't so likely to lose a whole day's travel if we have trouble along the way."

"Thank you, Morgan." Ruth said. "I can't tell you how relieved I am to have met you. I hope we get to be good friends."

Morgan smiled and said, "I think that's likely."

Mikey said, "Good night, Davey."

The Shipley wagon was solid, the red paint on the hubs and the yellow spokes still bright even after the hundred or so miles from St. Joseph. Bitter noticed the harness was new, and a well oiled saddle was parked on a log.

"Do you have a saddle horse?" Bitter asked.

"A Tennessee Walker," Ezra said. "Don't tell Ruth, but I won him in a poker game…saddle and all. Got him picketed down by the river, but I'll move him closer to the wagon before I turn in."

Bitter nodded, scratched the ears of a black and white mutt named Corky and asked, "Daylight?"

"Oh, man. I can't tell you how anxious we are to be gone. We been camped here for ten days. We'll be ready when you roll across the bridge."

Bitter grinned and held out his hand. "A pleasure, Ezra. A real pleasure."

11

Clabber and Sweet Cream Butter

AT THE SOUND OF WAGON wheels drumming on the wooden bridge, Ruth Shipley smiled at little David sitting beside her, slapped the reins of her mules and started for the wagon road called the Oregon Trail.

As he crossed the bridge, Bitter spotted Ezra mounted on a tall dark brown Tennessee Walker he called Lucky.

Bitter pulled Rockford to a halt and nodded approval of Ezra's big horse. "Morning. I see you're raring to go. What's that tied on behind your wagon, Mister Shipley?"

"That is Queeny, our milk cow."

"You didn't mention that last night," Bitter said. "She'll slow us down."

"Nah. She'll keep up…and she'll give us fresh milk for our oatmeal and our youngun's."

"I hope she does. We're starting late, so we have some distance to make up. I'm planning to average at least twenty-five miles a day."

"It'll be worth the fuss. Ruth makes clabber and fine butter. More than enough for all of us. What she does is skim the heavy cream, put it in a cold crock and let the wagon shake it all day. That way we got fresh cream butter at night. And if we camp by a crick, she sets the milk in the water. The crock cools down and the milk can last a couple days that way. The extra I feed to the dog."

Bitter shook his head in doubt, but held his peace. "Well…let's roll."

The trail was an up and down business…up one big rolling hill and down the other. There always seemed to be a few runty trees in each bottom, and Morgan watched Bitter, Ezra and Ethan break dry limbs from the trees and pick up dead wood where they could find it. When they each had an armful, they loped their mounts back to the wagon and stashed the wood in what was sort of a canvas hammock hung under the wagon box. The arrangement was intended to keep the wood dry in a rainstorm. And it kept the dirty wood out of the wagon box.

On one downhill stretch, feet braced against the front of the wagon box, Mikey said, "You never showed us what you got in the brown paper."

"Yes, I didn't. But I'll show you tonight. Okay?"

"Okay." he said. "Can I get out and walk? This wagon is getting my prosterrier sore."

"Can you keep up?"

"Uh-huh."

Morgan pulled the wagon to a stop and let Mikey climb down. She looked at his bare feet and shook her head. "Don't step on any horse apples, or I won't let you back in the wagon."

She looked back through the wagon top and waved at Ruth Shipley. The four Shipley mules were looking fresh and strong.

I think we can meet John's goal of twenty-five miles each day, she thought, *but we'll have to have some rest days, too…to do washing, air bedding and rest the animals. And us as well.*

Once the Bitter and Shipley wagons crossed the Big Blue River, they followed the deep rutted Oregon Trail parallel to the Little Blue in a roughly west to northwest direction. And except for a dry stretch of about twenty-five miles from the Little Blue to the Platte River, each evening camp provided plenty of water and forage for the animals, firewood for cooking, and evening skeeters for swatting.

Weary but entirely satisfied with the day's progress, Bitter led his party about a half-mile from the wagon road to a camp site on a grassy bank of the Little Blue. The draft animals were unhitched and allowed to find water and graze where they chose, and the riding stock was unsaddled.

Rockford found himself a narrow sandy beach to roll on and ease the itches while Lucifer watched the unseemly display with apparent disgust before plodding up the small stream to find shade and new grass. A rejuvenated Misery trailed along behind.

Harness and collars were hung on limbs to dry before sunset… and to be taken down and stowed in the wagons at night to keep gnawing squirrels, porcupines, and other salt seekers from chewing gaps in the sweat impregnated leather.

Bedding was laid out and inspected for chiggers, ticks, spiders and snakes. Morgan decided the next rest day would see a thorough cleaning of their bedding.

Ethan, Mikey and Davey gathered dried limbs from under the willow and cottonwood trees for the evening cook fire, stole a handful of dried apples from the apple barrel, and headed down the path alongside the stream. "Come on," Ethan said to the two smaller boys. "I want to see the creek, see what kind of fishing we got."

Ruth Shipley hollered, "You boys be careful now. Davey can't swim."

"I'll watch him," Ethan said.

The small procession, a big red hound, a smaller black-and-white mutt, and three boys, herded Morgan's memories in the direction of an earlier, innocent time when she and Harley had wandered the hills behind the Eagen farm, a time of finding a honey tree, of trying to find the cave the adults talked about, of picking blackberries and taking the haul back to Mama Eagen in a lard tin.

And a time of watching her mother's illness take her away from her children

Morgan had some glimmer of understanding when Harley felt the pull and early-on-excitement of the war. But she still resented her father's decision to enlist in the Union Army. Mainly she resented the fact he wasn't there to help when Mama Eagen had sickened and died from the flux.

Grandpa Crawford, Mama's father was there, but he was too grieving and too frail himself to pay much attention to Morgan. If Eunice and the ladies from church hadn't come and helped with the burial, Eunice holding her while she cried, Morgan was certain her heart would have broken.

And then Grandpa Crawford simply sat down in his rocker on the front porch, went to sleep and died. Morgan wondered later if he died of a broken heart when his darling daughter had left so young in life.

Eunice helped that time, too. But Morgan was too numb to feel the loss. They buried Grandpa alongside his daughter, next to the two small crosses. One read, "Eloise, Baby Girl." The other read, "Andrew, Baby Boy." Morgan wondered from time to time as she was growing up what her life might have been if Eloise and Andrew had lived.

Morgan was nine before she asked her mother why the babies had died. The only answer was, "I don't want to talk about it." Grandpa Crawford would say no more than it was God's will.

She sensed their grief and never asked again, but in a corner of her mind she also resented their reticence. When she asked Eunice what she knew, Eunice simply said, "Still born. Some people think it is God's judgment when a child is stillborn. But that's nonsense. Look at you and Harley. Both healthy as horses. If your mama was being punished for her sins, neither one of you would have lived."

The coo of a Mourning Dove and the first cool evening breeze shook Morgan loose from her memories. Using the tailgate for her kitchen counter, she unrolled the salted fish filets, sniffed, and decided the meat was still fresh enough to eat.

12

Gallopers

NOON OF DAY THREE FROM the Big Blue found the two-wagon caravan perched on a grassy hilltop. The travelers ate lunch while the animals rested and cropped grass. John Bitter ground hitched Rockford and scanned the hilltops with his field glasses, blaming unfamiliar territory for his uneasy feelings, but past experience taught him not to ignore his hunches. *Something's brewing*, he thought.

The three boys wolfed down their lunch and sped off to investigate the hillside, cautioned by Ruth and Morgan not to go far.

"My goodness," sighed Morgan, "to have that kind of energy after traveling all morning. They'll still be running circles around us by nightfall."

Ruth smiled and said, "Girl, don't you remember bein' a child? Why goin' slow was akin to dyin'."

"Oh, I know," Morgan said, "But these long days use up a lot of my energy. I'm not fussing. I just get to thinking about the long trip ahead of us, and I have to admit I'm amazed to find us all plodding along the trail to Oregon. It's unreal somehow. And a bit scary."

Bitter interrupted the conversation between the two women. "Riders coming," he said, and pointed back the way they had come that morning.

Bitter found the riders in his field glasses. "Cavalry," he said. "Better get the boys back to the wagons. And get them inside."

Dressed in Union blue, two riders on lather-streaked horses, leaned forward in their saddles, urging the laboring mounts to more speed. The bald truth for their urgency, a dozen galloping horses ridden by Cheyenne warriors broke over the crest of the big rolling hill the troopers crossed seconds before.

Bitter gathered Rockford's reins and swung into the saddle. He shucked the Henry rifle from the saddle scabbard, hammered his heels on Rockford's ribs and put him into a dead run in the direction of the troopers. He yelled over his shoulder to Ezra, "Gather the boys! I'll be right back."

As the two gallopers rode up out of the draw, Bitter yelled, "Keep comin', boys! Keep comin'!"

Not fifteen seconds later, a boiling, yipping mass of Indians rode up over the brow of the hill and into sight. Bitter pulled Rockford to a stop, lifted the Henry to his shoulder and shot past the galloping troopers. A big bay horse went down. He jacked another round into the chamber, fired again, and then slammed shot after shot at the Indians. The startled Indians pulled their animals to a sliding halt just as the blast of Ezra's big Sharps rolled across the hillsides.

A tall, handsome Indian was blown backwards off his horse and into the next life.

The two troopers slid their mounts to a stop beside Rockford, turned to face the Indians and fired their carbines. No horses or Indians went down, but Bitter saw one of the Indians flinch and touch his head. *Close enough to make him wonder*, he decided.

"Man, are we glad to see you, Captain Bitter," Corporal O'Grady panted as he reloaded his carbine. "I figured our goose was cooked."

"You aren't out of it yet." Bitter pointed in the direction of the Indians as the survivors split into two groups, obviously intent on surrounding the wagons.

The big Sharps fired again and a horse collapsed from under one of the Indians. The Indians halted their horses and one shouted something none of the English speakers understood.

"I think that'll do it for now," Bitter said. He watched two young warriors jump down from their horses and toss the body of Ezra's dead Indian on the back of another horse. The warrior Ezra put afoot caught the arm of another rider and swung up behind his friend. With two horses carrying double, the raiders shouted defiance, a note of frustration in their taunts, and rode over the crest of the hill and out of sight.

Bitter shook his head. "I didn't think I'd see you two again, O'Grady. What are you and Private Hackett doing out here?"

"Lookin' for you. We got word a band of Cheyenne, the ones chasing us I'm thinking, was working the road. So Sergeant Callaghan sent us ahead to warn you. Sergeant Callaghan also suggested we fort up and wait for him and the supply train."

"How far behind is he?"

"A day…day and half maybe. If he doesn't have trouble he should be here by tomorrow evening."

Bitter swung down and said, "Let's walk and cool your mounts. They look just about used up."

"They are," Hackett said and stepped out of the saddle. "We started with two horses each. These are the fresh pair. I imagine the Indians got the other two. They were just plumb worn out."

He patted the sweat-stained neck of his steel-gray gelding and shook his head. "I thought Old Blue was going down about when you showed up. He was laboring some, game but tired. Sure glad we caught up with you."

"Tell me that when the freight wagons and Sergeant Callaghan get here. I'm thinking the Indians will be back. So the question is who gets here first."

"I reckon that's true," Corporal O'Grady said, "but you'll be safer forted up than on the open road.'

Bitter looked around at the bare, grassy hillsides and shook his head. "We need to look for a stronger place than this."

"I don't know. Who ever was shooting that rifle knows what he is doing."

"That would be Ezra Shipley. He owns the second wagon. He and his wife Ruth and little boy Davey joined with us at the Big Blue crossing. I had some doubts about that at first, but I think those two four hundred yard shots blew my doubts away."

Corporal O'Grady pointed at the thin line of willow and cottonwood trees marking the course of the Little Blue River. "If we find a deep hole we can back up to, then we'd only have to defend three sides. And the timber might keep those bastards from making a massed charge. Make 'em fight on foot, and they don't like that kind of fighting. They're good at it, make no mistake, but if it can't be done a horseback, they might lose interest."

"Let's hope so," Bitter said.

Three little boys climbed down from the rear of the Bitter wagon, eyes big at the sight of the two troopers and the lather flecked horses. Davey nudged Ethan and said, "Your daddy saved those men."

Ethan didn't correct his use of the word "daddy," but he added, "Yep, he did, and it was your daddy that knocked that Indian off his horse."

The dogs barked until Ezra shushed them. Ruth and Morgan each laid pistols on wagon seats and each woman instinctively smoothed and patted hair in place.

Ezra held his big Sharps in the crook of his left elbow and watched the three lean men walk the horses to the wagon. He watched Bitter and thought, *He may not be a soldier boy any more, but he still be a soldier at heart.*

Bitter pointed to the horses led by O'Grady and Hackett and said, "Ethan, you and the boys walk these horses until they're cooled down. And then give them each a half bucket of water. No more than a half for now. Okay?"

"Are the Indians gone, Mister Bitter?" Ethan asked.

Bitter nodded and said, "Yep."

"For good?" Mikey asked.

"I don't know that. Truth is I think they'll be back. Their pride is hurt. But we'll be okay. Sergeant Callaghan's troop and all those teamsters will be along pretty soon."

The boys led the horses out a ways on the wagon road, and then Bitter introduced Ezra Shipley to Liam O'Grady and Paul Hackett, warily appraising the reaction of the southern-bred O'Grady to the Shipley's. All that earned was a heartfelt "thanks" from the two troopers. O'Grady shook hands and said, "I'm grateful. You sure can shoot, Mister Shipley."

Ezra nearly blushed at the praise, but all he said was, "You better call me Ezra."

Bitter let his breath out and moved O'Grady up another notch on the John Bitter scale of approval.

"And these two fine ladies," Bitter said, "are Morgan Bitter and Ruth Shipley. Don't take these ladies too lightly. Notice the pistols."

O'Grady grinned and said, "Nice to see you again, Missus Bitter. And nice to meet you as well, Missus Shipley."

When Bitter explained what was going on and about O'Grady's suggestion they fort up down on the creek, Ezra frowned and said, "I allow as to how I like open ground better for shooting."

O'Grady nodded and said, "I can understand that, but if they can hit us from four sides at once, that pretty well takes away your advantage. We can leave one open lane for long range shooting. That will be yours to take care of. We'll use the trees on either side to break up any horseback charge from those directions. And we'll have the women guard the back door. The river will give them some help if we can find a deep hole to back up to. And we can picket the animals in the trees."

Ezra nodded. "Okay. That might be the best we can do." He looked at O'Grady and asked, "You a praying man?"

O'Grady grinned, his blue eyes amused. "Yes…every time I get into a gun fight, I pray that I'm better than the other guy."

"Don't you belittle prayer," Ruth Shipley said and shook her finger at him.

O'Grady smiled. "No ma'am, I surely don't. My mama was a devout woman who raised me in the church. I'll have you know, I was once an altar boy."

"That's good, Mister O'Grady, because I think we'll need the Good Lord on our side when it comes time to chastise our brother heathens."

"I'm all in favor of chastising the heathens," O'Grady said with a broad smile. He pointed at the Sharps and asked Ezra, "How fast can you shoot and load?"

"If I take my time and make sure I hit what I'm aiming at, it takes me a good eight seconds between shots."

O'Grady nodded and said, "That'll do."

13
Forted Up

BITTER SCOUTED THE LITTLE BLUE River, a creek in reality, the big red hound keeping pace with Rockford, until he found a deep hole and a bank with a three foot drop off on the side he wanted for defense.

"This'll have to do," he said to no one in particular. He turned Rockford back toward the wagons on the hilltop and cantered up the slope.

"Found it. We got ourselves a big cottonwood log in back and a deep hole. We can climb a tree and keep watch for the Indians."

The draft animals were unhitched, watered and then herded into a corral made of ropes strung from tree to tree in a rough circle. Morgan helped Ethan unsaddle Lucifer and then simply turned him loose.

"You aren't gonna tie them up?" Hackett asked and pointed to the big mule and the old mare plodding through the trees to the little river.

"He won't stand for it, and she follows whereever he goes," Morgan said. "And he's as good as a watch dog. I pity anyone who tries to sneak up on us from that direction."

The men slipped cinch straps and piled saddles in against the base of the biggest cottonwood, ready to hand if needed. Bridles were traded for hackamores and the horses tied to a picket line strung between two trees.

Ezra and Bitter filled feed bags with cracked corn while O'Grady and Hackett carried buckets of water for the riding stock.

Manhandled into a "v," the wagons pointed like a spear out into the open prairie. Ezra and Bitter built a barrier of barrels and boxes in the gap between the wagons. When they were satisfied they had done what could be done, Ezra leaned his big Sharps rifle against the wagon box. He looked at Bitter with raised eyebrows and then shook his head.

"We'll get by, Ezra," Bitter said quietly.

The boys were set to gathering firewood, and Morgan said, "Might as well fix a good meal. The Indians already know where we are."

Bitter pointed to a big limb on the tallest cottonwood, a limb about twelve feet off the ground, and asked Ethan, "Think you can climb to that first big limb?"

Ethan studied the tree and nodded. "If you boost me, I can make it the rest of the way."

"Okay. I'll boost and you climb. Then I'm going to toss you a rope. We'll run a double line for climbing. That way we can shuck our rope off the tree when we leave."

High places, bluffs, cliffs, high bridges, and rooftops gave John Bitter the shivers. He didn't know why, but there it was. He could choke down his fear and do what needed doing, but he knew he would never like being very far off the ground.

He boosted Ethan up on his shoulders and said, "Stand on my shoulders and see if you can reach that first limb."

"Can't reach it," Ethan said.

"He's about a foot short of the limb," O'Grady said.

"Hand him the rope. If he can toss that over the limb, maybe he can get a start."

Ethan doubled the rope and pushed the looped end up and over the limb. "Got it," he said and pulled himself up on the first limb.

After that it was a simple matter of using smaller limbs like ladder rungs and pulling the rope up behind him.

Mikey said, "Be careful, Brother."

"Yes," Morgan echoed, "be careful."

Ethan straddled the big limb and dropped the double line on each side of it. "What can you see from up there?" Bitter asked.

"Two Indians."

That bit of information put eyes in motion and heads swiveling. Private Hackett unsnapped the flap on his holster and O'Grady walked to the carbine leaning against the backside of the big cottonwood.

"Where?" Bitter asked.

"Across the road…back where we came from."

"What are they doing?"

"Just layin' in the grass lookin' at us."

"Do you see any horses?" O'Grady asked.

"Nope. But there's a dip in the ground…right behind them. Horses could be there I guess."

"Okay. Get down out of that tree," Bitter ordered.

"They're standing up, Mister Bitter. One's old…got gray hair, and one's a boy…about as big as me."

"There they are, John," Ezra said looking over the barricade and pointing out to the prairie with the barrel of his Sharps.

Bitter focused the field glasses and studied the pair. "Old guy and a kid…look kinda rough. I don't see any weapons, and I don't think they've been eating regular."

Bitter handed the field glasses to O'Grady and said, "Take a look."

O'Grady fiddled with the focus and then pulled in a clear picture of an old man wearing a worn leather shirt and dirty canvas britches with big holes in the knees. The old man pushed himself upright with the help of a willow staff and staggered sideways until he caught his balance. Then he raised his hands in a gesture of surrender and started a limping shuffle towards the wagons.

"He needs help, John. He looks like he's going to fall down," Morgan said.

Through the field glasses O'Grady could see the boy was underfed and barefoot.

"Well, here they come," O'Grady said and handed the field glasses to Bitter. "Rough doesn't even come close. I'd say they're starved plumb down to gristle and bone."

Bitter hollered up to Ethan, "Look around and make sure you can't see any others before you come down."

"Yessir." Ethan scanned the hillsides and then looked behind the tree in the direction of the Little Blue. "I don't see a thing, Mister Bitter."

"Okay. Come on down, Ethan."

Ethan slid down the rope and Bitter caught him a foot short of the ground. "Good job," he said, and eased him on down.

The old man and the skinny boy, each with long hair packing what looked to be a half bale of grass and straw, crossed the wagon road and walked slowly down the slope to the wagon. The old man's dark eyes flitted from face to face and then settled on Ruth. He thought he could see a hint of compassion in her eyes, and he felt the need to have someone in this party of travelers sympathetic to him and the boy.

The smell of frying bacon sent a rumble through the old man's stomach, and the little boy, trembling slightly from hunger and fear, stumbled and nearly fell. That was too much for Ruth and Morgan who both walked out from behind the barrier. Each took an arm and helped the shivering boy shuffle to the fire. Morgan pointed to a small keg serving as a stool, and turned to the bacon sizzling and popping in the skillet.

Ruth hurried to the Shipley wagon and brought a tin cup and the milk crock back to the fire. Mikey, Ethan and Davey edged up in open curiosity and watched the boy hungrily drink the cool milk.

Ethan asked, "What's you name?"

They were all startled when he said in clear English, "Thomas."

The old Indian stumbled on past the men who were still holding weapons and wondering what the dickens was going on. He held out his hand for the milk cup and motioned to Ruth in imitation of pouring. She nodded and poured more milk from the crock.

O'Grady said, "I'd go easy on that, Missus Shipley, 'cause they ain't been eatin' much. Give a whole bunch of food and they'll get sick."

Morgan pointed at John and said, "Will you please get another keg for the old man to sit on. I'll see about feeding them."

Ethan watched in curiosity at his first up-close glimpse of wild Indians. When Thomas looked up at him, Ethan was startled by Thomas's blue eyes.

Ethan tugged at Bitter's sleeve and whispered, "I didn't know Indians had blue eyes."

"They don't," Bitter answered, "not that I know of.

He knelt down and looked at the bedraggled boy and said, "You aren't Indian, are you."

Thomas shook his head. "Indians killed my folks three years ago. I was seven. Old Owl took me in. He was a great medicine man, but when the favorite wife of Chief Wild Horse took sick a few weeks back, Owl couldn't save her. So Wild Horse burned everything Owl owned, killed Owl's horses and beat on us until we left camp.

"Owl said we would hide and wait until another white wagon came down the trail. We watched the fight and saw the wild ones ride off."

Thomas stopped talking long enough to chew hungrily on a strip of hot bacon, lick his fingers and reach for more.

"When Owl saw you getting set for another fight, he told me it was time for me to be white again. And he said you all should take your wagons and run back toward the rising sun until you find the soldiers."

"Why should we do that?"

Thomas said something to Owl that none of the travelers could understand. Owl took another biscuit and a piece of bacon from Morgan's plate and stuffed his mouth, chewed rapidly, and washed it all down with a cup of cool milk.

He wiped the grease from his fingers on his patched, dirty canvas pants and squatted down. With a twig he scratched a picture in a bare piece of ground.

First old Owl drew twelve parallel scratches in the earth. He pointed at Ezra and grinned. "Boom," he said and rubbed out one of the lines.

Then he drew a big arc out and away from the eleven scratches. He held up five fingers on his left hand counted them mutely with his right forefinger. He made a scratch at the end of the arc in the dirt and then held up five fingers again and made another scratch in the earth. He repeated the ritual nine times and made nine scratches in the earth. He pointed at the first eleven scratches and then at the nine scratches at the end of the arc.

Owl said something to Thomas, and Thomas shook his head and looked up at Bitter, the man he intuitively identified as the leader of the travelers. Thomas pointed to the nine lines in the earth and said, "Owl says that is how many men Wild Horse will bring back."

Bitter frowned and shook his head. Ezra looked at him and said, "I don't know if we can hold off that many. I think the old man is telling us this Wild Horse fella is bringing about forty five men back with him. Is that how you read it?"

Bitter nodded. "I don't know if it's forty-five or fifty-six, but it's a bunch. Okay, Thomas. What I can't figure is why he would take you to us if he thought we were all going to get killed."

Thomas turned to Owl who was stuffing his mouth with another butter lathered biscuit and another strip of bacon. Thomas didn't say anything until Owl chewed and swallowed the big gob of food. In English Thomas said to Owl, "Did you hear him?"

Owl nodded and then said in crisp Missionary School English. "Yes, Thomas. The answer to the problem is for you pilgrims to wait until dark, hitch the teams to the wagons and run like hell back in the direction of the army patrol headed this way.

"You'll have a nearly full moon and good light. Wild Horse will spend the night strutting and bragging about what a great warrior he is. Then he'll sleep until the sun comes up. By that time you will be long gone.

"If you are lucky, he'll think you've gone west…making a run for Fort Kearney. If you aren't, you'll still have a better chance than if you stay here."

"What will you do?" Ezra asked.

"I think Wild Horse will get himself killed tomorrow or the next day, and then I'll go back to my people and be a medicine man again. When Thomas and I got kicked out, I told Wild Horse he would die soon. And when he does, I'll be a big man among the people again. At heart, I'm a lazy man who likes to be fed on the best cuts of meat…and to have my bed kept warm by soft young women."

"You could go with us."

Owl laughed and said, "And get killed? Wild Horse can kick me out, but he's afraid to kill me. If I run with you, he won't be afraid any more."

Morgan asked, "Where did you learn to speak such good English."

Owl grinned. "I was Cherokee once upon a time. We grew up speaking English, learning to read and write. Hell, we even had slaves. But I couldn't stand to be pushed around, my property stolen, or sent to Godforsaken places because the Whites wanted what I had. Or because they were afraid of us Indians. I think there was just too much bad history between us and the whites for us to be peaceful neighbors.

"So I remade myself and became a Cheyenne. With the little science I know, and with some knowledge of medicine, it wasn't hard to become a great medicine man. I just never figured on getting old," he added with a laugh.

He looked at John Bitter with the hint of a smile on his dirty, wrinkled face and said, "You wouldn't have any vile liquor would you?"

"You found your calling all right," Bitter said, but he couldn't keep from smiling. He walked to the back of the wagon and rummaged a small earthen jug from under the load. He banged a metal cup against his pant leg to remove any trespassing dust and carried both back to the fire.

"I'm thinking we owe you," Bitter said, and then poured a good two inches of strong amber liquid in the cup.

14

Wagon Road Run

ETHAN SHIVERED AT THE CHILL air drifting quietly up the Little Blue River. He kneed Lucifer and reined him up beside the wagon. "Mikey," he said, "I need my canvas jacket. Can you get it for me?"

Mikey, who wasn't prone to wasting words, turned and climbed over the back the wagon seat he shared with Thomas and Morgan. He pulled Ethan's jacket free from the tangled coats and shirts, and crawled back to the wagon seat.

"Here, Brother," he said, and handed the coat to Ethan.

Thomas smelled a bit better since his bath in the Little Blue… and his first encounter with a bar of lye soap in several years.

Ruth, who was a better barber than Morgan, did the honors and cut the long strands of Thomas's hair away from his head. "There," she said, "now you be a white boy again."

Dressed in a pair of Ethan's pants and a long-sleeved shirt, he looked the part of an immigrant traveler.

Old Owl watched the moon peek over a hilltop and said to John Bitter, "Good luck, white man. You better get going. Just before sunrise, I'll build a big fire to make them think you are still here in the trees. That will buy you a little more time."

He said, "I thank you," and held up the burlap sack that carried a big chunk of bacon, dried biscuits, a small cook pot, some dried apples, and a packet of roasted Arbuckle. The matched pair of cigars Ezra had given him rode companion to a dozen Lucifer's in the pocket of his new blue shirt, the one Morgan had given him. Morgan's generosity left Bitter with just one spare shirt, a fact he noted with a shrug. *How much is a man's life worth after all?*

But he balked when Owl suggested he might like to have one of Bitter's pistols. "No…I'm going to need all the fire power I can get."

Owl shrugged and said, "It was worth a try. How about a good knife instead?"

Without a word, Bitter handed the old man a pocket knife.

"How does it work?" Owl asked.

Bitter opened the blade and Owl said, "Ah, I understand."

As the wagons pulled out from the trees and headed for the wagon road, Owl called, "Goodbye, Thomas. Remember Owl from time to time. And don't forget what I taught you."

Bitter brought up the rear, Hackett rode point, and O'Grady and Ezra took position on opposite sides of the wagons as outriders…posted about one-hundred-fifty yards from the wagons. Bitter had given orders to Ethan to keep Lucifer close to the wagons.

Owl cautioned them to go slowly and quietly until they were over the top of the first big hill, and then to hurry. "Wagons are slower than Indian horses," he said.

Ezra chuckled and said, "You sure know how to encourage a man."

They covered five miles back toward Sergeant Callaghan's supply train before Bitter decided the Indians really were going to wait until daylight to attack his party.

He put Rockford into a lope out to O'Grady. As the two horses walked quietly through the prairie grass, Bitter asked, "You think Hackett's blue horse is rested enough to make another run?"

"What you got in mind?"

"I'd like to send him on ahead. Let Callaghan know what we ran into and maybe hurry him in this direction. We might just hook up before the Indians hit us."

"I was wondering about doing the same thing, myself," O'Grady said. "I'll get him moving that way."

Bitter judged it to be midnight when he called for a halt to water the animals and to let riders rest after a long pull up to the crest of another steep hill. In the distance he thought he saw firelight and hoped it marked Sergeant Callaghan's camp. Rusty was limping, so Bitter leaned down and lifted the big dog up in front of the saddle. He rode to the back of the wagon and set Rusty behind the wagon seat. He said quietly, "Rusty's going to ride a while." An under-sized arm reached out and pulled Rusty under the covers. Bitter was too tired to protest.

The moon was headed for the western horizon when Sergeant Callaghan led a dozen mounted troopers to the Bitter-Shipley party.

O'Grady trotted his horse around the wagons and pulled to a halt in front of Sergeant Callaghan. He saluted and said, "Captain Bitter is scouting our back trail, Sarge, but we haven't seen any Indians yet."

The moon gave enough light for Callaghan to see that the mules pulling the wagons were tired to the bone, and the women driving the wagons looked weary enough to sleep sitting up. A little boy riding a big mule looked to be asleep in the saddle.

Morgan took the stop as a chance to stretch her legs and let her backsides rest from the jouncing the wagon doled out in pun-ishment for night travel. As she stepped down, Mikey whispered, "What's going on?"

"We just met up with Sergeant Callaghan's troopers. I'm going to find out what happens next."

She walked to the Shipley wagon just as Callaghan rode up.

"Howdy, Missus Bitter. I see you have traveling companions." Without waiting for a reply he added, "We're set up about three miles back. Just ease on up the road. The cook will have coffee on and food waiting."

"That sounds good, Sergeant," Ezra said as he pulled his horse to a stop by his wagon.

"And who are you?" Callaghan asked.

"I'm Ezra Shipley. Traveling with John Bitter to Oregon. We be glad to see you soldier boys. Mister Bitter has this fool notion of trying to lead the Indians away from the wagons. Said his Rockford horse could outrun anything on four legs…except maybe an antelope. Said he'd catch up later."

"I heard from Private Hackett there were too many Indians to fight, even if you forted up."

Callaghan could see Ezra nod. "An old Indian told us we were facing about forty- five braves. That just seemed like too many for us to handle."

Callaghan nodded. "You were right. But, instead of leading the Indians away, I'm thinking it would be a good idea if he let the Indians chase him up to us. With the teamsters, we number about twenty good fighting men. And we might have a little surprise waiting when they get here."

Ezra nodded. "I think you might have something. I'll ride back and help Mister Bitter, sort of let him know what you have in mind."

"We're set up about three miles back down the road. You get the Indians to follow and we'll do the rest."

Bitter wanted a cigarette and knew it wasn't smart. So he ignored the urge to smoke and dismounted to let Rockford graze while he sat in the grass and carefully glassed the hills to the west. There was enough bright moonlight, he thought, to spot any movement along the road.

He had a rough plan in mind, if you considered making it up as you went along a plan. Basically he planned to see if he could lure the Indians away from the wagons.

A low whistle brought Rockford's head up. He stared east down the dusty wagon road. Bitter focused his field glasses on a dark, long legged horse moving in the smooth gait of a Tennessee Walker.

What is Ezra doing back here?

Rockford nickered softly and Bitter cussed him as a no-account idiot that knew better. "Knock that off," he said quietly but intently. Rockford swung his head to look at Bitter and then went back to staring at the horse and rider coming up behind them.

Bitter said quietly, "Come on in, Ezra. I'm not going to shoot you."

Ezra swung down and asked softly, "Anything?"

"Nothing, yet. Why did you leave the wagons?"

"The women and kids are safe with your cavalry friends. Sergeant Callaghan…I think that's his name…says we should have the Indians chase us another four miles right up the road and into the boys in blue. Says he'll have a surprise waiting for them."

Bitter nodded. "How many men does he have?"

"I heard the number twenty used."

Bitter smiled and said, "Better than four…six if you count Morgan and Ruth. I'm glad old Owl showed up. I think he saved our lives."

Ezra held his Railroad watch to the moon and scrunched his face trying to make out the hands on the watch. "I think it's about three hours to daylight. Why don't you get some rest? I'll wake you in a couple of hours."

"What about you?"

"I learned to sleep in the saddle a long time ago. I'm good for now."

Without a word, Bitter pulled the stopper from his wool covered canteen and took a long drink of water before he pushed the stopper back and hung the canteen on the saddle horn. Revolver in hand, he crawled into a nest of tall prairie grass. The noise of two horses cropping grass was soft music in his ears, and he was asleep in minutes.

The sun was making shadows on the west face of the big hill occupied by John Bitter and Ezra Shipley before the Indians rode over the crest of a far hill and into the sunlight.

Ezra nudged Bitter's boot with his foot and said, "John, you best be awake now. Our Indian friends are headed this way."

Bitter pushed himself to his knees and stood up. "Where?"

Ezra handed him the field glasses and pointed west.

Bitter rubbed the sleep from his eyes and then looked through the field glasses at the long line of Indian horses crossing the skyline.

"Looks like a whole lot more than forty-five," Bitter said.

"I counted a couple more than fifty horses. That's a lot of fighting men."

"It is. You don't know if Callaghan brought that big Gatling along, do you?"

"No…all he said was he'd have a surprise waiting for 'em."

"Okay. How do you want to do this? What if we wait until they are about three or four hundred yards off. Then you knock one off his horse. I'll fire a shot with my pistol and if that doesn't discourage them, we run like hell for the next hump and do it all over again?"

Ezra walked over to his horse and pulled a forked willow limb about two feet long from a saddlebag and then slid his Sharps from the scabbard. He drove the limb in the middle of the road with the butt of his Sharps, and then laid down in a prone shooter's position, the barrel of the rifle resting in the fork.

"I don't suppose you'd want to ride out and set a four-hundred-yard marker, Mister Bitter."

"No…I don't think I'll do that. What I will do is picture a line of Johnny Rebs riding like hell right at me. I think I can remember what that looks like at four hundred yards."

"Okay. Now…you hold the reins of those horses so they don't spook when Old Thunder touches off. I don't want them leaving us stranded and at the mercy of the wild savages."

Even though he was expecting the shot, the roar of the big Sharps still made Bitter flinch a little. But that was nothing in comparison to the flinch of the Indian punched backwards off his trotting horse and under the hooves of the horses behind him.

"I sure hate killing people," Ezra said as he pulled his forked stick from the ground and hauled himself into the saddle.

Bitter watched the Indians mill about while two men pulled their dead companion from the ground and slung him face down across his horse.

Bitter pointed his revolver at the mass of Indians and pulled the trigger. He gave a holler and cussed the Indians in a loud voice.

Suddenly about twenty Indians bolted horses and rode hard at Bitter and Shipley.

"I think you irritated them some, Mister Shipley," Bitter said as they turned their horses back down the wagon road in the direction of Sergeant Callaghan and his troopers.

The Indian horses gained a good one hundred yards before Ezra and Bitter pulled their mounts to a stop on top of the next big hill. Bitter figured he had a chance of hitting the Indians at that range with his Henry. Three quick shots were answered by rifle shots from the Indians, wild punch-a-hole-in-the-sky shots. Bitter thought he saw one Indian grab his side and drop out of the chase.

The next three miles saw the fresher Indian horses gaining, but Ezra and Bitter continued to stop and pepper the hard riding band each time they reached the crest of another hill. And the Indians continued to waste ammunition, vainly trying to knock down a man or a horse.

At the top of the next hill, Bitter and Ezra rode into the waiting line of Callaghan's troopers. They were positioned at the military crest, just below the skyline on the back side of the hill. Callaghan was mounted to give him a better look at the chosen battlefield.

Bitter and Ezra wheeled their horses to face the Indians and fired again, but instead of running, they stood their ground. Bitter shook his fist at the sky and yelled, "Come and get it, you heathen sonsabitches!"

The hotheads in the bunch, led by a tall Indian on a painted horse yipped and kicked their horses to greater effort, confident they had ridden the white men to ground.

"Now!" Callaghan said. The line of troopers pushed forward, the Gatling in the middle of a line about fifty yards long.

"Wait, wait," Callaghan said, and when the Indians were within seventy-five yards of the line, he yelled, "Fire."

The first volley knocked the tall Indian off his painted horse, and wounded three others who might or might not survive. Five horses went down, and then the Gatling opened up to knock horses and men to the ground. All in all, twelve Indians would die in the first twenty seconds of fire from the Gatling.

The survivors gamely returned fire and one trooper went spinning backwards to fall in the grass. Four young warriors tried to sweep wide and get to the wagons behind the troopers. Bitter put Rockford into a gallop and pulled a pistol from the saddle holster. One young man tried to club Bitter with an empty rifle, only to be punched from his horse by a .44-caliber ball. Another went rolling when Rockford knocked his horse down, and at the sight of Ezra and Callaghan charging in from the top of the hill, the two survivors chose to cut and run. His dander up, Bitter fired until his pistol was empty. He thought he saw one of the horses flinch after his fourth shot, but it kept galloping down the hill in the direction of the main body of Indians.

Callaghan ran his horse back to the line of troopers. The men working the Gatling were still firing even though the hard riding Indians were nearly a half-mile away.

"Cease fire," Callaghan said. "You're just wasting ammunition."

Corporal O'Grady reported one casualty, Private George Hart, shot through the head. "And one civilian casualty," he added, "shot in his upper left thigh," and pointed at John Bitter.

John looked at his thigh in surprise and saw a streak of blood flowing through a small hole in his last good pair of britches. "Shit," was all he could think to say.

Ezra asked Sergeant Callaghan, "Do you have a surgeon?"

Callaghan shook his head. "No. We thought we'd be strong enough to discourage renegades and wild Indians from trying us."

"Well, in that case," Ezra said to Bitter, "let's get you back to our wagons and let me take a look at that leg."

Sergeant Callaghan ordered Corporal O'Grady to have the men clean their weapons and report on the remaining ammunition.

"Corporal Hackett," Callaghan added, startling Hackett with the news of his promotion to the rank of Corporal, "you assist Corporal O'Grady, and when that's done, form a detail to scrounge the battlefield for weapons and anything else of value, including anything that might tell us which band of wild heathens tried to rub us out."

Four small faces, eyes big with fear and wonder, and a small black-and-white mutt peeked out from behind a canvas flap on the Shipley wagon, stowed there by Ruth Shipley and Morgan Bitter during the fight. Ezra and Bitter rode their horses to the covered wagons, semi-protected by two rows of freight wagons, three to a row on each side. Rusty and Corky barked in greeting, and Morgan said, "Good Lord, John. You've ruined another pair of pants, haven't you."

In spite of himself, Bitter grinned. "I think I need some iron pants."

"Again?" Ezra asked.

Ethan said, "Yep. He almost ruined his knee last time, jumping off the train. It was moving when he did." There was a note of pride in his voice as he made the report.

"You shot, Mister Bitter?" Mikey asked.

Bitter nodded, wondering why the wound didn't hurt more, and why he hadn't noticed it before now. "Guess so," he said.

Ezra dismounted and helped Bitter from the saddle. Bitter said, "I don't think I'm hurt too bad," just before his knees hit the ground.

15
Owl's Prophecy

THE BURNING STING OF RAW whiskey in his open wound brought Bitter's senses back to life. He found himself on a blanket on the ground, stretched out in the shade of the wagon, his boots and pants off, Morgan holding his legs down while Ezra poured strong whisky over a bloody bullet hole. Four little boys hunkered on their heels in a half circle, and two dogs sat on their rear ends, watching in fascination while Ezra ministered to the needs of his new friend, John Bitter.

Morgan had to look away when Ezra used a large sheath knife to slice through the bullet hole in John's leg. "Got to make room to fish that bullet out," Ezra explained.

In spite of his intention to endure the pain in silence, Bitter muttered "Ow," through clinched teeth when Ezra pinched the muscle surrounding the bullet.

"Does that hurt?" Mikey asked.

"Caught me by surprise is all," Bitter said by way of apology.

"I'll bet it did," Ezra said. "Bullet wounds always happen by surprise."

"Did you get it dug out?" Bitter asked,

Ezra held a bloody lead ball up between thumb and forefinger for Bitter's inspection. "Spent bullet, I'm thinking. Only went in an inch…maybe an inch and a half. Stopped short of the bone or you'd really be hurting. You did lose enough blood to put you down, though.

"You'll need lots of beef broth and rest. Ruth is cooking up the broth. Ruth's broth will turn you good as new. You probably shouldn't ride your horse until you heal up. So we'll fix a pallet in the wagon."

"Thank you, Ezra," Bitter said, "What about the Indians?"

"Long gone. That Gatling took the starch out of 'em. The soldiers brought in a wounded Indian. Turns out our new friend Thomas can talk the Indian's talk, so he interpreted for Sergeant Callaghan. The captive told Thomas the tall Indian who got hisself killed in that first charge was Wild Horse."

"So Owl's prophecy came true," Bitter said.

"Looks that way. Owl can go back to being a big man among his people."

"What's Callaghan going to do?"

"He decided to wait until noon, and then move a few miles upriver to make camp. We need water for the animals. We'll have to make up a pallet in your wagon and figure out how to get you up there without breaking any stitches."

"Stitches?"

"It's either that or use a hot iron. What's your pleasure?"

Bitter endured the needle and the tug of linen thread as Ezra's stitches closed the wound. Ezra explained to the boys, "Blood poison is what you need to watch out for. I think as many soldiers died during the war from pussed-up wounds as from bullets.

"I had a surgeon tell me one time he always washed his hands with soap and warm water before he started in, and he always soaked his stitchin' thread in alcohol. We have no alcohol, but this moonshine comes close.

He tied off the first stitch while Morgan wiped the sweat off her husband's forehead. "How you doing, Husband?"

Bitter had to laugh at her question. "Hurts like hell, since you asked, but if this is the worst that ever happens..."

He winced as Ezra tied the second stitch. "Two more and we'll be good," Ezra said.

"Well, get on with it," Bitter growled. He looked up at Morgan. "Did I really pass out?"

"Well…I don't know. You did relax all of a sudden. We had to help you into the shade a bit."

"Yeah. What you mean is I passed out."

She shook her head. "Why pester yourself about it? You lost a lot of blood, and you haven't had much rest since the fight with Peale. Maybe you just need to slow down a bit."

Sergeant Callahan and Corporal O'Grady walked their horses to the wagon in time to watch Ezra tie the last knot.

"Y'all make a nice neat stitch, Ezra," O'Grady said, "although I can't say much for the material you're workin' on."

"I'll get you for that, O'Grady," Bitter said with a hint of a chuckle in his voice.

At noon the animals were harnessed and hitched to wagons, and horses were saddled. Teamsters settled in wagon seats, and little blond-headed Ethan climbed the stirrup on Lucifer's left side to pull himself into the saddle. "You ride close to the wagon, today," Bitter said.

The order of march set by Sergeant Callaghan was three freight wagons in the lead, the wheeled carriage proudly carrying the canvas covered Gatling gun, hitched behind the first freight wagon, ready for use, followed next by the Bitter and Shipley wagons, and finally the last three freight wagons following behind.

Sergeant Callaghan told Corporal O'Grady to set outriders on the flanks of the supply train. "And then you take one of the galvanized Yankees, maybe that skinny old man you know from back when. You and him ride point, and tell those other galvanized Yankees they did real good against the Indians.

"Corporal Hackett, you take that big reb, the one who stepped up first when we had those old boys surrounded in the basin. I want you two watching our back trail.

"We'll bury Private Hart down by the river. He loved to fish as I recall, so that's probably the best we can do for his poor soul."

Callaghan watched his corporals gallop off to put his orders into action and then hollered, "Roll 'em," as he led the eight-wagon train to the Oregon Trail.

Bitter, a cup of Ruth's beef broth in his stomach, spurned the pallet in the wagon. He allowed as how he would ride the wagon seat beside Morgan, his bandaged leg propped on the front of the wagon box in discomfort, the Henry leaned in a corner of the wagon box, and a pistol strapped to his waist. His dignity suffered some when Morgan had to help him pull the last of his undamaged britches over the bulky bandage hiding his wound, but he consoled himself with the idea that his dignity had already been damaged by an Indian bullet.

Ride through three years of the War without a scratch, and then let an uncivilized wild Indian shoot me. Plumb pitiful is what it is. I always figured other people got shot, not me.

Mikey climbed over the back of the wagon seat and squeezed in between them. "The gray mule with the white patch of hair between his eyes is Star. And the other one is Dusty," he announced without preamble.

Bitter grinned and said, "So they finally told you, huh?"

"Yep."

"That makes Rump, Windy, Star and Dusty?" Morgan asked.

"They might change their minds after while," Mikey said, "but that's their names right now. Thomas told me Indians change names as they grow up. So maybe mules do the same thing."

Bitter tickled Mikey in the ribs and said, "You're a little windy, yourself."

"Does Thomas have an Indian name?" Morgan asked. She snapped the long reins and said, "Haw, mules!" as the wagon ahead of her pulled in line on the Oregon Trail.

Mikey nodded. "Magpie is his Indian name. He said I could have an Indian name as soon as we find one that fits."

Ezra trotted his horse up beside the Bitter wagon and asked, pointing to Bitter's leg, "How does it feel?"

Bitter said, "Like a bullet punched a hole in my leg, and like a ham-handed surgeon pulled a hemp rope through my hide."

And then he laughed. "In truth, friend Ezra, I couldn't have asked for a better doctor. I'm lucky you were here. Thank you."

"Getting well will be thanks enough." He hesitated a few seconds before adding, "I'm wondering what we're going to do about Thomas. Any ideas?"

"Does he know his last name?"

"I haven't asked yet. Right now he's riding with Ruth and David and teaching 'em both how to speak Cheyenne. I thought that would give me a chance to talk to you."

"We're blood brothers, you know," Mikey said. "So that makes him family."

"What do you mean, blood brothers, Mikey?" Morgan asked.

"When the Indians were trying to kill us…again…Thomas said not to worry. If the Indians killed all the adults, he would swear Ethan, Davey, and I were his blood brothers. That would keep us safe."

"Pessimistic fellow, our Thomas," Bitter said.

"But smart," Ezra added.

"When we get to Fort Kearney," Bitter said, "I think we're duty bound to talk to the post commander. And I think we have to try and find his relatives. Maybe Mark Anthony can help with that."

"And if we can't?" Morgan asked.

"Three boys are no more trouble than two."

Morgan shook her head, but she grinned and said, "You're probably right."

"I'd raise him myself," Ezra said, "except it would make his a hard life. But I wouldn't mind if we lived nearby and could help out...be part of his family."

Bitter nodded. "I'd like that, Ezra. But first things first."

16

Across the Platte River

THE INDIANS FROM THE WILD Horse band scouted and harassed the column for four days. Random shots kept the teamsters, troopers, and civilian travelers on edge. At night, young bucks whooped and rode thundering tracks around the wagons. But during the day, they were respectful of the Gatling gun and kept their distance. They shouted taunts from hilltops, and fired random shots but never came within range of any rifle except Ezra's Sharps. And he wasn't in the mood to kill any more Indians. "Unless it comes down to it," he said to Bitter.

It was only when Queeny's lead rope came loose from the rear of the Shipley wagon and the cow took off across the prairie in a dead run that any of Wild Horse's warriors closed on the column. One young buck drove his horse straight at the cow and was reaching for her lead rope when a prairie chicken flew up in front of the horse with a great cackle and flutter of wings. That was enough to spook the horse which shied away from the sudden noise and left the young rider airborne a split second before he went plowing through the grass on his nose.

Ezra lowered his rifle and started laughing while he goosed Lucky in the ribs and loped after the free-running Indian horse.

Thomas recognized the young warrior sitting on the ground, spitting bits of grass and rubbing his shoulder. Thomas stood up in the wagon seat and hollered at him in Cheyenne, "Good one, Little Raven. Maybe you should ride the cow."

Little Raven scowled at this white boy who spoke Cheyenne and then said, "Is that you, Magpie?'

"Yes. I'm a white man now."

Ruefully, Little Raven watched Ezra chase the spooked horse, and then he laughed and pushed himself upright. "Yes. It was a good one. Maybe I should change my name to Prairie Chicken."

Ezra caught Little Raven's horse and led it back to him. "Here." he said and handed the reins to the young Indian. Ezra pointed with the barrel of the Sharps to the rolling hills north of the wagon road. "You best get back yonder. And leave my cow alone."

The young warrior jumped astride the bay horse. "Tell the black white man I thank him," he shouted to Thomas as he turned the horse and kicked him into a gallop.

The cow, which wasn't much of a runner anyway, stopped to sniff at some fresh grass and took up the business of grazing in an earnest fashion that might convince any watcher she hadn't been fed for a long time. Ezra caught up the rope and led her back to the wagon.

"Why didn't you shoot that man, Ezra?" Ruth asked.

"Just a young buck havin' some fun, Ruth. No harm done."

Thomas nodded. "His name is Little Raven. He says to thank the black white man."

Ezra shook his head. "Black white man, huh? I guess he would see it that way.

The Indians to the south call black white men buffalo soldiers. I'm no buffalo soldier. No soldier at all anymore."

Ruth looked at her husband and smiled. "I think once a soldier, always a soldier."

Afternoon of the fourth day saw the wagons led by Corporal O'Grady ford the Platte River in sight of the earth works of Fort

Kearney, Nebraska. A squad of mounted troopers trotted out of the main gate and down the bluff to the river, ready to lend a hand if any of the wagons should mire down in the silt-filled river bed.

A long-legged trooper riding a dark brown Morgan-mustang cross met O'Grady midstream. The muddy water lapped at his stirrups.

"Y'all have trouble, Liam? We been watchin' for you for the past few days. I wanted to take a ride and see if y'all were okay, but the Major put the kybosh to that."

O'Grady nodded. "Yep. We had a run in with some Johnny Rebs who stole our Gatling. We got 'er back. In fact we also got ourselves seven galvanized Yankees.

"Then the Wild Horse band jumped us. Must have been fifty or more. Sergeant Callaghan had us hiding behind a big rolling hill while two civilians pestered the Indians and led them right up to the Gatling. Whooeee! Pure damned murder is what it was."

He paused and hollered at the shouting, cursing teamster driving the lead wagon, "Head a little more upstream. Aim at those troopers on the bank, that's where the road is. And keep those mules moving so's you don't bog down."

O'Grady said, "Wagner, I'm plumb out of chaw. You got any?"

Lewis Wagner, O'Grady's longtime friend and another of the galvanized Yankees, handed Liam O'Grady a small block of chewing tobacco, marks deep in the tobacco where Wagner had gnawed a piece with his teeth.

O'Grady held the plug up and wrinkled his nose. "Messy is what you are Wagner, messy." He dug a pen knife from his pants and cut a plug from the clean end before handing the tobacco back to Wagner.

"We loose anybody to the fight?" Wagner asked.

O'Grady popped the tobacco in his mouth and said, "Hart caught one through the skull. Never felt a thing. We buried him back on the Little Blue. Callaghan said when we could we'd send a strong party back and bring his body to the fort."

"Too bad," Lewis Wagner said. "He was a good man."

O'Grady nodded. "He was."

He chewed Wagner's tobacco with satisfaction until he saw the Shipley wagon slip sideways in the current. He pointed and said, "Must have dropped a wheel in a soft spot. Come on, Lewis, let's lend a hand."

Ezra, a worried look on his face, caught Wagner's rope and tied it to the upriver front corner of his wagon. O'Grady ran a loop through the collar on the upriver mule, quickly took a turn around his saddle horn and put his horse to pulling the team. Ezra tied a rope to the upriver back corner of the wagons and put Lucky to straining on the rope.

O'Grady said, "Get 'em moving, ma'am."

Ruth slapped the reins and hollered in a fair imitation of a mule skinner, less the profanity of course, "Go mules, get now. Haw!" The cavalry horses and Ezra's big Lucky horse took up the slack in their ropes, the mules strained in the harness, and then the wagon lurched upright and was free of the sucking mud of the river bed.

"Thanks," Ezra said, as O'Grady and Wagner untied and shook out their ropes.

"Anytime, Mister Shipley, anytime."

Bitter, his sore leg adding to his helpless feeling, watched the riders pull the wagon free, and then said to Morgan, "Keep upriver a bit. We don't want to hit that same hole."

Morgan snapped, "I'm not an idiot, John."

"Oops. Are we testy today?"

She sighed, but she didn't apologize. She said, "I'll just be glad to sleep without worrying about the Indians."

"It is worrisome," Bitter said, "and I'll admit to the same. You know, it was different when all I had to worry about was just me.

During the war I had my scouts to take care of, but that was war, so I did my best and trusted to luck…for all of us.

"And then out of the blue, I have you and boys to worry about. That changed the picture. When one of my scouts caught a bullet, I felt bad, but I didn't feel like it was my fault. In war people get hurt. That's just how it is.

"But if you or Mikey, or Ethan…or Thomas for that matter gets hurt, that's my fault for not looking out for you."

He grimaced when the wagon wheels climbed out of the river and jounced up over the low dirt bank. The wagon slipped sideways into the deep ruts cut by countless wagons heading west.

"I saw that, Husband. Are you okay?"

"I'm okay. But I'll sure be glad to ride a saddle again instead of this iron seat."

"What? This wonderful spring bottomed seat? This marvel of the modern world? This seat that's bounced my backsides for days and days?"

Bitter grinned. "That's the one. I'll spell you off with the driving from now on. And I'm putting Ethan on Misery. I think she's ready to ride. So you can ride Lucifer now and again. Give your… ah…as Mikey says…prosterrier a rest."

Morgan started to correct him and then caught herself. "It'll be prosterrier from now on, won't it?"

"Lordy, but he's a rascal."

"Am not."

"You been listening from back there, Mikey?" Bitter asked.

"Yep. And I'm tired of riding this wagon, too. I thought I was gonna ride Misery."

"Oh, you will, Mikey, you will," Morgan said.

"But Mister Bitter just said Ethan would ride her."

Bitter shook his head. "Got a little ahead of myself with my planning. We'll find another horse up at the fort. You get Misery to ride, and Ethan can ride a different one. Okay?"

"No saddle."

Bitter took a deep breath and then said, "Okay…one more horse and two saddles. You keep this up and I'll go broke."

The Indians decided to stay on the south side of the Platte. One fired a shot that splashed upriver, wide of the last supply wagon, and then the warriors turned and rode south up and over the big rolling hills and out of sight, a long line of tanned, painted fighting men engaged in a losing battle to the ever increasing number of European and American settlers.

"There they go," Sergeant Callaghan said as he rode his tired horse up and out of the river, "and good riddance, I'd say."

The army supply wagons were driven inside the earth works for protection, and the Bitter and Shipley wagons, escorted by a blue clad rider, were led to a wooden shack sheltering a trading post that backed up to the low bluff overlooking the river. A dozen wagons were drawn in a semi-circle across the road from the trading post, a herd of mules, horses, and oxen grazing in the lee of a hill, watched by two armed men, civilians mounted on horses.

The young trooper involuntarily saluted and said, "Captain Bitter, sir, it'll be safe to camp here. Sergeant Callaghan said to tell you he will lead an escort for this party of Mormon wagons headed to the Utah territory. You can travel with us that far. I don't know if you'll have an escort beyond the Mormon cutoff."

"Thank you. Private. Tell Sergeant Callaghan I said thanks."

The young trooper saluted again. Bitter said, "You don't need to salute. I'm not in the army any more."

"No, sir, I don't. But I heard how you handled the Rebs."

"In that case…" Bitter said and returned the salute.

"Corporal O'Grady said he'll be riding with Sergeant Callaghan, and he'd appreciate it if you'd find room in your wagon for medical supplies."

Bitter shook his head and smiled before saying, "I can probably find a little room."

"Medical supplies?" Morgan asked.

"Liquid courage, for snakebite, is what he's talking about," Bitter said with a grin.

The young trooper turned his horse and loped back to the fort, low puffs of dust marking his ride.

Ezra rode up beside the Bitter wagon and said, "John, these folks is about to eat all the grass close by, and from the smell of their slit trenches, they been here quite a spell. Maybe we should camp up-river a ways."

"We'd be alone."

"Yeah, but the Wild Horse bunch is gone, and I heard a trooper saying the Sioux moved north."

"John," Morgan said, "I don't see any women or children with these men. I don't like that."

"Okay…you convinced me. We'll camp up river a ways. The dogs will let us know if anybody comes sniffing around."

They pulled into a grove of umbrella willows crowding the channel of a small stream that carried an anemic trickle of water to the Platte River. But there was a pool deep enough to water the horses and mules.

Supper dishes washed and stowed in the cook box, food and harness packed safely away from gnawing, salt-seeking critters, they sat on boxes and kegs around the small fire.

Bitter smoked a cigarette and sipped hot coffee laced with whiskey and a dab of heavy cream from Ruth's cream pitcher.

Mikey said, "Mama…I mean Missus Morgan…what's in the brown package? Did you forget?"

Morgan shook her head. "No. I was just waiting for the right time. Maybe this is it."

They all waited patiently while Morgan rummaged in the wagon. The package was about two feet square and about three inches deep, wrapped in plain brown paper. Morgan carried it to a small keg, sat down and unwrapped a shiny, rose colored stringed instrument.

"A zither!" Ruth said. "How nice! Can you play it?"

Morgan grinned and shook her head. "Not yet, but I plan to learn."

Ruth reached for the zither and said, "May I? I'll play and you sing. The keys mark the chord you want. You press the key and stroke the strings with a pick. Do you have one of those?"

Morgan took a metal guitar pick from a small box that came with the zither and handed it to Ruth.

The Bitter-Shipley party spent a pleasant hour singing with the zither. The boys asked for "Polly Wolly Doodle;" Ezra taught them the "Crawdad Song;" and Morgan's sweet, soft alto voice brought tears to Ezra's eyes when she sang "Aura Lee."

"Nuff to break a man's heart," he said.

Shadows filled the backsides of the rolling hills as the fire died and the coffee cooled by the fire. Ethan tossed a handful of small twigs in the ashes and watched as one curled and snapped and sent a trickle of smoke drifting up over the wagons.

Thomas yawned and started falling asleep where he sat. "You can almost hear his eyes clang shut," Bitter said with a smile. "I'm for bed myself."

17
A White Cherokee

RUSTY GROWLED AND CORKY STARTED barking just as the sun poked an eye over the horizon. Bitter rolled over on the pallet under the wagon and reached for his revolver. He swore when he banged his sore leg against an iron rimmed wheel getting out from the under the wagon. He saw Ezra emerge, the Sharps in his big hands.

"Hello the camp," a man called. "Can I come in?"

"Who are you?" Bitter asked.

"Owl."

"The medicine man?"

"Yes. I have decided to become a white Cherokee again."

Bitter grinned at Ezra. "Like a bad penny, he is."

Owl rode a big bay horse slowly into camp and eased himself out of a white man's saddle. He grinned at them, and pointed at his new buckskins and tugged at his gray braids. "I think I look a little better. Gotta new wife to take care of me."

While Bitter stirred the coals to start his fire and heat the coffee brewed the night before, Owl said, "The Wild Horse band has a new chief. A man called Buffalo Skull. He doesn't like me very much. Thinks I have too much power. But after you rubbed out Wild Horse, he is also a little afraid of my medicine.

"He's a big man, a bully. And he's also dumb as cold buffalo chips. Plans to join somebody named Red Cloud in a campaign against the forts.

"I know the Indians can't win. They'll get rubbed out or sent off to another reservation…until the whites decide they like that land better than they like the Indians…and then send us off to another useless piece of land.

"I don't want to see that. I think I'll ride with you and drink from the sea before I die. And I've decided I want to see this place you call Oregon."

"With just a horse?" Ezra asked.

"No. I have three more horses and a new wife waiting across the river. She didn't want to come in until she was sure you wouldn't kill me."

"What are you going to do for supplies?" Bitter asked.

"I have my medicine pouch."

"Medicine pouch?"

"I'll show you," Owl said. He slipped the leather thong from around his neck and pulled a leather pouch from under his shirt. With a grin he poured three large gold nuggets into his palm. "I'm thinking the man who runs the trading post will give me enough supplies to make the trip. In the white man's world, gold is strong medicine."

"Just one of the nuggets will get you what you need," Bitter said. "Do you have a rifle?"

Owl shook his head. "I think you'll have to buy me one. I don't think they want to sell me one, not even for the gold."

"After breakfast, we'll go to the trading post with you."

Morgan dressed using the far side of the wagon to protect her modesty. She stepped into the canvas britches she bought at Barton's Trading post, and buttoned her blue calico cotton shirt.

"I envy your pants and shirt," Ruth said as she climbed down from the Shipley wagon." Looking sideways at Ezra, she added. "I think I'll buy some for myself at the trading post."

Ezra grinned but didn't say anything.

Morgan said, "I know it's not ladylike to dress like a man, but it'll look like there are two men driving the wagons. It will give the appearance of a stronger party. Besides, it's more comfortable than a long dress for this kind of travel."

Old Owl took the warm coffee from Bitter and smiled. "Yes. With us Indians appearances count. No Indian wants to be rubbed out, but they are also like the white men. They think it will always be someone else who dies. So if you look strong enough to kill plenty of them, they will leave you alone…most of the time.

"They'll try to steal your horses and mules maybe, but mainly at night. And you have dogs. They are all like me…lazy. If it isn't easy or fun they won't do it."

"I'll need you," he said to John Bitter, "to be there when I go to the trading post. These clothes mark me as a Cheyenne, and right now the soldiers are not happy with the Cheyenne. I don't want to be shot before I can drink from the sea."

"What makes you think I'll take you to Oregon?"

"Because I speak Cheyenne and I have a strong reputation with other bands. So if I'm with you, maybe they won't bother us. I know something about white man's medicine, and I can set broken bones. I'm also a good singer," Owl added and then laughed.

"You were listening last night?" Morgan asked.

"Yes. You are a pretty good singer yourself. That Aura Lee song, that can make a man sad. Even a white Cherokee."

Morgan looked at Ruth and then they both laughed.

Book III – Trail's End

Once over South Pass, a sixteen-mile-wide gap in the Rocky Mountains, the Oregon Trail, never easy even in good weather, matched terrain against the determination of immigrants, cattlemen, miners, women, children and livestock.

But with its hard rocky road and scarce water, that section of the Oregon Trail from Twin Falls on the Snake River to Fort Boise was the worst. Some said you could count seven grave markers per mile, the accumulation of twenty-five years of sad endings for many hopeful travelers.

Arid miles of hot desert and temperatures reaching as high as one-hundred-fifteen degrees at the height of summer, left coyotes sitting in panting circles around dying water holes. Rattlesnakes by the dozens followed thirsty rodents to the same water.

Travelers found the hardships of travel across the Great Plains to be of no comparison to the hot, hard, rocky roads of the Idaho desert.

1
The Bishop

WITH A STRONG ESCORT OF twenty blue-clad troopers, two army supply wagons, and an army ambulance, the fourteen civilian wagons kept formation under a dust cloud rising behind hoof steps and wagon wheels. Corporal O'Grady made sure the Bitter wagon, followed by the Shipley's, was first in line.

A bearded brute of a man, a dusty broad-brimmed hat jammed firmly on his curly black hair, proclaimed, as though it would make a difference to Callaghan and O'Grady, he was a Bishop of the Mormon Church and entitled to lead the parade of wagons. Sergeant Callaghan's glare and Corporal O'Grady's sincere offer to take the man to "knuckle city" ended his protest, but not his grumbling.

Bitter, watching from the wagon seat, his sore leg protesting when a wheel dropped in a chuck hole, said to Morgan, "I don't think we can trust those men. I'll be glad when we're rid of them. O'Grady says they will go on to the Mormon settlements when we get to the cutoff."

"They have mean eyes," Morgan added. "I get the shivers when they look at me. I'm glad I have my pistol."

Bitter glanced at his wife, at the pistol on the wagon seat beside her, at the railroader's cap perched firmly on her red hair, and grinned. "I wouldn't want you mad at me."

When the leader of the Mormons cantered by on a sorrel horse, Rusty growled and Corky barked at the rider. Morgan said, "My sentiments exactly, Rusty."

Lucifer, big floppy ears laid back, nipped the sorrel in the flank, an act of hostility that set the Bishop's horse bucking and kicking at Lucifer. The Bishop fought to keep his seat, arms flailing and his hat sailing off on a puff of wind. Lucifer's bray grated on ears all the way back to Fort Kearney. Eyes big, Ethan reined Lucifer to a halt and then turned him back to the Bitter wagon. "I don't know why Lucifer did that," he said.

Corporal Hackett, a big grin on his face leaned down from the saddle, scooped the Mormon's hat off the ground, and then walked his horse to the outraged man. "Your hat seems to have blown away in the wind," Hackett said with a big smile on his face.

"I'll kill that damned mule before this trip is over."

"And hang, I reckon," Hackett said. Smile gone, steel in his grey eyes, Corporal Hackett pointed at Bitter, and said, "You are a puffed up jaybird who's gonna get himself killed if you keep this up. Don't you know who's riding in that wagon?"

"I don't know, and I don't care," the man growled. "I'm Jim Butler and when we reach the Utah country, what I say goes."

Unimpressed, Hackett said, "The mule belongs to Captain John Bitter."

Startled, Butler asked, "The gunfighter? I heard about him. He don't look so tough."

Hackett shook his head.

"I guess you could call him a gunfighter. He wouldn't call himself that, but several dead men would. So you behave yourself. If you get out of line and he doesn't shoot you, I will. Right after I hang you."

Butler glared at Hackett and jammed his hat back on his head. He backed his horse a few feet and pointed a finger at Bitter. "You keep that damned mule away from my stock. You hear?"

Bitter, his hand close to his revolver, nodded. "I hear you. And you and your men keep away from these wagons and our stock. I won't tell you twice."

Morgan looked over her shoulder as Butler loped his horse back to the Mormon wagons. "Why do we keep making enemies, John? I don't think we go out of our way looking for trouble."

"I think the Good Lord must have sprinkled a few mean ones in amongst the good…maybe to keep us on our toes. I don't know for sure. I do know I'm sick and tired of bullies. They're the kind to shoot you in the back."

"Well," Morgan said as she flicked the reins and put the wagon mules to pulling, "Rusty and Lucifer had him pegged, didn't they."

Camp the first night saw the Bitter and Shipley wagons about four hundred yards from the Mormons with a screen of Callaghan's troop camped in between. Just as the sun set, Rusty and Corky starting barking until Ethan shushed both of them.

O'Grady led one of the Mormons through the Union Army camp to the Bitter and Shipley wagons. The stranger was a tall young man, a wispy blond beard tugging at his face. He had kind blue eyes and a hat in his hands.

O'Grady said, "This gent wants to talk."

No friendly faces looked in the blond man's direction. He worked the brim of his hat with nervous thumbs and fingers, swallowed to clear his throat and then said, "I'm Abner Jones. I came to apologize for Bishop Butler's behavior. We don't all agree with his attitude toward outsiders, but you see, his wife was killed by a group of outlaws, Gentiles, and he hasn't been the same since."

Morgan nodded. "That would be hard on a person, but he needs to understand we aren't the people responsible for his loss. We look for no enemies. The trail is hard enough without bickering amongst ourselves."

With no friendliness in his voice, Bitter said, "Well, Abner, You keep him away from us , and we won't trouble your people."

Ethan, arms folded across his chest said, "If he comes here, I'll sick Rusty on him."

"And he'll do it, too," Mikey said from behind Morgan.

Abner tried to hold back a smile and then gave in. "I sure wouldn't want that red dog mad at me."

Owl said in Cheyenne to Thomas, "Tell him the big Mormon will die from a belly ache if they mess with us."

Thomas gave Abner a stern look, or as much of a stern look as he could muster. "Owl says the big Mormon, the mean one, will die from a stomach ache if he bothers any of us."

Abner cocked his head sideways and then grinned. "Might not be a bad idea to tell him that. For a God-fearing Bishop, he's more than a bit superstitious." He put his hat back on his head. "I'll say good night, then."

Contrary to tales told by men more interested in entertainment than in truth, Indians could count…sort of. What the Indians saw was a strong party of twenty army regulars and fourteen well-armed teamsters, plus Ezra and Bitter. They were wrong. Two of the wagons were driven by women. Not that it mattered much. They were both armed, even if only one had actually fired a weapon with malice at another human being.

That encounter led to the demise of Lige Duncan, a would-be rapist and bushwhacker. It was something his shooter disliked talking about. But talk about it or not, Morgan Bitter was one-for-one in the shooting department.

So the strength of the train kept the Indians at a distance, but it didn't keep them from riding silently on ridge tops, pacing the wagons from horseback, or from trying to steal the mules, the horses or the oxen. The loss of one horse belonging to the Mormons raised questions about whether it was the fault of a sneaky Indian or just a careless knot…a mystery never solved. But it heightened the sense of risk posed by the Indians.

The evening of day thirty-three from Fort Kearney, found the party making camp in a grove of Gambel oaks next to a clear, cold, rock-tumbling creek pouring down the south face of the Wind River Mountains. The Bitter and Shipley party chose a campsite a half-mile upstream from the Mormons.

"Here comes Corporal O'Grady and Sergeant Callaghan," Ethan said.

Bitter walked out from the wagons and said, "Howdy," when the blue clad riders splashed across the small stream and rode up to the camp site.

"Howdy, yourself, Captain Bitter," Sergeant Callaghan said and grinned. "We've come for some of that excellent medicinal elixir O'Grady keeps in your wagon." He watched Ezra and Owl mount horses and asked, "Where are you two going?"

"I'm going to be a father," Owl added as though that was explanation enough. "I will have to think about that. Maybe dream about it in the mountains. Up there." He pointed north at the distant mountains.

He kneed Horse and pointed him across the stream and uphill. Ezra shrugged and followed on Lucky, the big Sharps across his thighs, ready to hand if needed. Ezra's black and white mutt, Corky trotted alongside the big Tennessee Walker.

Bitter laughed and said to O'Grady and Callaghan, "Old Owl is notional, he is."

Sergeant Callaghan grinned and said, "I've been dealing with Indians for over two years and still don't know how they see things. I can't even tell how old they are. Owl could pass for seventy or better."

The two Union soldiers stepped down from the saddle and ground hitched their mounts. After shared troubles with the Rebs who stole the Gatling gun, the fight with the Wild Horse band, and a month of evening campfire visits, Bitter felt a strong friendship for the two men.

2
Owl's Gift

O'GRADY FOLLOWED ETHAN AND RUSTY through a thicket of willows to a pool below a small two foot waterfall. A gray green trout rose to snatch a mayfly from the surface of the pool before sinking into the deeper, darker water.

"Good one," O'Grady said. "You fish this pool, and I'll rig willow poles for the other boys. Then I'll show you how to find some hellgrammites for bait."

With rare and nearly priceless barbed hooks tied to heavy linen thread, hellgrammites for bait, the boys each caught a dozen small mountain trout before O'Grady decided that was enough for a supper mess.

"I don't suppose your mamas know how to cook trout," O'Grady said, "so I guess I'll have to show 'em."

"Does, too," Davey said. "My mama's the best cook in the whole world."

"I'm sure glad to hear that, Davey. What say we go find out? I'm hungry enough to eat the south end of a north-bound skunk."

"Are not," Mikey said. "Too stinky."

Bitter, Morgan, Ruth, and Sergeant Callaghan were sitting on upturned kegs sipping coffee and making small talk around the fire when the cavalcade of fish toting boys walked through the willow thicket above camp.

Woman, Owls dark-haired wife, rose from the scrap of blanket she used as a cushion while she worked a piece of leather into new moccasins. She put her awl and a leather punch into a deerskin bag, and walked the short distance through the trees to the small canvas tent she and Owl called home.

"Mama," Davey said, "look at what I caught."

He showed her a dozen or so small trout hanging from a willow limb. A fork at the bottom of the limb kept the trout from sliding off the makeshift stringer.

Ruth smiled and patted her son's head. "You are one fine fisherman. That's for sure. You help Mister O'Grady clean 'em and I'll get the skillet going."

Fresh trout, rolled in cornmeal, tails curling in sizzling bacon grease, filled two skillets as Owl and Ezra rode across the creek and up to camp. The little dog Corky was riding in Ezra's lap.

"It's a lot further to the mountains than it looks. Corky wore his legs out trying to keep up," Ezra said without preamble. "Owl found himself a hot springs and took what he calls a sacred bath, but there's so much heat in the spring it liked to burn his hide off. We had to stop and let him cool off in the stream."

"What smells so good?" Owl asked.

Bitter laughed and said, "A clean Indian."

Owl just grunted and swung down off his horse.

"I think he does smell a bit better," Ezra said with a laugh.

Owl ignored Ezra and said, "Who caught all the fish?"

"We did," the four boys said almost in unison.

"I caught the most," Thomas said.

"And I caught the biggest," Mikey said.

"Did not," Davey said, "I caught the biggest."

"I caught the first one," Ethan said, and no one disputed that claim.

Owl laughed and said, "Let's eat. Cold water bathing makes me hungry."

Woman carried an iron kettle filled with wild onions, sage, and pieces of dried elk meat and set it on the fire. "Tell them we help," she said in Cheyenne to Thomas.

Supper dishes were put away, a splash of medicinal elixir was added to the men's coffee cups, and the "Crawdad Song" repeated twice while Ruth played Morgan's zither.

Morgan smiled at Owl and said, "Do you want to sing for us?"

Owl shook his head. "I'll wait for the right time. This isn't the right time."

"Thomas," Morgan said, "please ask Woman if he really can sing."

Thomas grinned and said, "He's a terrible singer."

Owl grumped, but there was humor in his voice when he said, "His white blood prevents Thomas from knowing good Indian singing from bad."

Davey and Mikey started yawning, and Morgan said, "I think it's time the fishermen crawled in, don't you?"

O'Grady and Callaghan, stomachs content, puffed on cigars while the women tucked the boys in. Bitter rolled a cigarette and lit it with a small twig burning at the edge of the fire.

Callaghan and O'Grady are usually headed back to the troop by this time. I wonder what's on their minds.

Callaghan suddenly downed his coffee, set the cup on the ground and snubbed his cigar on a rock in the fire ring.

"How's your leg healing, John? You up to taking a short walk? I want to talk to the men."

Bitter slapped his thigh and said, "The leg is fine, and I've been thinking you had more on your mind than just a supper visit."

When the men were beyond earshot of the wagons, Callaghan stopped and looked at Bitter, Ezra and Owl. "You tell 'em, O'Grady."

"Well, I just happened to be passing the Mormon camp last night. They were holding some kind of powwow, and I heard our friend Abner shout, 'No!'

"I thought he sounded pretty worked up, so I sorta slipped up on 'em. Not hard to do since they don't have any dogs. Anyway I listened in and from what I could hear, Butler…the one they call Bishop…was arguing they should wait until us soldier boys start back and then kill you men."

He took a deep breath. "He wants the women and the children. I won't tell you what he had in mind, but I nearly shot Butler on the spot."

Callaghan fished the cigar stub from a shirt pocket and struck a sulfur match on the seat of his britches. He puffed on the cigar until the red coal was glowing in the twilight.

Callaghan took the cigar from his mouth and said, "What we are going to do in the morning, the Union Cavalry that is, is arrest Butler and take him back to Fort Laramie and then put him on trial for attempted murder, for slave trafficking, for theft, and for the attempted destruction of private property.

"In the meantime, I have two troopers keeping an eye on their camp…just to make sure they don't try anything tonight."

"Damn," Bitter said. "Trouble just seems to dog my footsteps."

"The price of life," Ezra allowed. "Try being a black man in this country."

"Or an Indian," Owl added. "Us Cherokees got kicked off our land…twice…and now the Cheyenne are having the same troubles."

Bitter nodded and said, "I know. I don't mean to complain, but it sure seems like I can't avoid trouble. I had fewer fights during the war. At least it feels that way sometimes."

Suddenly he was mad clear through. "What would the U.S. Cavalry say to a duel between me and Butler? Would you stop me?"

Callaghan nodded as if thinking and then said, "I suppose, since dueling isn't against the law in the territories, my troopers could sort of keep the others rounded up while you did your business."

"What kind of duel you got in mind?" O'Grady asked.

"I think pistols would be the way to go. If I shoot him in the knees, he won't be much inclined to travel."

"Let me tear his meat house down," O'Grady said. "It would be my pleasure to use my knuckles on him. Even the way he walks raises my hackles."

Owl turned and walked back to camp without saying another word.

Morning found Owl's tent missing and Owl, Horse and Woman gone. The smallest of Owl's horses, a compact bay was tied to a small oak tree. Bitter spotted a piece of white paper pinned to the ground by a rock. In clear Missionary school printing, Owl's note read:

John Bitter, Woman and I go back to the Cheyenne. The white world is too mixed up. I can't tell who the enemy is. My new son should be Indian, not a white Indian. I will miss son Thomas, but he should be a white man, not a Indian white man. Take care for him, John Bitter. The horse is for Thomas. The evil one won't bother you any more. Owl

Puzzled by Owl's last sentence, Bitter folded the note and put it in his shirt pocket. He really did intend to show it to Morgan, Ezra, and Ruth, and to talk to Thomas, tell him what Owl had said. But the splash of horses riding through the small stream sent him trotting back to his wagon. Instinctively, he brushed the handle of the revolver strapped to his waist.

Corporal Hackett and four mounted troopers pulled to a halt just shy of the campfire where Ruth and Morgan chatted as they fried bacon and soda pancakes.

Ezra came trotting back from the bushes where he had been tending to his morning "chores."

"Morning, Captain Bitter, ladies, Mister Shipley," Hackett said as he stepped down from his horse. "Sergeant Callaghan said I was to tell you that Bishop Butler is dead. Someone cut his throat last night…with his own knife. Whoever killed him left the knife sticking in his belly."

"And?" Bitter said, his sense of dread growing with each breath. *Owl said the big Mormon would die of a belly ache. I guess he did, sort of. After the fact.*

"The Mormon's think you did it."

"What does Sergeant Callaghan think?"

"He said you might have shot the son-of-a-bitch, but you wouldn't sneak up on him. The Mormons aren't so sure."

"Let them think what they will. Knife work isn't my style."

Hackett nodded. "It took a mighty sneaky person to pull that off. He was bedded down between two others."

Hackett looked at the empty ground where Owl's tent had stood the night before. "Captain Bitter, where's your friend Owl?"

Bitter took a deep breath and thought about the note in his pocket. *Old Owl's confession. But I'll be damned if I show it to these soldier boys. They'd have to hunt him down. Butler was properly detested, even by his own people.*

Callaghan will probably look for Owl anyway, but maybe he won't try too hard if I don't give them the note.

"He's gone, I think. I don't know why," he lied. "And he never said a word about leaving. Indians are notional. Owl might have decided it was too dangerous to travel with us anymore."

"No loyalty, I guess," Hackett said.

Loyal enough to kill Butler.

3

The Rock and the Hard Place

THE BITTER AND SHIPLEY PARTY camped an extra two days while Sergeant Callaghan, Corporal O'Grady, and four troopers, along with Abner Jones from the Mormon camp scoured every draw and brushy thicket for miles around. Bitter and Ezra put their time to good use greasing hubs, shoeing horses and mules, mending harness, and fixing a loose iron tire.

Ezra watched as Bitter lit a circle of limbs about the same diameter as the iron tire and fed the fire until he had a deep bed of coals, a process that took over an hour. When the coals were the right color and deep enough to suit Bitter, he laid the iron tire on the coals.

"How'd you learn to do that?"

"I worked for a blacksmith for a few days in St. Joseph. I earned enough to help pay for the wagon…army ambulance really. The smith taught me how to put iron tires on wagon wheels."

"You know, John," Ezra said, "that looks to be a lot more interesting than plowing behind a mule. You think you could teach me?"

"No. I know just enough to get into trouble. But you could apprentice to a blacksmith when we get to Oregon. I know a smith in a little town called Silverton. If I ask, he'll take you on."

"Would he be all right working with a colored man?"

Bitter nodded. "He's a black Irishman, and he's my friend. He'll take you on…if he doesn't already have an apprentice. You should know he isn't an easy man to like. Perfection is his standard."

"Don't know how to say thanks."

"No need." Bitter said, an eye on the iron tire heating in the fire ring. "You know Ezra, the truth is I don't like farming either. Too slow a business. And I don't like plowing, following the ass ends of draft animals either.

"I'd like to breed horses. We got a start. That Misery horse is still young enough to breed, and Ethan's pinto mare has good lines. She's a bit small, but crossed with Rockford, I think her colts would have good lines. And I can buy some more mares when we get home.

"I could even work in some time for this Pinkerton business I was telling you about."

Morgan and Ruth washed clothes, aired bedding, and rearranged the wagon loads. Between meals, Ruth taught Morgan to play the zither. "You got a sweet voice, girl," she'd say when Morgan had perfected the chords to Aura Lee. "Now we gonna work on the Gospels."

The boys explored the creek, found new fishing holes, and brought stringers of trout in to camp for evening suppers.

While Abner Jones rode with Sergeant Callaghan in search of Owl, the remaining Mormons were ordered to stay in camp, an order enforced by fourteen armed troopers under the command of Corporal Hackett. A couple of the Mormons grumbled about Callaghan hunting the wrong man and wasting time when the real killer was camped upstream, but the rest were convinced Butler's murder was committed by Owl.

Butler was not well liked, and it was clear he wouldn't be missed. By evening of the first day, Butler's body was buried beneath a cairn of rocks, and one man was chiseling Butler's name, a best guess as to his birth date, the date of his death, and the word "Murdered" on a flat piece of sandstone.

The first morning, O'Grady, acting as scout and tracker for Sergeant Callaghan, followed the clear hoof prints of Owl's horses in a deer path upstream from the Bitter and Shipley camp.

"Sarge," O'Grady said, "I think he's working to get some distance between him and us. But this clear trail won't last."

The hunters followed Owl's trail for a half mile to a rocky shelf. The white scar of a metal horseshoe on the rock shelf told O'Grady that Owl had turned west across the face of the mountains. When O'Grady reined his horse to follow Owl's trail, Callaghan shook his head no.

"He's too wily to let us see that. He wants us to think he's going west. Put two troopers on the other side of the stream to see where he crossed. I'm thinking he will go south to the next pass and then head east. Go back to the Cheyenne, maybe."

O'Grady was surprised by Callaghan's order, but he said, "Private Winthrop, you and Private Blair work the other side of the stream. See if you can find where he crossed."

O'Grady frowned, but held his peace. *Callaghan knows damned good and well Owl is going west and he knows damned good and well Owl killed Butler. Probably to keep his friend John Bitter from shootin the bastard and making enemies of Butler's friends...if Butler had any. Callaghan is deliberately taking us on a wild goose chase. He's going to make sure we don't find that old Indian.*

The third morning of Butler's death saw Sergeant Callaghan tell the Mormons they could be on their way and if any of them so much as thought of harming John Bitter, an innocent man, he would personally sell their scalps to souvenir hunters in the east.

"If the hair is black, it'll pass as an Indian scalp, and most of you are dark-headed. I figure your scalps could bring a hundred dollars apiece."

The sullen Mormons glared at Callaghan, but none challenged him. Finally Abner Jones said, "Let's get moving."

Callaghan's troopers rode escort to the first dip in the road and stopped. They kept watch until the dust cloud stirred by the wagons and hard pulling horses faded into the horizon.

Bitter led the wagons driven by Morgan and Ruth down off the hill to the main road. He reined Rockford to a halt as O'Grady cantered his horse to Bitter and pulled up. Ezra trotted Lucky past the wagons to Bitter and O'Grady. He was in time to hear O'Grady say, "A galloper from the small garrison south of here brought a message from Laramie. The Bannocks are attacking whites traveling the road from Fort Hall to Fort Boise.

"And this is as far as we can escort y'all. Orders from Laramie are sending us back. The Sioux and the Cheyenne are making that section of road hard on travelers, so we're needed.

"Word is a troop of Idaho Volunteers is guarding the road from Fort Hall to Fort Boise. I don't know if that's a fact or just a hope. We can send four troopers with you as far as Fort Hall. That's a good ten days' travel. But the rest of this escort will have to turn back. I hope you can find an army escort from there to Fort Boise.

"Or," he paused before saying, "I suppose you could wait here until another train or another escort comes along, or until the Mormons decide to come back and take your women. Now that Butler's dead, I don't think that's likely. But you never know.

"As for traveling with another wagon train, it's getting late in the year, and I don't know when or even if another train will be along. I hate to say this, but I reckon you're between a rock and a hard place."

Bitter and Ezra exchanged glances. Ezra nodded and Bitter said, "We'll take you up on your offer of an escort to Fort Hall."

"Good idea. Sergeant Callaghan thought you might see it that way. He recommends we take the Lander Cutoff. Shorter by several days. It's a little rough and the passes are high in the sky, but you've never seen a prettier place than Star Valley."

"We?" Bitter asked.

"Yeah. I'm going with you…me, Corporal Hackett, Private Winthrop and Private Blair. And a pack horse to carry our supplies."

Bitter smiled and stuck out his hand. "Welcome, but why do I think there's more to this than meets the eye?"

O'Grady grinned and took Bitter's hand. "My enlistment is up when we reach Fort Hall. I figure you need looking after, so I'm going on to this Oregon valley of yours. See what it's all about. Look for a place to call home."

"What about your farm in Arkansas?"

"I sold it to my stay-at-home brother. He'll wire me the money, if he ever has any, when I get settled. He loves digging in the dirt, watching the butt end of plowing mules and looking back at deep, straight furrows. He's a good farmer, and he loves growing things. Hell, I can't plow a straight line to save my soul."

"Whatcha gonna do in Oregon?" Ezra asked.

"Don't know yet, but I'm drawn to saloons. Maybe this Oregon country needs a nice, peaceful Irish Pub."

4
The Lander Cutoff

FOR THE FIRST SIX DAYS, O'Grady rode point and Bitter scouted their back trail, making sure the small party wasn't followed by miscreants, outlaws, or men of evil intent, men who were just a total embarrassment to the human race. Ezra and the three troopers rode the flanks and acted as the "Home Guard."

Alone, sitting on the trunk of a downed log, Bitter watched the road from a shady, open grove of young pine while Rockford grazed on brown, cured grass. "Rockford," he said, "why is most of the evil of this world the work of men? I suppose there are a few evil women, but they are a rarity, and I can't say I ever met one.

"Nope, the active works of evil on this earth are the works of the men. It's hard to accept, but there it is. I wasn't shot at even once by a woman. Not during the entire war. Women just don't do things that way."

He chuckled and added, "Unless you tangle with Morgan. Otherwise you're pretty safe from women."

The sun slipped behind the tall, rugged Caribou Mountains to the west, and Bitter, satisfied they weren't being followed, slipped the reins over Rockford's head and stepped into the saddle. "We best head for supper, horse. I'm getting hungry."

Bitter had ridden a mile, his attention to the road wandering a bit as he took in the sights of Star Valley, open meadow land, timber on the slopes, good water, and just plain nice to look at. "A man could run horses in this country, but I think the snows would plug the road in the winter time. That'd mean putting up a lot of hay. Could be done, I think. Maybe we better keep this valley in mind, Rockford. Might want to come back and build us a horse ranch."

Fresh horse tracks pressed on top of the wheel marks of the Bitter and Shipley wagons ended Bitter's daydreaming and wish-booking. Head swiveling, eyes scanning the cover on both sides of the road, he pulled his pistol, and growled, "How in the hell did anybody get by me?"

When he was satisfied no one was going to shoot at him, Bitter studied the tracks. "What we have here," he said to himself, and maybe to Rockford who stood with ears pointed front and center, "is one horse with iron shoes, a big horse, followed by an unshod horse small enough to call a pony…or a colt, I suppose. And tracks from a bigger unshod horse looking like it carries a heavier load than the first two."

There was something familiar about the tracks, but the loose dust didn't hold a print very well. He saw where the horses left the road, uphill in the direction of an aspen grove that backed up to the foothills east of the valley.

"Might be a spring up there. A man could camp and watch the road without being noticed. I'm not liking this, Rockford. Let's get out of here." He put Rockford into a ground-eating lope.

Five miles further on, Bitter spotted the red glow of a camp-fire. He slowed Rockford to a walk and gave silent approval of Ez-ra's choice of camp sites. Backed up against a grove of small bull pine, the camp was defensible…at least against a small force. The crystal-clear water of a small creek drifted easily out from the trees and into the lazy meander of a meadow stream.

The sad, soft cooing of a mourning dove from the top of a tall pine beyond camp stirred memories of evening fishing on Abiqua creek, of his big brother Luke tromping up the bank with a stringer of trout, of the two of them sitting on a downed cottonwood, rolling a smoke and talking quietly…about farming maybe, or horse breeding, or making home brew…and watching the shadows fill the evening.

I miss those times, but I swear I'm gonna break Luke's nose when I see him next. I haven't given him a thought for months. I guess I'd best send him a telegram from Fort Hall. Let him know I'll be home this fall."

And then sour thoughts of his brother drained away, replaced by the sight of four little boys wading in a small pool, splashing water on each other, their laughter drifting to his ears on a puff of cool evening breeze.

Bitter gigged Rockford in the ribs and put him in a trot across an open meadow to the bright campfire and the company of his wife, the boys and his friends.

"O'Grady," he said looking over Rockford's back as he unsaddled the big stallion, "I saw the tracks of three horses, one shod and two unshod. Somebody crossed the road after the wagons passed. We might have somebody following us. But if they are, they're sure taking a wind about way of doing it."

Bitter's statement had soldier's heads turning, eyes searching the meadow and the stand of pines, hands brushing pistol butts.

O'Grady frowned, puzzled by Bitter's casual report. "And?" he finally asked.

"I don't know how they got by me. Could be prospectors. Could be Indians. Could be an old mountain man just poking around like they do…looking for new country."

"Or old Owl, maybe?"

"What makes you say that?"

O'Grady shook his head. "That old Indian thinks highly of you. Enough to kill Butler to keep you out of trouble."

"You think Owl killed Butler?"

"John Bitter, y'all know damned good and well he did. And Sergeant Callaghan thought so too. Sarge took us out on two days of wild goose chases when Owl's track was as plain as the nose on your face. Just let that old Indian get away is what he did."

Morgan put her skillet on a big flat rock close to the fire, a rock that showed the scars of previous use by earlier campers. She walked over to her husband, searched his face, her blues eyes serious. "Do you think it was Owl?"

Bitter frowned and shook his head. "I don't know."

Hands on her hips, challenge in her voice, Morgan looked at O'Grady and asked, "What will you do if we find him?"

O'Grady winced and shrugged. "I wouldn't like it much, but I'd have to arrest him. He's a wanted fugitive."

"And if you weren't in the army?" she asked.

"I'd give him a big cigar and buy him a drink. But we don't know if it is Owl on our back trail. So we'll post a guard like we been doing."

After a supper of wild onions and fresh venison from a little buck Ezra killed earlier in the day, Bitter picked up his coffee cup and said to Morgan, "Let's walk out a ways."

Morgan nodded and said, "Let me get my shawl. It feels like frost coming on tonight."

He led her to the edge of the pine grove, found a downed tree and said, "Let's sit where we can watch the meadow."

She settled on the log next to him and scootched up against him. "Okay, John Bitter. Tell me what's on your mind."

He brushed her red hair back and kissed her on the forehead. "We've been so busy gathering up a family, we haven't taken much time to talk. There's some things you might want to know, sort of get ready for what we'll find when we get to the farm."

When he finished, she took his arm and pulled it around her shoulders. "So it was a woman that sent you running off to war. Your brother Luke stole your fiancée."

"Yep. And I intend to…or at least right up until today I did intend to bust his nose when I get back. But I think I put that to rest somewhere between sunrise and supper. It hit me. If I stay mad at Luke, it's a sour way of saying I don't like the way things worked out. I mean I wouldn't have the meanest, prettiest redheaded wife a man could want, and I wouldn't have Ethan or Mikey…or Thomas. I think it worked like it was supposed to. I think the Good Lord sent me what I needed the most."

Morgan slid out from under his arm and smacked him on the shoulder with her fist. "The meanest?"

He rubbed his shoulder, laughed and said, "Yep. And you just proved it."

5

Star Valley

MORNING FOUND A RIME OF frost on the water bucket and John Bitter up and stirring the ashes, looking for a hot coal to start the morning fire. O'Grady waved, awake, standing morning guard, his short barreled carbine in the crook of his left arm. Bitter nodded and O'Grady then shifted his eyes back to the string of timber running down a small ridge east of the road. He knew if trouble came, it would come from there.

Rusty crawled out from his nest under the wagon, watered a wagon wheel and then padded over to sniff a cold skillet. Not another soul crawled from warm blankets.

"Cold nights do one of two things," Bitter said to Rusty. "It either keeps people snuggled down or it gets them up and feeding the fire. This looks like a snuggle-down-and-wait-for-the-sun kind of morning."

Ethan eased down from the wagon, shoes in hand and barefooted to the fire. He sat on Morgan's skillet-rock by the fire pit, dusted the soles of his feet, and slipped dirty feet into a pair of worn, scarred shoes.

"No socks?" Bitter asked.

"Wore 'em out." Ethan said. "And these shoes are plumb tight with socks on anyway."

Bitter looked at the blond headed boy and noted the high-water britches. He said, "You know, Ethan, I think you've grown a good six inches since we left Missouri. You havin' any growing pains?"

Forehead scrunched in suspicion, Ethan shot a blue eyed look at Bitter and said, "Growin' pains?"

"Yeah. Achy legs at night, itchy scalp, runny nose, bed bugs, ticks or chiggers?"

"You funning' me, Mister Bitter."

Bitter tousled Ethan's hair and Ethan ducked his head. "I think I'd like you to ride scout with me today, Mister Sharp. You up to that?"

Ethan tied his shoe laces and jumped up from the rock and nodded. In a serious tone of voice he said, "I'd like that."

"Good. Go bring in Josey. That brown-and-white-painted mare has turned into a pretty good saddle horse. And bring your rifle. We'll see if we can get some fresh meat. Shoot some grouse maybe."

"Do I get to shoot?"

Bitter grinned and said, "That's the idea. We get to Oregon, you'll be our hunter. Keep the pot full and the smoke house goin'."

"Me?"

"Yep. There'll be some farm chores, but I'll see you have time for some hunting and fishing. And we need to get you some schooling. A man needs to read and write, know something about arithmetic, and learn the sciences. Even if you decide to farm, you'll need an education."

"Don't like school."

"And I don't care. You'll go when we get home."

Ethan turned and walked out to the meadow below camp. He kicked at the sod and muttered, "Darned old school."

In the meadow below camp, a lone black mule, aloof to the machinations of lesser creatures, kept his distance and discouraged any intrusion into his regal solitude. The wagon mules ignored him and focused on the chore of filling up on meadow grass. They hungrily ate this high mountain, sun-cured grass, somehow knowing it held the protein needed to fuel their strength for the upcoming heavy pull through the Caribou Mountains.

Rockford, secure in his unchallenged dominance of the small horse herd, watched Ethan kick his way through the dew-speckled grass, and then dropped his head and went back to grazing. The red hound was perfectly content to pad behind while the blond boy fumed and fussed over the imagined restrictions of a school room.

Ethan whistled and the pinto raised her head and nickered. The compact little mare ignored Rockford's stamping hoof and trotted toward Ethan.

She nudged him with her big velvet nose and lipped a scrap of dried apple from his palm. He rubbed her neck, and then Ethan's calm was restored. He held a hank of mane and walked the pinto mare quietly toward the wagons. "We get to ride with Mister Bitter today, Josey."

O'Grady's troopers pulled on boots, saddled horses, rolled bedrolls in ground cloths, and filled nose bags for each horse with a bait of army oats. Shivering in the cold, they surrounded the fire to kill the morning chill. Morgan and Ruth, each in aprons, set skillets to heating and coffee pots on handy rocks next to the fire.

"This is the last of our bacon," Morgan said to Ruth. "I hope we can buy some more in Fort Hall."

Trooper Blair walked to the pile of army supplies waiting to be loaded on the pack horses. He carried a slab of bacon back to the fire and said, "Miz Morgan, if you cook it, we can all eat it."

Ezra walked out to the edge of the frost trimmed meadow and banged on a bucket with a tin scoop. Heads lifted, and animals turned and headed for the grain. Ezra shook his head. "We just be funnin' you this morning. You ate every last grain yesterday. No oats or cracked corn till we get to Fort Hall. So y'all be needin' to make good time on the trail. You hear?"

From behind, O'Grady said, "We'll loan you some government oats this morning. Y'all can pay me back when we reach Fort Hall. If we don't have trouble on the trail, we should be there in another three days."

Bitter and Ethan, hands behind them, backed up to the last warmth of the morning cook fire, and watched while Ezra and trooper Blair led the small two wagon cavalcade back to the main road. Ruth's milk cow balked at the tug of her lead rope like she did most mornings. She rightly figured milk production was tied to lazy grazing and fresh water.

The teams splashed across the ford and pulled the wagons through the shade of a thin string of willow and aspen marking the meander of the little creek bubbling down from the foothills and into the big meadow.

When the wagons were beyond the ford, O'Grady turned and waved. Then he said something Bitter couldn't hear, and two troopers loped their horses out on the flanks of the wagons. Untied, the ever independent Lucifer followed behind, a better rear guard than most sleepy troopers.

And then they were gone. The busy, noisy campsite settled into empty silence, a silence accented by the pop of an ember in the fire pit. Bitter would never admit to the hint of melancholy each abandoned camp left in his soul.

"Well, Mister Sharp, let's kill the fire and go see what the rest of Star Valley looks like."

Bitter didn't want anyone to see their tracks crossing the road, so he and Ethan rode to the creek, and turned the horses upstream, keeping to the water. When they were two hundred yards up hill from the ford, Bitter turned Rockford up and out of the stream bed, riding at an angle to keep them above the road.

Noon found Bitter and Ethan sitting in the thin shade of a gnarled eight-foot mountain mahogany which, along with a half-acre of other stunted mahogany, claimed a grassy shoulder of the mountain. A light breeze cooled the thicket.

"The breeze explains why," Bitter said to Ethan, "mule deer like mahogany thickets. Shady and cool in the heat of day, and open enough to see any predators trying to sneak up on them."

Bitter sat with his rifle across his lap and watched the road a good three hundred yards below the steep slope. He and Ethan nooned on cold bacon and dried biscuits. Washed down with spring water from their canteens, the biscuits were almost edible. Ethan wrinkled his nose in disgust, but ate the biscuit one small bite at a time.

Bitter held up a dry biscuit for examination and said, "Plumb worn out on these things. I could use some fresh meat and fresh greens."

"Me, too," Ethan echoed. "How many hard biscuits do you reckon we've eaten so far?"

"Too many," Bitter laughed. "And Ruth's butter turned rancid. I didn't want to say anything and hurt her feelings, but it's almost enough to gag a man."

They could hear Rockford and Josey, each tied to a short mahogany tree, busy cropping grass, tails shooing pestiferous deer flies away. When one of the horses broke wind, Ethan laughed.

Without looking at Ethan, Bitter said quietly, "I heard Mikey crying last night. And I heard you shush him. Anything I should know?"

Ethan turned his head away from Bitter, and then in a halting, husky voice said, "He misses our mother sometimes…mostly at night."

Bitter nodded, but didn't say anything.

"I do, too. I don't mean…I mean…well…you and Miz Morgan are real good to me and Mikey, Mister Bitter. I'm glad you took us in and adopted us and everything, so we didn't get sent off to be orphans. But sometimes we miss Mama."

A lump in his throat, Bitter reached an arm around Ethan's shoulder and held him tight. "In the best of worlds, Ethan, you and Mikey would be home with your mother, and then your father would come home from the war. But that isn't how it worked out.

"On the other hand, from my own selfish look at life, you, Mikey and Morgan are the best thing that ever happened to me. The best people." He paused and added, "And I wish you'd just call me John instead of Mister Bitter."

"I'd like to call you pa, if that's okay."

"Oh, my. I'd like that best of all, Ethan. And I can call you and Mikey my sons." He paused, got his emotions under control again and added, "You want to know my favorite story?"

"What is it?" Ethan asked, too choked up to look up at Bitter.

"Stinging worms," Bitter said. He chuckled and repeated, "Stinging worms."

"Mister Bitter," Ethan asked, "you gonna adopt Thomas, too?"

Bitter said, "Well, what would you think if we did?"

Ethan didn't answer the question. Instead he said, "I see an Indian. Down on the road."

"Just sit still, Ethan. I see him."

A young boy led a gaunt gray horse carrying the sorrowful burden of a dead Indian out from behind a small stand of pine trees and stopped in the middle of the dusty road, staring in the direction the wagons had gone.

Bitter eased back into the thicket and in a crouch walked to his saddlebags to retrieve his field glasses.

Movement was a greater risk of discovery than noise, so he took his time working back through the thicket to where Ethan sat watching. "Still see him?"

"Yep. And an old woman showed up. She limps a lot. It looks like they're just talking about something. I'm gonna go get my rifle."

"Just sit tight. There'll be plenty of time to get your rifle if it comes down to shooting."

Bitter studied the two Indians through his field glasses. "They look starved down. I swear I can count that boy's ribs."

"What are we going to do?"

"We'll watch a bit and if no other Indians show up, we'll go shoot that little buck I spotted and feed 'em."

"What little buck?"

"See that aspen grove to the north? I saw a little buck slip in there while we were eating. We'll just ride up easy like on the horses. We need the meat, and those starving Indians need to be fed, too."

In later years Morgan delighted in telling the story of John Bitter and Ethan Sharp riding into camp just as the first evening star lit the sky. Bitter had a resigned look on his face. A tiny gray-haired woman, dressed in dirty buckskins that looked to carry more holes than leather, her arms wrapped around Bitter, rode double on Rockford. Bitter made a gesture to Morgan that said, "I didn't have any choice."

A small Indian boy on a tired old mare that stumbled now and again followed Ethan and Josey into camp. Ethan, head held high, his first buck tied on behind his saddle, said, "Thomas, can you talk to these people? I killed a buck and we fed 'em…after we buried the old man…and they kept saying 'fort' so we brung 'em along."

Ruth looked across the fire at Morgan, grinned and said, "He did it again, Morgan. That man gathers himself a flock, just like Jesus."

Morgan hurried over and caught the old woman as she slid off Rockford. *She's light as a feather,* Morgan thought, *and she looks starved down to skin and bones. And I suppose it's uncharitable, but she could sure stand a good bath.*

Morgan helped the woman to the fire and eased her down on a small upended keg. Ruth brought a scrap of blanket and wrapped it around the woman's thin shoulders.

Thomas asked in Cheyenne, "Who are you?"

The old woman was startled to hear this white boy speak her language. And then she looked up at Bitter and spoke. Thomas translated as she hurriedly told her story, her gaze never once looking away from Bitter.

"She says her name is Blue Flower…that's as close as I can come to her name in English. She says to thank the white chief for saving her life and the life of her grandson. And for helping with the burial.

"When her old husband died, her family told her to take his body away because they thought he died from the white man's sickness. They burned her teepee and everything she owned and then chased her away. Her grandson…his name is Little Badger… was angry about this, so he helped his grandmother load his grandfather's body on the old mare and came away with her.

"They were looking for a good place to bury the old man, but they spent a lot of time hiding from other Indians. She says it is a hard time for the Indians. They are hungry all the time. They would eat the horse if they found it. She was born a Bannock and hopes to find her family at Fort Hall."

6
Fort Hall

AFTER WEEKS ON THE TRAIL, Bitter was struck by the contrast of Fort Hall's white washed adobe walls against the dry, wind-blown landscape. The Stars and Stripes anchored to a tall flag pole whipped and cracked in the afternoon wind. *It's like a bright bruise on the countryside*, he thought, *but welcome for all of that.*

O'Grady, a big grin on his face, said, "John, you get 'em camped while I report in. I'll check for mail and see about getting my discharge papers. Ya'll get prepared to celebrate!"

Bitter led the wagons to a pool of shade downstream from a pioneer camp with a half dozen wagons. The number of canvas awnings and clothes flapping on rope lines told Bitter the travelers had been there awhile.

Blue Flower, smelling a lot better than when she rode double with John Bitter into camp, dressed in one of Ruth's old dresses, shiny salt and pepper hair plaited in two braids, said something to Thomas as she climbed down from the wagon seat she shared with Morgan. Then she pointed in the direction of the fort and said something to her grandson. The Indian boy led her old horse over, cupped his hands, and boosted her up.

Blue Flower settled on the back of her horse, her black eyes searching Bitter's face. She broke into a grin, nodded her head, and said something to Thomas who turned beet red. Little badger shook hands with Thomas white-man style, and with Blue Flower riding proudly erect, led his grandmother's horse across a used-up meadow in the direction of a row of seven aging teepees tucked in against a string of willow and cottonwood trees just downstream from Fort Hall.

"What did she say?" Bitter asked.

"She said I was to thank all of you for helping her."

"And that made you turn red?"

"No. She said she thinks you are a good husband. She said if she hadn't gotten so old, she would like to be your number two wife."

Ruth looked at Morgan and started giggling.

"Oh, my, John Bitter," Morgan said in a laugh choked voice, "you do have a way with women."

"Not nice," Ruth said, her brown eyes crinkling in mirth. And then she broke into giggles again.

Ezra grinned and said, "I think I'm gonna have to start calling you Chief."

Thomas said, "In the Indian world, you're a big man. You saved Owl, and you saved the daughter of a Bannock chief."

Bitter just shook his head in disgust and started unsaddling Rockford. He growled and said, "Let's get the mules out of harness, Ethan."

Morgan was surprised when Ethan said, "Yes, Pa. And then can me and the boys go check out the creek?"

Around their evening campfire, Bitter and Ezra agreed with Morgan and Ruth to rest a couple of days, get animals re-shod, grease hubs, mend harness, and have the blacksmith tighten one wagon tire.

"And get some clothes washed," Morgan added. "The boy's clothes are getting a wee bit ripe."

"Are not," Mikey said.

"And a bath," Ruth said, ignoring Mikey. "A nice, warm, tub bath."

Thomas said, "The Cheyenne bathe when there's enough water."

"I wonder what's keeping O'Grady?" Bitter said. "He told us to get ready to celebrate."

"Here comes a rider," Ethan said and pointed through the twilight in the direction of the fort.

Trooper Blair slowed his mount from a lope to walk and hollered, "Hello the camp."

"Come on in," Bitter shouted.

Trooper Blair slid from the saddle, a big grin on his face. "Let's she if I can remember what he shed." He cleared his throat, his tongue slightly twisted by whisky, and slurred, "Mishter Liam O'Grady, former corpal of the U esh Calvary, make that cavalry, requests your presence. We are shelbrating his dish charge."

Bitter grinned and said, "It sounds like you got an early start."

Blair gave them all a lopsided grin and said, "Yesh we have. Yesh we have." He gave Bitter a long look and said, "Well…you comin or not? You, too Mishter Shipley."

Midnight had come and gone before Bitter and Ezra walked into camp leading a long-legged horse with the former Corporal Liam O'Grady slumped in the saddle trying to sing an Irish shanty tune, but somehow losing the words midway through the chorus.

Bitter ground hitched the horse and Ezra caught O'Grady as he fell sideways out of the saddle. Morgan, wrapped in a blanket, crawled out from her bed under the wagon and barefooted over. She whispered, "Well…I'd say he celebrated. I laid out a blanket for him under the big willow."

Bitter grunted, slung the smaller O'Grady over his shoulder and carried him to the wool blanket waiting against the rough trunk of the willow.

When Bitter rolled him out on his bed, O'Grady woke enough to pull a corner of the blanket over his shoulders. He gave Bitter a sloppy grin and a small wave of his hand, and then fell instantly asleep.

Bitter slipped off his boots and crawled under the wagon. When he gave Morgan a hug, she whispered, "O'Grady wasn't the only one drinking tonight." And then she rolled and turned her back on the love of her life, but not before he caught the gleam of her white teeth through an involuntary smile.

He could hear Ruth say something to Ezra, her tone emphatic. Bitter smiled and then drifted off to sleep.

A shaft of early sunlight painted Bitter's face and brought him slowly awake. He turned in time to watch a bedraggled O'Grady, dark curly hair thatched with wild straw, stack a twist of grass and dry twigs on a hot coal and blow the pile into flame. O'Grady held his hand to the first small flame and shivered.

Bitter sniffed the thin hint of wood smoke drifting under his wagon. *There's something about a campfire that just never gets old.*

At the far off sound of reveille drifting across the meadow between the Bitter-Shipley camp and Fort Hall, Bitter rolled out from under the wagon, stood and tipped his boots upside down in case any rodents, snakes or spiders had nested during the night. Satisfied his feet wouldn't be sharing space with unwanted critters, he slipped the boots on and walked to the fire.

"Morning, Liam," he said quietly. "How's the head?"

"Don't talk so loud," O'Grady whispered, "my head feels like a drum."

Bitter laughed and said, "You sure celebrated."

"How'd I get here?"

Breakfast over, dishes washed and put away, the men smoked and drank coffee around the fire. Cane pole in hand, Ethan asked O'Grady, "You want to go catch a fish?"

O'Grady winced and said, "Almost any other time, but not this morning, thank you, lad," Ethan looked disappointed, but he shrugged and led a parade of boys and dogs to the creek.

Ruth and Morgan nodded at each other and disappeared behind blankets strung from ropes behind each wagon for the privacy of dressing. When they reappeared some fifteen minutes later, each was wearing a long sleeved dress and button shoes. Morgan's dress was slightly wrinkled from being packed, but the green dress set off her red braids to the point that only another woman might notice the wrinkled cloth. And Ruth's bright yellow dress gave her smooth mahogany skin a glow.

O'Grady gave a low whistle and said, "Look there, Ezra… John. I've never seen a more beautiful sight."

Morgan curtsied and blushed. The smaller Ruth stuck her chin out and said, "Thank you, Mister O'Grady, but you do have the Irish knack for blarney."

"I be telling you the truth, Missus Shipley. Now if y'all weren't taken…"

Bitter laughed and punched O'Grady on the shoulder. In an accent in imitation of the lanky southerner, he said, "Y'all keep your eyes to yourself, Liam, 'fore I have to blacken 'em."

"Amen to that," Ezra growled, a touch of jealousy nagging at his soul. He just didn't have the easy way with words like the Irishman.

"Speaking of y'all," Morgan mocked gently, "we want you to bring two mules with pack frames to the trading post. We are out of bacon, low on coffee, 'bout out of sugar, the hard biscuits are gone, the flour is weevily, we need salt, soap, stockings for the boys, cotton cloth, and just about anything you can think of. Oh… and some money."

Ruth said apologetically, "I'm hoping to trade fresh butter for some of what we need, Ezra."

Ezra nodded and said gently, "You order what you need, Ruth. We have enough left to pay for it."

O'Grady tugged Bitter's sleeve and nodded toward the wagon. "Need to talk."

"Okay," Bitter said when the two of them were out of earshot, "what's up?"

"Well, the paymaster is coming with a troop of Idaho Volunteers. They won't be here until tomorrow. So…I couldn't draw my mustering out pay. I'm temporarily without funds. And they won't feed me at the mess hall now that I'm a civilian."

"You can eat with us ," Bitter said, a smile tugging at his face. "What more do you need?"

"Well, I was thinking I might just replenish my poke by winning a few hands from the boys. There's a running poker game in the back of the trading post."

"You any good at cards?"

"Sometimes…if I stay sober…I win a few hands. But I need a stake. I…uh…sorta drank my poke last night."

Bitter shook his head, chuckled and asked, "How much?"

"I'm thinking twenty dollars would be enough. Stakes aren't very high until after pay day…which I'm hoping will be tomorrow. The boys will pay up on their IOU's then. I'm needin to buy a horse and saddle. The pistol is mine, but the rest of my gear belongs to the boys in blue. They let me keep my pants, my boots, my long johns, and my shirts. The rest the Army gets.

Bitter nodded. He walked to the rear of the wagon, pulled his saddlebags free of the tangle and extracted twenty silver dollars.

"Shame on you, Liam," he grinned as he handed the money over, "taking advantage of poor soldier boys."

O'Grady sniffed and observed, "They be full grown, and they'll take advantage of me in turn…if they can, so it's a fair game."

Bitter shook his head and muttered a quiet "good luck" at the retreating form of O'Grady stalking across the meadow in the direction of the Fort Hall trading post.

7
Blue Flower's Gift

AN HOUR AT THE TRADING post saw two matching piles of supplies stacked under the shed roof that served as shelter for the wooden porch.

The store owner, one James Pruitt, a bald-headed, ruddy-faced man wearing a stained canvas apron gave fair exchange for Ruth's sweet butter. "I have a buyer for the butter, and my wife loves fresh milk. Would you also trade for some hen's eggs?"

"Fresh eggs?"

"Gathered this morning."

"Let's talk trade," Ruth said.

Bitter bought a tanned elk hide for patching harness and a box of shells for the Henry. A yellow wide-brimmed hat tempted John. He tried it on and eyeballed his image in the store's small mirror. Morgan smiled and said, "Mighty nice."

"Yep, I agree, but it's too dang big."

"Ezra," Ruth said, "try the hat on. Yours is plumb worn out."

"Can't afford it, Ruth."

"Try it any way."

The tall hat was a comfortable fit for Ezra who couldn't resist peeking in the mirror and turning his head to examine his profile. Brown eyes twinkling, he said, "Plumb handsome is what it is. And the hat ain't bad either," he added with a chuckle.

Ruth shook her head. "Pride goeth before fall, Ezra," she said, but then she looked at the store keeper. "I'll give you two dollars for the hat if you throw in some cartridges for the Sharps."

"Two-fifty."

Ruth looked at the store keeper and nodded, "We'll take it."

Ezra kept peering at his image in mirror, fiddling with the hat, pulling the brim down, tipping it up, trying to turn his head to get a profile view.

Ruth shook her head and said, "Pride goeth before fall, Ezra." But she couldn't tame her smile.

He grinned and studied his face in the mirror. "I know. You keep reminding me, but this is the first new hat I ever wore."

Accounts settled, the store owner offered the use of a buckboard wagon to haul their supplies back to camp…for another pound of Ruth's butter. Ruth allowed that would be satisfactory if he threw in another dozen eggs. The store keeper grinned and said, "Make that a pound of butter and quart of sweet cream."

Ruth nodded. "I'll bring the butter and sweet cream around in the morning after milking."

Noon saw Blue Flower's grandson Little Badger riding up to camp. He spoke without dismounting. Thomas, who was stuffing his face with twice-baked beans and day-old bread, looked at Bitter, licked his fingers and said, "Little Badger wants you to visit his grandmother's lodge. She found a relative who knows where to find her brother. She wants to thank you before she leaves."

Bitter smiled and said, "Tell Little Badger there is no need for thanks."

Little Badger shook his head when Thomas translated for Bitter. He looked directly at Bitter and said something.

Thomas said, "Little Badger says his grandmother has something very important to tell Mister Bitter. And she doesn't want anyone else to hear. So please come now."

Bitter shrugged, looked at Morgan who was busy arranging gear in the wagon, and said, "I'll be back soon."

Morgan looked up, her blue eyes crinkled in humor. "Be sure you don't come back with another wife."

Ethan said, "I want to come. I've never seen a teepee."

"Me and Davey, too," Mikey said.

Ezra nodded okay. And so a troop of boys and dogs tagged along, the boys eager to see how the Indians lived.

Tiny Blue Flower sat on a downed cottonwood, cushioned by a gray wool blanket, and welcomed the warmth of the morning sun. She nodded at the sight of the boys and the two dogs following Bitter across the meadow guided by Little Badger and the old horse.

When they stopped in a semi-circle around the old woman, she patted the log beside her and spoke to Thomas.

Bitter looked at Thomas who said, "She wants you to sit with her and enjoy the morning sun. She has something important to tell you."

As though he was in a fancy parlor, Bitter removed his hat and eased down on the log beside Blue Flower. The top of her head didn't quite reach the level of his shoulder. She smiled up at him, patted his hand and started in on a story, stopping periodically to let Thomas translate.

"When I was a young girl, my father was chief of a small band of Bannocks...the northern Paiutes. We had a good life. Plenty of horses, lots of salmon to catch below the falls, camas to dig up in the high meadows, elk and buffalo for meat.

"But the Great Father sent us a dry year. Our horses ate all the grass in our home meadow and we had to follow the season into the high country to find grass for our horses.

"Other bands did the same. And so we traveled to a big meadow, the same one I think you found us in. I was young and so many years have passed that I can't be sure.

"But a band of Cheyenne also chased the dry season into the high country. And they wanted our meadow for their horses. When they tried to drive us out, my father and his best warriors fought back. The Cheyenne were too many. They pushed my father and his warriors back, and then attacked our village. The people fled into the steep canyons and made it hard for the Cheyenne to follow.

"But the canyon my mother took me and my brother to was too steep to climb. We were trapped and couldn't join the people. My brother and I threw rocks until all the good ones were gone.

"The Cheyenne laughed and stayed back until we were through. Then one big warrior rode his horse up to us, grabbed me and threw me across the shoulders of his horse. When my brother tried to pull me back, the warrior kicked him in the face and sent him rolling down the hill. He fell over a small cliff. I couldn't see if he was hurt.

"Yesterday I heard my brother survived and became a great chief. But I didn't know he had lived until now.

"Another warrior hit my mother on the head, threw her across his horse and rode away. She wasn't very big…small like me…so it wasn't hard for him.

"When we rode into the Cheyenne camp, my hands and feet were tied and I was tossed into a teepee. I listened and cried while the Cheyenne celebrated their victory over the Bannocks.

"Later that night, the warrior who had taken me tried to make a woman out of me. I bit the end of his nose. I tried to bite it off."

Blue Flower stopped her story long enough to laugh at the memory, and then caught her breath and continued on.

"After that he was called Split Nose. And he didn't like me very much. So at the fall powwow, he traded me to an eastern band of the Cheyenne for four ponies. I think Red Hawk, the warrior who bought me, thought I was pretty.

"And so I lived as a Cheyenne until Red Hawk died. I miss my daughters, but I'm glad Little Badger and I can live as Bannocks. Thanks to you, Little Badger and I survived. I sent word to my brother than I am alive, and that you helped me.

"The Bannocks will protect your wagon and the wagon of the black white man when you travel the road to Fort Boise."

Bitter was surprised to find the small woman sitting beside him had so much influence over the Bannocks, but the relief he felt was powerful. Impulsively he put an arm around her thin shoulders and gave her a gentle hug.

He looked at Thomas and said, "Tell Blue Flower we will always be grateful for the friendship of the Bannocks."

Mikey broke the spell with a tug on his sleeve. "Can we see the teepee now?"

8
A Change of Pace

W HEN BITTER AND THE BOYS trooped back into camp, Morgan said, "John, there is to be a party at the fort this evening. Ruth and I have been invited to entertain. I guess O'Grady has been bragging about us.

"There's to be a potluck dinner and dancing. And tomorrow, there will be apple bobbing and three-legged races for the kids, and a shooting contest…which Ruth says Ezra will win."

Most thought it was a glorious party. Ruth's zither playing and Morgan's singing started the entertainment. Both blushed at the applause, and after the crowd had eaten, a fiddle and a banjo struck up a tune while a trooper kept rhythm on a small Indian drum.

The dust rose as the dancers circled the bonfire built in the wagon road. Two young women from the wagon train, each suddenly in love with a healthy young trooper went for a walk down along the tree lined creek…for a while.

Hands clapped in time to the music and happy troopers stamped their feet and hollered "Eeehaw!" Ethan shouted "Eeehaw" in his little boy's voice, a shout echoed in return by the laughing troopers. "Eeehaw!"

A few troopers, a wee bit befuddled by the apple cider some calculating soul had surreptitiously spiked, wandered to the backroom of the trading post to try a few hands of poker.

O'Grady, encouraged by the arrival earlier in the day of the Idaho Volunteers and an army paymaster, followed them, confident that two things were about to happen…the IOU's he held from earlier games would be paid off…and fresh money would wind up in the poker pot.

As the bonfire died and the moon edged over the horizon to give the white walls of Fort Hall a pale gleam, weary dancers said their thanks to the post commander, Major Wells and his wife for hosting the party. Then they gathered children and empty bowls and headed home. The musicians, content from hours of playing music and from the thanks given by the dancers, packed instruments away, divided the coins in the hat a generous soul had taken through the happy crowd, and broke out a bottle of bad whiskey to celebrate a good time.

The fiddler, a thin middle aged man who had shaved a week earlier, said, "Did you see that redhead?"

The banjo player, a rawboned Kentuckian nodded and said, "I'd marry that un, but she be taken, and by a tough man. You ever hear of John Bitter?"

The emigrants walked the meadow to their wagons and tents, the trader and his wife to their living quarters in the rear of the trading post, and army wives and husbands back to their small houses.

Slightly miffed at John Bitter, who claimed he didn't know how to dance, Morgan had danced until the music stopped. She came away with sore feet and two proposals of marriage…both proffered even after she had shown her would-be suitors her wedding band.

Bitter found a bit of jealousy growing in his soul and was determined to have Morgan teach him to dance at some point when no one could watch. In the meantime he watched and drank from the cider bowl.

The only disruption was a brief fight between Corporal Hackett and a dark-haired drunk who made the mistake of allowing that he wasn't much impressed by John Bitter's reputation as a gunfighter. "If that's John Bitter, he don't look so tough. I think I'll just shoot the son-of-a-bitch."

That was as far as he got before Hackett said, "You'll have to go through me first."

Bitter heard later from O'Grady how Hackett had drawn his pistol and smacked the man on the head, rendering him immediately and almost permanently unconscious.

"Tell him I owe him, Liam."

Bitter only stumbled once crossing the meadow back to camp. He carried a sleeping Mikey in him arms and listened while Ethan and Thomas talked quietly while they followed behind. He over heard the word "fight," but had no idea what that was about.

Morgan carried her zither and didn't say a word until they were half way across the meadow. "I want to teach you to dance, John. It wasn't much fun dancing without you."

"You looked like you were having fun," he said quietly so as to not wake Mikey.

"I love to dance, but I would rather dance with you.'

"Okay. I'll give it a try, but I want to practice in private."

9

Beecher's Bibles

THE POP OF DRY TENDER in the fire pit, the soft hint of wood smoke and a little boy's whisper to "be quiet now," pushed John Bitter up from a dream where he was busy building a river-rock fireplace in the corner of his cabin and setting posts for a fence around his young orchard on Abiqua Creek.

He rubbed sleep from his eyes and thought about his farm. *It's bound to have changed some since I left. Luke said he'd look after it, but by gollies I don't know exactly what he meant by that. Well... we'll see when we get there. I hope he kept the blackberries at bay.*

He eased from under the blankets and fumbled along the edge of the tent until he found the wooden box that served as security for his shirt, britches, gun belt, and hat. He slipped into his clothes and boots in hand sock footed to the upturned keg by the fire pit.

"Up early, boys," Bitter said quietly to the three boys feeding limbs to the fire.

"Couldn't sleep," Ethan said.

"You want some bacon and some sweet soda bread?"

"I do," a sleepy-eyed Davey said as he edged close to the fire and held his hands out to the heat.

Ethan laughed and pointed at Rusty who pushed his way into the circle. "I'll bet he knows you're cooking hot cakes. Look at him drool."

Bitter dropped the tailgate and poured flour, brown sugar and, just for good measure, an egg into Morgan's mixing bowl. "Your mama got any buttermilk, Davey?"

Davey just turned and walked back to his parent's wagon.

"Don't talk much does he?" Thomas said.

A distant barking caught Bitter's attention and he looked in the direction of the Fort. Overnight, a dozen newly pitched skin lodges crowded the skyline along the creek.

Ezra came around the back of his wagon, stuffing his shirttail in his britches. "Hmmm," he grumbled. "You early birds get any worms? You sure got me up."

Bitter chuckled and shook his head. "I've never known you to be grumpy of a morning, Ezra. You worried about the rifle match?"

"You know, I think the army boys are okay shooting against a colored man, but I just don't know how the civilians will take it."

"Especially," Bitter said, "if you out-shoot them."

"That's what I'm worrying on, sure enough."

"Well, Mister Shipley, you'll have some strong friends there who will tend to the complainers."

Bitter dropped a spoon of bacon grease in the skillet and watched it melt, spread and them come to life. "You want to get the coffee going, Ezra, while I feed these hungry hombres?"

Ezra's worries were for naught. When he paid his fee and walked to the firing line where about a dozen shooters were waiting, a gray-haired old man with a bushy white beard, looked him over and said, "I think I'm in trouble. Unless my eyes are bad, you're shooting a .52-caliber Beecher's Bible."

Ezra frowned. "You got the caliber right. I just never heard a Sharps called…what did you say…a Beecher's Bible?"

"I take it you don't know that story. Beecher is a minister who holds strong views on slavery. He's dead set against it. So he smuggled Sharps rifles into Kansas. Packed them in wooden crates marked 'Bibles.' Said the Sharps was a strong moral agent, and that the pro-slavery boys saw greater moral persuasion and logic in a Sharps rifle than in the Bible. That's when some folks started calling those big rifles Beecher's Bibles."

'Well, I reckon I can echo his sentiments," Ezra said. "I'm sort of dead set against slavery myself."

The old man laughed and held out his hand. "Tom Beecher, at your service. Not related to reverend Beecher, but the last name did sort of focus me on the story. I'm a retired mountain man fallen on hard times. Got to scout for the Army just to make a living." And he laughed again. "Hell, for that matter, I'm a retired everything."

Ezra shook hands and said, "Ezra Shipley."

"Where you headed, Ezra?"

"Oregon. Got me a sharecrop job with my uncle in some place called Corvallis."

"Hell, take up your own land, Ezra. That Willamette Valley, I been there. It grows just about anything you want to plant. I grew melons, wheat, corn. I even tried tobacco. I think that's the only thing that won't grow. Anyway, I left my wife and our two boys on the place when this last ruckus started. Had to see the elephant, I did. The more fool I."

He looked out of the corner of his eyes in Ezra's direction. "When you figure to start for Oregon again? Maybe I'll trail along. Give up this scouting business."

Ezra held his gaze for a good ten seconds. "I think you would be welcome, but I have a partner who would have to give his okay."

"Well, we can have a drink and talk about it after the match."

A blue clad soldier with chevrons on his sleeves shouted, "It's time gentlemen. If there are no other shooters in the crowd, let's get started. You each have a target in front of you set at a measured fifty yards. The order of shooting will be from my right to my left. You will shoot one at a time. You will have thirty second to take your shot. At the shorter distances there will be no shooting from a rest.

"When everyone has taken his shot, we'll gather the targets and determine who will advance to the next round. I encourage you to be careful with your weapons. Do not point them in the direction of the onlookers or at any of my troopers. If you do, I may lose patience and just shoot you out of hand.

"Good luck. Is everyone ready?"

When they all said yes or nodded, the sergeant said, "You…in the green shirt. You may begin now."

The first shooter pulled his rifle to his shoulder, squinted and pulled the trigger. The sound of the shot rolled out across the open ground, and a cloud of black powder smoke marked the shooters position.

Of the fourteen marksmen, only two failed to punch a hole in the center of his target. Some shots were a little more centered than others, but 12 bullets cut the black. The shooters who had missed looked embarrassed and slipped back into the crowd of onlookers.

At one hundred yards, only five marksmen failed to hit the center of the target.

The Sergeant said, "The targets will now be moved to the one-hundred-fifty yard range. This is a measured distance you can rely on. Again this will be a shot without a supporting rest."

A skinny Kentuckian, the same one who played the banjo at last night's dance, Tom Beecher, Ezra and a red-headed trooper from New York were the only shooters to hit the mark.

"Congratulations gentlemen. We will now move up to the two-hundred yard mark. At this distance, you may use a rest, you may shoot from a prone or a sitting position, and you will be given a full minute to take your shot. Understood?"

Ezra's rooters were getting nervous. Davey squeezed his mother's hand and whispered, "I can't watch. I can't even see the black dot any more."

Ethan whispered back, "He'll make it, Davey. I think your dad can hit anything he looks at. Remember that big Indian he shot so far away? Well, this is easier."

"And he doesn't have to kill anyone," Ruth said. "Have faith."

Thomas tugged at Bitter's sleeve and said, "The Bannocks are watching the shooting, Mister Bitter. If Mister Shipley wins, they'll think he has big medicine."

Morgan winked at Thomas and said with more confidence that she felt, "He'll win."

"Yes, yes he will," Bitter declared.

At three hundred yards, only the two shooters with Beecher's Bibles were left.

"The gentleman in the beard will shoot first," the sergeant said. "You may take as much time as you wish."

Tom Beecher tapped the forked stick he had driven in the ground to make sure it was solid. Then he lay down on the blanket he used for cushion, set the barrel of the rifle in the fork, and pulled the rifle butt into his shoulder. He took a deep breath, steadied his aim and slowly let his breath drift from his half open mouth. He squeezed the trigger, braced for the concussion…and nothing happened.

He shared some vulgarity with the waiting crowd that had Ruth covering Davey's ears. He got to his feet, looked at the crowd and said, "I apologize for that. I just never had Old Bessie fail me before."

"You still have a shot," the sergeant said. "May I suggest you reload and try again."

Beecher replaced the errant cartridge with a fresh one and settled back into his prone shooter's position. This time the gun belched fire and smoke filled the air.

Beecher look at Ezra and shook his head. "Pulled it, I did. I think that misfire rattled me. You make the shot and get this thing over, you hear?"

"Yessir, Mister Beecher, I intend to do just that."

Ezra went through a routine almost identical to Beecher's, only his rifle didn't misfire.

The sergeant pointed at the two troopers who were setting targets for the match and said, "Go get 'em, and let's see what we got."

By the time the troopers brought the targets back, Ezra had introduced Tom Beecher to the Bitter and Shipley party. "He says he wants to travel with us back to Oregon. Got hisself a place in the Willamette Valley."

Bitter eyed the man, shook hands and said, "What are you doing so far from home?"

"I did a fool thing. I hired on to scout for the Army. I had this notion about seeing the big fuss in the East, but I got a tad sidetracked right here among the heathen redskins. I been a scouting for the Army for the past two-and-a-half years.

"But the way I see it, I'm too old to watch the next chapter in this here upcoming war with the savages. I think I'll sit this one out from the comfort of my rocking chair on the front porch of my home on the big Willamette River."

He stopped for a minute and then asked Bitter, "You know the French Prairie country?"

"I do."

"I own a big chunk of that."

The sergeant's voice cut their conversation off. "Gentlemen, I'm prepared to declare a winner."

He held the targets up for the onlookers. "The target in my right hand is Tom Beecher's. You will see that his bullet is low and left about two inches from the bulls eye.

"The target in my left hand belongs to Ezra Shipley. As you can see, his bullet punched the center out of the black."

The sergeant looked at Ezra and said, "That's fine shooting, Mister Shipley. I think we could use you in the 10th Cavalry."

Ezra grinned and shook his head. "I'm sure they are fine troops, but I done my time."

The sergeant smiled and said, "I figured you were taught to shoot by an intelligent army sergeant." And then he laughed and held out his hand while the crowd applauded.

"And the fifty dollar prize is yours."

Ruth pushed to the front and held out her hand. "I'd be pleased to take that."

The distant ringing of a bell gave notice that the events set up for the youngsters were about to begin. Mikey said, "Can we get going. It's about time for the apple bobbing."

The apple bobbing just didn't hold Ethan's interest. *Once you own a rifle, you just sort of outgrow this kid stuff,* he thought. But he and Thomas were good sports and hung out with Mikey and Davey, who were having good fun chasing the red apples around the big water-filled galvanized tub Hall's cook and his crew set out.

10
Debits and Credits

SEATED BY THE EVENING FIRE Ezra lit a cigar purchased with a bit of prize money Ruth had reluctantly dug from her hidey-hole. Bitter lit a roll-your-own after adding a splash of whiskey to his coffee. He held the bottle out to Ezra who looked at Ruth until she reluctantly nodded her head and said, "Go ahead. I reckon you earned it."

Bitter grinned and said, "You know, I bought our mules from Black Jack Jefferson back in Missouri. I found him down on the banks of the Missouri, catching catfish, singing gospel songs, and drinking whiskey. When I asked him how he worked that out, he said it was sinful to disrespect the good things God provides. I think Mister Jefferson included moonshine in his list of the good things."

Ruth pointed her right index finger at Bitter to give her statement the emphasis she felt she needed. "Don't you go giving Ezra any excuses to drink the devil's brew. He already knows how to do that."

"And here I thought it was his first taste," Bitter said and chuckled.

Thomas belched and then got up from the round keg he was using as a seat. "Mister Bitter, Blue Flower invited me and Ethan to sleep in her teepee tonight. Would that be all right?"

Bitter looked at Ethan. "You want to do that?"

"Sure. That would be fun."

"What about me and Davey?" Mikey asked.

"Not enough room for all of us ," Thomas said.

"Well, I reckon you'll have to sleep with Rusty tonight, Mikey."

Morgan frowned, but Bitter winked at her and added, "There's a world of comfort in having a big hound nearby. But…I think Mikey and I should take him down to the creek and give him a bath first. What do you think, Mikey?"

Mikey nodded, but didn't say anything else.

"All right, then, Ethan. You and Thomas can stay with Blue Flower, but I want you back here at the crack of dawn. We'll be packing up and getting ready to follow those Idaho Volunteers across this next stretch of desert to Fort Boise."

Just after dark, O'Grady rode into the firelight on a tall, rose-and-gray-dappled gelding.

"Howdy, y'all," he said as he swung out of the saddle.

Morgan walked over and patted the rose-colored horse on the shoulder. "He's beautiful. I've never seen a horse this color. What is he?"

O'Grady was grinning from ear to ear. "The Nez Perce breed 'em. Call 'em Appaloosa. I don't know what the heck that means in Nez Perce, but they are special. I guess he was just too danged pretty to be male, so they gelded him. I don't know, but he has an easy gate and he can run.

"I traded a keg of whiskey, a good blanket, my cavalry boots, and a twenty dollar gold piece for him."

Bitter shook his head and smiled. "I suppose you can pay me my twenty dollars back now?

O'Grady laughed and pulled up another small keg for a stool. "I don't suppose you have any of that liquored-up coffee left."

Bitter pointed to the pot and said, "Help yourself.

O'Grady dug into his pants pocked and produced a twenty-dollar gold piece and handed it to John. "Thanks for the grubstake."

Ruth and Ezra watched the exchange and Ezra winked at Ruth. "And what else you been up to, Liam?"

O'Grady reached for his cup, took a sip of coffee and set the cup on the keg he had been using for a stool. With a smile he pulled a new leather wallet from his hip pocket, opened it up and pretended to peer inside. "Well, what have we here?" he said as he took a stack of Yankee dollars from an inside compartment.

With an air of concentration, he counted, "Twenty, forty, sixty, eighty, one hundred, one hundred twenty, one hundred forty, and ten makes it one hundred and fifty dollars belonging to none other than Ruth Shipley, wife of our unequaled sharp shooter. I could only get three to one odds, but even so…"

He looked at Ezra and asked, "How in the world did you hit the target, Ezra? I couldn't even see the bull's eye at that distance."

Ezra shrugged and smiled. "Old Thunder just knows where to look. Besides, I saw where he put it…just over the top of that big red rock. I have to tell you, I'm plumb grateful Tom Beecher's rifle misfired. Rattled him, it did. I was beginning to think he was gonna to outshoot me."

Morgan looked at Ruth and asked, "You bet fifty dollars?"

"I only bet on sure things. And as far as I know there is nothing in the Bible that forbids a little wager now and again."

Bitter laughed and held up his cup. "To the victors."

11

Hard Scrabble

DAY THIRTEEN ON THE OREGON Trail from Fort Hall to Fort Boise saw Bitter lead a lame Rockford back toward the wagons. Morgan pulled her mules to a stop, and Ezra rode up on his Lucky horse. He stepped down and walked over to watch.

Bitter tugged on Rockford's right front leg and lifted his hoof. A little blood seeped from the pad.

"Stone bruised," was Ezra's opinion. "Sharp rock maybe."

Bitter nodded agreement, patted Rockford's neck and said, "Well, Rockford, you old bag of bones. You know what this means? It means you can't be ridden until you heal up."

Ezra pointed in the direction of the Idaho Volunteers, a unit of about sixty men led by a Captain Bradford. "The captain says we'll make Fort Boise before dark. It means we'll camp on the Boise River tonight. Think your black horse can make it that far?"

Morgan said, "He'll make it." She wrapped the reins around the handle of the wagon brake and got down, stretched and walked to the back of the wagon. She dropped the tailgate and started moving boxes and cook gear. Over her shoulder she said, "We'll use some of that elk hide leather you bought in Fort Hall to make a boot. We'll pad the boot and lace it on. I saw Daddy do it for one of his horses, so you let me make it. It has to fit tight enough he doesn't chew it loose or step out of it."

Ruth pulled her mules in beside the Bitter wagon. "Whoa now," she said. "How bad is it, Ezra?"

"Rockford has a bruised hoof. Morgan says she can make a padded boot for it. We get to Fort Boise, we can rest him a couple of days and he should be all right. And I'm for bathing in something other than dust."

"How far is it, Ezra?"

He pointed in the direction of the Idaho Volunteers strung out along both sides of the trail as guards for the nine wagons in the little pioneer caravan. "The Captain says we'll make it before dark. I reckon that means anything between five and six hours."

Ethan, a boy watchful and leery of the world, a skill honed to a fine edge when he and Mikey were living alone, whistled up Rusty and then loped Josey to the wagons. He watched Morgan measure and mark a pattern on the tanned elk hide. Worry in his voice, he asked, "Is Rockford all right?"

Morgan nodded. "Stone bruise. Gimped up a bit."

He glanced at Bitter and said in a quiet voice, "You want to ride Josey, Pa?"

Bitter grinned and shook his head. "Thank you Ethan. But, no. You go round up Mikey and Thomas. I want 'em close."

Ethan turned Josey and with a holler kicked her into a lope out to where Thomas and Mikey rode their horses trying to keep out of the dust kicked up by horses and wagons.

"You need to get back to the wagon," he said as he pulled Josey to a stop. "I don't know what's happening, but Pa looked pretty serious."

"Indians?" Mikey asked, a slight quaver in his voice.

"Maybe. Let's get moving."

A grizzled sergeant galloped back down the trail to the Bitter and Shipley wagons. Much too old to still be working at the business of war, but welcome anyway because experienced troopers were hard to come by, Sergeant Ambrose brought ages of wisdom and years of experience to the cadre of troopers he led.

He pulled his horse to a dusty stop. "You having trouble, Captain Bitter?"

"Lame horse. We'll get a boot on him and follow along. Have you seen Mister Beecher?"

The sergeant pulled his brimmed hat from his head and wiped the sweat band with a once white piece of rag he carried in his hip pocket. Without looking directly at Bitter he said, "Well…he's off doing a bit of scouting. Can't help hisself. Said he found some fresh horse tracks a few hundred yards off the trail that he needed to satisfy hisself about."

"That might cause us to worry some, Sergeant. Let us know what he finds. And would you let O'Grady know we might need him."

"Sure. The minute he gets back. He's out scouting with Beecher. In the meantime, I'm going to keep a squad with your wagons until you catch up."

"Did Beecher mention Indians?"

"No. Didn't have to. We're in Shoshone country. It just figures the only people not using the wagon road are Indians. If they act friendly and want to get close to your wagons, you keep your weapons handy, cause they ain't friendly. Killed the Ward party a few years back…or most of them anyway. The rest danged near died of starvation trying to walk out after their wagons was burned and wrecked. The Indians killed or stole all their animals. In fact some of those poor souls may have indeed starved to death."

He shook his head. "Pilgrims, defenseless pilgrims is what they were. You know it sometimes surprises me that any of you every finish this trip alive."

"This isn't my first time over the trail," Bitter said.

"I know. And you ain't no pilgrims." He reined his horse around and said, "I'll get a squad of troopers headed this way." With that he gigged his mount in the ribs and cantered down the road.

"And welcome they'll be," John said in a quiet, worried voice.

The seven wagons that made up the rest of immigrant train rolled by with nary a howdy-do nor an offer of help. Not that help was needed, but the indifference of the people in the other wagons rankled Bitter. When he mentioned it to Morgan, she shrugged and said, "If they are as weary of this hot, dry, rocky, treeless desert as I am, they just might not have the energy to do more than plod ahead. I think people just sort of sink into themselves. Just endure. And all those grave markers. It gives me the shivers. I stopped counting at one hundred."

She clamped her lips and then blurted, "My Lord, John, I'm not sure we'll ever see trees again. Or take a bath."

He put his arms around her shoulders and said, "Tonight we camp on the Boise River. We'll heat a tub of water and you can have a nice warm bath. And sleep sound because all those troopers at the fort will keep the Indians away."

She sighed and went back to punching holes in the elk hide with her awl. "Tell me about Abiqua Creek again," she said to her husband. "Tell me how cold and clear it is… how sweet tasting… and about the farm. I really hope the apples are ready for picking when we get there. What I wouldn't give for a fresh, juicy, fall apple."

Ezra had just finished watering Queeny and giving her a little grain in a nose bag when O'Grady on his rose colored horse and Beecher riding a mouse-colored mustang came trotting up over the brow of the big rolling hill that carried the wagon road. They glanced behind from time to time.

Ezra spotted them first. "John, here comes O'Grady and Beecher. I reckon we'll know what they found soon enough." He shaded his eyes and asked, "Is that a dust cloud moving behind them?"

Bitter nodded. "It sure looks like it. You know, Ezra, it hasn't been much over a month since our last fight, and I'm not looking forward to another."

"Wishing won't make any difference, John. Trouble is part of living."

John turned and saw Morgan and Ruth shading their eyes, looking east, concern etched in their brows. He looked at Morgan and asked gently, "How you coming with that boot for Rockford?"

"I'm about done. Need to cut a boot lace and then you can put it on." She paused. "Do you think those are Indians behind O'Grady and Beecher?"

"Could be." He watched the boys aim their horses at the wagon and said, "I know it's hot under the wagon tarp, but when they get back, I want them in the wagon in case we have to make a run for it."

Rusty and Corky started barking and Ruth said, "Look what's coming," and pointed west. Sergeant Ambrose, a young lieutenant and a troop of twenty men were galloping back up the trail pulling a mountain howitzer. The mules packing the shells and the powder were having a hard time keeping up.

"Well," Bitter shouted when Ambrose slid his horse to a stop, "I'm guessing you have some news."

Sergeant Ambrose saluted, and in mindless reflex Bitter returned it. "This youngster is Lieutenant McCall. Lieutenant let me introduce Captain Bitter."

McCall saluted crisply and said, "A galloper met us just as we started down off Bonneville point. The Major sent him looking for us. The wire sent word that Chief Pocatello is doing his best to kill immigrant travelers."

"And that," Sergeant Ambrose interrupted, "got me to thinking about Beecher's horse tracks out in the sagebrush, so Captain Bradford decided to send a detachment back to sort of look after you and your wagons."

Bitter pointed east at the dust cloud hanging over the trail and said, "I think Beecher and O'Grady found 'em and decided to bring 'em back."

Ambrose chuckled. "You suppose?"

"Maybe not on purpose," Ezra said, "but the results are the same."

Bitter looked at the Lieutenant and said, "Why don't we block the road with our wagons," Bitter said, "and leave a gap for your howitzer between the wagons. You might use the wagons to screen your troopers, have them dismount and stay out of sight until the Indians get within range.

"My friends and I will cover the men with the howitzer. We have two Sharps rifles, a Henry repeater, and a Sharps carbine. And we all have pistols. Does that suit you, Lieutenant?"

The young lieutenant glanced at his sergeant who nodded. "Yessir, but you need to understand Pocatello has more than sixty warriors with him. And some if not most are armed with rifles. These are first-class fighting men."

Bitter said, "Then we'll have to hit them hard before they discover they outnumber us so badly. Any help coming?"

Lieutenant McCall shook his head. "No. But I'll send a galloper after the rest of our troop and have them turn back. Captain Bradford will have to agree since he's in charge. But he's a…how to put it…a cautious man. So while we can hope, we best plan on taking care of this business without help."

Bitter looked at the dust cloud that was getting closer. "Well, Lieutenant, it's time to get your boys in position then, and get that cannon loaded. You shooting explosive rounds or solid shot?"

Lieutenant McCall smiled and said, "Explosive, sir, explosive. Makes a terrible racket and a worse mess of human flesh…or horse flesh for that matter."

Bitter shook his head. "West Point?"

"Yessir. Artillery is my specialty."

"Well, it's your show then."

O'Grady and Beecher pulled sweat-stained horses in behind the wagons just as a squad of troopers rolled the light mountain howitzer in between the wagons.

Bitter looked up at O'Grady and asked, "What have you brought me this time, O'Grady?"

O'Grady gave him a tight grin and dismounted. "Well, John, I think we be facing about sixty or seventy well-armed and well-mounted Shoshone. I believe that's a few more than I brought you last time."

Beecher swung down from the saddle and asked, "Last time?"

O'Grady laughed. "Yes. Last time it was only a dozen Cheyenne chasing me and Corporal Hackett, not sixty." He looked at Bitter. "And don't you go charging this bunch like you did last time."

Beecher said, "You'll have to tell me that tale sometime," and led his horse around behind the wagons. He handed the reins to a big a blue clad horse holder with the reins of four other horses wrapped around his hand. Beecher pulled the Sharps from the saddle scabbard, lifted the strap of his bullet pouch from the saddle horn and walked back to the wagons.

12

Bradford's Glory

LIEUTENANT MCCALL STOOD BEHIND THE four man squad manning the twelve-pound howitzer. He had trained them himself and was proud of their proficiency, but they had yet to be battle tested. For that matter, Lieutenant McCall was also about to engage in his first fight, and he was just a little nervous. He wasn't exactly sure what he was nervous about …maybe getting killed or just failing to do his duty…which might get him killed anyway.

Above all, he did not want to let his troopers down. So he said quietly, "Steady now. Let the savages get a little closer. Remember to shoot as we've trained."

McCall watched the Shoshones maneuver into a two hundred yard front across the open hillside, spread out, getting ready to charge and overrun the small party. "Mister Beecher," he said, "how far do you judge them to be?"

"Five hundred yards. They'll walk their horses until they are within about two hundred yards and then they'll charge."

"How good are you and Mister Shipley with those things?"

Beecher smiled and said, "What you got in mind, Lieutenant?"

At four hundred yards, or at least Ezra and Beecher's best guess at the distance, each quietly picked an Indian to shoot. Ezra said back over his shoulder, "Ruth, pray for their souls."

From behind the wagon, Ruth said, "I will Ezra. Now you shoot straight."

Four little boys lifted the side of the canvas top on the Bitter wagon and took a peek at the mass of Indians. Ethan had his Clemens rifle primed and his knife in his hand.

"I'm scared, Brother," Mikey whispered.

"Me, too," Davey chimed in. "That's an awful lot of Indians."

Ethan whispered back, "Not to worry. Our papas will whip these Indians just like last time."

"Yeah," Thomas said, "but we don't have the Gatling."

"Don't matter," Ethan said. "We got a cannon this time."

"You boys be quiet," Morgan said outside the canvas top. "No matter what happens, don't let the Indians know you're in there. And stay below the side boards."

The muzzle blasts of two Sharps rifles, followed almost immediately by the concussive force and noise of the small cannon, startled everyone, but most of all the boys. They saw an Indian on one end of the line punched off his horse, and on the other end of the line a horse went down leaving his rider afoot.

"Damned horse raised his head up just as I touched off," Beecher muttered as he hurried to reload.

In the center, the force of the explosive cannon shell killed three horses and their riders and wounded four more riders and their mounts.

And then the Indians charged. The nervous gun crew reloaded and then overshot the charging line. "Easy now, boys," McCall shouted. "By the numbers. Reload!"

Ezra and Beecher each fired again, and then Sergeant Ambrose yelled to the soldiers hiding behind the wagons, "Spread out, lads, and give 'em hell."

Two eight-man squads moved out from each side of the wagons and knelt in the short sage and dusty bunch grass, carbines aimed at the mass of charging Indians. "Wait, wait," Ambrose shouted over the thunder of at least sixty horses, and when the Indians were within one hundred yards, he shouted, "Fire!"

The howitzer roared again and then O'Grady and Bitter joined the fight, Bitter's Henry pounding shot after shot into the charging line.

Morgan, pistol belt strapped around her waist, moved up beside her husband and took a quick, ineffectual shot with the carbine she had taken from good old Lige's pappy.

"Take your time and aim," Bitter gritted as he swung the Henry to take another shot. And then the yelling, yipping Indians split and raced along both sides of the wagons firing rifles at the defenders.

They pulled animals to a quick halt, reversed direction and charged again. Just as the Indian's horses reached a full gallop, a bugle sounded and forty or so troopers, led by Captain Bradford, came boiling up out of a wide draw just north of the Bitter and Shipley wagons.

The Indians hesitated, surprised by the sudden appearance of more soldiers. The howitzer, quickly reversed just like McCall had practiced, roared again, knocking another big hole in the line of charging horses. And then Bradford's troopers were among them shooting pistols at close range until the pistols were empty, then clubbing at Indians with pistol barrels. Horses collided with horses and went down in tangled piles of shouting men and squealing animals.

The boys hiding in the wagon could hear the bark of pistols, the sharp crack of rifles and the shouts of men trying to kill each other.

 Captain Bradford's saber flashed in the sunlight and then the dust and powder smoke made it almost impossible to see who was friend and who was foe. When one of his troopers fired a rifle into the mass of fighting men, Ambrose was apoplectic and shouted unkind things and made predictions of dire calamity "if any of you fire again without my permission!"

A group of Indians, about thirty strong, broke free of the wheeling mass of men and horses and bolted to the south out across the barren hills. Beecher and Ezra each fired and knocked two more Indians from galloping horses.

A bugle sounded recall and Bradford's troopers pulled back from the fight to rally on Captain Bradford. He shouted, "Let 'em go, boys. Let' 'em go. We stung 'em today. They won't be back for more, I'm thinking."

Another fifteen or so Indians galloped away, some shouting frustrated taunts at the blue clad soldiers. One turned and fired his rifle, the lead ball skipping across the ground, leaving a trail of dust puffs before losing momentum.

Bradford led his troops up the wagon. "Lieutenant, that was a fine job. Get me a count of casualties and report back. Have Sergeant Ambrose take a squad and search the field. I want to know if any of the dead is Pocatello."

Bradford, stepped out of the saddle, took a deep breath and said to Bitter, "You folks wouldn't have any medicinal elixir would you?"

Bitter grinned and held out his hand. "I'm John Bitter. You're welcome to all we have, Captain. You wouldn't be Irish by any chance?"

Bradford smiled and shook his head. "I don't know what makes the Irish think they have a monopoly on whisky drinking."

O'Grady from behind Bitter, in an exaggerated Irish accent said, "Sad to say, we all did until the English robbed us of that honor."

Morgan lifted the back cover and peeked over the tailgate into the wagon. "You can come out boys. The Indians are gone. And get those dogs out of there."

Morgan lifted Davey down, felt him tremble as she sat him on the ground. She watched in pity as he ran crying to Ruth.

Mikey held out his arms and she lifted him down. "You're getting too big for this, Mikey. You okay?"

"Sure." He watched Ethan and Thomas climb down and added, "We knew Pa and Mister Shipley could whip 'em. Didn't we, Brother?" It sounded more brag than question.

"A cautious man, Lieutenant?" Bitter said quietly as they watched Captain Bradford drain a cup a whiskey.

"I'm embarrassed to have so misjudged him," the lieutenant admitted, his voice still shaky from the adrenalin rush…and the fear.

Captain Bradford watched his troopers scrounge the battle field, picking up souvenirs, retrieving Indian rifles, and looking for Pocatello among the dead. All told, the Indians lost fourteen warriors, and had several wounded who managed to stay mounted long enough to ride away from the fight.

When a trooper decided the Indian he found was playing possum, he fired his pistol into the ground close to the man's ear. No amount of personal discipline could keep the warrior from jerking his head away from the concussion. Hands in the air in surrender, the Indian rolled quickly over on his back and gave in to capture.

The cavalry had three killed and five wounded, four of whom were ambulatory, and one seriously injured when a big Shoshone had run a short lance into his side.

Captain Bradford said, "Ma'am, we'd like to load our worst injured in your wagon. The rest can ride, but he's hurt pretty bad."

Morgan nodded. "We would be glad to, Captain. How far is it to Fort Boise?"

"Four hours should do it."

Sergeant Ambrose rode up and saluted. "Captain, you're a brave man. I'm thinking we might not have made it if you hadn't showed up when you did."

Captain Bradford returned the salute and smiled. "I'm afraid you were the bait, Sergeant."

"Huh. In that case I take it back, sir. That was cold blooded."

"No. The opportunity came and I took it."

Bitter and O'Grady watched the exchange and looked at each other.

"It sounds like something a certain Captain Bitter might have done, doesn't it?" O'Grady allowed.

"I don't know," Bitter said. "It wasn't my decision to make."

"Sergeant," Captain Bradford asked, "did our boys find Pocatello?"

"No sir. I think he got away…again."

"Well, bring that injured Shoshone in. We'll patch him up and see if he can tell us what Pocatello is up to."

Ambrose pointed a finger where a small group of Shoshone had died. "What about those, Captain."

"Pocatello will come back for them. They'll be gone by morning."

"You want to try and ambush him again?"

"Not in the dark. We'd likely shoot ourselves. Let's mount up and head back to the fort. I'm worried about those other wagons. "

13

Fort Boise, Cool Water and Old Friends

DARKNESS SAW THE BOYS TUCKED in bed, sweeter smelling after a swim in a slow backwater pool of the Boise River. Their privacy guarded by a big red hound, a black –and-white mutt, and a loaded revolver, Ruth and Morgan took a lantern down to the river to wash away the grit gathered from two weeks on the trail.

"Lord Almighty," Ruth said as she dog paddled in the deep pool, "cool water and good soap. I was beginning to think they had disappeared from the face of the earth."

Morgan laughed. "John says that last stretch was the hardest part of the trail. I sure hope so." She waded until she was shoulder deep and then pushed into a glide and side stroked out to Ruth.

They treaded water and Ruth grinned at Morgan. "You beginning to show, girl. Either that or you been eating better than I have."

"You think I'm pregnant?"

"Aren't you?"

"I don't know yet. I missed my time, but hard traveling might have something to do with that."

"Girl, you got the glow that comes from being with child."

Morgan laughed softly and said, "I hope so. I love the boys, but I think a child of my own…especially a girl child…would round out our family."

Morgan turned and swam for the bank. "Come on, Ruth. I have something special I've been saving back. At Fort Hall I bought two bars of Sunlight soap. It's for a lady's hair."

Ruth laughed. "Anything sounds better than lye soap."

Morgan and Ruth walked back to camp, refreshed, dressed in clean clothes and happy with Morgan's secret.

"You sure look better," John said with a grin as they walked into the firelight. "Feeling better?"

"Here you go," Morgan said, and handed him the cardboard box that protected her Sunlight soap. "You men could benefit from a bath. Ripe is what I call you."

She looked at O'Grady and Beecher and said, "That includes you two as well. I don't know if you have any clean duds, but if you have, it would be nice if you wore them. Bring your old clothes back and we'll wash them tomorrow."

"And you as well, Ezra," Ruth ordered.

Beecher started to protest that he'd had his spring bath, but when Ruth allowed a skunk smelled better, he settled for "yes ma'am," and followed Bitter's lantern toward the river.

"Bathing in the dark, being skeeter food," Beecher grumbled. "I'll be lucky if I don't step on a rattlesnake. Ezra, my friend, Ruth may not be very big, but I'll bet she can be a hellcat when she gets going."

Ezra laughed, "You know, one time back in Maryland, a big old white boy told me to step aside and let him continue his morning constitutional. By the time Ruth finished, he was saying 'sorry,' calling her 'ma'am', and he damned near apologized to me. He caught himself in time to avoid that indignity, but I had a hard time to keep from laughing."

Rusty got up from where he had been lying by the fire and started growling. Nose twitching, teeth bared, he looked with un-blinking eyes at a patch of brush beyond the wagons.

Morgan edged over to the wagon box and pulled her Navy revolver from its holster.

"Hello the camp. Can I come in?"

"Who are you?"

"It's me, Owl."

Surprise in her voice, Morgan said, "Owl?"

Looking a bit gaunt, his buckskins no longer new, Owl stepped from behind a bush and said, "Rusty, don't you remember me?" He patted his knee and said, "Come here boy."

Rusty edged forward, sniffed Owl's outreached hand, and then started a tail wagging greeting.

Owl grinned at Morgan and Ruth. "Whew. I thought he was gonna bite me. Us Indians don't like to get bit by dogs."

Morgan put her pistol back in the holster and said, "Come on in. Where's Woman?"

"She's back in the trees with Horse. Said she wanted to make sure you didn't shoot me. That wild Irishman with you?"

"Yes. He's going on to Oregon with us."

"Good. I heard him promise me a cigar and a shot of whiskey."

Ruth started laughing, and then sputtered, "You were listening?"

Owl grinned and said, "I've never been too far away. Sometimes I slip up close at night and listen to you talk. I need to keep my white man's talk polished up, and that's a good way to do it.

"But we've been hungry some, me and Woman. It's hard to hunt with so many Indians around. You got any bacon? I miss my bacon. And coffee."

Morgan gave him an unfriendly look. "Nope."

"Why not?"

"You leave Woman out there alone and then figure we'll feed you. You get her in here first."

Owl whistled and waited. A dead branch popped under a hoof, and then Woman walked into camp leading Horse, the unnamed mare she rode, and their smaller pack animal.

"Ask her to sit by the fire Owl. You go take care of your animals, and then we'll have coffee and fried bacon. Got it?"

"You white women could learn from us Indians. Then you wouldn't be so rude to your elders or to your men."

"And you could learn to treat your women with more respect."

With an exaggerated sigh, old Owl untied the bundles on the pack horse, slipped girths and unsaddled both horses. The women heard him say something in grumbling Cherokee…or what they thought must be Cherokee…as he led the horses out to the open ground where he could picket them on a little patch of bunch grass.

The celebration grew a bit after the bathers returned to camp. Kegs for sitting surrounded a fire encouraged by dry cottonwood limbs. Owl chewed on one of O'Grady's cigars, sipped whiskey from a tin cup, and told lies about his adventures as he dogged the wagons through Starr Valley, Soda Springs and on to Fort Hall.

"The passes got too narrow. We couldn't stay up and off the road, so we traveled by night. Moonlight is best for that kind of traveling, but the really dark nights were hard. I just had to let Horse have his head and trust to his eyesight some nights."

"Did you cross the road ahead of me in Starr Valley?" Bitter asked.

"That wasn't good. I thought you were ahead of us."

"So you were in that little stand of aspen above the road. Right?"

Owl nodded. "Yes. Good thing we're friends, huh?"

"So, Owl," O'Grady said, "y'all gonna be a white man again?"

"Woman wants my son to learn the way of the whites. She says our days as wild people is about over. She says we have to learn new ways or the people will disappear.

So I think we will find a nice reservation…someplace in Oregon. I'll teach the young people to speak English, do their numbers and read and write. I can make a living that way."

Morgan said, "I didn't think Woman spoke at all."

"At night I can't keep her quiet. She has a busy mind."

"Doesn't she have a name other Woman?" Ruth asked, exasperation in her voice.

Owl nodded. "It doesn't translate well. It means the change in the color of a magpie's wing when it flies. You know…from black to a shiny dark green. That's Woman…sort of hidden until she talks. Maybe her name is Quiet Talker…or Seldom Speaks. Something like that."

"Oh, you old rascal," Morgan said. "You're just teasing us."

Owl grinned and said, "Maybe."

Beecher laughed. "You speak any French?"

Owl shook his head. "I only know three languages…Cherokee, Cheyenne and English. I can cuss a little in French, but that doesn't count."

"Don't matter," Beecher said. "On French Prairie we live with what's left of the Kalapuya. My wife is Kalapuya. Being married to me kept her from being sent to the reservation, not that many survived the sickness. Malaria is what they called it. Killed a lot of Kalapuya.

"Anyway, my new Indian friend, if you would like, you could build a nice cabin on my land and teach good English to the descendants of the Métis and Kalapuya. How does that strike you?"

"Well…first I have to go see the ocean. Taste the water. How far is it to the ocean from French Prairie?"

Beecher laughed. "You know I've never taken the time to see the ocean, but I'm told it's about two days by horseback. Hell, I'll go with you."

Owl tilted his head and studied Beecher's face. And then a smile creased his weathered face. "I think I'll drink to that."

Owl watched John Bitter light a roll-your-own, and then asked, "You find Thomas's people?"

Bitter shook his head. "The Pinkertons are looking, but no word yet. In the morning I'll go the fort and check for messages."

"That's good. He needs to be with his people."

14

The Bitter and the Sweet

THOMAS AND BITTER WERE UP early, anxious to visit the fort and see if Mark Anthony had any news about Thomas's relatives. They skipped breakfast and walked a river bank path a short distance to the fort. A morning Robin sent his "cheer up, cheerily, cheer up" out through the willow trees.

When they were out of sight of the wagons, Bitter stopped, knelt down and looked Thomas in the eye. He took a deep breath and said, "I don't want you getting your hopes up, Thomas, but if anybody can find your people, Mark Anthony can. He's got detectives working for him it seems like everywhere."

Thomas nodded and said, "I don't know…our close family was all killed but me when the Indians…" He blinked back tears, and then started in again. "I don't remember any other family. We were all going to Oregon together."

Bitter nodded and said, "You're a brave boy Thomas."

He stood back up and brushed the grass and dust off his pants. "If we can't find any relatives, you can always live with us."

The main gates were closed, but a sentry posted on a catwalk inside the walls called down and asked them their business. When Bitter identified himself, the sentry said, "Good morning Captain. Use the pilgrim's gate."

When Bitter told the trooper who unlocked the pilgrim gate he needed the telegraph office, the trooper pointed across the compound to the main headquarters building.

"Over there," he said. "Knuckles should be up watching the wire this time of day."

"Knuckles?"

The trooper grinned. "I think his given name is Stanley, Stanley Sweet, but he's called Knuckles because when he gets drunk, he picks out someone twice his size and says 'I'm taking you to knuckle city.'"

Bitter laughed. "And how does he do?"

The trooper grinned and said, "He always looses, and when they let him out of the guardhouse, he always says he through drinking. That lasts until payday. And then he starts all over again."

Bitter chuckled and shook his head. "I don't know if it takes all kinds, but it's a fact that there are all kinds."

"Ain't that the truth."

Bitter smiled. "Well, Thomas. Let's go see Knuckles and find out if Mark Anthony sent us anything."

A young trooper, all of five-feet-four or five-inches tall, wearing a bruise around his left eye, answered Bitter's knock.

"What do you want?"

Bitter showed him his Pinkerton badge and said, "I'm John Bitter. I'm expecting a wire from the Pinkertons. Has anything come in?"

"As a matter of fact...I do have something. Come on in."

He walked to a plank counter that held his telegraph key, a pad of paper and several pencils. "Here you go," he said, fishing two slips of paper from the pile in a cigar box.

Thomas watched anxiously as Bitter read the two slips of paper. When Bitter frowned, Thomas felt his shoulders sag.

"Well, Thomas. The news is good. Mark Anthony found a family who claim to be distant cousins to your father. It's a short message, but it says they are coming to Oregon next year, and asks if you can stay with us until they get there. They don't want me to send you back. Okay?"

Thomas felt a new pang of anxiety. The Bitter's were friends, but these new people were total strangers. He swallowed the lump in his throat and nodded.

"The second one says, 'Coming by ship, send directions. MA.' I think that means my friend Mark Anthony is coming to Oregon."

He looked at the small trooper and couldn't keep the smile from sneaking onto his face at the sight of the man's black eye. "Well, Mister Knuckles, I need to send a wire to Mark Anthony in Washington D.C., care of the Pinkerton National Detective Agency."

"Who told you my name was Knuckles? You tell me and I'll fix him, I will."

Bitter laughed and said, "Don't get your dander up, Mister Sweet. I think I'll let you figure that one out. Now…here's what I want to send."

Sweet talked while he worked the key in a foreign sounding pattern of clicks and clacks that made no sense to Bitter. "The Pinkertons have their own telegraph in their office in Washington City. This will go direct." He stopped working the key and in less than twenty seconds, the key clicked in a slightly new rhythm. Sweet spelled out each letter as quickly as he could with a newly sharpened pencil and then said, "They acknowledged receipt."

He looked up from his chair and asked, "Anything else I can do for you, Captain Bitter?"

"No. I think that'll do it. Thanks. How much do I owe you?"

"If it was up to me, I'd say it was free, but the Sergeant says I have to charge one dollar."

Camp was astir by the time Bitter and Thomas walked back up the river. The fire was going and the tang of salty bacon seasoned by wood smoke drifted through the tangle of willows lining the river. Bitter noted the bedding airing on rope lines strung between two big umbrella willows.

"That's smells pretty good, Thomas. You hungry?"

"Yep." And then the blurted, "I don't know those people, Mister Bitter. What if they don't like me? What if I don't like them?"

"We'll work that out when the time comes, Thomas."

Rusty and Corky started barking as a chestnut horse carrying a blue clad mountain of human flesh splashed across the shallow riffles of the Boise River and up on the bank. The rider pulled the horse to a stop just beyond the wagons, swung down, and dropped the reins to ground hitch the horse.

Morgan said, "Quiet, you two," to the dogs.

Bitter decided the horse looked a mite small to be carrying so large a man. *Large… but there's not an ounce of fat on him. What? Six foot five or six? Tall and broad as an axe handle,* Bitter thought. *And a Captain of cavalry it looks like. A fighting man to judge by the scar on his jaw. Saber scar maybe.*

"Good morning, folks," the big man said to the people eating breakfast around the fire. "I don't mean to disturb your breakfast, but I wanted to see when your party will be ready to tackle the next stretch."

Bitter looked at the freshly washed clothes drying on ropes strung between two willow trees, the bedding airing on other lines, took a deep breath and said, "Why do you want to know?"

"Excuse me. I should have introduced myself. I'm Captain Bidwell. I lead the Oregon Volunteers that will accompany this train on through to The Dalles."

Bitter looked at Ezra who was sipping coffee and chewing on a cigar stub. "I think we need about another two days to rest these animals, John. They look pretty gaunt."

"Okay, then," Bidwell nodded. "We have to resupply as well, and our horses also need some rest. Daybreak two mornings hence, then. "

O'Grady asked, "You expecting Indian trouble?"

Looking less than happy, Bidwell said, "We've forty troopers. That plus the wagon party makes us pretty strong. It's no guarantee, but once we hit the Grande Rhonde, I think we should be in good shape."

"What about the Cayuse?" Beecher asked. "They giving travelers trouble?"

Bidwell took his big hat off and rubbed his forehead. "Is that coffee I'm smelling?"

Over coffee he reviewed the history of the Cayuse and the Umatilla and the 1851 treaty between the U.S. Government and the Indians. "And so, they all moved onto the reservation about fourteen years ago."

Beecher nodded. "I heard about that, but you know damned good and well that doesn't keep the hot heads, the young bucks from sneaking off the reservation and holding up wagon trains and stealing horses…or women for that matter."

"That will not happen on this trip. I guarantee it," Bidwell said emphatically.

"Any place to buy hay or grain or to graze our animals?" Ezra asked, changing the subject.

Morning of day three saw the Bitter and Shipley mule teams pulling directly up the Oregon Trail past Fort Boise to join seven other pioneer wagons and two army supply wagons

In spite of the season, it was a cool morning. "Good for the animals," Owl said from atop Horse as he eased up beside Bitter's wagon. "That lame-footed Rockford horse will ready to ride in a few days. Then you won't have to do woman's work."

"Woman's work?" Bitter said with a touch asperity in his tone.

"Yes. Men ride horses. Women drive wagons."

A private wheeled his horse from the head of the line and trotted back to the Bitter wagon. "Captain wants you and your friend's wagons up front."

"What's the reason for that?"

The private shook his head. "The captain doesn't share his reasons with me. I'm just relaying his orders."

Sergeant Ambrose touched the brim of his broad hat in a casual salute and nodded when Bitter's wagon reached the head of the line. "Good morning, Captain Bitter. Let's roll 'em."

"You going with us ?"

Ambrose nodded. "I'm getting too old for this army business. Time to find a rocking chair and a fishing pole. But the time we get to The Dalles, I'll be a civilian again. This is the safest way I know to make the trip."

15
Farewell Bend to LaGrande

MIDMORNING OF DAY FOUR FROM Fort Boise saw Bitter pull the mules to a stop, wrap the reins around the wagon brake, and step down from the wagon seat. He stretched and looked back at the flat, gray water of the Snake River at Farewell Bend. A team of oxen pulled a wagon from the ferry and up the small embankment, and the ferry reversed and headed for a cluster of wagons on the Idaho side of the Snake River.

"Hallelujah," he shouted to Morgan as she rode up on Lucifer. "Oregon, Morgan. We are in Oregon at last. I feel like I just got out of prison. We have some miles to cover, but by the grace of God, we are home."

Morgan smiled at his enthusiasm. "And how many more miles have we to go, John Bitter?"

"A few, Morgan Bitter, a few. We'll camp on the Burnt River tonight, the North Powder next, and then on to LaGrande. Some French trapper named the Grande Rhonde valley LaGrande, and grand it is. And then it's only about two weeks to the Willamette Valley and home."

She pointed to the big, bare hills, sun baked, sere and dry, the bunch grass brown and long past cured. "Is it all like this?"

Bitter smiled and said, "No. In two days we'll be in the Powder River valley. You'll see tall mountains again…covered with pine.

And we'll have good grazing, cool mountain water, and an easy grade for a couple of days."

"We've been very fortunate, John. There have been no breakdowns, no lost animals, no sickness. Do you think we'll stay lucky?"

"I think we will. You see, I'm a very lucky person. I have a good wife, good boys, good friends, strong mules and a good wagon. What could go wrong?"

Young Lieutenant Benjamin Riley, who had been spending more evenings at the Bitter-Shipley campfire than seemed necessary to John Bitter, loped his horse up the long grade. He pulled his mount to a halt and saluted, a salute that went unanswered by former Captain John Bitter.

Lieutenant Riley said, "The captain told me the crossing is going to take the rest of the day. If you wish to go ahead, there is good graze and good water at Express, a stage stop on the Burnt River. I'm to take Sergeant Ambrose and a squad with you, if that's your wish."

"What I wish is the ox teams pulling those other wagons were a little faster. But, I'll settle for going on ahead, and I thank you for your company. By the way, what have you done with Beecher and O'Grady?"

"They were across the river at first light, scouting the road. Unless they run into trouble, they'll be back before dark."

"Good. I always feel better if that old mountain man is in camp. He knows things, senses things before the rest of us…with maybe the exception of old Owl. And Liam O'Grady comes a close second to Beecher." He paused and then added with a chuckle, "Except for one notable time."

"When was that?" Lieutenant Riley asked.

Bitter grinned. "I think I better let him tell that tale. Ask him about the Franklin campaign some time, and bring some good whiskey when you do."

Lieutenant Riley nodded. "I will."

Beecher and O'Grady found the Bitter-Shipley party camped on a rocky flat in a bend of the Burnt River where Dixie Creek added a low summer-water trickle. Wagons half surrounded by the army's "A" tents, Sergeant Ambrose was barking orders to string ropes between the sumac trees to hang privacy blankets and to dig a private latrine for the ladies, a courtesy that would be repeated each evening until they reached The Dalles. The metallic sound of shovels banging rocks told the story of an alluvial fan where the two streams became one.

Bitter waved to Beecher and O'Grady as he led the mules back to camp after watering them from the river.

A thicket of sumac trees, some about twenty feet tall provided shade. Woman was standing on an upturned bucket reaching as high as she could to pick the last of the red berries from the trees.

"She's going to make a drink," Owl explained as he sat on an upturned keg while he carved willow whistles with the pocket knife Bitter had given him back on the Little Blue. "It's good for the stomach. Her morning stomach has been complaining."

"You mean she has morning sickness, from being pregnant," Ruth said from beyond her wagon as she milked Queeny, the white streams of warm milk shushing into a clean bucket.

He shook his head. "No. Indian women don't get morning sick. Only white women."

Morgan spooned some bacon grease into her iron skillet and set it on a flat rock by the fire. As soon as the fire had a good bed of coals, she intended to fry the little rabbit Ethan had shot earlier in the day.

The boys were down on the creek with one cane pole and three willow poles trying to catch trout for supper. Uneasy for some reason, Ezra followed them to the little river, a leather gun belt carrying one of Bitter's extra pistols strapped to his waist.

Bitter's other extra pistol kept O'Grady and Beecher company on their scouting trips. Earlier when he offered O'Grady the pistol, Bitter had explained, "I'd loan you my Henry, Liam, but if I needed it…"

O'Grady nodded and said, "I'm grateful, John. If I find one like it in The Dalles, I'll buy it." O'Grady patted the pistol butt and said, "In the meantime, I'll pepper any outlaws or wild Indians trying to pester us while Beecher reloads."

O'Grady and Beecher rode to the campfire and dismounted. "Whew," Beecher said to no one in particular. "I'm getting a mite long in the tooth for this life. I keep thinking about my rocking chair and warm biscuits with wild blackberry jam."

Lieutenant Riley and Sergeant Ambrose left troopers digging latrines and starting cook fires and walked over to the Bitter-Shipley wagons.

"See anything," Riley asked?

"I'm glad to see, you, too," Beecher said. "We're just fine, thank you. Still got our scalps."

"I think the Lieutenant wants a report," Sergeant Ambrose said.

"Oh, I see," O'Grady added, ignoring Riley. "He just wants a report. Well, y'all can tell him we found a sad group of Cayuse… or at least that's what Mister Beecher says they are…digging roots and gathering grass seeds along the Powder River. Mostly women, younguns and old men. A couple of teenage boys were trying to spear fish."

Bitter's attention sharpened. "No grown men?"

"No," Beecher and O'Grady said in unison.

"What does that mean?" Lieutenant Riley asked.

Beecher finished tamping his pipe with an awful smelling concoction he called tobacco, dragged a thumbnail across the head of a wooden match and sucked the stem until the bowl was lit. He waved the match until the flame died and tossed the dead match in the fire pit.

"Well, Lieutenant," the old mountain man said, "it could mean a couple of things. For one, it could mean the warriors are off someplace on a big hunt. Or it could mean they're off someplace else stealing horses, raiding settlements and trying to kill travelers."

"I thought you said the Indians in this part of the world were on reservations," Morgan said.

"They are," Beecher said, "but they're allowed to hunt, fish, and gather on their traditional grounds."

"And there ain't enough soldiers to keep 'em on the reservations to begin with," Ambrose added in disgust.

"Any horse herd?" Bitter asked.

"A few ponies running loose in the south end of the valley… probably enough to pack their possessions and whatever else they gather up."

Ruth set a bucket of fresh milk on the tailgate of her wagon, up out of reach of the dogs and asked, "Do they just go off and leave their women and children unprotected?"

Beecher nodded. "Sometimes…for a few days…if they are satisfied there are no raiders nearby."

Rusty's barking and growling, accented by Corky's sharp yapping tugged their thoughts from the nagging worry of warrior bands. They heard Ezra shout and then Bitter, followed closely by O'Grady and Beecher was running for the river.

A pistol shot followed by two more echoed off the hills. Bitter and O'Grady pulled their pistols as they ran. Bitter shouted, "Ezra! Where are you?"

"Over here, John," Ezra shouted. The river bank blocked all but the view of Ezra's yellow hat. They heard him say, "Keep back, boys, and get those dogs under control."

Bitter and O'Grady topped the bank in time to see Ezra poke a dead limb at the headless, writhing body of a rattler all of four feet long. Ezra looked up and took a deep breath to calm his nerves. "Dang, but this big old rattler scared the bejesus out of me. I almost stepped on him, and he coiled up and went to buzzing. Had to shoot him. I'll bet he's a good five feet long."

"Boys," Bitter said, "I think we best get up off the river and back to camp. We'll let the snakes have the fish in this river."

Ethan shuddered and said, "Yessir, Pa," and started climbing the bank. "Come on Mikey…and you two. We don't like snakes."

Around the supper fire, Owl asked, "You gonna eat that snake?

"Lord, no," Ezra said. "They be ugly and stink to high heaven."

Owl, nodded. "Yes, they do. Did you bury the head?"

Ezra nodded. "I did."

"That's good," Owl said. "An old, old story tells of a huge yellow jacket that ate the head of a rattle snake and drank all of the snake's poison. When he stung one of The People, that person died from the rattlesnake poison. That's how yellow jackets became our enemies. And that's why we always bury the head of the snake when we kill one."

Ezra nodded. "There's a similar story told in the South."

For those sleeping on the ground or in tents that night, sleep was disturbed by dreams of buzz tails and dripping fangs.

16

A Galvanized Yankee

THE BAND OF CAYUSE BEECHER and O'Grady had seen camped on the Powder River the day before were gone by the time Lieutenant Riley led his troopers and the Bitter-Shipley wagons to the Powder River.

Riley called a noon halt, and his troopers dismounted and loosened saddle girths, checked horse hoofs, fiddled with personal gear and looked for snakes. No cooking fires were lit, but Ruth offered the grateful troopers fresh milk for their tin cups and butter for their dried biscuits.

"Mighty, good Miz Shipley," one trooper said before wiping away his milk moustache. "Makes me homesick, it does."

"And where would that be?" she asked.

"Ohio. My folks have a farm back there."

"You going back?"

He shook his head. "No. I like this Oregon country. I'll build me a home out here someplace when my enlistment is up. Then I might send for my brothers."

The horses and mules were watered and allowed to graze for an hour while O'Grady and gray haired Tom Beecher rode a wide circle through the tall rye grass growing along the river, scouting for tracks to see where the Indians had gone.

They pulled their horses to a stop and Beecher pointed to a wide swathe of trampled grass. "I reckon even a Johnny Reb could follow that sign."

"I'll have y'all know I am now a genuine galvanized Yankee, not a rebel."

Beecher, who had grown to like the young O'Grady, grinned and tugged at his white beard. "Now tell me, O'Grady. How did you get to be a galvanized Yankee?"

"I blame it all on Captain John Bitter."

Beecher raised his eyebrows and waited while O'Grady used his skinning knife to cut a slice of tobacco from a plug he carried in his shirt pocket. "Well?" Beecher said.

"Well," O'Grady said, and bit down on the tobacco. "You see, I was scouting the Union lines at Franklin, me and about twenty good ol' boys, a horse back, trying to locate their right flank. We were sorta easing along this old road that wound through the hardwoods, and the next thing you know, we had blue bellies in front of us , blue bellies in back of us , and blue bellies on both sides. They just appeared out of nowhere. They pretty much had us boxed.

"And then this Union captain feller rode out from behind a big old walnut tree and said, in a really pleasant manner I should add, 'Howdy, boys. Welcome to the end of your war.' And that was it. The union boys went to laughing and collecting our weapons… and our horses. And they made us walk to the Union lines. Plumb humiliating, it was. Besides, I hate to walk.

"Anyway, that's when this Union captain offered me a drink. He said, 'You probably won't find any whiskey where you're going.'

"And then, later when I heard about the battle and the number of good men General Hood squandered, I got to feeling pretty grateful to that Union captain. I figured he probably saved my life.

"I sat around in a prisoner camp for two months, feeling sorry for myself. No whiskey, no tobacco, and no women in a prison camp. So then this Union Army feller offered me to get out of the prisoner stockade if I would swear allegiance to the Union and go fight the savages in the West. I did not want to spend any more time in a stockade, so I became a galvanized Yankee.

"We was at Barton's Trading Post when I ran into Captain Bitter again. I hadn't known his name up until then, but I recognized him, and he remembered me. Anyway, that was the time we rescued the Gatling Gun and convinced about twenty good ol' southern boys the war was over."

"Gatling Gun?"

"Yeah, you see these ol' boys were hiding in a little valley…" Beecher spent most of the ride back to the river and the wagons entertained by O'Grady's tale of the adventures of Captain John Bitter.

As they walked their horses through a shallow ford on the Powder River, Beecher said, "It sounds like John Bitter rode to war a youngster and came home a man. I think he'll do just fine when he gets home. Maybe I'll talk him into running for governor…or senator even. Now about you, my young friend, I'm thinking an enterprising soul like yourself would do well in French Prairie with a nice tavern. Can you cook?"

17

Blue Mountains and Hard Times

G RAY STORM CLOUDS THREATENED TO ruin the morning, and a strong breeze brought the cool scent of rain as the travelers broke camp in the LaGrande Valley. Morgan stood on a short wooden keg to saddle Lucifer and said over her shoulder, "I never thought I'd smell rain again. I don't want to get wet, but some clean, dust free air would be nice."

"Amen, to that," Bitter said as he finished harnessing the mules. "I think I'll dig out our slickers.

"Ethan, you help Mikey saddle Misery. You boys can ride horseback for now, but I want you to stay close to the wagon."

"You want me to drive the wagon, Pa? Then you can ride Josey," Ethan said.

"I think I'll save you for when we're over the Blues. Okay?"

Ethan looked disappointed, but he said, "Sure, Pa."

Bitter heard Thomas say, "Told you," as the boys turned their horses and started up the trail.

Lieutenant Riley turned his mount and trotted over to the wagons. "Trooper Smith came in at first light. Your dogs must have been asleep. Anyway, Captain Bidwell sent him ahead of the main party. I guess about half the people in the other wagons have come down with something. And to make matters worse, a couple of their oxen died. Just up and died, mysteriously.

"Captain Bidwell said we could either wait on the main party or just keep going. Me and the boys will stay with you either way."

Ezra looked at Ruth, and Bitter looked at Morgan. Both women nodded. "We'll keep going then, Mister Riley," Bitter said.

Riley nodded. "Good. I'm anxious to get away from these skeeters. And I'm not keen on being around sick folks."

Wind and rain ambushed the party just as they hit the first steep grade in the Blues. Most of the troopers were drenched before they could pull ponchos from bedrolls.

Over the noise of thunder and pounding rain, Bitter whistled the boys over and reached for his slicker. "Tie your horses on behind and get under the top."

Morgan wrapped the reins around the Lucifer's saddle, turned him loose and climbed up beside Bitter. "Are you glad you didn't try Rockford today?"

"Day's not over," he grinned. "Quite a storm."

"Where's O'Grady and Beecher?" she asked.

"Scouting again. I imagine they'll hunker down under a big tree and ride the storm out."

Four troopers in rain-slick, rubberized ponchos, sat on their mounts under a big pine until the wagons pulled even. Blinking the water out of his eyes, a young trooper said, "Howdy. Sergeant Ambrose said we was to rope two horses to each wagon to give you some help with the next grade. He says it's all steep ground for the next five or six miles."

The increase in elevation gradually brought a mix of soft snow and cold rain. By the time they reached the first summit, and the troopers untied their ropes to leave the wagon pulling to the mules, quietly falling snow replaced the rain, and the boys could see Rusty's tracks in the snow.

Rusty snapped at falling snow flakes, trying to catch them in the air. Ethan laughed until Mikey took offense and said, "It's his first snow storm. He don't know any better."

"Well, I think it's your first snow storm, too. And you know better."

Corky's short legs just made it too hard for her to keep up with the mules, and Ruth suspected she was carrying a litter of puppies, so she rode behind the wagon seat, snug under the wagon top with Davey for company.

A puff of wind blew snow through the front flap of the wagon and Mikey said, "It's sure cold, Miz Morgan."

"Wrap up in a blanket, Mikey," Morgan said. "I see a fire up ahead. I think we're going to take a rest and try to get warm."

O'Grady and Beecher were grinning when Ezra and Bitter brought the mules to a halt in a stand of mixed pine and fir. The heat rising from their big fire was bouncing the lower limbs of a leaning fir tree.

O'Grady laughed and said, "What a sight. From roasting heat to snow storms. We figured you'd be along pretty soon."

"Where's your slickers?" Morgan asked.

Beecher shook his head. "In the wagon, of course. You know that was kinda careless of us."

Sergeant Ambrose rode back down the road. "Lieutenant Riley figures to stop for an hour. Give you a chance to water your stock. Rest a bit. We won't share your fire. There's too many of us. We'll build our own."

Bitter nodded. "An hour then, Sergeant. But I'm hoping we pitch camp before dark."

"Twelve miles to Immigrant Springs…more or less. Good wood and water there. And Meachum Stage Stop nearby. The boys figure on having a drink there tonight. And if there's room, we might get to bunk in their nice dry barn."

"What's the road like?"

"Well, as I remember it, there's some ups and some downs. But from Meachum, it's all downhill to the Umatilla River. We'll keep doing like we been doing…rope up and help your teams on the uphill stretches."

Owl rode Horse, followed by Woman and the packhorse up to the fire and slid down without so much as looking at Woman.

"You look like a wet hound, Owl," Bitter said.

Owl looked exasperated. "You white men are too dumb to camp and wait the storm out. If we want to travel with you, we get wet."

Woman, her black hair dripping cold water, looked blue around the lips. Morgan hurried over to help her down. Woman pushed her away and slid off her horse, but her knees buckled when she hit the ground. Morgan caught her and helped her to the fire. "John," she ordered. "Go get something for Woman to sit on. And bring our heavy blanket."

Ruth said, "Morgan, she's got a fever. I can see it from here. We can't camp here. She should ride in one of our wagons."

Hands on her hips, Morgan turned on Owl. "Why didn't you say something? She could have ridden with us. Now she's wet and cold and sick. And don't give me any of that 'us Indian you whites' nonsense either."

Owl, who had lived more than sixty years, mainly by his wits, knew when to keep his mouth shut.

When they pulled off the road into the timber at Immigrant Springs, the snow measured six inches deep. But just at dusk, the skies cleared, the first evening stars rode the eastern sky, and the temperature dropped. While the boys gathered firewood and pine cones, and broke dry limbs from trees, Ezra and Bitter watered and grained the mules, tendrils of steam from wet mule hides drifting into the air.

"Mules," Bitter said quietly while he rubbed each one down with a scrap of blanket, "you get me to Abiqua Creek, I'm gonna turn you loose for a month. Fatten you up. You may have to pull a plow now and again, or take a short trip, but no more killer trips like this one for you."

"I'll say amen to that," Ezra added while he rubbed his own mules down.

O'Grady and Beecher helped Owl scrape away the snow and pitch his tent, the flaps open to the fire. Owl admitted to himself he was ashamed he hadn't noticed how Woman was suffering, but he was too proud to say so aloud.

In atonement he rolled out Woman's moth eaten buffalo hide as a ground cloth and helped her down from the Shipley wagon. He wrapped her in two thick Hudson's Bay wool blankets and pillowed her head on a rolled up scrap of blanket.

When he laid a hand on her forehead, Owl could feel the fever. "I'll make some willow tea. Bring the fever down. Help you sleep."

Woman said something in Cheyenne, and Ethan nudged Thomas and raised his eyebrows in question. Thomas whispered, "She said she was sorry to lose the baby."

"What?"

Thomas listened to Owl and Woman talking and then said, "She just told him she lost the baby. Buried it back on the river bank. Owl just thought she was taking a long time to relieve herself. He sounds like he is crying."

Morgan looked at Thomas and asked, "What's going on."

Tears formed in the corners of his eyes and then over spilled and started down his cheeks. "Oh, Miz Morgan," he said in a choked voice, "she lost her baby."

Owl stepped out of the tent and said, "Boys, I need some big rocks." He held his hands about six inches apart. "About this big. We'll heat 'em up in the fire and put 'em around her bed. Keep her warm. While you find some rocks I'll make Woman some willow tea."

18
Owl's Medicine and Ruth's Prayer

BEECHER AND O'GRADY SPELLED EACH other off through the night, feeding the fire and warming gray rocks for Owl to tuck in and around Woman's bed. They watched while he gently fed Woman a bitter willow tea one spoonful at a time. "You got any sugar?" he asked Morgan when he was first brewing the tea. "This tea is bitter as gall. Sugar helps. Most people can't drink it, but if I add a little sugar it makes it better."

Morgan brought out the can holding the last of her sugar. When Owl mixed three heaping teaspoons of sugar in the little pot of tea and then ate a spoonful himself, Morgan couldn't help but wonder if he wasn't a little less than honest about the need for sugar in the tea.

Once during the night, Ethan, barely visible in the firelight stuck his head out from the back flap of the wagon and whispered, "Mister O'Grady, can me and the boys have a couple of rocks. It's colder than hell in here."

O'Grady suppressed a smile and said quietly, "Watch your language, young Ethan."

"Well? You got any warm rocks?"

The cold drove Bitter from the tent where he and Morgan endured the night. He whispered to O'Grady he'd take over the chore of tending the fire. Just before the sun pushed the gray light from the sky, he saw the canvas flap stir and watched Ethan drop a rock behind the wagon, and shoes in hand, slip to the ground. Rusty leaned over the raised tailgate, jumped and hit the ground with a quiet grunt. He tail-wagged to the fire and bumped Bitter's hand with his cold nose, asking for something to eat. Bitter absent-mindedly rubbed the dog's head.

"I wonder, Ethan," Bitter, said in a quiet voice, "if we can find you some socks at the stage stop over at Meachum. What say we saddle up and ride over there? Test Rockford's hoof on a short ride."

Ethan wiped the wet pine and fir needles from his dirty feet and nodded as he tugged his worn shoes on over bare feet. "I wouldn't mind some socks. How is Woman doing?"

"I don't know. Owl hasn't stirred yet."

"Sunshine will make her better," Ethan said.

"You could be right. Well, let's stoke the fire and go see if anyone is up at Meachum. I don't know what they have for supplies, but we'll find out."

Horse hooves crunched through a layer of frozen snow as Bitter and Ethan, their breath visible in the cold air, rode out of camp. It was cold, but a blue sky gave promise of a warmer day. "You know, Ethan," Bitter said, "I'll bet this snow is gone by tomorrow. And I'll bet the trail is dusty the day after."

Ruth and Morgan were turning sizzling bacon strips in cast iron skillets by the time Bitter and Ethan rode back to camp.

Bitter stepped out of the saddle and said, "Looks like Rockford is ready to ride. He doesn't limp at all. And he tried to buck me off."

Bitter held out a small paper bag. "And we found four pairs of socks for the boys. I paid a quarter for each pair, but I think it'll prove worth it. Ethan has stinky feet. Maybe wearing socks will fix that."

Ethan scowled and said, "Do not."

Morgan smiled and said, "Yes you do."

O'Grady poked his head out from under the poncho he used to cover his bedroll and said, "Hold the racket down. I'm trying to get some sleep. How's Woman this morning?"

Sometime during the night Owl had closed the flaps to the tent he and Woman shared. "I don't know," Morgan said, "but we'll let them sleep for now."

"Amen," Ruth said. "Sleep is healing." She paused and then added, "I want to say a prayer to our Lord and Savior, so you heathen man-childs take off your hats and bow your heads."

For some reason Bitter always felt like smiling at Ruth's pronouncements. *It must be the contrast between her iron will and her small size*, he thought. *Lord, she can't be five feet tall, but she could run the devil out of camp if she put her mind to it.*

He almost always managed to hide his amusement, but this time he grinned and took the hat from his head. "Yes ma'am, this heathen man-child will join you in prayer."

By the time Ruth's sincere prayer of thanks for the friendship of Morgan and John Bitter, for the acquaintance of Liam O'Grady, fighting man and drinker though he was, for Ezra's strength and marksmanship, for the friendship between Tom Beecher and Ezra, for Owl's help in escaping the heathen Indians on the Little Blue River, for the friendship of the boys with her little Davey…all of that had Bitter blinking away tears.

"With all these blessings, Oh Lord, we ask one more…that you heal Woman in body and in spirit and lift her up in spite of the grievous loss of her child. Amen."

To his manly disgust a tear leaked out from the corner of Bitter's left eye. *Always the left eye*, he thought.

A hearty "Amen" startled them. "Amen," Owl said again. "Thank you, Sister Ruth."

"You be Christian?" Ruth asked as Owl walked to the fire and held out his hands to the warmth.

Owl nodded and said, "Sometimes."

"You best be constant in your devotion. Part-timers might not get past the Pearly Gates."

Owl grinned. "Maybe I'll have to enter through the tepee flap."

Beecher crawled out of his bedroll and asked, "How is Woman this morning?"

Owl nodded and said, "Her fever is gone and she's asleep. Thank you for the rocks."

Morgan looked at her husband and said, "John, I know you are anxious to move on, but we might want to stay put for a couple of days to give Woman time to heal up and gather her strength."

"What about making a bed in the wagon?" Bitter asked.

"No," Ruth said. "The jouncing might start the bleeding again. I think two days here and then a bed in the wagon."

Bitter looked at the steam rising from tree limbs as the sun melted the snow and lit the orange bark of the big pine trees. "All right, then. We'll lay over for a couple of day. I best go tell Lieutenant Riley."

Beecher nodded. "Good. That'll give us some time to hunt. There's some big, open slopes a few miles ahead that might hold some elk. I'm hungry for a good elk steak." He looked at O'Grady who nodded.

"We'll need a pack horse. You coming, Mister Shipley? We might need you for some long-distance shooting. Any of your mules good for packing?"

Ezra nodded. "The blue one will stand still while you shoot, and he'll carry a good load."

O'Grady said, "That'll be the one then."

"Can me and Thomas come, too?" Ethan asked.

Beecher nodded. "You have to be quiet, and you have to do what I say. And no shooting with that light rifle of yours. Elk are just too big for that little gun."

Ruth watched Ezra and the two bigger boys make energetic preparations and thought, *We all need a change of pace. A few days rest will be a help.*

Bitter had to call Rusty back as the hunting party left camp.

Mikey sat by the fire with his arms crossed and a pout on his face. "They get all the fun," he said. "Me and Davey don't get to do any fun stuff."

"Well," Bitter said, "what say we saddle Misery and we all ride over to the stage stop. We might find some stick candy. I like red-striped peppermint myself. And I think we'll see if we can buy some hay for the animals. There's not much graze to be had right here."

Bitter carried Mikey's saddle to where the animals were picketed. He set the saddle in place, and when he caught Misery swelling up he thumped her belly with a knee.

"Not too hard, Mister Bitter. She's got a colt in there."

"What?"

"She is going to have a colt. Rockford did it to her. And to Ethan's horse, Josey. Josey is going to have a colt, too. That way we'll have a horse ranch, just like you want. You won't have to follow the ass end of mules plowing ground."

"Mikey, have you been listening in on my conversations?"

"Yep. I listen at night. Otherwise I wouldn't know anything. Big people never tell kids anything."

Bitter had to think a minute about that and then nodded. "I think you're right, Mikey. Okay…here's the deal. Anything you want to know, ask, and if I can give you an answer, I will."

Bitter mounted Rockford, and when Rockford bunched up and started to crow hop, Bitter grinned and said, "Go ahead, Rockford. Let's see what you got." A keen observer might have concluded horse and rider were having a good time.

When he was satisfied Rockford had the kinks out, he reached down and swung Davey up behind the saddle. "You hang on, Davey. Your mother will have my scalp if you fall off this horse."

Mikey led Misery to a big downed tree to give him enough height to climb into the saddle. "And Miz Morgan is going to have a baby."

"What? How do you know that?"

"The baby told me."

19
Downhill Grades

S OMETIME DURING THE NIGHT, CAPTAIN Bidwell and the rest of his company rode into Meachum and made camp next to the Meachum horse corral. Alexander Lafollette, the station manager heard the commotion, and pistol in hand tiptoed to the window. A pale moon and the white snow gave enough visibility to convince him the men outside were friends, not hostiles. *Soldiers*, he decided.

He found a match and lit the lantern on the long table, and then walked barefoot across the cold, bare planks to the corner of the big room where Cookie was snoring his way through the night. Lafollette stepped behind the blanket that served as partition and privacy and nudged Cookie with his foot.

"Get up Cookie. We got company."

"What?"

"I said we got company. You get some grub going, and some coffee. Some soldier boys just rode in. They'll be cold and hungry."

Cookie was a perpetual morning grouch, and his middle-of-the-night personality was, if anything, worse. "Let 'em fix their own grub," Cookie growled, and then rolled over to go back to sleep.

Lafollette kicked him in the butt with the heel of his bare foot, and said, "You get busy, George, or I'll send you out on the next stage."

Cookie knew Alexander was serious when he called him George, so he rolled over and sat up. He used a knuckle to rub the sleep from his eyes. "Okay. Okay. How many?"

"I don't know. I'm guessing about thirty."

Cookie nodded. "We got biscuits I made up for the morning stage. That means I'll have to make up some more. We got some duck eggs we can scramble. And there's some gravy left. And I can fry up some of that fresh elk you bought from those immigrants over at the spring. Plus the leftover coffee."

"Well, you get the fire going and I'll go see if they want to be fed."

Lafollette stepped into his boots, slipped into a jacket hanging from a peg, lit the second lantern and stepped out onto the porch. He could hear orders being given and see soldiers setting saddles on the top rail of the horse corral.

A man called across the yard, "Did we wake you up?"

Lafollette nodded and said, "You did." He walked the lantern across the yard and held it up so he could see who he was talking with. It damned near put a crick in his neck to look high enough to see the man's face.

"I'm Captain Bidwell," the big man said. "We ran into some trouble or we'd have been in before dark. A flash flood worked over the road in that first canyon coming up out of LaGrande. Took out part of the road. So we had to wait the flood out. And then we had some road clearing to do."

"How many troopers do you have?"

"Thirty."

"Do they need to be fed?"

Amazed by the offer, Bidwell asked, "Can you do that?"

"Yes. I have some fresh elk meat. And we can scramble some duck eggs, heat some biscuit and gravy, and warm up what's left of the coffee. As soon as Cookie gets the fire going again, we'll warm it up."

"Lordy," Bidwell said, "hot coffee sounds mighty good. We'll get our tents up and take care of the horses. Then we'll be in. What's this going to cost?"

"Well…how does twenty-five cents a head sound?"

"You take military scrip?"

"I do, but it'll be thirty-five cents a head if I have to take scrip." Lafollette was proud to run a profitable station.

Bitter found himself getting more and more impatient the closer he got to home, so he chaffed at Bidwell's decision to rest the cavalry mounts until noon of the second day. Morgan shook her head and smiled at her husband. "Patience, Husband. Woman can use the time to heal a bit. And I take comfort from the presence of Captain Bidwell's troopers."

"Amen," Ruth said. "I've gotten so I'm scared at even the thought of Indians."

Shortly after noon, Captain Bidwell told Lieutenant Benjamin Riley to mount the troop. Riley nodded at Sergeant Ambrose who barked, "Column of twos. Mount."

Bidwell, riding the biggest calvary horse he could find, back erect, led the parade through the sunlit ponderosa pine and down the Oregon Trail. In the sunny patches the snow was already gone and stretches of the road were beginning to dry out.

Ethan guided Josey in alongside Rockford. Bitter nodded and said, "I told you this snow would be gone. We'll eat trail dust before the day is out."

Beecher and O'Grady, drawing scouting pay, were somewhere up ahead. Bitter thought about his own scouting forays during the war and felt a twinge of jealousy at the freedom *that meant. It feels like I've been tied to these wagons forever. Two weeks, just two more weeks and we'll be home. Maybe we should have a 'burn the wagons' celebration,* he thought. And then he laughed out loud.

Ethan looked at him and said, "What?"

"Two weeks…fourteen days to home."

"You sure? I get to wondering if we'll ever get there."

When Bitter asked Bidwell about the other seven wagons, Bid-well spat and said, "Quitters. They just up and said they weren't going any further than the Grande Rhonde Valley. Said they were sick of the trail. They met one of the early settlers in that area, and he talked them into taking up land right there."

"You could do worse," Bitter allowed. "That's nice country." Captain Bidwell pulled a cigar from his pocket and held it out for inspection. "My last one until we get to The Dalles. Meachum didn't have any." He struck a match and sucked on the cigar until the end was cherry red. He took a puff and sighed. "Well…at least we'll be able to move faster and cover more ground without oxen to slow us down."

The nooning took place on a big gravel bar where willow, cottonwoods, and the Umatilla River wrapped their arms around a deep pool fed by a hundred yards of shallow riffles. Big Chinook salmon heading upriver to spawn finned their way through the riffles or let the current drift them back to deeper water.

Beecher and O'Grady had a six foot bed of coals going and a half dozen salmon on the bank. Captain Bidwell rode his big horse to the fire and stepped down. "You trade for the salmon?"

O'Grady looked up from the chore of scaling the fish and shook his head. "No. Beecher just shoots 'em in the head and I catch 'em before they float away."

Troopers led their horses to the river for water, while Beecher packed each fish in river bank clay. He laid salmon in a trench dug in the coals, and then raked mounds of red coals over each one.

"They'll be ready in about an hour, Captain. Then we'll have ourselves a feast. The clay keeps the juices in the fish."

Bidwell pointed at the biggest mud-packed fish and asked, "How big do think that one is?"

"I'd say about fifty pounds. There's some bigger fish in the river, but I didn't want to take the biggest brooders."

An hour later, Beecher borrowed a shovel from Bitter and rolled clay-baked salmon from the coals one at a time. Hungry troopers lined up with tin plates in hand, waiting for Beecher to crack the clay and expose the baked fish.

Morgan asked, "Is Abiqua Creek like this?"

Bitter looked around at the bare, sun-baked hills and said, "No. We have an oak grove, fir trees, sub-irrigated meadows, fruit trees, and…"

Morgan interrupted, "I meant, like this…brimming with salmon."

Bitter thought for a few seconds and then said, "You know, Oregon really is a land of milk and honey. On Abiqua Creek, we've got wild blackberries for fruit and jam, a good run of silver salmon, trout fishing year round, back tailed deer…who work hard at eating my garden and my fruit trees, by the way…and ground that will grow just about anything you want."

The scent of baked salmon drifted to where they sat, and Morgan reached over and patted the back of his hand. "I'm anxious to be there, husband. It smells like the salmon is ready. Let's go get a little of that 'milk and honey.'"

20
Celilo

THE CAVALRY TROOP AND THE Bitter-Shipley party were drawn to the roar of the Columbia River as it poured over a series of waterfalls and rushed through narrow chutes on its way to the Pacific Ocean.

Captain Bidwell told Lieutenant Riley to post guards on the wagons, and have the horse holders wait on the road with the mounts. Riley nodded at Sergeant Ambrose who heard Bidwell's request. Ambrose barked orders to dismount, pointed at four troopers and said, "You boys guard these wagons. Horse holders, watch the mounts. We'll spell you off in a few minutes. The rest of you can go look at the waterfalls."

Bidwell led the troopers and the wagon party to a path worn into the rocks by centuries of foot travel. A low basalt bluff offered a good view of the upper falls.

Beecher pointed at a dozen natives standing on fragile looking scaffolds out over the river, netting and spearing salmon from the boiling water below the falls. He looked at O'Grady and said, "I been here a half dozen times and I still can't get over the sheer guts it takes to fish like that. Ever once in a while, maybe once or twice a year, one of them falls in and is never seen again. They never even look for the body."

To no one in particular…or maybe to everyone in particular, Beecher shouted over the sound of the rapids, "They been doin' that for hundreds of years…maybe thousands. The Wascos call this place Celilo. Kinda of a nice sounding word, ain't it?

"Anyway, near as I can make out Celilo means the sound of water pounding on rocks. Something like that. They dry salmon to trade with other bands of Indians."

Mikey started to walk down the path leading to the river, but Morgan called him back, "No, Mikey. That's too dangerous. If you fall in, we'll never find you."

A bearded photographer, his large wooden-boxed camera perched on a tripod at the edge of the bluff, head under the black cape of the camera, peered at the upside down image in the lens. When he was satisfied with the picture of Indian men perched on precarious looking scaffolds spearing and netting salmon, he tripped the shutter. He liked human figures in his landscapes. *This*, he thought, *is dramatic.*

Ethan's voice pulled him from under the cape. "Whatcha doin, mister?"

The photographer, a large young man with blue eyes and a flowing blond beard looked with surprise at the blond-headed boy and then at the wagons and the troopers.

"Well, I sure let you all sneak up on me, I did. What I'm doing is photographing the wonders of the Columbia River and the Columbia River Gorge."

'Photographing?" Ethan asked.

"Let me show you," the man said. He walked to an oak box about two feet square and unlatched the top lid. "Here." He pulled an eighteen-by-twenty-four-inch picture from a divider in the box. "I like this one." The clear, black-and-white photo showed a waterfall plunging over the top of a tall, tree covered rim, and then over a second, shorter water fall. The tiny figure of a woman in a white jacket could be seen standing at the edge of the lower waterfall.

Ethan stared in amazement and then said, "How tall is that waterfall?"

"About three hundred feet."

Stunned, Ethan said, "I want to make pictures like that."

The photographer looked at the disheveled, blond-haired boy and nodded. Later in life he could never quite figure out what he saw in the boy in that instant, a sudden passion for photography maybe. But whatever it was, he dug into the pocket of his vest and handed Ethan a card that read, "A. G. Brown, Landscapes and Portraiture Studios, Vancouver, Washington."

"You hang on to that card, and when you finish school, if you still want to be a photographer, come to Vancouver and I'll teach you what I know."

Ethan shook hands and said, "Thanks. I will. Can you take a picture of me and my family? My pa will pay you. We live on Abiqua Creek. Come on, I'll introduce you."

Brown posed the Bitter-Shipley party along the bluff, with Bidwell, Riley and Ambrose on one end of the line, Owl and Woman sort of in the middle and Beecher and O'Grady on the far end. He said, "Hold it, hold it," and snapped the shutter. He took two pictures and promised to have the photos delivered to Abiqua Creek.

When Bitter offered to pay, Brown shook his head. "No. When Ethan goes to work for me in about eight or nine years, he can pay me then."

"To work for you?"

"I'm going to be a photographer like Mister Brown," Ethan said.

Brown held out his hand to Bitter. "It was nice to meet you folks. I heard about a waterfall on your Abiqua Creek that's supposed to be pretty special. When I'm through with this trip, I'll bring you these pictures. And I want to photograph Abiqua Falls."

Morgan said, "The least we can do is feed you a good meal when you come. You like apple pie?"

A short, muscular Indian carrying two salmon by the gills, one in each hand, scrambled over the rocks and up the path leading to a collection of rough-looking houses across the wagon road, some made from cut lumber, others from rock and slabs of cedar bark, and some made from canvas stretched over wooden frames.

Beecher greeted the man in the Chinook trade language, and the Indian nodded. He looked the troopers over and, sensing no hostility, nodded again without saying anything. But when he caught sight of Woman standing beside gray haired Owl, he laid the fish on the rocks, pointed to her, and said something that made Beecher laugh.

"Owl," Beecher said, "he wants to know how much to buy your daughter."

Troopers laughed and made catcalls before Bidwell frowned them into silence.

They loitered on the bluff for half an hour, watching the Indians pull salmon after salmon from the river before Captain Bidwell asked Bitter, "You folks ready to roll? It's about four easy hours to The Dalles."

Bitter nodded and looked at Ezra who said, "I'm ready." And then he asked Captain Bidwell, "The Dalles be how far from the Willamette Valley?"

"About ninety miles if you float the river."

Ezra looked at the pounding water and shook his head. "I wouldn't trust a boat on this big river. I'll be going with John Bitter over the Barlow Trail."

21
Home

THEY WERE WITHIN THREE MILES of The Dalles settlements, the snowy peak of Mount Hood poking the sky in the southwest, when Bitter caught sight of a compact, medium-sized man trotting a long-legged bay horse upriver on the wagon road. He dressed for all the world like Mark Anthony, right down to black wool trousers, a long sleeved, white shirt, red sleeve garters, black string tie, and a black bowler hat.

He could pass for Mark Anthony's brother, Bitter thought. He gigged Rockford in the ribs and loped the horse to the front of the column. Bidwell signaled a halt, and as Bitter rode up, he heard the stranger ask for John Bitter.

"I'm John Bitter. You wouldn't be related to Mark Anthony, by any chance?"

The young man, maybe in his mid-twenties, laughed, his brown eyes amused, and said. "I'll have to tell Mark what you said. No, I'm Ralph Comstock, but I do work for Mister Anthony. If you are John Bitter, I have a message for you…a personal message."

Bitter pointed at the shade of a sumac tree about twenty feet tall and said, "Over there."

"Lieutenant Riley," Captain Bidwell said, "let's take a break."

Bitter and Comstock dismounted, horses ground hitched, before Agent Comstock produced his Pinkerton credentials. "Now, if I could see yours."

Bitter shook his head. "I don't carry them. They're in the wagon."

"Okay then, what color is you wife's hair."

"What?"

Comstock laughed. "Mark Anthony said that was the test question."

In disgust Bitter said, "Red. Now why all the games?"

"Because it is vital that you are John Bitter. It seems our mutual friend, Mark Anthony has been to your farm. Squatters, all men, are living in your cabin, eating your fruit and grazing animals on your pasture."

"What?"

"It appears that your brother gave them permission. I don't have the facts behind that, but if you will give Agent Mark Anthony your power of attorney, I will hurry back and he will proceed to evict them."

"Why doesn't he just wait until I get there?"

Comstock smiled. "Because he's afraid you will want to 'reason' with them. He said you always seemed to break your nose on someone's fist when engage in 'reasoning.' Not that you don't win your arguments, but he wanted to save you the trouble."

"I'll do my own reasoning, but I thank him for the kind thought. Now, how in the hell did he get here ahead of me?"

"I traveled with him by ship from Baltimore. By the way, I'm to be the Pinkerton Agent for Seattle when my business here is finished. With the completion of the rail line between the Atlantic side of the Isthmus of Panama and the Pacific side, travelers no longer need to sail through the Magellan Straight and around the South American Continent.

"So the whole trip, counting the run from Panama to San Francisco on the *SS California*, and ten days to Portland on the mail packet, took us a mere fifty days…well, fifty-one actually."

"I'd say that's a lot faster than plodding along with a wagon. And he sent you looking for me?"

"Yes…and he put another agent to watching the Barlow Trail. He figured you would probably use that one if you had gotten here ahead of me."

Agent Ralph Comstock nodded like he had made up his mind about something. He pushed the brim of his derby back on his dark brown hair and looked at Bitter with a smile. "Since you are determined to do your own 'reasoning,' and Mister Anthony said you would want to, I can have you home in two days if you travel by steamboat to Portland and then up the Willamette River to Salem."

"How much will that cost?"

"It's expensive…five dollars per person and five dollars per animal to the Cascades, and then ten dollars per person and ten dollars per animal from the Cascades to Portland."

"That's more than I want to spend. We have eighteen animals and twelve people."

"Mister Anthony advanced me enough money to pay the fare. He is anxious to have you home. He needs your help on an important case."

"I was planning on using the Barlow Trail."

"I'm told that's a much harder and a more time-consuming trail to the Willamette Valley. If we go by steamer, you can disembark at Salem. My maps say it's only about twenty-five miles to your farm from there. And you can take your wagons and your animals. The steamships push barges for just that purpose."

Bitter let out his breath slowly and nodded. "I have to tell you that two days to home sounds unreal. Nice, but unreal. We've been on the trail for over a hundred days. I'll have to talk it over with Morgan and with the Shipley's first, but it sure sounds good to me. Let's go meet my family and my friends. Ezra can't swim, so he'll be the toughest to convince. I think he's scared of the water."

22
Down River

THE TRIP FROM THE DALLES on the side wheeler *Oneonta* to the Cascades took the remainder of the day. Passengers, animals, and cargo had to be driven or hauled the six odd miles below the nearly impassable rapids…impassable except during high water…and then onto a barge waiting to be pushed downriver by the paddle wheeler *Multnomah*.

The comfort of state rooms was morally off limits for the Bitter and Shipley party when Edsel Ross, Captain of the Multnomah said there weren't any state rooms available for coloreds or Indians. So they all wound up camping overnight on the barge, a cold fireless business. Captain Ross did relent the next morning enough to say they could all ride downriver on the deck of the steamer. "Better view," was the only explanation he offered.

Morgan thought his conscience might be bothering him just a little.

They lined the rail on the bow of the ship, amazed by the speed of the sternwheeler, and warmed by the sunshine and the amazing scenery. Tall fir trees climbed steep talus slopes until sheer rock cliffs discouraged tree growth. Above the talus slopes grew moss, ferns, and an occasional determined scrawny fir or a lost maple tree. And lining the cliffs, like massed armies guarding the parapets, stood mixed stands of fir, tamarack, and cedar.

Dark bluffs, some looking to be a thousand feet high, lined both sides of the Columbia River Gorge, draped every few miles by waterfalls that seemed to just appear out of the sky, falling sometimes three hundred feet or more to carve basin pools in hard layers of basalt.

Beecher nudged Bitter and pointed down river. "That big rock right on the river there, standing by hisself is over eight hundred feet tall. Somebody named it Beacon Rock. Biggest rock I ever saw."

Ethan watched an Osprey fold its wings and hammer the water. Wings beating furiously, it rose from the surface of the river with a fish almost too big to carry. He watched until it flew out of sight, wondering where the nest was.

He walked over to Morgan and asked, "Can I have a piece of paper and a pencil?"

"All I have are in the wagon. I'll go ask the ship's captain."

Captain Ross looked puzzled by Morgan's request to buy paper and pencil. In an effort to salve his conscience and make amends, he climbed to the pilot house and returned with three sheets of writing paper and two lead pencils.

"Here you go," he said. "No charge."

Morgan smiled. "Thank you."

Ethan accepted the paper and pens, and disappeared into the passenger area and out of the wind.

Further downriver on the Oregon side stood another smaller monolith, but Beecher said he wouldn't name it in front of the ladies.

In spite of the scenery, Bitter still fumed at the treatment of Owl and of Ezra's family. In a way, he understood the animosity many immigrants felt towards Indians. The Europeans and the Indians had been killing each other for years. Not that it made Ross's behavior toward the Shipley's any better.

"Sonofabitch," he growled without meaning to.

"There you go again, John," Morgan said and raised her eyebrows in question.

"I don't know why I didn't stick a gun barrel up the Captain's nose and insist on state rooms for all of us."

Agent Comstock overheard John and shook his head. "Not worth it, Mister Bitter. We'll be there soon. That's what all of this trouble is about."

'I'll think I'll get out of the wind," Morgan said. "How about you, Ruth?"

They found Ethan at a crude table bolted to the deck. He was so intent he didn't notice Morgan and Ruth move up behind him. There in clear relief on the paper was a drawing of a bird in flight. And there was no doubt that it was an Osprey.

"Oh, my," Morgan said. "That's wonderful, Ethan. How did you draw that?"

Ethan just shrugged. "I didn't. It was just there on the page. Like these," and he pulled two other drawings out from under the Osprey picture. The first showed John Bitter and Morgan, backs turned, standing at the rail of the steamer, staring down river at Beacon Rock. The second was of Ezra with his arm around Ruth's shoulders, both watching a distant osprey in flight.

Tears in her eyes, Morgan gave Ethan a hug. "Oh, Ethan…" was all she could say. "Can I show these to the rest?"

Ethan shrugged. "I guess it'll be okay."

A light rain greeted them the morning of day two of their down-river trip, as wagons, people, and stock boarded the steamship *Corvallis*, a two-ended side wheeler built pretty much like a ferry boat. The *Corvallis* was tied to a dock on the east side of the Willamette River a mile or so above Willamette Falls waiting for goods and passengers wanting transportation upriver as far as the town of Corvallis.

Robert Kelly, captain of the *Corvallis*, greeted Tom Beecher with a shout, a back slap and a hug. "You old hound dog. It's about time you got home. I was thinking I'd have to marry your wife if you didn't show up soon."

Beecher grinned and held Kelly at arms length. "Well, Bob, how is Martha?"

"She ain't pregnant, if that's what you're asking."

Beecher guffawed and slapped Kelly's shoulder hard enough to make him stagger. "I'll get to work on…oops…ah. Sorry ladies. This rascal is Bob Kelly, one of my close by neighbors on French Prairie. Martha is my long-suffering wife."

"Let's get out of the rain," Kelly suggested and led them to a passenger area complete with a wood burning, potbellied stove and benches anchored to the deck. When the dogs tried to sneak through the door, Kelly said, "No, you dogs. You stay outside." Rusty looked at Ethan who pointed out the door and said, "You guard the wagons, Rusty." Rusty managed a forlorn look, but he led Corky back out the door.

The boys edged up to the stove and held their hands to the warmth.

"Damn," Ethan whispered. "Feels as cold as all that snow in the Blues."

"Don't cuss, Brother," Mikey said. "Ruth will rap you on the knuckles."

Ethan frowned at Mikey, but didn't say anything.

"Bob," Beecher said, "let me introduce you to this ragged bunch of émigrés. Let's start with old Owl here. After he and I get back from having a drink of the Pacific Ocean, he's going to teach our younguns how to read, write, and speak English, Cherokee, and Cheyenne…and how to cuss in French.

"He doubles as a medicine man. That pretty young woman over there is his wife."

Bob Kelly reached out and shook hands. "Nice to meet you Mister Owl. You'll be welcome in French Prairie. You, too, Ma'am."

Beecher pulled Liam O'Grady over by the arm, and said, "Don't be fooled by the blue he's wearing, or that damned southern drawl. He is a genuine Irisher, and if we treat him right, he'll open a pub. Is that piece of land across the road from Saint Paul's church still vacant?"

Kelly grinned. "It is, and I think it's a good location. We can draw comfort from heaven while we're having a drink."

Ruth stepped forward and poked Kelly's chest with her forefinger. Barely five feet tall, she had to tilt her head back to look the lean six-footer in the eye. "Don't you be sacrilegious about a house of worship…even if it is a misguided Catholic Church. The Good Lord expects us to respect His house."

Kelly raised his hands in mock surrender. "And who might you be, Ma'am?"

Beecher laughed and said, "Let me introduce Missus Ruth Shipley, wife of the only man to ever beat me in a shooting match. Get over here Ezra. Bob here is my best friend. I'd trust him with anything but my wife."

Ezra grinned and held out his hand. "Mighty proud to meet you, Mister Kelly."

Kelly nodded. "I'd like to hear about you outshooting Tom. I don't think it's ever been done before."

"Just luck," Ezra said.

"Luck, hell. He centered the bull at three hundred yards," Beecher said. "Terrified me he did. I decided I needed to keep an eye on him in case he took a dislike to this old man.

"And this fine young couple is Mister John Bitter, an Abiqua Creek farmer until he turned Union Army Captain, and his wife, Missus Morgan Bitter. She owns that big black mule standing up front…all by his lonesome. A word to the wise, Bob. Leave him alone. He only tolerates children and Missus Morgan. And that black horse ain't a whole lot better."

Kelly tipped his hat to Morgan and shook hands with Bitter. "How long have you been traveling with Tom?"

"Since Fort Hall," Beecher interrupted. "I like these people. Ezra's going to be a blacksmith. I tried to talk him into setting up shop next to my place, but he says he needs to learn the trade first. After that I hope he'll take up his own farm and be the blacksmith for French Prairie.

"Missus Shipley is also a school teacher, so she can fix whatever Owl messes up."

They all laughed and Bitter felt the tension of the long months starting to slip away, and he was suddenly aware of how sore the muscles in his neck were. *Huh. I didn't know how tense I was.*

"And he doesn't know it yet, but Captain Bitter is going be the state representative for our district."

Bitter frowned and said, "Who decided that?"

Kelly laughed and said, "Tom Beecher, one of the wealthiest men in the state of Oregon. He owns a big piece of French Prairie, and the Wheatland Ferry, not to mention this little boat. And that's just for starters."

Bitter shook his head, but a smile creased his face. "You forgot to mention that."

Beecher nodded, and then grinned. "You are a natural leader, John Bitter, and unlike most of the political skunks in Salem, you have the courage of your convictions. Besides, for some reason I can't figure out, I like you."

"And I don't have a say?" Bitter asked.

Beecher ignored him and said, "Now for the youngsters. Get over here, boys. This blond-headed rascal is Ethan. He's a mighty fine mule skinner and a good brother to this other blond-haired rascal, Mikey. Ethan's going to be a fine artist and a fine photographer.

You should see the drawing he made of an old Osprey fishing the Columbia. We are going to need someone to record and preserve a visual record of our times. Ethan's my choice for that job.

"Mikey here knows things the rest of us can't understand. He can talk to animals. He knows what they think. Kinda scary, come to think about it. I see him learning to be our veterinarian.

"Thomas here is or was an apprentice medicine man. Old Owl took him in after some Cheyenne stole him from his family. He's a hell of a rider. And he's smart as a whip. How many youngsters do you know who speak three languages?

"Anyway, I'm sending him to school in Salem. As people start filling up this big valley, we are going to need a good lawyer to help us protect our land, and Thomas is my pick."

Thomas swallowed hard and turned beet red. For starters he knew the story about him being stolen from his family was just not true. They had been killed by the Cheyenne, and it was only a notional Cheyenne that had kept him alive. And second, he wasn't used to such high praise. It embarrassed him a little, but it also pleased him a lot.

"And little Davey here is a dreamer. He notices almost everything and stows it away for a time he'll need it. I don't know what he'll become, but observant people make out all right in this life. Shoot, Agent Comstock, maybe he'll become the first black Pinkerton detective."

Bitter shook his head. "You got it all worked out. What if I don't want to be a state representative?"

"I know you won't be able to stand the shenanigans of those hucksters holding public office. All they want is to get rich, and they'll skin the average man to get there. And the only legitimate tool you'll have to fight them is public office."

"Oh, bullshit," Bitter said. "I already have a job…farming, raising a family…"

"John Bitter," Ruth scolded.

"And he's a Pinkerton," Ralph Comstock said, and squeezed into the circle.

Beecher just grinned. "All the better. Know thine enemy. Who better to know thine enemy than a Pinkerton?"

Comstock laughed, but Bitter frowned and shook his head.

Kelly's first mate stuck his head in the door of the passenger area and said, "We're loaded, Captain Robert."

"We'll talk later," Captain Kelly said to Bitter and then grinned as he walked out the door, headed for the wheel house.

Amazing. How did Tom Beecher get to know us so well? Bitter thought.

Captain Kelly took the boys to the wheel house, and when the landing next to the Wheatland Ferry was in sight, he said, "You boys want to blow the whistle? We need to let folks know we're here."

The blast of the steam whistle carried out across the bottoms, and up and down the river, eight times all told, by the time Captain Kelly nudged the *Corvallis* in against the low wharf on the east side of the big river.

There were hugs and handshakes and invitations to come calling before Horse, Woman's horse and her pack animal, O'Grady's rose colored Appaloosa, and Beecher's mouse-colored horse were all led ashore. "Y'all come," O'Grady hollered from the wharf as the Corvallis backed into the current of the river.

"You, too, Liam O'Grady," John Bitter shouted. The boys waved from the back end of the ship, and the dogs barked until the wharf was out of sight.

Bitter looked at Morgan, Ezra, and Ruth, before saying, "I hate goodbyes."

23
Abiqua Creek

SOMEHOW EVEN THE MULES PULLING the wagons seemed to sense the excitement of their owners. Heads up, nearly at a trot, Ruth's mules followed an eager Rockford down the wagon road in the direction of Abiqua Creek.

You'd think they knew we're almost home, Morgan thought. She slapped the reins on mule rumps to hurry them after Ruth's wagon.

A new one-room school built in an open stand of scattered white oak trees surprised Bitter. It hadn't been there when he left for the war. The fresh shiplap lumber nailed to the sides of the building waited for its first coat of white wash, but polished window glass and the little bell tower standing proudly over the small porch were visible testimony to local pride and to local determination to educate the young.

Bitter reined Rockford to the side of the dusty road and waited for Morgan to catch up. When she started to pull the mules to a stop, he said, "Keep going."

He walked Rockford alongside the wagon, its spokes long past paint, but sturdy yet…even after two thousand and some odd miles.

Bitter pointed at the school building and said, "That's new… the building is new. I guess that's where the boys will go to school."

Morgan grinned and said, "I think Ethan and Thomas are a lot more interested in school than they were…especially Thomas now that Beecher has given him…what? A mission?"

"I've thought about that. He simply opened the world up for Thomas, and photographer Brown might have already done that for Ethan. I had no idea Ethan had such talent."

"Too busy surviving, maybe, to let it show?"

Bitter nodded. "That's for sure." And then he grinned. "Stinging worms, Morgan my love, stinging worms."

The road to the farm led off to the south, winding in and around big fir trees, and then through a thicket of scrub oak to Bitter's lower pasture, a good twenty-five acre sub-irrigated meadow of native grass.

Bitter pulled Rockford to a halt and waited until Morgan and Ruth drove the wagons into the open meadow. The boys and Ezra, Davey riding double on Lucky rode to each side of the wagons and halted. Misery, her belly filling out, a healthy sheen to her coat, immediately started cropping grass.

Arnold Comstock who had chosen to ride rear guard, rode up on his big bay. "Is this your place?" he asked Bitter.

"Part of it. The house is just beyond that little orchard, the barn is in behind that, and you can see the cottonwoods along the creek to the left of the orchard. There's a forty-acre piece across the creek. Yep. This is ours."

He grinned when he saw Ethan fidgeting with impatience. "Go ahead boys, ride for home!"

"Eeehaw!" Ethan shouted and spurred Josey into a gallop. And the race was on. The cap Ethan wore…some days…blew off half way across the pasture, but he didn't stop to pick it up. Misery and Thomas's horse were too close behind. Bitter was grinning and Morgan was frowning as the boys disappeared into the trees beyond the orchard.

Agent Comstock was laughing when he rode out and retrieved Ethan's cap.

"They're going to get hurt, John Bitter," Morgan said.

Bitter grinned and shook his head. "The ground is soft and they've been riding those horses for the past thousand miles. They'll be fine."

"You lead," Ruth said to Morgan. "We'll follow, but for the Good Lord's sake, Morgan, get a move on!"

The wagons rounded a turn in the road in time to see a laughing Mark Anthony lift Mikey from the saddle. Mikey wrapped his arms around Anthony's neck and squeezed until Anthony thought his neck might snap.

Ethan was holding Josey's reins and staring at the log cabin, liking the looks of it, the rock foundation, the porch running across the front, smoke coming out the chimney. He shifted his gaze to the dapper person he called Uncle Mark, stuck out his hand and said, "Well, we made it."

"You sure did. Who is this fine lad?" he asked, nodding to Thomas.

"Thomas. He and old Owl saved our hides back on the Little Blue. We had to run, but the army had this big old Gatling gun. Pa and Mister Shipley led the Indians right up the hill to where the soldiers was hiding and then they started shooting the Gatling and killed a lot of Indians. Pa got shot, but Mister Shipley sewed him back up. That was the second time Pa got hurt.

"We fought the Indians three times after we saw you, Uncle Mark. But Pa and Mister Shipley whipped 'em every time."

Anthony nodded. "That must have been quite a trip. Can you save the tale until after I say hello to your folks?"

"Oh…sorry."

"No. Don't be sorry. I'm very interested. Got shot and fought the Indians three times. Amazing."

When his friend John Bitter and a well set up black man he didn't know stepped down from their saddles, Anthony walked forward, hand outstretched. "Welcome home, John."

Bitter shook hands, noted Mark Anthony's black eye and asked, "What about the squatters?"

Anthony laughed and said, "I took a page out of your book. I reasoned with them. Your bother Luke held a shotgun on three of the brothers, while I reasoned with the fourth, who is also the eldest and the biggest.

"It reminded me of the fight you had with Peale, except I only promised this squatter a whipping before I ran him off. I whipped him all right, but not without beating on his fist with my nose. They cleared out yesterday.

"Actually, I'm still not sure they would have left but for your brother Luke. He had fire in his eyes and a double barreled shotgun. Turns out he told them they could use the barn for a couple of days…not squat on the place and use your cabin. He sort of reminded me of you. No back-up in him.

"Anyway, Luke's wife came over and cleaned the cabin yesterday afternoon and left a Dutch oven full of venison stew." He raised an eyebrow and cocked his head. "She seemed quite solicitous about your health, and she wanted to know all I could tell her about Morgan."

Bitter shook his head. "It's a long story. I'll tell you later." He waved Ezra up and said, "This is my good friend Ezra Shipley. We hooked up in Marysville and have kept company since.

"Ezra, this dapper citified looking dude is Mark Anthony. He's another close friend."

The men shook hands without more than a nod.

Bitter put an arm around Ezra's shoulders and said, "We saw the elephant, and we fought the Indians three times. But we made it, old friend."

Ezra gave John Bitter a weary smile. "You made it. Ruth and I have some miles to go yet."

"Not right away, Ezra. Take your time. We'll rest up, maybe do a little hunting, let the animals fatten up. Rest…really rest."

They walked to the wagons and each helped his wife down. Morgan smiled and when Mark Anthony held out his hand, she pushed it aside and stepped close for a hug. She kissed his cheek, tears in her eyes and patted his shoulder before pushing on by and up the steps into the neat, two-room cabin.

The smell of venison stew steaming in a Dutch oven hung on a spit over the coals in the fireplace made her mouth water. *Mark's doing,* she thought. And then she sank down on one of John Bitter's kitchen benches, let her shoulders slump, and silently wept.

Ruth slipped down on the bench beside her and put a hand on her shoulder. "Plumb worn out, aren't we Morgan."

Morgan dabbed at her tears with a sleeve and nodded, "But overwhelmed with joy."

"That man of yours know about the baby?"

"He will tonight. I didn't want to say anything until Woman left us."

Ruth nodded. "There's time, girl, there's time."

While Ruth and Morgan made biscuits to go with the stew, the mules were unharnessed and turned loose in what Bitter called his upper pasture, a fifteen-acre meadow he had fenced to keep his stock in before he left, not that he had much to start with. Just a couple of mares and a runty milk cow. None of his stock were in sight, but he decided that could be left for another day.

The wagon mules and the horses waded belly deep in native grass, busy filling empty stomachs. Rockford worked his way down to the creek for a drink of cool, clear water, snuffling and snatching at tufts of grass along the way. Queeny looked to be in hog heaven as she grazed on belly-high grass before following Rockford down to the creek.

Lucifer, true to his cantankerous nature, chose to wander the road back to the lower pasture, Misery tagging along behind.

While Ralph Comstock conferred with Mark Anthony, Ezra, and Bitter pushed the Shipley wagon though the doors of the barn. There was room for all four boys in the cabin loft, but Ruth and Ezra would have to sleep in the wagon again.

Ezra gazed at the barn in approval. Whoever built it had made it strong and square. "You build this?"

"Luke helped, and a couple of Scots living over on Butte Creek. Mill wrights. They helped with the framing, but I did the rest."

Ezra nodded approvingly. "Nice barn."

Ezra hung the harness on pegs in the tack room, and then latched the tack room door. "I think my stomach is rubbing my back bone. Is that food I'm smelling?"

Supper over, the boys took Ethan's cane pole down to the creek. Rusty got up off the spot he already claimed on the front porch and tail wagged after them, Corky bouncing along side. "I hope that cat gut leader works," Anthony shouted after the boys.

Morgan watched them disappear into the trees along the creek and nodded to herself. "This will be a good place to raise a family."

Ruth and Morgan washed the supper dishes while the men sat on the edge of the porch talking and spiking cups of coffee with some kind of French whiskey supplied by Mark Anthony.

Bitter lit a roll-your-own and asked Anthony where he got the venison and the spuds. "Didn't," Anthony said. "You brother's wife brought that Dutch oven over earlier. All I had to do was warm it up."

"How did you know when we'd be in?"

"I didn't, but I figured on eating before dark…with or without you."

Drying her hands on a clean piece of flour cloth, Ruth walked out the door with Morgan in tow. "Gentlemens," Ruth said, "Morgan wishes to announce she is with child. I think our homecoming, a new child coming to join us in about seven months, and our new life in Oregon calls for a prayer of thanks and the need to ask God for his blessings on this house and our beloved friends."

Bitter tossed the stub of his cigarette in the yard, set his coffee cup down and mounted the steps. He took Morgan in his arms and kissed her to the sound of good natured catcalls and heartfelt clapping.

Bitter held her and whispered, "I wondered when you were going to tell me."

"You knew?"

He nodded, "Mikey said the baby told him."

"Bow your heads," Ruth ordered. "Dear Lord…"

24
Home Again

A RIFLE SHOT JUST AT DAYLIGHT startled the two Pinkerton Detectives sleeping in Bitter's barn loft. They hurriedly stepped into their pants, pulled suspenders over their shoulders, and, pistols in hand, slipped barefoot down the ladder to the ground floor.

Ezra poked his head out from under the canvas flap guarding Shipley privacy and said, "What's going on?"

"We heard a shot," Mark Anthony said.

"That must be what woke me up," Ezra replied.

Agent Comstock opened the man door and peeked out in the general direction of the rifle shot. "Here comes John. He's toting his rifle and wearing a big grin. I wonder what that's about?"

Bitter spotted Comstock and said, "Did I wake you up?"

"If that was you doing the shooting, you did."

"I decided to see if I could catch a pestiferous deer eating my fruit. I spotted a little three point buck eating windfall apples, so I added him to the larder. Nice and fat he is. I need a horse to bring him to the barn."

Morgan wasn't amused at the gunshot and Ethan was disappointed. "I thought I was going to be the hunter," he huffed when Bitter told him about the little buck.

Bitter looked a tad embarrassed. "I did say that, didn't I? Well, you can hunt the next one. Okay?"

"Well, okay I guess."

Morgan smacked Bitter's shoulder with a fist and said, "You scared the dickens out of me, John. Gunshots make my heart pound. Too many Indian fights."

Bitter rubbed his shoulder and frowned. "That hurt." And then he nodded and said, "I'll tell you what I'm doing next time so I won't scare you."

The sun was barely nudging the sky when Mark Anthony and Agent Comstock led saddled horses to the front porch and ground hitched them. They knocked on the cabin door and entered with a "Hello the house."

"Come on in," Morgan said. "There's coffee in the pot and cups on the table."

Bitter asked, "You leaving?"

Anthony nodded. "Ralph is anxious to get to Seattle and start his new job. And I'm working a case in Portland for a Mister Benson. His daughter is missing. Young woman, wild and headstrong. Ran off with a man Benson describes as a 'riverboat gambler.' He wants me to find her. Bring her home."

"Why didn't he go to the Sheriff?" Bitter asked.

"Too proud, Agent Bitter, too proud. Pride makes the detective business very profitable.

"Now, I want you to take a month to get settled, and then I'll be back to help you open an office in Salem. Mister Pinkerton's plan is to have a man in every major city and town in the whole country. For Oregon, that's Portland and Salem. We'll expand as the population grows."

"I know I took the retainer, but I didn't know you wanted me in an office."

"No, no. The office will be run by a clerk. When we have a case, you'll be the investigator. But once the office is open, your salary will be one-hundred dollars a month. And if you don't have a case, you'll be free to do whatever you want."

"What if I want to look at that country east of the Cascades? Look for a horse ranch. I might be gone a couple weeks at a time."

"Not a problem. Just let the office know."

"And you'll pay me anyway."

"Yep."

"Well, sit down have some breakfast before you leave," Morgan said.

25
Luke and Lydia

LUKE BITTER, DRESSED IN A white linen suit, white shirt and black tie, his black low-heeled boots polished to a high shine, drove his leather-topped buggy off the main farm road and down John's lane to the fence bordering the orchard. He pulled the team to a stop by the fence bordering the orchard. His pair of matched blacks stared for a few seconds at two women picking apples and then dropped their heads to feed on the roadside grass.

Lydia, Luke's blond--headed wife pointed to the two women filling apples buckets with low hanging fruit. "They're wearing men's pants," she said. "That's not very lady like."

"It's practical, though," Luke suggested.

"Is that John's wife?" Lydia asked. "That red head?"

Luke studied his wife for a quick couple of seconds, and decided Lydia was hoping John had brought home a crone instead of this pretty young woman. "I think so. Let's go ask."

Lydia sniffed and said, "I'll sit here with baby Eloise, if you don't mind."

"Suit yourself, but I expect you to behave. This is my brother's wife, after all. I won't put up with any of your snits today."

Ruth watched the exchange between Luke and Lydia, and even though they were out of earshot, concluded they were in a less than harmonious discussion. She nudged Morgan with an elbow. "I think that's John's brother. They favor each other."

Morgan brushed hair out of her eyes and set her bucket down, watching Luke walk through the orchard. "He looks to be fairly well off, not at all like a farmer," she whispered to Ruth.

"Ladies," Luke said when he was closer, "I'm Luke Bitter, John's brother. My wife Lydia and I have come calling. Is John around?"

"I'm Morgan, John's wife and this is my best friend, Ruth Shipley."

Luke tipped his broad brimmed hat and said, "How do, ma'am."

"Well," Ruth said, "he surely does favor John."

"If you'll help us with these apple buckets, we'll go back to the house," Morgan said. "John and Ezra, Ruth's husband, have gone to the woodlot. We have a lot to do before winter sets in, and your squatters burned most of the woodpile."

Luke winced and said, "I'll have my hands bring you some firewood tomorrow."

Ezra slapped the reins and laughed when Windy let go with his to-be-expected cloud of gas. He nudged John with his elbow. "I'll bet those two mules are both wondering why they been singled out to pull a wagon load of wood while the rest get to graze."

"Gotta have wood, Ezra."

"You be too restless to rest, John Bitter."

"You know, Ezra, I'm so damned glad to be home I want to get all the chores done at once. I got three years to make up for."

"I know farming, John Bitter. It's never caught up. There's always a chore waiting for when you get up."

Luke was standing on the porch when Ezra pulled the wagon into the yard. "You go ahead, John. I'll take the wagon around to the wood pile and get the mules out of harness."

Luke came down the steps, his eyes wary, uncertain about John's feelings over Lydia.

John grinned and slapped Luke's hand aside and wrapped his big brother in a bear hug. "You old outlaw," John said, "I'm mighty glad to see you."

Luke stepped back blinking tears that threatened to spill from his eyes. "Me too," was all he could get out before the tears flowed down his cheeks. "I worried, John. Oh, damn, how I worried. We'd get word, late of course, about all the men killed in one the big battles, and I knew those damned rebs would kill you, sure as hell. And here you are at last, hale and hardy."

John laughed, "Hell, I never got a scratch during the whole war. Took a wild Indian to puncture my hide on the way home."

Luke grabbed John's hand and pumped it a few times. "Mighty glad, John, mighty glad." He wiped his tears with a shirt sleeve and pointed to the orchard. "Let's walk out a ways. I need to talk."

John and Luke stopped under the outspread branches of an apple tree John had planted five years earlier. Luke faced John and said, "Where to start? First, I'm sorry about taking Lydia. I know that's why you went to war. But it just sort of happened."

John shook his head. "No, Luke, it didn't just sort of happen. Lydia decided you were a better catch and deliberately stalked you. I had a lot of campfires to think about that. Hell, she was probably right. Look at you.

"And I don't want you being sorry. I have a beautiful wife, two strong sons…or three…depending on whether or not I can find Thomas's relatives…and a baby on the way. Besides, I think I was looking for a good excuse to go see the fuss anyway."

He stepped back and said, "What about you? You're limping, but otherwise you look to be prospering."

"I am…and all because I fell off a ladder and broke my ankle the first year you were gone. I couldn't walk for several months, and I guess the ankle will be a bother the rest of my life.

"But, little brother, it gave me time to do what I really like. I love to work leather. I make saddles mainly, and people pay me as much as two hundred dollars for my best ones. I opened a store in Salem. We make harness, bridles, belts, knife sheaths, wallets, purses, quirts, braided leather reins, braided leather ropes…we upholster buggy seats, easy chairs, you name it.

"I have six people working for me who make the basic items while I work on the things I like. A wealthy rancher in California is paying me one thousand dollars to make a woman's saddle for his daughter's wedding. It's all gilt and curlicues, silver plated stirrups, you name it. Can you imagine paying that for a saddle?"

Bitter shook his head. "No. No I can't."

"Well, the upshot is that while I was laid up, I hired a couple of hands to do my haying, and sold all the stock except my horses and your mares. By the way, you own eight head of horses now. I bred your mares to a good stud. But, I owe you for the milk cow. She got out and I could never find her."

He looked away before saying, "Lydia and I built a house in Salem on Mission Street. We'll be moving into it day after tomorrow. I'm going to sell my farm. I guess that means we won't be neighbors after all."

John grinned and said, "That your idea or Lydia's?"

Luke looked uncomfortable. "Well, I want to keep the farm, but Lydia says she needs the money to furnish her new house."

John didn't say anything for a few seconds, and then asked, "How much for the farm, Luke?"

Morgan was bouncing Eloise, age eighteen months on her knee and Lydia was sitting on a kitchen bench looking uncomfortable when John and Luke walked into the cabin. Ruth had taken Ezra for a walk after introductions were made. It had taken Lydia all of thirty seconds to ask Morgan, "Are these coloreds yours?"

It wasn't a question Lydia would ever ask again, not of Morgan, nor of anyone else. Not ever. And in fact, Lydia would spend the rest of her life trying very hard to never be alone with Morgan again.

Morgan raised her eyebrows and shook her head when John asked, "Where's Ezra and Ruth."

Morgan looked at Lydia and said, "They felt the need for fresh air, so they decided to go for a walk."

Luke didn't say anything, but his anger was obvious.

The tension passed right over John's head. In an excited voice, he said, "Guess what? I'm going to buy Luke's farm. I have enough reward money left to pay him off. He's leaving all the furniture but Daddy's grandfather clock. And he is leaving all the tools…plows, harness…all of it…dishes and everything."

"And…Ruth and Ezra can live in it. Be our close-by neighbors. Ezra and I can farm both places and split the profit. Oh, I don't know…he might not want to. I haven't all the details worked out, but I figure you and Ruth can fix that."

Eloise started to fuss, and that was enough excuse for Lydia. "Luke," she said in a sharp tone, "I think it's time we left."

Luke shook hands with John and said, "I'll have my attorney draw up the papers. I'll bring 'em out next week. You can pay me then. And your friends can move in day after tomorrow. Anything we leave is yours…or theirs for that matter. That's up to you."

John looked at his big brother, older by three years, heavier by thirty pounds, some of it flab coming on, and taller by an inch. He glanced at Lydia and then grinned at his brother. "Thanks, Luke. For everything."

From the shade of the orchard where they had walked to get away from Lydia, Ezra and Ruth saw the matched pair of blacks, their stocking feet flashing in the sunlight, pull the buggy up the road and out of sight.

Ruth squeezed her husband's arm. "Morgan told me John was once engaged to that woman. I guess he didn't notice her hard mouth."

Ezra raised his eyebrows and then nodded. "Neither did Luke, I imagine. Why don't you say a prayer for them both Ruth, but especially for Luke."

Epilogue

Winter on Abiqua Creek was a rainy one, interlaced with Christmas snow that lasted about four days. Much to the disgust of the boys, the snow was really never deep enough for decent sledding. Bitter showed them how to make snowmen, and to throw snowballs. Thomas had the strongest arm and hit Bitter square between the shoulder blades as he climbed the steps to the cabin. "Uh, oh," Mikey said, but Bitter just laughed and went on in to warm up by the fire.

The Sharp Family Bible and the Eagan Family Bible stood on the mantle over the fireplace. Morgan baked Mikey a birthday cake, months late according to the Sharp Family Bible, but he was proud to finally be six years old.

The teacher hired by the school board wrote a letter saying she had married and wouldn't be coming to teach at Oak Grove Grade School after all. That left them in a fix, until Ethan told the substitute teacher, a young woman all of fourteen years old, that Davey's mother was a teacher,

The board members, all elderly men, were skeptical of hiring a black woman, but they agreed to an interview. She impressed them. In an open meeting, they agreed to offer her ten dollars a month, half of what they were prepared to pay the white teacher.

John Bitter stood up and in a cold, hard voice read them from the Good Book. The fact that he was wearing a pistol at the time, and the fact that his exploits on the Oregon Trail had begun to slip into the folk lore of the Valley, might have had something to do with a change of heart. The Chairman of the School Board, Joseph Maupin apologized and augmented the offer by ten dollars a month.

Ethan punched an older boy, a student at the school for making unkind remarks about Missus Shipley's ethnic origins. Ethan wore a shiner for a week, but the older boy was always respectful after that…especially around Missus Shipley and around Ethan. And in truth the boy grew to like and respect Missus Shipley. All he ever said was said in private to Ethan. Out behind the schoolhouse where no one could hear, he held out his hand and said, "Ethan, I'm sorry for what I said about Missus Shipley." Ethan was glad, but it wouldn't be the last fight he would have with bigger boys who said things they shouldn't.

On the whole, the local farmers and the merchants were accepting of the Shipley's. Doc Hardy, the local blacksmith took Ezra on as an apprentice, and was overheard telling Oliver Oster, owner of the Silverton Saloon, that Ezra had an uncanny knack for working metal. "And strong. I'm telling you, he has arms like tree trunks. But he has a delicate touch. He's making sled runners for his boy's Christmas present. And andirons for John Bitter's fireplace.

"I tell you, Ollie, that man can work with metal. Did you know he fought in the Civil War? He's a wounded war hero. Anyway, set that aside. What would you think if I brought in a boring machine? I want to branch out. We'll start making pistols and work our way up from there."

Oster, a quiet man who was often asked by local business men for his advice, nodded and said, "Good idea, Doc. Now there's something I want to talk to you about. We need a new Sheriff in Marion County. I heard how John Bitter and one of his Pinkerton friends found Benson's daughter and took her home. I'm thinking about running him for County Sheriff."

The only real trouble came from a few dried up old prunes at the local Baptist Church. The first Sunday Ezra, Ruth, and Davey entered the little church, four of the women got their husbands by the ear and walked out. The minister, a Kentuckian who liked preaching more than working asked Ezra and Ruth to leave.

When Morgan heard about it, she was ready to lynch the minister, but Ruth shook her head. "It won't help. They are beyond redemption."

"Well," Morgan said, "We'll find a minister and start our own church."

Ruth nodded. "As Christ said, 'For where two or three are gathered together in my name, there I am in the midst of them.'"

"Amen," Morgan said. "I'll sic John on that. We can build a church right out there by the road."

O'Grady's letter sent from Saint Paul said the building for his pub was nearly complete, thanks to a loan from Tom Beecher, and that Owl and Beecher were gone a month "drinking from the ocean," and that Woman was fully recovered and getting to be a nuisance. Bitter and Morgan both laughed at that. "I guess he got my letter," Bitter said. "Come Spring let's go pay a visit."

Morgan's shape left no doubt as to her pregnancy, and also left John with the sure and certain knowledge there would never be another baby unless he expanded the house.

"We'll turn our bedroom into a dining room. I'll add a new bedroom on the other end of the cabin, and I want to build a bunkhouse for the boys. What do you think?"

She nodded, walked to where he was sitting on a stool by the low burning fireplace, and down sat on his lap. She kissed his cheek and then smiled. "Not until I have my new cook stove you won't. In the meantime, John Bitter, there will be time for us after the baby is born. The boys will be in school most days. We'll work something out."

Christmas brought them a post card from Jack and Wanda Bellamy saying they'd be out next summer. The boys were in bed, and John and Morgan were sitting by the fire.

"Read it to me, again," he said.

"Okay. It says, 'Dear John and Morgan, See you in August. We are coming by ship. The Pacific is supposed to be smooth that time of year. We are anxious to see you and the boys, and Abiqua Creek. Love, Jack and Wanda Bellamy.' "

"So Wanda married him after all. Good. I liked them," Morgan said. "And Wanda likes the boys."

"Still nothing from Harley?"

"No. He's not much for writing, but I think it's time for another letter. Maybe I'll include one of Ethan's drawings."

John looked at Morgan, the gleam of firelight in her red hair. "I want to ask you something."

"Go ahead."

"Why wouldn't you let me kiss you when we went for a walk in your orchard?"

She studied his face and said, "I wanted you to, but I was afraid of you. Afraid of what I was feeling. But when you left, I knew I couldn't leave it at that."

"So you followed me. Are you glad you did?"

"Forever, husband, forever."

Thank you

Vi Collins, for hours of patient listening and valuable criticism, and for your unwavering tolerance and faith that Bitter's Run was worth the time and effort invested in the story.

Jerry Barrowcliff, for being an early reader and a willing researcher. And for your expert advice about and insight into the arms and customs of the times. I'm especially grateful for your story about Beecher's Bibles and for the quiet hint that maybe I should do some judicious pruning of the manuscript. (I did.)

Dale Casey, for sixty eight years of friendship, for spotting typos and other errors, and for being a Bitter's Run protector and offsite storage site.

Eva Long of Long on Books. (I was very dependent on my editor Eva as we brought book six of our partnership to life.)

Jeff Duckworth of Duck Of All Trades for interior layout and cover design. (Nice job, again.)

Jim Goble for being an early reader. (Your enthusiasm for Bitter's Run helped me keep going.)

Lise at Mohawk Paperback Plus for years of support and confidence in my story telling. (And for selling a lot of my books over the past years.)

Peter Flowers, scholar, historian, theologian and friend.

Note: I frequently give thanks to my cadre of loyal readers, so if I fail to mention you by name, know that I am nonetheless grateful. If it wasn't for you, I'd have given this business up a long time ago. (The fish are grateful I didn't.)

Author's Note

The number I used in the introduction to Book II: The Oregon Trail is a "soft" estimate that reads, "Between 1840 and 1860 **more than** 100,000 people set out to travel the Oregon Trail..." In my research, I found differing historical accounts of the number of people who traveled what came to be called The Oregon Trail. Estimates range from 100,000 to much higher figures ranging from 200,000 to 400,000 people. I believe no one knows the actual number. And I suspect the number varies depending on how many years of Oregon Trail travel the estimators chose to include.

I also found no consistent record keeping until the military started escorting wagon trains and guarding the road. But before then, I think it safe to use the vague word "thousands" in describing the number of people who walked, rode, pushed hand carts, carried packsacks, and drove teams of oxen, mules or horses on their way across The Oregon Trail.

Rod Collins
July 1, 2015

Rod Collins is an award-winning author and the creator of the fictional Sheriff Bud Blair series, a set of contemporary Western murder mysteries staged primarily in Oregon's High Desert, but which also stray into the Puget Sound area in Washington, and as far south as Alamos, Mexico. Readers are saying nice things about *Spider Silk*, *Stone Fly*, *Bloodstone*, and *Mariah's Song*.

Bitter's Run is a departure from the Bud Blair novels. Collins says, "I've always wanted to write a frontier novel, but the notion of a quick draw Western rapidly evolved into an historical novel set in the early months after Lee surrendered to Grant at Appomattox."

After a thirty-year career with the U.S. Forest Service, he set out to pursue his lifelong ambition to be a writer. Five novels later (and one non-fiction work, *What Do I Do When I Get There?*) his writing projects include another Bud Blair novel with Detective (Retired) Dell BeBe leading the way.

9 780996 539487